Having spent most of his life trapped in the frozen tundra of upstate New York, Daniel Cohen decided to dream himself somewhere new. It was from this quest for heat that the scorching world of COLDMAKER was born.

www.danielacohenbooks.com
🐦 @saxophonehome

Also by Daniel A. Cohen

Coldmaker
Coldmarch

C◈OLD MYTH

DANIEL A. COHEN

Book Three of the Coldmaker Saga

HARPER
Voyager

Harper*Voyager*
An imprint of HarperCollins*Publishers* Ltd
1 London Bridge Street
London SE1 9GF

www.harpercollins.co.uk

First published by HarperCollins*Publishers* 2020
1

A catalogue record for this book is available from the British Library

ISBN: 978-0-00-820728-1

Set in Meridien by Palimpsest Book Production Limited,
Falkirk, Stirlingshire

Printed and bound in the UK by CPI Group (UK) Ltd, Croydon CR0 4YY

MIX
Paper from
responsible sources
FSC™ C007454

To Jardin

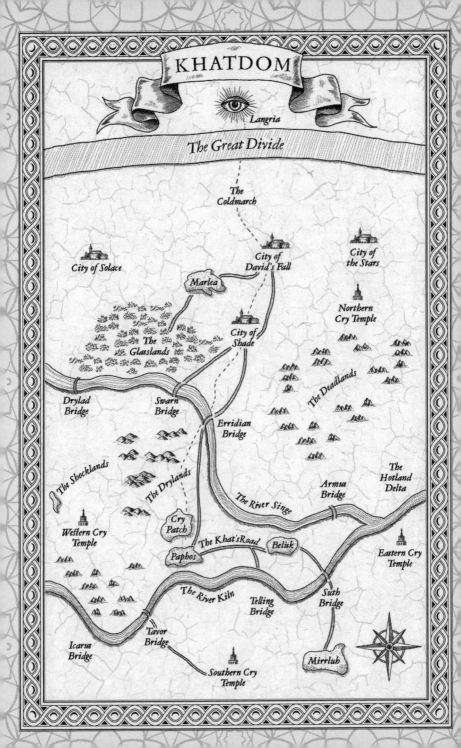

PART ONE

PART ONE

Chapter One

The stars looked brighter while I was recruiting.

Pins of light became luminous spears, puncturing the darkness and pointing to the cracks in the barracks walls. Loose stones big enough to crawl through were hard to find on purpose, keeping the passageways secret. I found it impressive that even with the stone boot of the Khat on our backs for eight hundred years, heavy enough to crush granite to sand, some Jadans were always willing to risk death just to sneak out and take a small breath of freedom.

Those particular Jadans were the first to join our cause.

Tilting my head back, I stared into the night sky and drew two fingers down my cheek. My ancestors once used this gesture to honour the World Crier. Tears acknowledged the pain and sacrifice that went into creating something beautiful, something full of life and wonder.

The world was a different place now.

Eight hundred years ago the Great Drought had struck, and the land began to die. Cold, which had always fallen from the sky, began to disappear. Eventually the pieces became so scarce that they only fell in one place – the Khat's Cry Patch.

Without nourishment from above, the Sun took free rein

and burned the land to sand and dust. Animals, plants and entire civilizations withered away under its merciless, scorching power. The Khat claimed he was the only one worthy of relief, and the world had to accept chains of death. Any trace of culture from before the Drought was burned or buried. Songs were silenced. Dancing feet were bound. Even the smallest traditions were stamped out in in order to cleanse the past from the present.

The crying gesture had been one of the many things made illegal after Cold stopped falling for my people.

Shilah looked over at me and mimicked the movement, letting her fingers linger on her cheek. Her knuckles touched her long braid, which hung on the front of her shoulder. Her dark skin had a luminous glow, like it was drinking in the starlight and shining from the inside out.

'After you, World Partner,' she said.

I looked down at my left hand, flexing my little invention and stretching the bronze fingers straight. The guiding rings that went around my middle finger tended to slip, but it felt good to once again look down and see the shape of a full hand. Ever since I'd lost the last two fingers I'd felt somewhat incomplete – I couldn't have them back, but tinkering had at least made me useful again.

I rubbed my metal pinky, checking the friction of the rubber-strip finger pads. The grip was still quite sticky, which let me know I'd picked a good material. I couldn't tinker as well as I used to, but at least with bronze fingers I could hold the glass chalice during our recruiting ritual.

'Unless,' Shilah said, tracing a jagged crack in the barracks wall. Her almond eyes wouldn't meet mine. 'Leah holds that position now. How are things with your new shadow, by the way?'

I paused, my stomach clenching tight. 'You mean how she won't give me a moment's peace?'

'I'm sure you just hate the lingering touches.'

Heat rose into my cheeks. 'What do you mean?'

She shrugged. 'I mean she lingers.'

'She doesn't linger.'

Shilah turned and tapped my shoulder, her palm gently resting along my collar bone. '"Meshua. How does this potion work? Meshua can I help you make that crank-fan? Meshua you've made the cave so cold that I wish I had someone to sleep next to." She's not even being subtle anymore.'

I turned my concentration back to the barracks wall, searching for any telltale signs of a secret panel. 'I've made it very clear that I'm not interested in her. I've got enough to worry – *we've* got enough to worry about with everything – with the cave – and the recruiting and—'

Shilah squeezed my shoulder. 'Shivers and Frosts, Spout, I was just kidding around. I know.'

I swallowed hard.

She paused, a teasing smirk coming to her lips. 'But she does linger.'

I chuckled. '"Shivers and Frosts," huh? You've been spending too much time with Cam.'

Shilah blushed. 'It's not like he invented the saying, and it's got a nice ring to it. Also, know thy enemy, right?'

I gave her a stern look. 'Cam is hardly the enemy.'

She looked down at her sandals. 'I didn't mean it like that. He's been teaching me more about Noble life. About his father and brothers, and how those bastards think and what they say. Got to know all the loose bricks in the Pyramid if you want it to come crumbling down.'

'Poetry.' I nodded, tapping my knuckles gently across a curious patch of wall.

'Boy or girl tonight?' Shilah asked.

I gave her a look. 'Girl. Definitely.'

'Why so confident?'

I thought about all the new recruits back in our caverns. We were twenty-six Jadans strong. A true Flock. Still nowhere near close enough to take on the Khat's army of thousands, but we were at least approaching the numbers we'd need to begin my next Idea.

'The strongest Jadan I know is a girl,' I said. 'And if we're going to do what we're planning to do, we need all the strength we can get.'

Shilah paused, facing me and taking my broken hand in hers. She gave the bronze fingers a squeeze, but she wasn't gentle with the rest of my hand. She knew better then to show me pity. 'Well then I hope it's a boy. The most brilliant Jadan I know is a boy.'

I looked away, blushing. A large rectangle of stone seemed to protrude just a hair from the wall. 'I think we found our spot.'

Shilah glanced up at the stars. 'Perfect timing, too. The Crying will be happening about now.'

I looked over my shoulder. Wind howled over the cliff, carrying up a light dusting of sand from the desolate land far below. High dunes and Sun-bleached rocks spread as far as the eye could see, in every direction the only sign of life being the odd patch of boilweed now and again.

Just like everywhere outside of Paphos, the land here was dead.

And with dead land came dead spirits.

I thought whispers of Ice might be enough to change things here in the City of David's Fall. It should have been enough to do something. I'd hoped the rumors would cause rebellion. I hoped word of the miracle material would spread throughout every house, shop and barracks, causing the Jadan people to rise up and toss our oppressors over the same cliff they once forced us over.

My thoughts had proven optimistic.

In the City of David's Fall, fear ran deeper than hope.

Ever since our battle at the Sanctuary, the Khat's forces had been showing up in droves. The city had grown tense and overcrowded. Streets teemed with Khatfists and armoured guards, doing everything they could to prove their superiority.

The night air shook with the sounds of cries and lashings, worsening with the arrival of each new Noble caravan. If any Jadan so much as mentioned Ice, the taskmasters would brand their tongues unusable. Most of my people shrank deeper into their shells. Most stepped tighter into line.

Most, but not all.

I nodded for Shilah to join me. The large stone of the barracks gave under my palm. This was the right spot.

Now all we had to do was wait.

Shilah reached into the sheath I had designed and retrieved the blade. It was still strange to see the weapon of the Vicaress without a wreath of flames, or without the merciless blue eyes sizzling behind it.

Abb used to tell me that revenge is an empty journey; that there can be no satisfaction until one has the courage to let go of the past.

The Vicaress stabbed him to death with this very blade.

She'd been killed in return, by the hand of my Flock. And I didn't regret my revenge.

I only regretted not getting more of it myself.

Shilah sat down at one side of the secret panel, crossing her legs and waving the Vicaress's blade in front of her face. I took the opposing side, my back hovering right up against the wall. The brick was terribly hot as after being battered by the Sun all day.

We waited patiently. The wind laughed across the nearby cliffs.

The City of David's Fall was set on a series of plateaus. It struck me as purposeful that the Jadan barracks were usually built as close to the cliffs as possible. Not only would it keep the unworthy masses away from the city centre, but it was a subtle reminder of what happened here the last time our people tried to rebel.

Shilah scraped the blade across the ground and picked up the handful of dirt and sand. She rolled the land around her fingertips and then opened her hand, letting the grit be carried away by the wind.

I pulled out the chalice, staring into my choice of glass – Glassland Green. I owed a great debt to desperation in my journey to becoming an Inventor, but it was quite refreshing to get to use the best things for my work instead of just what I was able to scavenge. For the chalice, I'd needed something that wouldn't shatter.

'I hate that we have to scare them,' I said.

'I scared the crap out of you at first too. You turned out all right.'

'You absolutely did not scare me.'

She wrapped an arm around her chest and pretended to shiver. 'Ahhh, don't kill me, sand wraith! I don't know how to get my own invention off!'

I shushed her with a smirk. 'Quiet. We don't want to scare anyone back inside.'

She thrust the blade into the ground by her feet, sitting back and closing her eyes.

The wind up here was lovely. The Nobles had been wrong in their placement of the barracks. The air was much more bearable, cool and fresh, and the views were spectacular. This location was a gift.

I relished this time, just Shilah and I, more than anything.

Having so many Jadans look to us as saviours was exhausting. It was nice to get away. I breathed a little easier looking out over dead land and dreaming of a better world. Together.

A sound from inside.

I held a finger to my lips, Shilah and I simultaneously rising to our feet. After a moment the brick scraped backwards. Scabbed hands took its place, grasping at small freedom.

Shilah flattened herself against the wall, which didn't take much effort as her back was as deadly straight as always. She held the Vicaress's blade in one hand, a fresh rip of boilweed dangling from the other.

A shock of curly black hair appeared in the opening of the wall. A girl. Perhaps fourteen or fifteen years old, only slightly younger than us. On the back of her neck was the tattoo all Jadans were forced to wear, denoting our barracks and slave number. The ink was always black as a starless night, so it could be read on our dark skin. Her elbows were cracked and ashen, and her ears were rather large for her head. I wondered if she'd already heard us.

We kept flat until the girl crawled out and then turned.

She opened her mouth to scream.

Shilah hopped off the wall, holding out the knife and hissing through her teeth. 'Make one sound and I use this.'

The girl's eyes flashed wide. Arms immediately wrapped around her chest in protection.

I hated this method of introduction, but we couldn't have the girl screaming. Harshness was the quickest path out of the confusion.

Shilah let the blade fall to her side, putting on her most charming smile. 'I'm just kidding. I would never do that. I'm Shilah. This is Micah. We're here to change your whole life.'

The girl looked at me. Her face flushed with terror. She was unsteady on her feet, poised to flee.

'Hello,' I said, giving her a friendly wave with my damaged hand.

I knew the rumours spoken in the shadows – a Jadan with golden fingers, gifted from the Crier so he could make and touch Ice. I hoped this girl had heard at least some version of the tale.

Fear continued to darken her face.

'Please. I wasn't going anywhere,' the girl said, a lump visible in her throat. Her lips were cracked and bleeding. Her nightly rations were probably withheld. 'I was just checking for—'

'Really, we're not going to hurt you,' I said. 'We just have to be private.'

'I don't have any figs or anything.' The girl's voice was meek; her fingers rubbed her elbows. 'I never save rations.'

'What's your name?' Shilah asked sweetly. It was not a tone I was used to.

The girl's eyes flashed to the blade. 'Whatever will keep me alive.'

Shilah stared at the girl with pinched lips.

'Cassay,' the girl said.

Shilah angled the blade to catch more starlight. 'You recognize this blade, Cassay?'

Cassay thought about it for a second and then nodded. Her curls did not sway with the motion, crusted over with dirt. 'How'd you get it?'

Shilah gestured to me.

'Cassay,' I said, handing over the green glass chalice. 'Please hold this.'

Cassay kept her arms wrapped around her torn shirt. 'Why?'

'Please,' I said gently.

Eventually she yielded, taking the cup in trembling hands. I tipped my waterskin over the top and filled the glass precisely halfway.

Shilah stepped in front of the girl, slicing off a tiny sliver of abb.

A part of me winced. We only had so many abbs left, and

the Coldmaker, the finest invention I'd ever created, couldn't produce them forever. The machine was dying, and if we didn't find a Frost to power the charge inside soon, we'd lose what little advantage we had. Abbs may have been the most powerful form of Cold in existence, able to make Ice, but they were finite, like every other piece of Cold.

I wished the recruits could fully understand the honour we were bestowing. These were the last of the abbs we were giving them. Sacrificing power for family; although my father would have said they were the same thing.

Shilah held the abb sliver over the cup between her thumb and forefinger.

'Cassay,' Shilah said in a dramatic voice, 'ever heard of Langria?'

Cassay nodded, the water trembling in the glass. 'Yes?'

I rested my hands gently beneath Cassay's. Our first three Jadan recruits had dropped the chalice when witnessing the Ice. And I needed them to *feel* the Cold instead of just seeing it. The gap between knowledge and understanding could be as wide as the Great Divide.

'Welcome to real freedom,' Shilah said.

The fleck of gold dropped into the water.

The reaction was instantaneous.

I'd tried Glassland Blue and Glassland Black for the chalice, but neither could withstand the pressure. I'd thought about just using bronze – to match the Coldmaker, as well as my fingers – but the material needed to be translucent, so our recruits could fully see what was happening.

Crystal arms reached the lip of the glass as the Ice expanded. Shilah and I had to practise the sizing of the slice of abb, making sure it was small enough to ensure there was still some water left to drink.

The girl gasped.

'You're them,' Cassay said, her body ready to collapse.

'You're real. I didn't believe what Hadim was saying, but you're real.'

'Drink,' I said, filing the name 'Hadim' away for later. We needed as many recruits as possible. 'We're just Jadans, like you.'

'Drink,' Shilah echoed. 'Drink and be free.'

Guiding her shaking hands, I brought the glass up to her lips. Cassay closed her eyes and she sighed with her whole body. It was quite a long moment before she opened them again, tears dotting the corners of her eyes.

She turned her face to the stars.

I imagined they looked brighter.

Chapter Two

A shout from the crowd: 'Put on the dancing vest!'

I didn't need to see the mouth to know who it had come from. I cleared my throat, trying not to crack a smile. 'As I was saying—'

'The vest! Put it on! You'll look dashing!'

Shilah glared down off the platform by my side. She also struggled to keep the laughter off her lips. These daily gatherings could get rather bleak, and Cam always tried to infuse the room with laughter. It practically never worked, and tonight I'd hoped he would refrain.

Because tonight's discussion was going to be different.

We'd reached thirty recruits, and so finally Shilah and I were going to reveal the Idea.

The Idea was something Shilah and I had been working on since we'd taken up residence beneath the city, turning the Coldmarch caverns – once an underground haven for Jadans escaping north – into living quarters for our Flock. This vast space had a source of clean water, and plenty of room for those who needed to heal. It even included my very own tinkershop, isolated from everything else and brimming with materials we'd gathered.

But the new Idea wasn't something physical, something to be tinkered together. The Idea was to be a shift in our identity. It was a mad dash to the dead-carts in nearly every sense. It was scary, daunting and seemingly impossible.

Which meant we were probably doing the right thing.

One cannot change the world without risk. I used to think differently, until it was time to effect real change. In creating the Coldmaker, even in the relative safety of the Tavor Manor, I had put many lives in danger. First and foremost my own, but more importantly, the lives of Shilah, and Cam and my barracks family.

This Idea would imperil every Jadan in the City of David's Fall. It would be like collectively ripping all the pages out of the Khat's Gospels and spitting at the Sun. We would be invoking the wrath of the entire Khatdom, and even if all went well, there was a large chance that many or all of us would die.

Which meant Cam's outbursts were out of place.

'Like I was saying,' I said to the crowd. 'I know there has been a lot of confusion lately about what we're actually—'

'Dashing, I say!' Cam shouted. 'Totally dashing!'

A collective murmur of disbelief ran through the crowd. Many of the recruits still didn't understand why we were hosting a High Noble with blonde hair, fair skin and a silly grin in the first place. A few stunned children looked at their new parents, trying to decide how to react.

Shilah and I thought that the whole idea of 'parents' and 'children' might dissolve down here in the caves – considering we were all one Flock now – but we'd been proven wrong. Pairs naturally formed. Rebelliousness served as a surprisingly unifying trait around which to build relationships. The younger Jadans looked to the older Jadans for guidance in their dissent. The older Jadans looked to the younger Jadans to be reminded of hope. Family could mean a lot of things. I thanked the Crier every day for putting me in the same barracks as my father, Abb, the best Jadan I've ever known.

My smile finally broke. 'Cam, I'm not going to put on the dancing vest.'

'No offense, Spout,' Cam said. He pointed a thin finger toward the beadwork vest, draped over the cone of rock on the platform. 'But I was talking to Shilah.'

Shilah ran her tongue across her back teeth, her eyes alight. She waved her fist at Cam. 'I'll wrap this around your face if you interrupt again, Camlish Tavor.'

'Anyway,' I said, stifling a laugh, 'I know a lot of you have been asking about Langria lately, and why we continue to hide down here instead of continuing the Coldmarch . . .'

'Bunch of priss nonsense!' Ellcia shouted out, her face darkening to the colour of her freckles. 'Langria ain't no bettah than what we got. Langria being just stories.'

Ellia gave an affirming nod from behind her sister's shoulder.

This was a common belief. Even I doubted the existence of Langria, and knew we couldn't count on the legendary city to help. For all I knew, our Flock was the only community of free Jadans in the entire World Cried, and what mattered was finding more Frosts here in the City of David's Fall.

'We're honouring the Coldmaker,' Leah shouted out, her fingers dancing through the air in front of her. Whenever she spoke, others went quiet. I was used to her incomparable beauty by now, which included large eyes and a full bottom lip, but I understood how others could still get stunned into silence. 'We're honouring you! You've saved us all, Meshua.'

Heat rose into my face. I kept my gaze off Shilah. 'Thank you.'

'You look Cold, Meshua Shilah!' Cam called, clapping his

hands in a fast beat. 'If only there were some dancing garment you could put on to help with that. If only there was some way to move your body to warm up, with rhythm and a shaking of the hips.'

Shilah blushed, but there was also a smirk beneath it.

'You put it on!' I called back to Cam, feeling slightly annoyed.

We had an Idea to share; something that would change the shape of the fight to come. I wanted to laugh and joke as much as everyone, but now was not the time. There was work to be done.

'Okay, I will,' Cam said with a shrug and began nuzzling his way through the crowd. Some of the newer recruits flinched away before he could make contact, hunching tight and returning to their slave stances.

Cam tried to keep his tone light, but his pain was clear every time they shirked away. 'Make way,' he said. 'Amazing dancer coming through. My moves are only accurately described as dangerous and intoxicating. They call me "Old Droughtweed Feet".'

'This is serious,' Shilah said, biting her trembling lip. It looked like anger from afar, but I knew the shaking was from laughter.

Cam stopped next to one of our newest recruits, a bony girl named Rivkah. Cam nudged her with his elbow. 'That half of Meshua's pretty attractive when she's being serious. Am I right?'

Rivkah curled into her slave stance.

Cam slumped even deeper.

'Camlish!' This time the shout came from Split the Pedlar, our other resident High Noble. Split had been the one to guide us along the Coldmarch, and I owed him everything. 'You're not a part of this, son. Let the Jadans have their moment.'

Split's doughy belly, thin hair and constant layer of dirt made him more approachable to the recruits than Cam, as Split lacked the stately look common in High Nobles. Still the Flock generally kept their distance from him as well; unless of course they wanted to see Split's dwarf camel, Picka.

Cam went to say something, his expression defensive, but eventually he slunk away and gave a conceding nod.

'It's okay, Split,' I said. 'The moment belongs to all of us.'

I turned to Shilah with a go-ahead look.

'You sure you don't want to do it?' she whispered out of the side of her mouth.

I shook my head. 'You'll do it better.'

She smirked, keeping her voice down. 'Because . . .'

'Because without you I'd still be tinkering crank-fans in the dark.'

'Good answer.' She put a hand around my waist and pulled me against her, the two halves of Meshua coming together as one. Leah shot Shilah a look of pure distain, turning to whisper something to Ellia.

Clearing her throat, Shilah stood a little taller, which I didn't realize was possible until I looked down at her feet and saw she was standing on her toes.

'Jadans of the Flock,' Shilah said. 'Some of you are new, and some of you have been down here with us for weeks now. We appreciate you leaving your barracks families; for taking a chance on hope. Our Jadan ancestors have been waiting the last eight hundred years for us to be in this position.' Her face contorted with anger. 'The whole Khatdom is built on lies!' She breathed deep and the fire faded just as quickly as it had arrived. 'Lies that have eroded down, and we've already begun to expose the truth beneath. The Nobles tell us that we are unworthy, yet we have a Frost inside the Coldmaker! We have a machine that *makes* Cold more powerful than anything the Khat has. For the first time since the

Great Drought, the Jadan people have Ice. You have all tasted the Ice, and you know what power it holds.'

A collective whisper rushed through the Flock. It was close to a cheer, but not quite there. Everyone was on edge, waiting.

My stomach went tight. I wasn't ready to admit that our Frost, which powered the Coldmaker, had dwindled down to the size of a Shiver. We'd overworked the holy Cold, and were no longer giving the daily rations of Ice of which Shilah spoke. We'd switched over to using stolen Wisps and Drafts, the two smallest denominations of Cold, to keep everyone alive. The abbs had become ceremonial, only used while recruiting.

Which is why we so desperately needed the new Idea to work. There was no telling how many Frosts were in the Sanctuary. They wouldn't solve all of our problems, but they would at least buy us plenty of time while I worked on the biggest Idea of all.

Flight.

'The Nobles tell you that the Crier keeps his Eye closed to us,' Shilah continued, gesturing around the Coldmarch cave. The stone walls were painted with dozens of Opened Eyes, representing our salvation. 'But we have been safe within our new home!' Shilah boomed, making the crying gesture down her cheek. 'Our numbers continue to grow. Even with all these eyes staring at us, it is the Nobles who cannot see us. The Crier obviously does not want us captured; He wants us to succeed.'

The murmuring grew louder. Cam's face went slack with awe as he stared. I couldn't blame him for the admiration. Shilah's ferocity entranced us all.

'The decree of unworthiness tells us that we should be tortured and be made to feel like lesser beings,' Shilah said, her confidence swelling. She unsheathed the flameless blade from her belt and waved it in front of the crowd. 'But we killed the Vicaress of Paphos and took her weapon. She can't hurt us any longer.'

'Mostly because she's dead,' Cam added, wiggling his eyebrows but somewhat hushed.

Shilah rolled her eyes but ended the gesture with a wink. 'And you know what? The Vicaress of David's Fall will be next.'

A few mouths gasped, but not everyone seemed surprised to see Shilah make such a declaration. Some fists even clenched along with her.

'Is that the plan?' Samsah called up, a dark excitement piercing his words. Samsah was a stout Builder, his skin like the underside of a stone at night. He was vocal and proud, constantly trying to prove himself. 'To kill the Vicaress here?'

'The sooner that happens the better,' I interjected, looking over to our weapon wall. I'd heard plenty of stories that claimed this Vicaress was even more unsettling than the one we'd slain, but I'd yet to witness her in person. 'But the plan is actually much bigger than that.'

Shilah approached the sacred pool, which swirled next to the dancing platform. The pond was moving slowly, unlike when, not too long ago, the whole thing had been forged into Ice. I could still see the black-clad body of the Vicaress sprawled lifelessly across the surface, her terrible blade extinguished. It was one of my favourite memories.

Shilah took one knee. She steeled her jaw and held that very blade over the water.

I gave her a nod to start the reaction.

I'd rigged up a little bit of tinkering on the blade earlier in the day, to give us a small spectacle to go along with the Idea. I'd smeared a thin layer of honey across the metal and then sprinkled it with abb gratings, small enough they kept their form.

Shilah dipped the blade in the water.

The water tinged gold for a moment. The point at which the metal touched the water gaped with colour and crystals, like a beautiful wound. The entire blade was immediately enrobed in a thick layer of Ice.

Shilah struggled to pull the blade back out of the water. She looked to me with a helpless grin, digging her heels into the rock as she strained. I hadn't known the metal would gather so much Ice – we couldn't test it earlier, it case the blade broke – and so I went to her side and tried to help her shoulder the weight. We couldn't lift it, but we were able to slide the huge block of Ice the blade had gathered onto the dancing platform. The metal was now lost deep within a glistening mass the size of a small pyramid stone.

Shilah and I looked at each other, our faces lit up with happy embarrassment. We only intended for the blade to cover itself in a thin layer of Ice so we could shatter the whole thing with a hammer, but there was something wonderful in such small failures. They reminded us we weren't perfect. We weren't saviours. I suddenly didn't feel so heavy.

Shilah wiped her face and stood up, squinting one eye as she thought.

'As you can see,' she said, gesturing to the Ice, 'this is what we are going to do to the Khatdom. Cover them with our might. Show them how something that only seems like a few specks can still have real power.'

I stood by her side, impressed by how quickly she'd come up with something believable.

Excited chatter sprouted across the cave.

'The plan is,' Shilah said, reading the crowd, 'we're going to take the City of David's Fall, and with it, every Frost hidden here.'

The Flock went silent.

'What does that mean?' Samsah asked.

'It means,' Shilah said, 'with more Frosts come more

Coldmakers. So we're going to drive out the Nobles. All of them. And take their Cold.'

Cam bristled.

Shilah cracked her knuckles. 'Almost all of them. As you know, Split and Cam are most valuable to our Flock.'

Another murmur. Cam looked at his feet, his cheeks going red.

'How are we to do such a thing?' Samsah asked. 'We are yours to command to the death, Meshuas, but how do we drive them out? There are at least five hundred Nobles in the city, including all of the Khat's forces from Paphos. Even with the Hookmen—'

'We have no Hookman,' Shilah said, glaring. 'We only have the Five.'

A shudder ran through the cave.

The Five stood off to the side, silent as usual. They were once the most trusted guard to the Vicaress of Paphos, and even though they had betrayed her and turned to our side most of the Flock still didn't trust them. Behemoth frames and Closed-Eye brands on their foreheads didn't help. I was beginning to understand the Five as Jadans, and not as monsters, but many still saw them as the nightmares our parents warned us about should we wander too far from obedience.

'I'm working on a few things,' I said, gesturing to the tinkershop tunnel. 'And it's going to come down to convincing everyone's old barracks to rise up when the time comes. There may be five hundred Nobles in the city, but there are twice as many Jadans, and sometimes it's not only about bigger numbers. One Chill is as Cold as a hundred Wisps. One storm can shift a hundred dunes.'

Abb used to tell me that. I always listened to his words, but only recently have I begun to understand them.

'Within the next week,' I continued, 'we will be taking the

Sanctuary. After that, we'll take the city itself. We have the Wraiths, and when we liberate the Frosts from the Sanctuary, we will have all sorts of new power. If there's any Jadan in here who doesn't want to fight for that power, don't be ashamed, because there's plenty to do here in the cave—'

'If there's any Jadan in here who doesn't want to fight,' Shilah said, her face going stern and her voice as Cold as a hundred Wisps, 'it must be because they have forgotten what life is like outside of the Flock. The fear. The beatings. Gasping for Cold as the Sun burns you to the bones, the Nobles lighting up Droughtweed and laughing at our pain.'

My stomach tightened. I didn't want to force the Flock to put their lives in danger, but we needed as many of them as we could get to fight. Our situation was difficult to say the least, and a single warrior could mean the difference between victory and defeat.

Single fingers are good for poking, but only together can they make a fist – another one of Abb's sayings.

'Is there anyone here that won't fight with us?' Shilah asked.

No one made a sound. Not even the youngest recruits.

'Good,' Shilah said, her jaw sleek and defined. 'I only ask out of love. Love for our people and for the Crier. And I promise, when the time comes, we'll be ready.' She made the crying gesture down her cheek, which the Flock returned in unison. 'For now, Micah and I have work to do.'

And then with a heave, she kicked the handle of the blade, the block of Ice sliding into the water. She kissed me on the cheek and then stepped off the platform, manoeuvring into the crowd. Cam cut her off before she could get far, giving her the first hug. She seemed self-concious in his grip, but eventually she squeezed back, her hand cupping the bottom of his golden hair. She held on for longer than normal.

The crowd turned to each other and embraced with feverish

holds. I stepped off the platform and returned all the waves and worried smiles sent my way. Leah began to rush towards me, and I quickly looked around the room.

Dunes, my ally and friend, broke free of the other Five. He rolled his shoulders together and bent his knees, making his massive frame as small as possible. He always walked around the cave like this so as not to intimidate, even though it never worked. The other Five remained in place on the side as always, waiting for my command.

Dunes rushed onto the platform and embraced me. He smelled like sweat and sand, and had the intense musk I found only in older Jadans. His arms were much broader than my father's, by for a moment I could pretend.

'Hold on!' Samsah yelled, clapping his hands for attention and breaking the din. 'I'm sorry. I'm not trying to undermine you in any way Meshua, both Meshuas, but someone has to say this. What about the last time the Jadans tried to hold this city? Are we forgetting about the Fall itself? Right now we have Cold and food and a semblance of freedom. Shouldn't we protect this beautiful thing. We have our own, little version of Langria down here.'

Shilah turned to me and gave a wry smile.

I had a feeling someone was going to bring this up. We encouraged the Flock to speak their minds.

'It's a good point,' I said, stepping back up on the platform. I kept my voice soft, as Split had taught me, to get people to really listen. 'But it will be different this time. Back then the Khat had a weapon that he used to boil the land. Desert. He planted it outside of the walls.'

'Do we think that, or actually know that?' Samsah asked.

'It's the only explanation that makes sense,' Shilah said, holding up Split's copy of the Book of the March: the one with all the prophecies and secrets the Jadan people had gathered over the centuries. 'For now we have to have faith.'

'And what happens if he uses the Desert weapon again?' Samsah asked. 'Do we really need more Frosts that badly?'

'Yes. We Do.' I took a deep breath. 'And if the Khat tries to use Desert again, I could get a hold of some, then I could study it. If I figure out how it works we can use it against him.'

Samsah absently rubbed his hand over his forearm, which was thick with scars. The Builders always had rough skin. 'And if we all burn in the process?'

Dunes came to my defense. 'Then we burn together.'

'Then we burn together, priss!' Ellcia cackled. 'But no worrying because we won't burn.'

Leah slunk her way to my side, her hand resting gently on my lower back, sending a shiver up my spine.

'And we all believe that you'll succeed,' she cooed.

I put my hand over hers and patted in a friendly manner. I still couldn't really look at her directly, as her skin was like smooth chocolate and her hair was thick as yarn. I had to be the most cautious when looking at her eyes. Light green: the colour of life itself. So seductive they could heat me up to the point of melting.

'Weapons?' Samsah asked hopefully. 'The Wraith weapons, is that how we will win?'

'Yes,' I said, looking away.

'And they are strong enough to—'

'Leave him alone, Samsah!' Leah lashed. 'This boy – the beautiful Meshua! – is responsible for the Coldmaker. For showing you Ice and freedom. You owe him blind allegiance.'

Shilah almost gagged.

Samsah lowered into a bow. 'Of course. And he has it. I just thought a bit of perspective from someone a little more . . . experienced might be welcome.'

'And what experience do you have tinkering miracles?' Leah asked, her voice like a whip with a dozen tails. She lowered her hand to a dangerous position on my back, her nails digging into my skin.

Samsah quickly backed down. 'Apologies. I feel ashamed for—'

'It's okay, it's good,' I said, tapping Leah's hand for release, which did nothing in the way of getting me released. 'We should all speak our minds. Part of the Opened Eye is seeing the world from other perspectives.'

'Divine,' Leah said, hand going up and teasing the back of my neck. 'You really are the Crier's son, aren't you?'

My stomach crawled with heat, sinking downward.

Shilah came over and yanked me from Leah's grasp, putting her arm around my shoulder and leading me away.

'Like I said,' Shilah began, angling towards the tinkershop tunnel, 'we have work to do.'

'Can I come?' Cam asked.

'You never need an invitation,' I said.

'Actually I think Micah and I need some alone time.' Shilah winked at me. 'World Partner to World Partner.'

Leah scowled.

Cam sagged into himself. 'That's okay. I have some reading to do anyway.'

Shilah and I made our way through the crowd, members of the Flock stopping to declare their allegiance or congratulate us on a fine plan. To their credit, not a single Jadan told us they wouldn't fight.

Shilah and I were nearing the tunnel to the tinkershop when I stopped and squeezed back towards the Five. Their need for formality still never sat right in my stomach, but they always insisted. I couldn't have them standing menacingly in the corner, not so much as moving their chests to breathe.

'Dismissed,' I said, bowing to them.

The Five bowed back in unison.

'By your command,' they said together.

Then they snapped out of attention, breaking rank.

Even though I was closest with Dunes, Jia was the first to scoop me into a hug, his thick belly getting in the way of skinny arms. He'd been the most rotund of the Hookmen to begin with, but since coming to the cave he'd filled out to quite the impressive size. He always offered to share the candied figs he got on raids, but none outside of the Five or I ever wanted to eat with him.

'Micah, you delightful genius,' Jia said. His voice jiggled nearly as much as his haunches. 'The crumbling of the Khatdom is near.'

'We can't get overconfident.'

Jia released me and I took a deep breath. He smelled like roasted honey.

Het, the second shortest of the Five, put a hand over his heart and made one of the many secretive warding gestures he knew; smuggled over from the other side of the Drought. 'I will give you all the wards I know. The protection of the Ancestors will be upon you.'

'Thank you.' I didn't quite believe in the mystical sort of inventing, but still I said: 'I'll need them.'

Kasroot stepped up next, holding out a greasy lump. 'Want some soap?'

These weren't insults like I had originally thought. To Kasroot, cleanliness and hygiene were signs of divinity: a gift from the Crier. Especially in Jadans. The first time we'd spoken – after he did his part to kill the Vicaress and then pledged his life to me – he'd offered me a sprig of Khatmint to rub over my teeth.

I took the soap. 'Thank you, Kasroot.'

Cleave gave a small twitch of his neck that I took as a respectful greeting. He was the strongest, fastest and tallest of the Five. Dunes told me he'd made a vow not to speak until he saw the holy land of Langria. I had a feeling his voice was too deep for normal ears to hear; like the sky before a sandstorm.

Dunes reached out and touched my bronze fingers; the ones replacing the ruined flesh I'd commanded Dunes to cut off.

'Every day I regret this,' he said. 'And every day I'm proud that you chose me to do it.'

I moved the brass digits with the ring around my middle finger. It was the next best thing to real, and considering the Cold accident that had burned the two smallest fingers on that hand, I was just grateful I still had so much of my original hand left. 'Well they were only getting worse, and since someone had to stop the infection from spreading,' I said, staring up at the long scar on Dunes' cheek, 'I'm glad it was friend.'

Dunes stepped back and gave a bow so low that anyone else would have toppled. 'I'll take this city for you myself. I'll maim every Noble and bring you their fingers as tribute.'

'I know you will.' I smiled.

Kasroot reached into a pocket and removed the pumice rock he used for scraping away dead skin. He tried to hand that over as well, but I politely declined.

'Micah!' Shilah called, waving me back over.

I gave the Five another bow. As I turned, I glanced at the swirling pool. The block of Ice floated on top, a glint of steel buried deep at its core.

Chapter Three

My tinkershop kept me from going mad.

The place had everything I needed. Space to experiment. Thick walls that kept the clangs and churning confined. And enough materials that I could attempt inventing whatever idea called to me.

Best of all, however, was that the tinkershop had solitude.

I'd come to realize that time alone was as important to inventing as the materials themselves.

I had initially done all my tinkering out in the main chamber, set up so everyone could see and help. The Flock had watched me at my craft, and I'd answered questions about materials while I worked. I'd tinkered special requests like crank-fans and indulged Leah's constant distractions of lounging beside my worktables and offering to hold things for me. Asking me if there was anything I wanted to hold of hers.

I was able to get about an hour's worth of tinkering done each day.

After the first few weeks, I felt drained, disillusioned, and with my ideas waning with every moment my hands were idle. The confidence in me had congealed to insecurity. Everything felt as hollow as the passageways. Some days my chest was so tight that I couldn't breathe, having to lay on my back and force my lungs to find air. I'd thought maybe it was a leftover sickness from the time in my life addled by Droughtweed smoke, but the episodes always subsided when I found my space. I had to turn Cam and Shilah down on multiple scouting missions, claiming I had to work on the Coldmaker, when really I was just filled with unrecognizable dread.

So one day I strapped the Coldmaker bag around my shoulder, took a few figs from the communal barrel, and headed out tired and deflated to explore the caverns without saying a word to anyone.

I came back with a plan.

Within hours, Cam and the Five had helped move everything through the damp caverns and into my new tinkershop. Metals, trinkets, vials, clay urns, gears, scrolls and countless other baubles salvaged during the night. Everyone knew where I'd gone, but the Flock respected me enough to let me pretend it was a secret.

I was able to disappear, and through the solitude, find myself once again.

Today's session in the tinkershop started off as most others did, although how it ended would hold much more weight. In a few hours' time, the Flock was either going to take the Sanctuary or end up back in chains.

I just hoped my Wraiths would be enough.

I began with my morning ritual of sawing chunks of salt crystals from the walls. The crystal cones were a beautiful pink, and didn't release without a fight. I ground the salt down in my churning wheel or powder bowl, and the repetitive motion helped centre me. Often my best ideas came while I was churning salt, but right now I wasn't searching for ideas so much as courage.

The Wraiths were ready. And they were the most vicious piece of tinkering I'd ever done.

The Crier help whoever got in their way.

Shilah entered the tinkershop, pushing aside the two shields that I'd bound end to end to form a door across the fissure. It was the only entrance or exit to my secret space. The shields were heavy and thick, useful for keeping sound inside.

I turned back to the salt wall, sawing another piece. There had been Opened Eyes painted on the crystals when I'd discovered the room, and I made sure never to defile any salt chunks with the symbol on them.

'How you feeling?' Shilah asked.

I gritted my teeth, the muscles in my arm straining. 'Truthfully?'

'I didn't know you and I spoke anything else. Just tell me, Spout.'

I breathed a little easier at the sound of my old name. The teeth of the saw caught halfway through the salt. 'I'm terrified.'

'You stormed the Sanctuary once before,' she said. 'To try and rescue a certain someone. Someone who was in the process of rescuing herself, but was grateful for your timing nonetheless.'

I didn't turn around. I was in no mood to joke. Smiling was a window, and I wanted to keep my fear hidden from everyone, including her.

Shilah came across the tinkershop and laid a hand on my shoulder. Her touch felt different from anyone else's. There was no jolt of dangerous excitement like I got from Leah, but this was somehow better. Shilah wasn't pressing into me. She was taking away some of the weight.

'We're going to win,' she said. 'Those bastards will never see it coming. And the Five are all eager to fight. Imagine Cleave barrelling down on you with a Wraith in front of him.'

'*That* would actually scare me.'

Shilah squeezed me playfully in the shoulder. 'The whole

Flock is ready, and there can't be more than fifty Nobles still in the Sanctuary, not with all those rumours we've been spreading. The guards are starting to give up and get confused, thinking that we've escaped to Marlea. Last time Cam and I went out, we saw—'

'When was that?' I asked, trying not to sound sullen. It was my own fault for not going, as I'd turned them down the last few times. But I had to work on the Wraiths.

'Two days ago,' she said.

'You take Jia with you?'

'Kasroot actually. He's better at the sneaking. All that nervousness makes him extra careful.'

'That's good.'

Shilah paused. 'What are you scared of?'

'I'm not scared about the Sanctuary,' I said, idly gesturing to the three stout Wraiths in the centre of the room. 'We're going to win.'

Shilah went over and ran her hand along the reinforced sides of the Wraiths. The design wasn't terribly complex, but it was effective. More or less they were large transportable basins, able to spray out a terrible bit of alchemy. I'd covered the interior clay chamber with steel in case the Nobles tried to shoot at them with arrows. Clay could shatter. Steel would not. I almost chiselled Opened Eyes into the metal like I'd done with the Coldmaker, but decided against it. The Opened Eye was a symbol of hope and paradise. The Wraiths were symbols of pain and agony.

I kept sawing the salt.

'Meshua,' she said.

I turned around slowly, wiping my forehead, saw dangling by my side. Shilah never called me that, especially since we tried so hard to keep the Flock from seeing us in that light. I squeezed the handle of the saw tighter, a dense rock settling into my stomach.

'Is that what you want?' Shilah asked. 'To be the legendary child of the World Crier? The invincible warrior that was sent here by prophecy to free our people?'

I swallowed hard. 'No. You know that.'

'Well then who do you want to be?'

'Me.' I leaned over the nearest table and rested my body weight on my knuckles. I finally let out a sigh that had been building over the long, sleepless night. 'I just want to be me.'

Shilah came to my side. 'So be you.'

'But—'

She took my cheeks in her hands and made me stare her in the eyes. 'Meshua is just a story, Spout. Just a pretty story to make us feel like there's an ending to our suffering. It gives people comfort, but it also made them believe that someone is coming to save them. But you and I both know the only way our people are going to get free is if we save ourselves. It's obvious that the Crier, real or not, hasn't been able to intervene. Eight hundred years has made that very clear. Meshua isn't real. *You* are real.'

'Real can fail.'

'Yes,' she said, plucking at my lip with her thumb. 'But a story has no chance of success in itself. Words can't lift a single grain of sand. Stories can change people, but it's only people who can manifest change.'

I lifted an eyebrow.

Shilah shrugged, giving me a guilty smirk. 'Cam's been having me read some of the old philosopher texts we found in the—'

'But if we fail – not at the Sanctuary, but if . . .' I felt my hands begin to shake. 'You know what can happen as much as I do.'

Shilah took my hands and gave them a squeeze.

'I assume you're talking about the extermination of our people.'

I nodded. 'Things are balanced for now. Terrible, but balanced. At least we exist. At least the Khat keeps us alive.'

'Don't you forget where you come from. Don't forget like the others.'

I pulled up my shirt to reveal all the scars from when the Vicaress had tortured me. Shilah had saved me that night, and if not for her I'd be dead.

'*I* know where you come from,' Shilah said. 'Just checking that you do to.'

'When we win,' I said, 'when we take the Sanctuary and show our strength, the Khat's not just going to roll over and accept our victory. He's going to fight with everything he has. He's going to send armies from all across the Khatdom, calling on forces we don't even know about. He's going to use every trick the Nobles have learned since the Drought. He's got far better inventors than me in the Pyramid, and worse of all, he's going to take it out on our families. You know that, right? He's going to send his taskmasters into our old barracks and slaughter our families by the hundreds. To draw us out and make us collapse with grief.'

Shilah gave a hard nod. 'I'm aware.'

'He doesn't need to keep *any* of the Jadan people alive,' I said softly. 'That's the sad truth. He could kill every single Jadan, wipe us out, and the world would go on. Cold will still fall for him. Yes, the Nobles would have to do all the hard work in the Patches, and building the monuments, but that might be a sacrifice he's willing to make. The Khat's Anthem has a point. We only survived because of his mercy.'

'Sun-damn screw the Khat's Anthem,' Shilah spat. 'I've never even sung it.'

'How is that possible?'

'I don't know, maybe I have. The point is that, yes, he could exterminate us all.'

'And that doesn't terrify you? That our small little Flock,

started by me and you, might end up destroying the entire Jadan race?'

Shilah's eyes sparkled with intensity. 'Scares me to my bones.'

'So then what if we fail?'

'Exactly, *we*. What if *we* fail. You have me to lead beside you,' Shilah said. 'All this time I've been trying to get it through to you that you're not alone.' She toyed with her braid. 'I thought Cam was the one with the thick skull.'

I kept my face flat. 'He does have a big head.'

Shilah smiled, a secret begging to come off her lips.

'What?' I asked.

She glanced over her shoulder and then back. 'What if we win? What if we're the ones who end the Drought?'

'I don't know how to end the Drought.'

'How many Frosts are in the Sanctuary you think?' she asked.

'Split thinks dozens. Maybe none, though.'

'Even if it was only a few. Imagine having more Coldmakers while we figure out how to fly! Abbs everywhere, cooling water, and making gardens so big that we could all finally grow some fat on our bones. We could take in hundreds of runaways. The rest of the Jadans across the Khatdom would look at us, at our stand, and wonder how. Wonder why. How long has it been since our people have had something to wonder about? Terrible answers have been forced down our throat for so long, that we forget how to hunger for truth.'

'Another old philosopher?'

'Hell no.' Shilah slapped her stomach, the firm skin resounding with a flat sound. 'From the gut.'

'You've thought this through.' I scraped the salt on the pillar with my bronze finger and then brought it to my tongue. The tip stung. 'I hope you're right.'

'When have I not been? And besides, you don't think the

Jadans of Langria didn't worry about the same thing? About provoking the Khat? And they're still there, still fighting.'

'We don't know anything about Langria.'

Shilah crossed her arms over her chest. 'Excuse me, tinkerer, but I believe I created my own Little Langria once. You were there.' Her eyebrow raised playfully. 'You don't remember the taste of my Khatmelon?'

I threw my hands up in defeat. 'Right again.'

'Damn right.'

At last, ease in my stomach. 'You always know what to say to calm me down.'

She slapped me lightly on the cheek, leaving her hand to linger. 'Enjoy it while you can. Tonight I set you ablaze. I want to see the Micah who trapped a hundred sick bastards into a room and Iced over their dead bodies.'

'Can you kiss me?'

The words came out before I could think about their impact. I went stiff, but Shilah didn't so much as flinch. It had been quite some time since we'd explored anything in the realm of romance, and it wasn't something I dwelled over. There were too many other, bigger concerns to worry over.

'Sorry,' I said, heat rising to my cheeks. 'It's just that—'

Shilah shrugged like it was no big deal. 'Of course I can kiss you.'

She leaned in and pressed her lips against mine. Her mouth was cold and wet, as if she'd just drank her rations. Our lips took a moment to stop sliding about before they held firm. She pressed hard, her hands coming to the back of my head and scraping through my hair, her fingernails massaging my scalp.

After a moment we parted and looked deep into each other's eyes.

Then we began laughing.

It was simple laughter; of recognition; of connection. The

chuckles came from our hearts more than our mouths, and it was a wonderful moment.

I didn't feel a thing.

It appeared that neither did she.

I took her hands again in mine and gave them a powerful squeeze. 'I really am so lucky to have you.'

'I'm the lucky one. Also, I think Cam's outside,' she whispered. 'Want to call him in so he doesn't feel left out?'

'Cam!'

Silence.

'How do you know he's out there?'

Shilah gave me an obvious sort of look.

'Cam!' I called, giving her hands one final squeeze before letting them go. 'You can come in!'

A crown of golden hair popped around the shield-door. Cam kept his gaze averted as he entered, looking around wildly. I could see the pain in his eyes. There was unsteadiness in his step. He must have heard what we'd done.

'Bigger in here then I remember,' he said, surveying the decoy boxes, voice boomers, Cold-Charged clay urns, and every other thing I was in the process of tinkering. None were as impressive and menacing as the Wraiths.

'Is it?' I asked.

He nodded, whistling a soft tune and gently slapping a fist into his open palm.

'What's going on Cam?' I asked, wiping my mouth with the back of my hand.

Shilah took another step away.

'Just figured the three of us should have a quiet moment together.' He ambled about the workshop, his movements rather awkward. 'A lot's about to change.'

He stopped at the nearest table to pick up a half-filled vial and examine the contents. He looked at the venom inside with a studious expression.

'For the Stingers,' I explained. 'Going to top them off before tonight.'

He picked up one of the Stingers – one of my old weapon designs, more or less a dagger that could inject poison – by the long handle, examining the triangular blades at the end. Scorpions were more than plentiful in the damp, sprawling Coldmarch caves, and so I had enough poison to make a Stinger for every fighter in the Flock. The design was simple enough, back from the times in my youth when efficiency and ingenuity were the only things in large supply. But simple didn't mean ineffective. Stingers could deliver a lethal dose of poison: their blades were sharp and their springs were tight.

'So are you ready?' Shilah asked. 'There might be other High Nobles in the Sanctuary. Other Tavors.'

Cam gave Shilah a pained look. He put the weapon back down. 'I probably shouldn't have intruded. You two have the quiet moment and just find me later if you want.'

I wanted to say something to reassure him. To remind him that Leroi, the High Noble who'd taken me in and taught me how to be an Inventor, the one who'd died holding off the Vicaress so we could escape, was a Tavor.

I was about to open my mouth but Shilah beat me to action. She stormed through the tinkershop and grabbed Cam by the arm. 'Get your bony butt over here, you whiny baby. You know I didn't mean it like that.'

Cam looked down at his feet, his face red.

Shilah yanked him closer to where I was standing, sighing as she pulled. 'I'm sorry. I apologize. I'll make it up to you later.'

I could see the lump forming in Cam's throat.

I lit a candle and filled three chalices with water, dropping a Wisp into each from our stockpile of Cold. The abbs were now too precious to use for drinking. I wished we could use Cold crossbows in the upcoming battle, like when we stormed the Sanctuary the first time, but considering the Frost's shrinking stature, it seemed like the poor Coldmaker might only be capable of making a few dozen abbs more. We couldn't stall any longer; we had to take the Sanctuary not only so we'd have another stronghold – one that could fit a lot more Jadans – but to harvest the Frosts hidden somewhere in its depths.

'To a quiet moment,' I said, lifting my chalice.

Shilah gave me a playful nudge with her elbow. 'You can do better than that, Micah. Just think where we were a year ago. Just think about how the future free Jadans will celebrate our gathering.'

'Then to a quiet moment with my closest friends,' I said, tipping the cup towards Cam. 'Who happen to be my family.'

'Thank you,' Cam said softly, staring at his feet.

I didn't remember him ever being so distant. He'd been respecting my tinkering space ever since I told him I'd been working on something big. I tried to recall the last time Cam and I had spent time together and came up blank. He and Shilah had been spending most of the last week in disguise, inviting me out to ransack the city for materials, and I'd been a terrible friend, telling them to stay away.

'Cam,' I said, 'I'm glad you're here.'

He gave me a tentative look, pushing the golden rim glasses back up his nose. 'Yeah?'

'I was going to come find you anyway,' I said, nodding towards the centre of the tinkershop. 'I'm putting you in charge of one of the Wraiths. One for me, one for Shilah, and one for you.'

He cocked his head to the side. 'I'm honoured. But I don't even know how they work. I figured you were putting the Five in charge of them.'

'Remember I told you I had that idea about enhancing the Cold Charges?' I asked. 'Or at least trying to.'

'Of course,' he said, looking away.

Clearly I'd forgotten to tell him. I wanted to kick myself for not celebrating the breakthrough with him sooner, especially since I'd figured out something that not even his cousin Leroi could.

'I figured out how to make the Charge stronger,' I said. 'And turn it into a weapon.'

Cam gestured towards the three Wraiths. I nodded.

'Sorry I didn't tell you earlier. I should have given you more warning so you could practice, but I don't think you'll need it. They're easy enough to use.'

Cam looked to Shilah for reassurance, and she gave him an excited nod.

'It was always the plan,' she said. 'That's kind of why I made that bad joke.'

'Really?'

'Really.'

'I get to lead one of the secret weapons?' he asked.

'You were good with that Cold crossbow last time,' I said, severity taking away all semblance of humour. We hadn't talked much about the battle at the Sanctuary, and I wondered if Cam had been having an easier time than me processing it all. Those bastards deserved it for what they did to Shilah, but the ability to viciously kill was a serious thing to find out about yourself. 'So if you think you can handle it.'

He straightened up and puffed out his chest. 'Absolutely I can.'

Hurrying over to the middle Wraiths, he ran his hand over the front hose coming out of the body. The hose ran about an arm's length and ended in a custom nozzle. 'How does it work?' He slid a finger across the inside of the nozzle and immediately let out a yelp. His whole body jerked. Reflexively, he went to put the burning finger in his mouth, but Shilah was already next to him, catching him by the wrist.

'You don't want to do that,' she said.

Cam's face clenched with pain. He stared at his finger, dancing back and forth between feet. 'Shivers and F-frosts that hurts! It's – it's – it stings. It's melting me!'

I rushed over to him. A clean piece of boilweed and the antidote vial were already out for exactly this. I wiped his finger dry with the boilweed – he winced and grimaced at the pressure – and then I smeared on my special mixture of groan salve, oil and wax. It took many burning splotches on my arms and legs to figure out a correct mixture to quell the sensation. My antidote didn't take away the burn fully, but it dulled the sensation to a throb.

Shilah let Cam's wrist go. She brought the slimy finger to her face to investigate.

'What just happened?' he asked.

'Feel better?'

He met my eyes. 'I'm fine. That was really painful. How'd you invent burning water? You mix in that scorpion venom?'

I waved Cam over to my clay urns where I'd had my breakthrough with the Cold Charge. I lifted the lid off one of the urns, but placed my hand against Cam's chest as he leaned in to take a closer look. I'd learned the hard way that the fumes burned something fierce.

'Really all I did was continue Leroi's work,' I pointed to the bowls of crushed pink salt next to the urns. Leroi used only white salts to mix when experimenting with Cold, but I don't think colour had anything to do with it. It's all salt in the end. 'Okay, so remember how the Cold Charge works? The salt dissolves in the water first and then the Cold dissolves next. But they fight each other, right? Since they're opposites. Salt being a product of death and Cold life, the mixture collecting the energy?'

Cam nodded, keeping his finger by his side. He kept twitching, and I could tell he wanted to nurse it. My skin had been sore for days after my testing.

'Remember how Leroi had hit a point where the Charge couldn't get stronger?' Shilah asked.

'Yes,' Cam said, tapping his bottom lip. 'Fifty-six Wisps. Thirty-five Drafts. Thirteen Shivers. Five Chills.'

I thought my jaw might hit the ground. 'You remember the exact number?'

Cam shrugged, rapping his knuckles against his head. 'Thick skull. It traps things I overhear.' He wouldn't meet my eyes. 'Anyway. I'm guessing you dissolved in a full abb, and that's why the Charge bites like a Sobek?'

Shilah gave him an impressed look.

I put the lid back on the urn. My nostrils were starting to burn. 'How'd you know?'

'I've learned a lot from you both,' he said. 'And that seems like something you would do, Spout.'

'You've got a smudge, and you're going to need to see this.' Shilah took Cam's glasses off his nose and removed a fresh rip of boilweed from her pocket, giving the lenses a polish. Cam held still but didn't seem surprised, as if this wasn't the first time she'd done this.

'You're exactly right,' I said, going over to the table where I tinkered the bulbs for the Sinais – the lights that needed no fire, and ran on only the Charge. The table was covered in wicks, glass and raw materials, ready to be tinkered together. I grabbed a Sinai bulb already fastened on the long copper rod. 'I dissolved in the abb, and it pushed the Cold Charge over the edge. I was originally going to try and use this new blend to power all sorts of inventions, but when I tried . . .'

I nodded to Shilah who slid the lid off the urn. I let the copper rod hover over the opening, careful not to touch metal to liquid. The fumes alone were potent enough.

The Sinai light sprung to life, bright and blinding.

'Shivers and Frosts,' Cam said, shielding his eyes. 'What happens if you put the copper rod in the water directly?'

I nodded to Shilah who passed out a few pairs of tinted eyewear. She always seemed to know what I was going to ask her to do before I did. Next I strapped a pair of thick boilweed gloves over my hands.

'Watch yourselves,' I said, shoving the rod in the liquid.

The light became bright as Sun itself. It burned inside the glass, orange and white teeth gnashing their way out. Our eyewear was barely enough protection to keep from wincing, and after a moment the glass bulb cracked in half, fire shooting up from the filament.

I yanked the copper rod away from the water and everything calmed.

Shilah slid the lid back over the urn.

'Wow,' Cam said, taking off his glasses. 'Wow.'

Shilah took her protection off as well. Char smattered on her cheek. Cam eyed it, his hand moving as to wipe it away. He thought twice, keeping his hand to himself, looking at his finger with regret.

I cocked my head to the side.

And then realization fell like a slab careening off the top of the Pyramid. It bashed me over the head.

How had I not noticed until now?

I was clearly the one with the thick skull.

'And so the – Wraith,' Cam said, looking away. 'It holds a lot of the Charged water?'

I had to shake myself back to reality, my head fuzzy with embarrassment. 'Yes. Wraith. Water.'

We all moved to the centre of the room. My legs were a bit unsteady, but not from fumes. I pointed to the different parts of the Wraith as I explained what they did, but my voice was droning. I couldn't focus, too busy sifting through memories to see if there were any signs that I'd missed.

It was so obvious.

'So the Charged water sits in the main body here,' I choked

out, tapping the reinforced clay. 'The pump here on top has a tight plunger that lets in air one way and then compresses it into the body of the Wraith, into the water, and creates pressure. It can get pretty intense, since it's airtight after I sealed the holes with Dybbuk grease. The hose in front has a lever on top here that releases the pressure and shoots the water out of the spout.'

'Spout,' Cam chimed with a smile.

'Hmm?' I asked, blinking a few times. 'What?'

'Your name,' Cam said.

'Oh right. Anyway, it's all pretty simple.' I pointed to the bottom of the Wraith, at the legs on bearings and springs, each sitting on wheel on the end. I'd made the wheels double-tiered and wide as possible, with rope nettling in between to spread out the weight over sands.

How did I not know about Cam and Shilah's feelings for each other?

'I put four spring-assisted legs on each Wraith so we can wheel them easier and quieter. They're quite heavy.'

'And how far can they shoot?' Cam asked, wincing as he touched his finger.

'It's good,' I said, missing his question. 'Oh, they can fire the water about a hundred or so paces. And sorry you got some on you, but it's probably better you know what it feels like.'

'I've been shocked by it too,' Shilah said, lifting up her shirt and revealing her stomach. There were patches of angry skin where she'd rubbed the Wraithwater away.

'Oh no,' Cam said, his face twisting with horror. He reached out to touch her but stopped at the last second, giving me a furtive glance. 'I'm so sorry.'

Shilah gave a cool shrug, not looking my way either. 'It's okay. I wanted to know.'

I nearly collapsed into the nearest chair.

How had I missed the signs?

I cleared my throat. 'The blast doesn't last particularly long, ten seconds at most before it needs to be pumped again. But even if enemy has taken cover, or they have shields in front of them and we can't fight them with arrows or swords, there's really no way for them to protect themselves against the Wraithwater. And the shock doesn't stop. I don't know at what dose it's lethal yet, but the burning can last for hours, only getting worse without the antidote. I imagine the Khat will hear Noble screams in Paphos.' I pointed to the end of the hose, where I'd put the metal mesh cap that flips over the nozzle. 'This is if you need to spread the stream.'

Cam nodded. 'This is going to be quite the weapon.'

'Only if necessary,' I said, my throat burning. 'I don't want to use it unless we have to. But we might have to. We can't lose.'

Shilah put a hand on Cam's lower back. 'Only if necessary.'

Another of Cam's fingers went inside the hose, gathering up some Charged residue.

Shilah went to stop him. 'Idiot! What are you—'

Cam waved her off, closing his eyes. He brought his finger out, his cheeks shaking as he stared at the burning skin.

'I want to feel it,' Cam said, his teeth clenched so hard that his jaw nearly locked. 'My father always called me weak, you know. He always said that it must have been one of the Domestics he violated who gave birth to me, not my mother. It was a joke for him. He used to actually joke about that sort of thing. Jadans were just things for him to have fun with and toss aside.'

He breathed deep, staring at his finger with an intensity I rarely saw.

'One day he caught me sneaking a young Domestic some leftover bread. She was shaking because she was so hungry. Our house taskmaster whipped her for something or other recently, and so I snuck her down to the kitchens and brought her back some bread and Cold water to her quarters. My father strolled in just as she was eating the last piece, but honestly he didn't seem surprised, almost like he planned the whole thing. He grabbed us both by the arms and took us into the garden. I was ten at the time. I think. And the Domestic was twelve maybe? I don't remember everything to be honest. I remember the heat the most. How angry the Sun was.'

Shilah picked up the antidote vial and a clean strip of boilweed, trying to grab Cam's hand, but he stopped her. Tears formed at the corners of his eyes.

'But my father was smiling. He told me "Camlish, today is the day I finally teach you how to be a Tavor. You've made a mistake, and you have to fix it. That's what High Nobles do." I was young, and of course looked up to my father then. He didn't seem so angry, and I just nodded and told him I was sorry. That I'd do whatever he said. He told me to simply get the bread and water back, then I could go. I didn't know what he meant, so he took the Domestic and wrenched open her mouth and pressed his fingers on the back of her tongue. He pulled his hands away right before she started gagging. "Like this," he said. "Get the bread and water back." I shook my head, and then he took out his knife. "You get the bread and water back or I cut it back." Again, he was smiling.

'I shook my head, confused. So quick that I barely saw, he sliced into the skin of her stomach, just enough to draw blood. I remember thinking how the red blended with her dark skin. My skin was so pale, and blood was always so apparent if I cut myself. The girl didn't scream at all. She just gave me a pleading look. My father cut into her again. Eventually I relented, yelling for him to stop. And so my father held the poor girl's hands behind her back and I shoved my fingers down her throat until she gave back the bread and water. She vomited and gagged as softly as she could, and most of the bile splashed on my feet. I was crying and I took my hand away, wiping it on my shirt. "All of it," my father said calmly. And so I choked her again. I made her give back the bread and water. After she was empty he gave her a soft pat on the head and sent her on her way. I never saw her around the manor again. I never asked about her. I was too ashamed.'

'Cam,' Shilah said softly.

'You say we should only use this weapon if necessary,' Cam said, staring at his finger, his eyes burning with sorrow. 'I say it's been necessary for a very long time.'

Chapter Four

I lifted my hand for stillness, bronze fingers glinting in the starlight.

The Flock halted in the sands behind me, making much less noise than I expected. The only sounds were a few clanging weapons, a couple of knocking knees, and the groan of the Wraiths coming to a standstill. For such a patchwork army, I hadn't expected everyone to move with such stealth. But we'd made it here without raising alarm.

The Sanctuary was in our sights.

Giant, gated and thick-walled, the Sanctuary was one of the few buildings in the City of David's Fall with multiple floors. Four long wings made the place a sprawling stronghold, with guard towers and sharp staircases. It wasn't quite as stately as the Khat's Pyramid, but it was expensively adorned with statues, stained glass and wrought iron. There was a dark grandness about the place; like a High Noblewoman with a silk dress and blood under her fingernails.

Traversing the plateaus to get here would have been no problem at all, if not for the unwieldy Wraiths. After the first flight of stairs along the rocky mountainside, I'd suggested leaving them back, but Shilah and Cam both insisted we couldn't afford not to have them. In the end, it took five of us carrying each machine to get them up the stairs and hills. The clay bodies were watertight, so no one carrying the machines got shocked – this seemed like a small miracle in its own right – but it had taken a few long, painfully silent hours to navigate into position.

So far we'd made our way through back alleys and deserted streets. By now the Khat's armies had bought the bait of our disappearance to Marlea, and the city was nearly empty at night. We'd found shelter in the shadows so far, but the Sanctuary was surrounded by open land.

There would be no place to hide within a hundred paces of the gates.

The Nobles had designed it like this to catch runaways, to dangle the lure of freedom and lace the bait with a hook.

I looked to the rooftops around us and smiled at each pair of eyes. These were future recruits, their dark and withered bodies pressed tighter against the hot stones. Some of them scattered away at my acknowledgment, some of them gasped and pointed at my bronze fingers.

I used to be just as skinny as these slaves. Just as scared. Just as broken. I hoped they would tell their friends what they witnessed here tonight.

We were now gathered in stillness. Our small force managed to nearly all fit in the shadows behind a Cry Temple, which only reminded me how few of us there were. Soon we'd enter the moat of visibility around the Sanctuary. There would be no turning back. It was win or chains.

I surveyed our ranks lined up on the soft ground behind us.

First were the Five, two assigned to each Wraith. They were likely to be the only ones in the Flock strong enough to push the inventions without any help. Kasroot and Het partnered up. Cleave and Jia did as well. Samsah volunteered to partner with Dunes for the third Wraith, Samsah looking like a scrawny child in comparison – although he'd held his own when it came to pushing. Cam and Shilah were both hovering in front of their respective Wraiths, the hoses in their gloved hands. I would be in charge of the third Wraith, rolled along by Dunes and Samsah.

I still couldn't look at Cam and Shilah without feeling a dizzying sense of my own ignorance. I should have been focusing on the battle ahead, but I kept thinking about this glaring development.

Behind the Five were the Builders and Street Jadans we'd recruited, weapons at the ready. Equipped with Stingers, swords and crossbows, they almost looked menacing. Hadim was fidgeting, his thick fingers twitching over the crossbow trigger.

At the very back were the Domestics and children.

I shook my head, reminding myself that 'children' was the wrong description. They were the youngest, but not children. All over the age of ten, they'd seen horrors that Nobles wouldn't even witness in a lifetime. They'd been forced to grow up too fast.

Not children.

Young warriors.

I'd been hesitant to fit them with weapons, only wanting them to carry the burden of supplies, but in the end I'd relented. They deserved a chance in case the Nobles broke through our ranks. Each young warrior shouldered a bag of supplies and a razor-sharp dagger.

Shilah came up to my side and stood as straight as I'd ever seen. Her long braid was tucked on the side of her proud face. A blade was concealed in those locks, the way she used to, and tonight the steel would taste blood.

I made the Crying gesture down my cheek.

The Flock returned the gesture in unison. Split used his dagger hand, but then remembered not to slice up his face.

'Anybody want to say anything?' I asked, my eyes on the sky. 'For inspiration.'

Shilah leaned in and put her lips against my ear. 'I think we're supposed to do that.'

I nodded, trying not to faint. My imagination was beginning to play tricks on me. I had to look away from the Flock. All I could see were faces bloodied by battle, half of them lying in the dead-carts. All I could see was suffering.

I almost called for retreat then and there. I couldn't live with myself if I was responsible for any of their deaths tonight.

Shilah nudged me with an elbow.

My throat barely agreed to make any sounds. 'I think you're all going to be great.'

A few nods of respect crossed the front rows, but fear ran rampant through the ranks.

Shilah sighed and took an abb out of her pocket, raising it for the Flock to see. She held it between her thumb and forefingers and the golden colour caught the starlight. I didn't know Shilah had any abbs left.

'Creator and Crier of everything we see,' Shilah said, her tones serious, arm stretching high. 'Here we stand before you, ready to take your world back from tyranny. Eight hundred years is too long to be subject to whip and flame, and it is finally time to set things to how you intended. To freedom. To justice. To Cold falling across the land. To all the animals and cultures that will spring back to life from the bounty of your tears.' Her face went hard and menacing. 'If this is not your will, strike me down now, because I will not stop until the Jadans are free. I promise you, I will not stop until the Jadans are free.'

The Flock went tense. A few tilted away from Shilah like plants leaning away from the Sun. The Five remained perfectly rigid. All accept Jia, who was clearly chewing something.

'If you do not want to see a Jadan with her own Cold,'

Shilah continued, 'Cry a Shiver from the heavens and send me to my death. Let it strike me between the eyes and close them forever. Knock this miracle from my hands and bloody the sands with my open veins. I promise I will not stop.'

I'd never heard her talk in such a serious way. With such poetry.

Cam started coughing, his face turning red as he tried to stifle himself.

'Sorry,' Cam said. 'I was so impressed I forgot to swallow and choked on my own spit.'

The night air became clouded with anticipation.

Shilah's hand was tense around the abb, her forearm shaking. At last she lowered her eyes and faced the Flock. 'By taking the Sanctuary, we are inviting the Sun to come at us with all the fire in the world. We are inviting the Khat to bathe in fear. He will do everything he can to snuff us out.' She held the abb out as far as she could. 'But if you feel scared, think of this Cold. This is *our* Cold. This Cold belongs to the Jadans. Their Frosts belong to the Jadans. Here is undisputable proof that the Khats have lied to us and stran- gled the world. The Crier has always believed we are worthy. Now let's prove it.'

Leah tentatively raised the banner she'd fashioned. The flag was originally supposed to have an Opened Eye, but she'd stitched on a hand with two golden fingers underneath. I don't think Shilah minded because it was obvious, especially in the moment, that there was more than one leader of the Flock.

'We fight for the Crier,' Shilah said, raising her sword.

'For the Crier,' Dunes said, slapping his meaty hand on the Wraith.

'We fight for the Jadans,' Shilah said, licking her lips and then kissing the abb. She passed it to me, giving me a go-ahead sort of look. I pressed it to my lips and found her spit having stimulated Cold throughout the golden bead. I passed it next to Cam, who kissed it the same, his eyes lighting up at the sensation. The abb made its way through the ranks of our Flock, everyone tasting what they were fighting for.

The abb found its way into the hands of Split. He hesitated, looking at the Five with disdain, who'd all handled the Cold before him.

'Split,' I said. 'You too.'

He gave me an apologetic nod, kissing the abb and passing it on.

'From now on, you do all the speeches,' I whispered to Shilah.

Her cheeks blushed.

'Okay,' she said next to the group, taking out a loop of rope. Each of us was equipped with similar pieces. 'We take the eastern gates and secure the guard room and outer wall. From there the Five will lead each faction outward into the Sanctuary, and we'll secure the hallways one by one. Bring the prisoners back to the guard room bound. Dunes?'

Dunes snapped to attention and raised his cudgel, which was padded with boilweed. The rest of the Five did the same. I advised them to wrap the weapons in boilweed, because I wanted to have our prisoners unconscious rather then dead. Merciless killing for the sake of merciless killing made us no better than the Nobles.

'After a Noble is knocked down and bound, don't just assume anything,' Shilah said. 'Those bastards will probably pretend to be dead and then bite your throat out if you don't stay sharp. Remember, every Noble we capture is a bargaining chip, so try to keep them alive. We know the layout of the Sanctuary.' Shilah gave Ellcia and Ellia a thankful look, offering only a slight nod to Leah. 'But they don't know anything about us, or how many we are. Use that to our advantage, and none of us will shed blood tonight. Most of the Nobles will be asleep, and we expect the majority of the taskmasters to be bunking in—'

A piercing scream cut her off.

The eerie sound echoed off the bricks of the Cry Temple, reverberating through the alleyway in which we'd gathered. The Flock broke rank, everyone trying to discern where the sound had come from. Weapons slid out of scabbards. Ellia dropped her Stinger. Faces hardened under threat. Rooftop onlookers twitched back into the shadows.

Cam's knuckles went pale around his Wraith's hose. 'What was that?'

'I don't know,' I said. 'Maybe a runaway?'

Shilah nodded to me. 'Let's go check it—'

Another scream. This one was followed by a chorus of throaty cheers. The sounds were distant, so I couldn't estimate any numbers, but it sounded like a full crowd.

Which made no sense.

We'd scouted for eight nights straight, and the Sanctuary was supposed to be quiet at this point in the night. It was too late for gatherings. If it was a Domestic trying to run away, she'd be tracked down by a few taskmasters or soldiers, not an entire battalion.

Dunes abandoned his post at the Wraith and knelt in front of Shilah and I.

'Let me go out there ahead of you,' Dunes said. 'There are still Hookmen in the Khatdom, and if it is a runaway out there maybe—'

Next came noises with the cadence of a speech. A voice rose and fell like a gentle wind. The tone was irritatingly familiar.

'No,' I said, taking out my Stinger and waving Dunes on. 'But you can go with me.'

Cam went to open his mouth. I nodded before he could say anything.

'Wait here,' Shilah commanded of the Flock. 'Stay sharp.'

The four of us disappeared around the building, with Dunes in the front. He looked far less threatening with the cudgel in hand instead of the hooked blade he used to carry, but he still cut a dangerous silhouette.

We sped across the empty space of dirt and sand as quietly as we could, sweeping towards the massive Sanctuary. The place was spacious and well guarded; it would serve as an excellent fortress for us.

The eastern gates were abandoned and there wasn't a single flicker of movement from the watch towers above. The shouting continued – low and growly, almost like a chant – coming from the northern area of the Sanctuary, which was just out of view.

Dunes waved us behind him as we pressed against the stone outer wall, sliding along so we wouldn't be seen. We side-stepped as fast as we could, trying to keep our clothes from rustling. My chest thundered but my hands were surprisingly steady.

The collective murmurs died and the single, airy voice returned. It became more clear as we neared the edge. There was a wet sort of rattle in the middle of the voice, but that wasn't what grated on me.

My vision went red as I realized who was talking.

'One last chance, my beautiful darling,' he said. 'Tell me where they are, where they are, or your neck gets a scar.'

The moist clacking was new, as if his tongue was dipped in clay and left to harden, but still I recognized the tone.

Panic shot into Shilah's face, and she tried to hide her fear, but it was apparent. Her hand went to the scars on her stomach.

'Please, I don't know,' a delicate voice answered back, one crack away from shattering. 'I'll do anything you want. You can make me more beautiful, more like you. I swear to the Crier that I don't know!'

'She swears to the Crier!' the voice rang out, coming from above us. It was like burnt sugar. 'How delightful is that?'

The crowd beneath answered with laughter.

Cam grabbed my wrist and mouthed: 'Ka'in.'

So all of us recognized the voice.

Ka'in. The High Noble who used to be in charge of the Sanctuary. The one who'd stolen Shilah and tried to torture her into submission. The one who picked a different Domestic to burn to death each month, making a betting game out of it, played by himself and a faction of masked High Nobles.

We'd stormed the place and locked them in a room with a deadly dose of Ice and Cold. He wasn't supposed to be alive.

'Ka'in,' I said.

'That's not possible,' Cam gasped.

'And how would the Crier hear your swears, my black-haired vision?' Ka'in called out. 'He doesn't listen to Jadan-kind-of-Jadans. Next are you going pray the Sun kisses your skin and makes you pale? Kissy kissy. You want the Sun to make you beautiful, love? There are easier ways.'

'Please,' the girl shouted. 'Please, I'll do anything! Let me prove myself!'

Someone else shouted from ground level. 'Show her, Ka'in! Show her like the others!'

'The new Khat!' someone screamed, full of righteousness and fervour. 'Ka'in is divine!'

Dunes finally skirted to the edge of the wall. He got down on his stomach and shuffled forward, just enough for him see what was happening. His large back remained still for a moment and then he returned to his feet, unsteady.

I went to take a look around the corner. Dunes pressed a hand on my chest. His look of complete sorrow also held me back.

'This is my fault,' he whispered.

'In no way is it your fault,' I said. 'If anything, it's mine.'

'What is it?' Cam whispered, his face as pale as bone. 'Should we not look?'

'I *am* divine!' Ka'in shouted from the top of the building. 'I have been made perfect! Chosen by the Crier's touch. I am the most beautiful in the World Cried. I am his most perfect creation! And dirty little slaves should know better than to lie to His most perfect creation!'

Dunes shook his head, his eyes going as dark as I'd seen. 'I should have gone back in and slit his throat. This is my doing. These are my deaths, Meshua.'

'I would never have let you go back,' I said. 'That much Ice and Cold would have killed you too.'

Kneeling down, Dunes thrust out his arm and turned over his wrist. I nearly fell over from shock and confusion. It was the same gesture my friend Matty used to make when he was nervous, offering up his 'Calm Spot' for me to touch and ease his worries. With trembling fingers and a mind clouded with disarray, I began to reach out, thinking of Matty, my lost friend. My heart squeezed. Dunes ignored my hand and took out his small dagger. I was yanked back to reality.

He pressed the blade against his wrist.

I nearly shouted for him to stop, but then I realized what he was doing.

His wrist was one of the few patches of skin on his body left without a death tally. Most everywhere else was riddled with marks from all the Jadan deaths he felt responsible for. Before I could silently protest, Dunes made three tiny nicks in his dark skin, the blood welling up. The cuts were ugly, but nothing serious.

'Don't do that anymore,' I whispered. 'I need you strong.'

'One last chance!' Ka'in cackled. 'Or you will be protecting your friends right into the flames!'

Not able to wait any longer, I peeked around the corner.

A hundred guards and soldiers and taskmasters were

assembled at the base of the Sanctuary. They had a few fires roaring and were roasting large Sobek lizards over the flames. Many Nobles held plates piled high with decadent foods.

The guards were having a feast.

Everyone had a wineskin, and smiles abounded on every face. Their attention was gathered upwards.

I looked up at the balcony and nearly vomited.

Once there had been a stained-glass mural there. The artwork had depicted the grisly scene of David's Fall, where the Jadans had been made to jump to their deaths. I'd destroyed it the last time I was here, shattering the glass with an abb from my crossbow. The world needed to be rid of such horrible things.

I never thought its destruction would give rise to something worse.

Now, instead of just glass depictions, there were actual Jadans.

Dead Jadans.

Three bodies hung off the balcony, dangling at the end of ropes. They were lifeless and charred. Small flames clung to melted skin.

The victims looked young, but I couldn't tell how young, as their bodies had become unrecognizable.

Ka'in was standing on the hollowed out balcony where the tops of the ropes had been tied around pillars. A few Nobles lingered at his back, all wearing black velvet masks. Each one held a flaming torch. Three more Jadans, these ones alive, were poised at the lip of the balcony, their hands bound behind their backs and ropes already around their necks. Two women and a boy. The boy was the only one not trembling, his expression vacant, clearly in shock.

And Ka'in stood there, lording above everyone.

His skin was now blackened and ugly, looking almost purple in places. Parts of him were bandaged, but most of the gruesome flesh was revealed for all those below to witness. His head was now without hair, and his face was covered in stitches and scars. He looked like something freshly risen from the dead-carts.

All those shards of glass and Ice had only served to reveal his true self. He finally looked the part of a demon.

'The Crier has touched me!' Ka'in said, waving his torch in front of the girl's face. 'Do you like when I touch you? It's like the Crier is touching you! Here, taste some holiness.' He put his blemished forearm in front of her mouth, and she eagerly thrust out her tongue, placing it on his Cold-burned skin. Her expression looked hopeful, as if this act might save her.

It was then when I recognized her face. I also recognized the fingers on her left hand. They'd healed in terrible directions, looking gnarled and unusable. She was the Domestic who'd betrayed us by screaming our presence in the Sanctuary the first time we were there.

That fact didn't dampen my pity in the slightest. She was family. She should be with the Flock, not standing at the border of death with a rope around her neck.

A yellow stream trickled off the balcony next to her. The boy was beginning to show signs of life.

'Now that you have my Chosen-ness on your tongue, lovely love,' Ka'in said, clearing his throat, the rattle getting worse, 'you can tell no more lies. Your only lying will be on a lovely bed or in a dead-cart. Your choice. Where did they go?'

'I swear I don't know,' she pleaded. 'I was loyal to you. I'll be loyal.'

Ka'in turned to address the crowd. 'Do you believe her?'

The crowd answered in unison. Wine spilled as hands raised. Roasted lizard flecked off fat lips. 'No!'

'And what happens to those we don't believe?' Ka'in called, almost a chant.

I couldn't take it any more. It was obvious was what about to happen.

I turned around to begin running.

Shilah was already halfway across the expanse in front of me. She was so quick it was frightening. I waved to Cam and Dunes to follow, but I didn't look at them.

I couldn't have them seeing my shame.

Ka'in should be dead. And it was *my* fault. I'd have to cut into my flesh and start my own death tally, just like Dunes.

All of us reached the Flock just as the Noble cheering reached a maddening level behind us. Shilah was already gesturing wildly, forming an attack plan. She called out orders for which unit to go where. I couldn't hear her clearly over the blood boiling in my ears. I got behind one of the Wraiths and began pushing out into the moat with every ounce of strength I possessed. I shouldn't have been able to move the massive thing by myself, as it weighed more than Jia; but maybe there was something of the Crier in the air. Maybe rage doesn't care all that much about shouldn't have.

I barrelled across the expanse. The Wraith flowed across the land in front of me like the River Singe. I pushed with all of my might, and a loud noise pierced my ears. It took me a moment to realize it was a battle cry coming from my lips.

But it was also coming from the lips of those behind me.

Before I knew it, my Wraith was moving twice as fast. Cam and Shilah were pushing on either side of me. I chanced a glance back and saw the other Wraiths keeping pace, pushed by the Five and Samsah, their faces serious and deadly. The rest of the Flock was screaming, their daggers and Stingers and crossbows at the ready.

We rounded the corner, shouting murder.

The Nobles had heard us coming. Everyone was already scrambling, their plates and wine cups down, weapons up. Most of them were simply guards, but there were a few real soldiers and Khatfists from Paphos in the crowd. Their armour gleamed and their swords were sharp. The soldiers were first in line when we rounded the corner, ready for battle, forming ranks and lifting their pikes.

It didn't matter.

Four Jadan bodies now hung off the balcony. The girl with the gnarled fingers was burning, her body hanging taut. She wasn't squirming. Her neck must have broken in the fall.

Each and every one of these Nobles would die. My heart commanded it so.

The Warrior in me had returned.

'You!' Ka'in shouted, pointing the torch down at me, kicking the rope at his feet. 'I *knew* you and Hillia here were in cahoots. She protected you till the end, but I have been made most beautiful—'

I grabbed the Wraith hose and wrenched back the release lever almost hard enough to break it off. The stream wouldn't reach Ka'in, but that was okay. I wanted to kill him with my hands.

Charged water erupted from the spout, blasting with such power that the hose almost bucked out of my hands. The guards and taskmasters watched the water arcing towards them and laughed.

Laughter turned to screams.

I screamed along with them: theirs of pain, mine of glory. I sprayed their faces and hands and aimed down their chest plates, hoping to inflict as much pain as possible. Their bodies jerked and sputtered and they begged for mercy.

I showed none.

I doused half of the crowd with the Wraithwater before the pressure gave and the stream died. By that time, the other Wraiths had flanked mine, and Cam and Shilah were in position with their hoses. They both released the levers and two new streams attacked the Noble crowd.

Shilah's teeth were bared. Cam's face was stricken with horror. Their accuracy was divine.

The clinking of metal led me to find Split furiously pumping the pressure back into my Wraith. His face was blood red and he moved faster than I'd ever seen, his wispy hair flying in all directions.

'Thanks,' I said, the word coming out oddly soft and tender.

Forces clashed inside of me.

The gears in my brain had ground themselves loose; I was awash with sharp ideas. Some were of honour. Others were of anger. The frantic thoughts stabbed at their barriers, aching to push into the real world through actions. I was full of sensations screaming at me, telling me new ways to inflict Noble pain. My arms buzzed with pleasure. My hands itched as I waited for Split to ready the Wraith.

The Pedlar seethed with effort, the muscles in his forearm bulging back to a former state. His eyes lost years of sorrow. There was a flash of a younger Split; one not yet plagued by so much loss.

I marvelled in Noble destruction, watching the crowd writhe and flail. Most were lying on their backs now. They clawed at their faces and arms, trying to get the Wraithwater off their skin. They shouted of burning and going blind. Their tears were glorious. I could smell their shocked flesh.

Then I realized it was just my poor Jadan family still roasting off the balcony.

I needed vengeance. I needed the Nobles to suffer and die.

Ka'in and the masked followers had disappeared into the Sanctuary, but I wasn't worried. I'd find them. I'd deal with them accordingly.

Split finished priming the Wraith. My voice nearly broke as I bellowed my next war cry, loosing the next volley of caustic water. Cam and Shilah's streams had dried up, waiting to be primed, and my new attack arrived just in time. The Noble agony remained fluid.

Pretty soon the whole crowd was one part flailing and one part screams. They tried stripping away their clothes and armour, but their faces only grew more panicked. Wraithwater couldn't be cured without an antidote; they were only making things worse for themselves.

The pain wouldn't stop.

Neither would I.

I grabbed a sword from our supplies and ran over to the nearest Khatfist. I stabbed sharp metal into any naked flesh I could find. Metal hit bone and the blade reverberated in my hand. I clutched tightly. The Noble's screech was high pitched and tickled my ears.

Wraithwater dripped into the wounds and sunk under his skin, and the man's eyes rolled backwards. He fell unconscious, which was a mercy I wasn't intending. I moved to the next body rolling on the ground. I found vengeance. And then I found more vengeance.

I would have thought my actions might come with guilt or remorse, but I felt nothing of the sort. The tip of the metal cut through Noble muscles and fat with delightful ease, like carving designs into clay.

The Five were immediately at my sides, cudgels abandoned and swords in hand. They sought their own revenge. Het and Dunes killed the bastards with reckless abandon. Jia wore a deep frown, apologizing under his breath to each victim as he sliced their necks. Kasroot snarled at each spurt of blood. Cleave killed methodically, dispassionate as death itself.

I kicked hands trying to grab at my ankles, keeping off the Wraithwater. A few flecks burned into my flesh, but I'd worn long sun-robes. Most of the water fell harmlessly against the thick cloth.

Soon enough, everyone had been either sliced or skewered, and I doubted we'd be taking any of them alive.

'Everyone fall back!' Shilah called, waving our Flock away from the fallen Nobles. Blood seeped from a cut on her arm, but otherwise she was unharmed.

The Flock retreated, leaving the writhing mass to suffer alone.

I did not.

I went back to the Wraith and I started pumping, moving air into the clay stomach of the machine. Madness stirred in my blood now. I looked up again at the hanging Jadan bodies, their burning stench unbearable. I was stricken by fever. I wasn't finished with these Nobles yet. Only death would save them.

A hand grabbed my shoulder.

'Micah.'

I kept pumping.

'Micah,' Shilah said again. 'It's over. Now we go find Ka'in.. That's what matters.'

I kept pumping. The pressure was almost ready.

Split came over to me next. His dagger was thick with blood, and he scratched at the back of his neck.

'Son,' he said. 'Come on. You did good, but she's right. If we don't catch that Sun-damn blister of a Noble he might get away.'

I pushed past Split, moving to the front of the Wraith and grabbing the hose. I couldn't stop. Stopping meant facing the truth. Stopping meant cutting down bodies from ropes; the one who died because I'd been too weak to finish off Ka'in in the first place. I wouldn't be weak now.

Cam came beside me next. 'The Wraiths worked perfectly, Spout. This is just the beginning.'

His words didn't register. They might as well have been in Ancient Jadan.

I clapped on the filter on the hose to broaden the spray.

'Micah!' Shilah chided.

I aimed a wordless scream at the Nobles, unleashing the torrent of charged water. The twitches and groans were less frantic than last time, but there were still a few satisfying screams. I aimed for the wounds and growled so loud that my voice broke. The sound continued, from a much deeper place than my lips.

Leah waved the banner high above her head, cheering me on.

The Wraith finally ran dry. Dunes had to pull me away from the hose.

I dropped to my knees and wept, my tears burning into the sand.

We couldn't find Ka'in.

It was my fault.

We spent hours securing every room, every hallway, every tower, but there was no sign of him anywhere. I had Samsah and a few others guard the secret escape door that led out into the sands, but he'd not gone that way. There must have been other passageways out of the Sanctuary, which would be good for us in the future, but bad in the meantime.

The rest of the night was spent securing the Sanctuary. This involved disposing of twenty more Nobles and taskmasters who'd slept through Ka'in's ceremony. It didn't take much effort. The Five knocked them unconscious and bound them faster than I could point. We hauled the limp Nobles through the basement and tossed them in the cages in the 'Beauty Room'. I hoped the Nobles would wake with fear in their hearts. The walls were lined with terrible pictures of severed body parts and diagrams of naked bones. There were clay representations of organs and jawbones, and the whole place looked like a dead-pit sorted out and pinned for examination.

To make things worse, there were cages in the corner. Ka'in used to keep the Domestics locked up before exposing them to his curiosities. Shilah, Ellia, Ellcia and Leah had counted among those victims.

Shilah had been tortured on one of the tables, which were made of clean metal and had camel-leather straps on the corners. I had Dunes and Cleave take the tables out and bury them in the sands.

I was tempted to have the Wraiths brought in so we could lock our prisoners in the cages and spray them, to make them suffer like they'd made Jadans suffer, but I knew Shilah wouldn't go for it. She'd barely met my eyes when we were in the room.

There were ten Domestics left alive in the Sanctuary, including the three young Jadans that Ka'in had almost hung and burned over the balcony. There should have been thirteen.

When no one was watching, I'd taken a scalpel from one of the Beauty Room drawers and cut four thin slices into the back of my leg.

Shilah tended to the Domestics in the Sanctuary's central gardens, offering Cold water and groan salve for their wounds. The necks of the three Jadans from the balcony had serious abrasions from being dragged around with the rope, but the balm would help. Almost all of them were in some state of shock. It was going to be a long battle back to health, but I wouldn't let them fight it alone.

The Flock helped move the Wraiths to the guard towers and barred the entrances to the gates. Shilah oversaw everything, keeping everyone focused. Her steely commands and upright demeanour quelled any fears over the Khat's impending reaction. While Shilah was busy being a leader, I took Dunes, Cam and Split on a sombre mission.

There was one thing that needed doing before the night was over.

Dunes lifted the charred Jadan bodies back up to the balcony. He was strong enough to do it by himself. Cutting them loose from their ropes and letting them fall would have been easier, but they were family. They had died for our cause, even if they didn't know it at the time.

We found a cart in one of the guard towers and used it to bring our kin out into the sands. Shoving boilweed up my nose was the only thing that kept me from breaking down or vomiting. It was long, arduous work, and we were silent the entire time.

We dug three graves into the warm sands and lowered the bodies. Then we gave them an Ancient Jadan funeral. Split had shown me the rituals in the Book of the March, and I was glad to revive the tradition. Eight centuries later, some aspects of old culture would survive.

Funerals were taken very seriously by the Jadans of the past. Family members often presided over their dead for weeks. The Book of the March taught us that they would even perform rituals over the graves for generations to come, often bringing children to the burial spots of their ancestors and telling stories. The ancient Jadans had a penchant for humour, and would sing funny songs about their ancestors, but most were tender and emotional. They planted red alder and Rose of Gilead petals over the sites, which we could not do, as all we had to work with was dust and sand.

I wished with all my heart that I could have done this for my father, that I could have had a place where I could go and sing for him on the nights when the stars were brightest and the wind was most playful.

Dunes put a protective arm around my shoulder.

We laid a Wisp over each of our fallen kins' eyes, or at least where their eyes would have been. The fires had claimed most of their faces. We didn't have access to most of the burial seeds and fruits that the Book of the March called for

– a lot of the species the pages spoke of were believed to be extinct – but the Crier would understand. I laid some of Jia's candied figs in whatever folds of clothing I could find.

'What are the Wisps on the eyes for?' Cam asked, standing back a few feet.

Split gave me a look, telling me to go ahead.

'The Khat twisted the old stories to serve his claim,' I said, sounding strange in my own ears. My voice was high pitched and nasally from my loaded nostrils. 'They say that we go to the Black if we misbehave, right? And if we're good we get to serve Nobles in the afterlife.'

Cam gave a guilty nod. His face had taken on a pale tinge from vomiting so many times. He looked like a painting of himself that had been left too long in the Sun.

'The lie worked because it was born out of our own myth,' Split said.

'What myth?' Cam asked.

Split took out his copy of the Book of the March and held it against his chest. 'You know I never got to do this ceremony for my daughter. She was only half Jadan, but still I would have done it.'

'I'm so sorry, Split,' I said. 'That they took your family.'

He gave a sad laugh. 'You're the last person in the World Cried who has to be sorry. I just hope my little girl found her Frost. She was so tiny and her hands were so small. I worry she couldn't have picked one up if she tried.'

I put a hand over the Book. 'I'm sure the Crier doesn't care about that.'

Cam was silent.

I started to sprinkle sand over the first body.

'The old myth goes like this,' I said. 'When a Jadan dies, they wake up in a long black field. It's quiet and Cold and dark, because it's the one place the Sun can't reach. A secret place just for us.'

I continued pouring buckets of sand over the girl, hiding her ruined flesh. 'Death carries us there, and then flies away on raven wings.'

The Pedlar gave me a reassuring nod, joining me on covering the grave with sand. The girl's body slowly faded into the earth. 'Hillia,' Ka'in had called her. I hoped she would find her peace.

'So you wake up in the field,' Cam prompted.

'Yes,' I said. 'And the dark land is vast and long and peaceful. And you wander the field and you hear the songs of your family. Time is different in the black field, so sometimes the songs are from the past, sometimes they haven't been sung yet. And your feet sink into the cool earth as you smile and laugh at the stories in the music. There's no Sun, and it's quiet, and all the things you loved seem all the lovelier. You stare at the stars and eat the foods that your family puts in your pockets. You plant the seeds of the fruits so the next Jadans to arrive have something to eat, just in case they didn't have anyone. And you drink from sweet rivers and wander the black land, until one day you finally come across your Frost. It shines through the black soil, and you kneel down and start to dig it up. It was made just for you. Ever since the Crier was blinded by Sun, this is how He finds the Jadans. This is how He shows you you're one of His children, even if he's never been able to see you. Every Frost is unique, each one special. And when you touch the Frost, the Crier knows where you are, and the Cold takes you up into the heavens so you can be with Him forever, with your family. With the spirit of the Jadan people.'

Split wiped away a tear. 'Anyah and Lizah found theirs. I know they did.'

'We put the Wisps in the eyes,' I told Cam. 'Because they help the dead see their way to the Frost. Cold can always find Cold. The Wisps make it so the dead don't have to wander aimlessly in the black fields. Loved ones put the Wisps in the eyes so, when those in the black feel ready, they can always find their way home.'

Sand covered the last of Hillia's body.

'Did I get it right?' I asked Split.

'And then some,' the Pedlar said quietly, looking up at the stars.

Cam was clearly thinking up a storm. 'The Noble story of the afterlife is so different. It's all about decadence and indulging in pleasures forever.'

I shrugged. 'With the Jadans serving every Noble need, right?'

Cam swallowed hard, his face cycling through a series of emotions.

'I think I get it now,' Cam said. 'The Khat has made it a threat instead of something natural – getting sent to the black – because he claims the Crier deemed Jadans unworthy. So if there's no Frost in the fields, no light, then there is no hope of going home. If you get sent to the black, you'll be stuck forever. That's probably why he also doesn't let Jadans sing anything other than the Khat's Anthem. So there's no more songs from your family.'

'You got it,' I said. 'But in the Khat's version, if we serve the Nobles well, then we at least get to go where the Nobles go after we die. Because even an eternity of serving is better than an eternity abandoned.'

Cam knelt down over the second small grave. The fire had been merciless on this one's body. I still couldn't tell if it was a boy or a girl. Or how old they'd been.

'Hold on,' Cam said, fishing through his pockets. He pulled out a few almonds and put them on the body, giving me a sad look. 'It's all I have on me.'

I touched his shoulder. 'I'm sure they'll go a long way.'

We finished the burial and I sent Cam and Split back.

I told them that Dunes and I were going to perform a few more ceremonies out of the Book of the March. That we were going to sing a few private songs for the dead, and not to worry if we didn't come back for a while. Split's arm was over Cam's shoulder as they walked: a family of their own.

Dunes and I exchanged a silent nod.

The rest of the Five showed up out of the shadows, dragging empty carts behind them.

One by one we took the dead Nobles and threw them off the southern cliff.

Chapter Five

I found no sleep that night.

I was too busy searching for salvation.

Dunes and I covered the entire Sanctuary three times, looking for Frosts. Each time though, I noticed the paintings of the beautiful Jadan women on the walls were fewer – Ellia and Ellcia having proceeded with their own mission. I didn't know if the sisters were burning the canvases or storing them somewhere, but either way I left dealing with the portraits up to them.

Dunes kept his cudgel out at all times in case we found any lingering Nobles. I hoped we'd stumble across Ka'in, but I would have settled for any of the masked bastards; it would at least have given me an outlet for my rage.

We went into every room, secret or otherwise, turning out the entire place. Without a Frost, taking the Sanctuary meant little more than a slight delay in our deaths. If I was going to uncover the secrets of flight, to figure out a way to break the Drought, I needed a secure situation. I wouldn't be able to focus on anything if my people were dying by the droves, having nothing to keep the Sun at bay.

Hours passed with no Frosts, although we did find useful items.

There was every kind of food imaginable in the kitchens. Loads of supplies were stored in salt barrels and Cold boxes, which would last the Flock months. We found an entire armoury full of weapons, including tar to burn and thousands of arrows to shoot. We found a library full of scrolls, ancient books and a magnificent collection of Jadan art from before the Drought. Apparently Ka'in was a collector.

There were fine linens, and three water-well reservoirs, and even an entire closet of musical instruments. A few harps rested in the back, and my chest squeezed at the thought of Leah with the strings. There were so many useful things that would bring joy and security to the Flock.

But there was no excitement for me. Food and supplies were just bandages, the wound underneath festering.

There wasn't a single Frost anywhere.

It was maddening, especially since we'd discovered Ka'in's Coldroom early on in the night. The cavernous space was filled floor to ceiling with different crates of Cold, meticulously separated by type. Thousands of Wisps and Drafts. Hundreds of Shivers. Dozens of Chills. All resting in golden chests with no keys. My heart leapt in my throat each time I easily picked one of the locks, expecting a Frost.

But there was only disappointment.

The last time I was here, Ka'in admitted to having a Frost. The confession had been accidental, but it rang with the sound of truth. And if Ka'in had admitted to having one Frost, it was likely he had several. But now that I had come up empty so many times I had to come to terms with three options, each equally disheartening.

One: Ka'in never had any Frosts in the first place.

Two: he took them with him as he fled.

Three: they were too well hidden for us to find.

Dunes tried to console me, assuring me he'd get me a Frost somehow, but my mood only soured as the night went on. Cam and Shilah joined the hunt, but their presence made me feel more ashamed. I should have been happy we at least had a defendable fortress and enough Cold to keep the Flock alive for months, but I could only concentrate on our inevitable demise. Without a Frost our revolution would end. Our power didn't come from Wisps or Drafts or Chills or high walls. It came from the promise of change; and without the Coldmaker, our significance would eventually boil away.

I sifted through Ka'in's private quarters for the fourth time. The rooms were sequestered deep in the basement of the Sanctuary. I insisted on being alone.

The Sun would be rising soon, but it couldn't reach me directly through so many layers of shadow and stone. The air was luxurious in here, tempered by the Cold Bellows in the corner. There was a private drinking well too, its stone rim studded with tiny Closed Eyes made of clay. I tried to remove them, but they were cemented on.

Vials of precious honey were spread across a few pedestals; and dusty spaces glared at me from the wall, places where portraits of unfortunate Domestics had recently been torn away.

I slammed my palm against the wall by Ka'in's bed, my bronze fingers rattling. I'd scoured ever inch of the room, hoping to find some secret hiding place. I was aware of the hate and anger festering in my chest, and of the voice that didn't even sound like my own, whispering: You're missing it. You're weak.

I was unbearably tired. I'd never felt so frustrated. Violence seethed in my chest, like a nest of sand-vipers all tangled up and trying to bite their way free.

I didn't even want Ka'in dead.

Dead meant the Sun-damned bastard might find peace.

The Crier was supposed to be merciful and good, and there was a chance He might Cry a Frost for even the most despicable of Nobles.

I couldn't let Ka'in have peace. I wanted Ka'in alive. I wanted to lock him in the belly of a Wraith and slam the lid on his screams. I wanted to flay his purpled skin and pour charged water in the oozing slits. I wanted to take all my tinkering knowledge and skill, and develop a machine so brutal, so terrifying, so precisely effective, that I might drive away every memory of the sick pleasures he'd taken at the expense of my people, replacing them with repentance. It would be an Idea so vicious that—

'Micah.'

'What?' I didn't turn around, continuing to wrap my knuckles along the wall. I was in no moment to see Cam's pale face. To look at the fair skin and yellow hair that Shilah obviously found more entrancing than mine.

'Leave me alone,' I spat.

'Spout.'

I narrowed my eyes and turned. Cam leaned against the door, his body hunched and tight, almost like a slave stance.

'WHAT!' I shouted, anger plaguing my words. 'I'm trying to save us!'

'I know.' He recoiled. 'But you can't save us on an empty stomach.'

Turning over his palm, he revealed a plump orangefruit.

I finally broke.

He came over to the spot on the floor where I crumbled, and wrapped his arms around me. His body was warm, and I felt his heart beating through his chest in a calming rhythm. My head was tucked under his chin, and for a moment I knew relief from his soothing touch.

'Shhhh,' he said. His fingers were tight around my neck, pressing against my tattooed numbers. My father's numbers.

Sobs wrenched from my chest.

'It's okay,' he said softly. I could tell from his grip that he wasn't planning on letting me go yet. I accepted his kindness, and by doing so, I could finally see the extent of the hole. It was there inside of me. It was so black and deep that it might take a thousand Frosts to fill. It might not have even been possible.

'I killed them,' I said.

Cam squeezed the back of my neck. 'I know.'

'Cam, you don't understand. I killed them. They're dead. I killed so many of them. I did things.'

His voice remained just as calm. 'I know. I did too.'

'You don't—'

'Shhhh,'Cam said, holding me tighter. 'We were all with you.'

'There's something growing inside of me and I – I don't know how –' I sniffed. My face was on fire, and I was glad my nose was pressed into his chest so he couldn't see my tears. 'I miss my dad.'

'I know,' Cam said. 'But Shilah's here. Split's here. I'm here. I'm always going to be here. Even if you try and push me away, or ignore me, or lump me in. There's no way I'm going to let you save the world alone. I'm too vain and I need the recognition.'

I sobbed out a laugh. Cam smelled different than he used to. He used to smell like spicy flowers, and now he smelled like sweat and the deep sands.

'I just want you to know,' Cam continued. 'You've done something good. Okay, maybe *good* is a tough way to see it, but you've done something *right*. Micah, you're doing everything right. You are saving us.'

My voice sounded meek, like it used to sound after my first few whippings. So much had happened since the last time I'd felt the lash of a taskmaster, yet once again I felt small and vulnerable. Abb used to say that time was like the wind, pushing sand over all our pain. He said it could take hours, days, or years, but eventually everything would be covered. He was right in a way; but I also knew a strong enough wind could scrape that pain back into the open. I used to see bones in the dunes behind my barracks, back when I snuck out at night and dreamed of doing something more.

'I just wanted to make things,' I said. 'I never wanted to hurt anyone.'

'I know,' Cam said, closing the orangefruit into my hand. 'I wanted to be a singer.'

'Huh?'

'Yeah.' I felt his shrug through my cheek. 'I love music; you know that. I've always loved music. When the troops from Belisk would visit the Tavor Manor, damn, those were the happiest days of my childhood.'

'I've never heard you sing,' I said.

'I used to. My favourite Domestic Jadan used to teach me. She had gray hair and big old cheeks that puffed out when she was frustrated.' Cam touched his throat. 'She showed me how to make my throat vibrate the notes without sounding like a warble. But my father caught me singing a song I wrote and he put an end to it. He said the arts were for those too weak to do something real.'

I sniffed, gently pulling away and wiping the snot from under my nose.

'You know,' I said. 'Your father is a real asshole.'

Cam gave a dark chuckle. 'You know what I'd say to him if he was here?'

I shook my head.

'I'd point to the Coldmaker and say, "look dad, art", and then I'd smash him over the head with a rock.'

I smiled, feeling slightly less dead inside.

Cam took out a fresh piece of boilweed and began wiping

the back of my hands. He worked a gob of spit on the boil-weed and then rubbed, the red stains coming away slowly. The Noble blood had dried on good.

'I came to show you something,' he said.

I was about to ask what, but then thought of a more pressing topic. 'Wait. You wrote a song? How did it go? What was it about?'

Cam smiled. 'A girl. What else?'

I got to my feet and brushed the creases out of my robes.

Cam pointed to the orangefruit. 'So you going to share or be greedy? You know, I worked up quite an appetite myself. Big battle and all.'

I laughed and peeled the rind. I split the tender fruit in half and put a slice in my cheek. The sugary juice tingled and I wished it would stay forever. Silence passed as we ate, but soon an uncomfortable truth parted my lips. I had to look down at my feet as the words erupted from my heart.

'She likes you, you know,' I said. 'Shilah.'

Cam paused, his body going stiff. 'I – I—'

'It's okay. It was never our future to end up like that anyway. We have something different.' My eyes flicked up to his with a small challenge. 'It's still special. Just different.'

'Yes, um.' Cam swallowed hard, clearing his throat and looking rather uncomfortable. 'But seriously, I came to show you something. You should probably see this right away.'

I nodded. If he wasn't ready to talk about Shilah, I wasn't going to prod.

We left the room and he led me around dark corners, picking up the pace. Shadows backed away as we ran, a Sinai in Cam's outstretched hand.

'Is it Ka'in?' I asked as he led me up a spiralling staircase. There was no one else around.

'No,' Cam said.

'Tell me.'

'You just have to see it.'

I shook my head with frustration. 'That doesn't help. Just tell me. Did the Nobles here raise an army already? Did someone betray us?'

'No, but it's interesting that that's where your mind goes.'

I shrugged. 'My trust isn't easily won.'

'You trusted the Hookmen immediately.'

I thought about it for a moment. 'Dunes has kind eyes.'

'What about me? High Noble and all. Why'd you trust me?'

I took the stairs two at a time, following after him.

'I didn't.'

'What are you talking about?' Cam asked, shooting me a perplexed look over his shoulder. 'We did all that awesome stuff together. I took you to the apothecary, and got that music box, and didn't we get chocolate?'

'Cam,' I said blankly, 'I was a Street Slave. I had to do that stuff since you wanted me to.'

'No, I know. But I could see it in your face. You were having fun. We were bonding.'

I looked at the back of my knuckles, which were now clean. 'Yeah, I guess so.'

Our walk was brisk, not quite a run, heading to the balcony where Ka'in had set up the ropes. A place of Sunlight and darkness.

'Speaking of bonding. Who's your favourite of the Five?' Cam asked. 'Jia?'

'You mean besides Dunes,'I said.

'Obviously besides Dunes.'

'Jia,' I admitted. 'Although it's probably going to be Het if all of his warding actually works.'

'You think they will? Doesn't seem like you to believe that sort of stuff.'

'No,' I said. 'It doesn't.'

Cam shouldered open the door in front of him, leading

out to the balcony. Light was just beginning to crest the far side of the world. The Sun would be rising soon. When it got high enough it would surely see the pile of dead Nobles at the base of the Southern cliff.

On the balcony in front of me, Shilah and the Five were silhouetted by the rising light. Their backs were to Cam and I, listening to some sort of commotion down below. Shouting clouded the air, but the voices didn't sound mournful. I made my presence known with heavy feet and Shilah swivelled with the proudest face I'd ever seen her wear.

The Five snapped around to me as a single unit next.

Shilah was so skinny compared to the Five that she looked like a needle surrounded by swords, but still somehow retained the commanding air. The Coldmaker waited at her feet. It was out of canvas bag and catching some of the morning light.

'Hey,' Shilah said. 'I wanted to wait for you before we say anything.'

'Say anything about what?'

She waved me over next to her, making a space. Cam gave me a go-ahead look. I walked forward and took my place by her side, the noises becoming a little clearer. They sounded like conversations; like chattering in a marketplace.

Shilah looped her arm through mine and we walked up to the balcony together, taking in the astonishing sight.

Hundreds of Jadans were kneeling in front of the Sanctuary.

The bodies stretched out across the empty expanse, holding bags, tattered clothing and meagre possessions. Young, old, Builders, Domestics, Patch Jadans; there were so many of all different ages. They began to rise to their feet as they took notice of Shilah and I, rousing each other, their voices dripping with hope. Tears fell across cheeks.

'Meshua!' someone shouted.

One by one the Jadan arrivals rose to their feet. Their arms stretched out to us.

'MESHUA!'

Those lurking on the rooftops must have spread word of our battle. Hundreds had apparently abandoned their barracks this morning, coming to us instead of going to their slave posts.

Shilah's eyes were alight with hope and pride.

I turned to the Five.

'Unlock the doors,' I said. 'Let them in.'

The Five bowed as one, Dunes bowing lowest, and then disappeared back into the Sanctuary. Shilah and I stepped up to the edge of the balcony. Down below, arms opened wide, eyes wept with joy and strangers hugged one another. Some of them had already drawn Opened Eyes onto their clothing. Some of the older Jadans dropped to their knees and kissed the sands.

All of a sudden our Flock numbered in the hundreds.

'MESHUA!'

Things were changing.

'MESHUA!'

I turned to Shilah and dropped my voice to a whisper. 'You do the speeches, remember.'

Shilah laughed, opened her arms, and then launched our revolution.

PART TWO

PART TWO

Chapter Six

'Lechem et Shemess chetman herad – Naass grosh lo chiss,' Split read, his accent throaty and unsure. He scratched at the thread-like hair clinging to his bald head. Eventually he shrugged and translated. 'And the Sun took his next payment, and that's how snake lost his feet forever.'

A collective whimper spread throughout the young Jadan audience. One child at the end of the front row began to full-out cry.

Split was quick to flip around the pages to show the illustration. The snake was headed for a hole in the sands, fleeing from the evil Sun. The drawing in the ancient book was rather faded, but it was clear that the snake was happy.

This book was part of a huge array we'd uncovered in the Sanctuary library. The children liked the ones with the crude illustrations best, and those became the ones Split used for his story time.

'It's okay!' Split said in desperate tones. 'Look, see. It turned out for the best, because the snake could get around quicker and dig faster without feet! The Sun could never find him down under the sands, and so in the end, the snake won the bet!' Split pointed to the creature's mouth, which may or may not have been smiling. The picture was too faded to tell. 'You see how happy he is?'

Most of the kids relaxed, and some even giggled, although the one in the front row kept crying. I placed the boy around five or six. I didn't think he was sobbing because of the story.

I looked for any signs of broken bones or angry wounds that we might have missed, but he seemed in decent health. As healthy as could be expected at least – considering the circumstances of where we'd found his particular group of children.

Picka began braying behind Split, nudging the Pedlar with her snout. The children loved the dwarf camel, and Split made sure to bring her to every story time.

'Shhh,' Split said, looking around the room with desperate eyes. 'I'm telling you, snake was better off, kids. He was faster now without those bulky legs. It's okay. It's okay!'

'Quit it,' one of the girls in the second row said to the crying boy, smacking him in the back of the head. 'Don't waste water, Niles.'

It was difficult to keep track of all the children's names, as there were now hundreds of Jadans taking refuge in the Sanctuary. About fifty Jadan kids were in the room listening to Split's story.

This group was one of six which we'd found locked in the schools, after the Nobles had begun abandoning the city. The Priests had left them with no Cold, food, or water, barring them into the hot stone buildings in the middle of the day.

Their torture was a message for Shilah and I.

It was their first retaliation.

There would be many more.

The Jadan children had all been next to dead when we found them. They weren't screaming or moaning, and their silence only spoke to how close to the black they were. I'd picked the lock and found them patiently in their seats, blood on their faces and Closed Eye pendants sewn into their clothes.

It had been the same at each of the six schools.

Shilah careened through the rows, stopping at Niles. Niles continued to weep with abandon.

'What is it, Niles?' Shilah asked, her tone soothing. 'What's wrong?'

Niles shied away from her touch, his hands going into fists and rocking back and forth. He began whispering under his breath.

'It's okay, Niles!' Split said gently, snapping his fingers and then stroking Picka's snout. 'You want to touch her? She's really soft and doesn't bite.'

Picka fluttered her black lips at the sound of her name, showing large teeth. It was a friendly expression, but Niles probably hadn't had much experience with beasts yet. It only caused another wave of tears.

The girl behind Niles lifted her fist to hit him again – the Khat's Priests encouraged violence against other Jadan children – but Shilah caught the strike before it landed.

'No, Juniss!' Shilah commanded. 'None of that.'

The girl, Juniss, looked confused, staring as if boilweed smoke was coming out of Shilah's ears.

'Whass wrong?' Juniss asked her.

'You don't hit your brothers,' Shilah said. 'The Nobles did enough of that.'

Niles' whispering was getting more frantic. The tears made the dark skin on his face glisten like pebbles on the banks of the Singe. Shilah went to put a hand on his shoulder, but he smacked her touch away. His small body continued to rock.

Shilah stood up in frustration, grinding her teeth.

Picka's braying got shriller.

Cam filtered through the ranks of children next. Niles took one look at Cam's golden hair and immediately the young boy's expression softened into obedience.

'What's wrong?' Cam asked, kneeling down.

'We – sniff – we's sposed to say our promises. We didn't say our promises today. The Crier's gunna b-be angry with us, and the Sun's gunna take our f– feet too.'

A few of the other children nodded their agreements, suddenly remembering the predicament they were in. Their faces bunched, turning at the ceiling in fear.

It was so incredibly awful that I almost laughed. A surge of fresh rage careened through my chest.

Shilah knelt, but this time didn't try and make any contact. 'You don't have to say the Khat's promises anymore. You're safe now. You're with your family.'

Niles wouldn't look her in the eyes. 'But t-the promises keeps us safe. If we don't say them we d-don't get our Cold. The Crier will be angry.'

It wasn't that I'd forgotten about the promises – saying something twice a day for years practically imprints it on the tongue – it had just been such a long time since my life with the Priests. But now, having been reminded, I could feel the candlewax burning onto the backs of my hands. The Priests had done that every time they thought my promises didn't sound sincere. They used blood-red wax so we'd get used to the colour.

'They were lies,' Shilah said, making a halting gesture towards Picka, which actually got the camel to quiet down. 'Everything they taught you. Everything they made you—'

Niles began bawling again. This time two other children joined in. Juniss looked like she was about to hurl her sandals at the weeping children.

Shilah stood up, a look of deep bewilderment crossing her face. She looked to me for help. I shrugged. All of a sudden battle plans and Cold-charged inventions seemed much easier than dealing with children.

Cam reached out and put a hand on Niles' cheek. The kid went rigid, bowing into a slave position. It nearly broke my heart.

'I have a new promise,' Cam said, wiping away the tear. 'Right from the Crier Himself! You believe me, right?'

The whole group of children went quiet, the whimpering and worry all but disappearing. Their attention was rapt.

They had no choice but to believe Cam, as listening to Nobles was promise number three.

I curled my hands into fists, the bronze fingers wrenching out a nasty squeak. I'd been working tirelessly through the nights, and I'd forgotten to oil the joints.

Cam gestured for Split to give him the old book and he flipped to a random page, pointing with a finger at new picture. His face lit up.

'Aha,' Cam said, clearing his throat. 'Schelmes herrer ada adamnaths shilustus. *Promise* granat schloss. Yep, here's the answer to your question, children. Right from the Crier Himself.'

My head tilted with curiosity.

Split read the children stories in Ancient Jadan in case we were ever able to bring it back, but unless Cam had been getting lessons, he didn't know how to read the lost language. I had a strong feeling he was making the words up.

The children's mouths were agape with wonder. Shilah's was as well.

'It says "I promise to love my new Jadan family,"' Cam said, tapping the page, his cheeks going red. His eyes were buried in the text.

'I promise to love my new Jadan family,' the kids repeated.

It was an eerie sort of chant, monotonous and severe.

Cam looked over to Shilah. He thrust out his bottom lip

and gave her an agreeable nod. Her face was caught in a complex flurry of emotions.

All of a sudden I felt the urge to study the wall, a knot in my stomach.

'Hchhemesh lethat Meshua,' Cam read. 'I promise to listen to Meshuas.'

The kids didn't hesitate. Their chant was even more monotone this time. 'I promise to listen to Meshuas.'

Split's mouth curled into a wry grin as he scratched Picka behind the ears. 'Yes of course,' he said in a leading way. '*That* promise. Good memory, Camlish.'

Shilah leaned over and whispered into Cam's ear. Cam bristled.

'Rhth nuath schelsmon loh esh,' Cam read. 'I promise that I'm *worthy*.'

The kids became confused, tripping over themselves to get the words out. It was a contradiction to everything they'd been taught. Watching them try to make sense of such a thing was like watching a scorpion trying to sting itself.

Cam tapped the page. 'It's right here. "I promise that I'm worthy." It's from the Crier, so you kids might as well promise it.'

'Worthy?' Juniss asked. 'But we're not worthy. The Priests told us we're not.'

Cam gave an innocent shrug. 'I guess you are now. The Crier must have left these new promises for you to find here in the Sanctuary. It's like a game. And I bet you there's a bunch more of the promises to find. Right Split?'

Split nodded. 'Absolutely. And more stories too. Do you kids want to hear about the beetle and the honey jar again?'

The kids giggled and clamored their 'yesses' and settled back in like everything was normal. Cam handed the book back to Split and then came to stand at my side.

'How'd I do?' he asked out of the corner of his mouth.

Cam was still taller than me, but I was closing the gap. I slapped him on the back. 'I promise to never doubt you again.'

I nodded to the hallway, beckoning for Shilah to join, and the three of us left Split to his lessons, closing the door just as the Pedlar was describing the beetle's insatiable sweet tooth. The Jadans of the past had given wild personalities to the animals of the world. I enjoyed listening to Split tell the stories just as much as the children, but we had more pressing work at hand.

'So I checked with Dunes this morning,' I said leading them through towards the balcony. 'He said there weren't any Frosts in the Suth Manor either—'

'What was that, Cam?' Shilah asked, cutting me off.

Cam didn't slow his pace. 'What was what?'

'New promises?' Shilah asked, toying with her braid. 'That was ingenious. I went blank and you figured out how to calm them down. And your Ancient Jadan has become very authentic-sounding.'

She winked and Cam blushed, giving her a flimsy shrug.

'I have to pull my weight somehow,' Cam said

'This from the same Camlish who accidentally set fire to that stack of boilweed in the kitchens three days ago?'

Cam chuckled. 'When are you going to let that go? I told you. That wasn't my fault. I thought I heard Cleave behind me.'

'You always think Cleave is behind you,' Shilah said, shaking her head, her smile wild.

Cam threw his hands up. 'Can you blame me? He walks like a shadow.'

'He's harmless. To us at least.' Shilah nudged Cam with an elbow. 'Unlike that whiptail scarab that definitely fell on your nose in the courtyard.'

'It was real,' Cam said. 'It was on me!'

'It was a freckle,' Shilah said, laughter pinching her lips.

'I think I know my own freckles.' Cam pointed down along his elbow. 'This one is Bart. And this is Mordechah. And these twin Freckles are Ellia and Ellcia. Just don't tell the sisters I named freckles after them.'

I hadn't heard about the boilweed fire or the freckle spider. I'd been confined to the tinkershop all week, working on the new Idea to try and crack Flight. Without a Frost, the skies were our only chance of survival.

'So I was saying,' I cut in. 'Dunes said the Five scoured the Suth Manor and still found no Frosts. If any Frosts were in the city, then the High Nobles are taking them as they leave.'

'But we're finding all sorts of other Cold, right?' Cam asked. 'Even Chills?'

'Yes,' I said begrudgingly.

'And all of our new Flock are bringing the Cold here?'

'Yes,' I said.

'And the Five uncovered a practical *mountain* of Cold when they raided the Tavor Manor?'

I nodded.

'That all sounds good to me,' Cam said. 'Especially since the Tavor Cold technically belonged to my father, and taking it away from him feels wonderful.'

'Yes,' I said, practically a whisper now.

'Micah, what is it?' Shilah asked.

We passed a trio of older Domestics hobbling down the stairs slowly, all who stopped to bow. Their red-rimmed eyes began to water and their hands went over their hearts. One of them looked like she might stop breathing, overtaken by awe.

'Meshua,' the oldest-looking one said, her hair grayer than even Old Man Gum – the mad loon who babbled back in my childhood barracks, always about how 'they put it in the ground' – and her face as wrinkled as a Sobek lizard.

'We are saved because of you,' she continued. 'Bless the Crier for the gift of his two beautiful children.'

Cam backed out of the way, flattening against the wall. A tender look softened his face.

'Hello,' I said with a meek wave, still rather uncomfortable with such reverence. 'Thank you.'

Shilah put a hand under the oldest woman's chin and raised the wrinkled face up to her own. They exchanged a powerful glance, full of something I didn't quite understand. Something feminine and strong and possibly even magical.

'It's the other way around,' Shilah exclaimed, grabbing her hand and squeezing. 'You have lived long and bravely, and showed us our people can survive anything. You give *us* hope, Mothers.'

The oldest woman began shaking with emotion. She kissed Shilah's hand, gave me a low bow, with her poor back cracking in a dozen places, and their group tottered along.

'What's wrong,' I said, taking the stairs two at a time, 'is how terrible those children have been treated.'

'I know,' Shilah said. 'We just need to think, and come up with things like Cam's promises. We'll get them to come around.'

Cam looked like he was going to spill over with happiness.

Shilah squeezed his lower back. 'You did good, Freckles.'

'Even if we find all the Cold in the City of David's Fall,' I blurted. 'It won't be nearly enough.'

'It will keep everyone here alive,' Shilah said. 'And that's something.'

'For now,' I said. 'And I appreciate you keeping everyone's spirits up. But you know as well as I do what's coming.'

'It won't be like last time.'

'Why wouldn't it be?' I fired back.

'Because,' Shilah said, 'it's different. We know more now.'

'Things are only different because of the Coldmaker,' I said, checking for Leah. She usually followed me whenever I was outside of the tinkershop, and I wasn't in the mood to deal with her. 'And the Coldmaker doesn't work anymore. It's broken, dammit. It made its final abb last night. The Frost is gone.'

Shilah stopped in her tracks, only showing surprise for a moment. Then she shook her head. 'The Coldmaker is not broken, it's just incomplete. And the machine isn't even the most important thing. What's more important is the *feeling* that our people have now. Remember, Jadans outnumber Nobles in the Khatdom three to one and—'

'But the amount of weapons they have outnumber us a hundred to one,' I said. 'And their training for battle and ruthlessness outnumbers us a thousand to one. I'm not the only Inventor in the Khatdom, either. The Pyramid will have things – send things – that we won't understand. The Khat is going to strike hard and we're not going to be prepared.'

We rushed into the high hallway and made our way towards the balcony.

'Micah, slow down,' Shilah said. 'Let's talk about this.'

I kept walking, shouldering through the doors and out into the morning air. The Sun's light slapped me in the face like sizzling coals. I sucked in a gasp. The heat was greater this high up, on the top plateau of the city, making the air thick and hard to swallow.

I walked to the edge of the balcony. I could see the scorch marks from the ropes across the stone.

'Look,' Cam said, pointing outwards to the eastern gates of the city, far below the plateaus, on dune level. 'More Nobles leaving.'

The fleeing caravan was smaller than usual. I doubted there were many Nobles still even left in the city. They'd been evacuating since we had taken the Sanctuary, more of them fleeing every day.

As we stepped into clear view on the balcony, a smattering

of cheers and prayers were sent our way. Word of our appearance caught on amongst the tents and blankets, and soon enough the moat below was flooded in holy gestures and falling tears.

There were more newcomers than yesterday. The Jadans around the city were taking shelter around the Sanctuary, all so they could be close to 'Meshua'.

Shilah and I had sent word that we had enough Cold and food for everyone in the city. Our stores were plentiful, our water wells deep, and the fig trees in the courtyard stout and healthy. Samsah and some of the Builders were doling out rations by the gates, but with so many Jadans in the City of David's Fall we couldn't last indefinitely under siege. Especially if the Khat still had access to Desert.

I waved two knuckles at the caravan carts.

Cam did the same.

'How's it coming along, by the way, Micah?' Cam asked gently. 'Flight.'

Shilah shot him a warning look.

'What?' Cam asked under his breath. 'I was just asking.'

'Nothing new yet,' I said, my mind immediately turning over my possible solutions. None of them seemed promising. 'But I'll let you know.'

'Can we help at all?' Cam asked.

I shook my head. 'It's something I have to figure out on my own.'

Shilah bopped me on the head.

'No you don't,' Shilah said. 'You're just being stubborn.'

I sighed. 'Fine. Please help. I do need it. I'm running out of ideas.'

Shilah examined her fist. 'Hmm. Maybe Juniss was on to something.'

Just then the Five shot out from behind the nearest Cry Temple and careened across the moat, marching in between all the new kneelers. The cheering immediately died down at the sight of the hulking figures.

Each one of the Five carried a large bag that would be filled with Cold. Jia had a second sack tied around his waist, jiggling along with his stomach. I was quite confident it was another large batch of candied figs.

The Five stopped at the bottom of the balcony and lined up. Dunes kept his eyes on the ground, which let me know the answer before I even asked the question.

'Didn't find any Frosts?' I asked, heart already sinking.

'No,' Dunes said, his chin still tucked against his chest. 'The Erridian Manor was bare. But we found plenty of Cold. And something . . . else.'

That piqued my attention.

'What is it, Dunes?' Shilah asked.

Dunes glanced over his shoulder. The hundreds of Jadans in the expanse were paying close attention. All eyes were on the Five. A blare of heat seared down from the sky, as if the Sun were watching closely as well.

'I'd rather show you in private,' Dunes called up. His voice was just loud enough to reach my ears.

I nodded, gesturing back to the hallway inside.

Dunes broke rank and rushed around the building.

'And the tunnels?' I called out to the remaining Four. 'How are they coming?'

Het drew a ward over his chest, but he wouldn't meet my eyes. 'Dozens of Builders working diligently at your command.'

'Good,' I said. 'Make sure they all get plenty of Cold water.'

'Consider it done,' Kasroot called up, looking at his hands as if they'd been dragged through a rubbish heap.

'Micah, Shilah, Camlish!' Jia called up, wiggling the bag on his hip. 'I brought you Khatmelons. Ripe and juicy! Plumper than the Khat, and all the tenderness that's missing from his heart.'

He spoke in gracious tones, as jovial as always, but there was something different about Jia. A third thing, besides the Cold and figs, weighed him down. It showed in his eyes and his posture and his voice. It pulled heavy, and for a moment, he looked just as tired and scared as all the other Jadans in the moat.

'Thanks, Jia,' I said, cocking my head slightly. 'Why don't you share them with the rest of the family out there?'

Jia looked around, his cheeks beginning to sag. Soon enough his expression matched his demeanour. He opened the Khatmelon bag and waved it around, but no one dared step closer to him. If anything, they retreated.

'My people,' I called out. 'Remember the Five are not Hookmen anymore! They're just as Jadan as the rest of us.'

Heads nodded with assent. No one looked particularly assured.

'Yes of course, Meshua!'

'Thank you, Meshua!'

'Bless you, young tears!'

I gave a wave dismissing the Five, and then went back inside to meet Dunes.

'What do you think he found?' Cam asked. 'It didn't look like he was carrying anything other than his Cold bag.'

'Maybe he found out some sort of secret,' Shilah said. 'About Langria.'

Cam gave her an astonished look.

'What?' she asked.

'Nothing,' Cam said. 'It's just that you don't talk much about Langria anymore. Not as much as you used to.'

'I think for me, Langria was always the only path to freedom. I didn't know that we might find another way out of the Drought, with flight.'

'*If* I can figure it out,' I said.

Shilah nodded. 'We. If we can. You're not alone.'

'Did you see their expressions?' I asked. 'They looked terrified. I have a bad feeling.'

'We can't let everything rattle us,' Shilah said. 'But I saw
it too.'

Soon enough Dunes was padding up the stairs inside the
Sanctuary, his footfalls all but soundless. He stopped in front
of me and lowered with respect.

'You know you don't have to bow,' I said, my throat
clenching up. I couldn't take the suspense. 'We're equals.'

'A bow is not always subservient,' Dunes said. He was
oddly cold in his movements. It was like a light had gone out
inside of him, so dim it was almost extinguished.

I could tell he didn't want to share what he found, and I
didn't want him to either. The air between us grew tense and
paralysing. The empty walls, dust lining the spaces where
Jadan portraits once hung, pressed inward. I felt the rug under
my feet start to tilt, the floor unbalanced, and while I could
still hear the chants of 'Meshua' outside, they had never
sounded less true.

'So what did you find?' Shilah asked finally.

'Cheese?' Cam added. 'Cheese that didn't get mushy from
heat on your way here?'

'Be serious, Cam,' I said.

Dunes took a piece of folded parchment from his pocket,
holding it out. His hands trembled. The self-inflicted cuts on
his wrist had healed nicely, so the shaking wasn't from that.

'It's exactly as you feared,' Dunes said. 'The Nobles are not
fleeing the city because they're scared. They're fleeing because
of these letters. I'm surprised it took us this long to find one,
but I imagine the enemy doesn't want us to know their
reasons.'

For once I hadn't wanted to be right. The parchment was
thick and official-looking, with the Khat's seal on the front.
Shilah unfolded it slowly.

'What's it say?' Cam asked.

'For all of my chosen,' Shilah read slowly. She seemed ill at ease as well, and I wondered if we were going to collapse together. 'Abandon the city at once, for the Crier has spoken. He shall punish the Jadan filth in the way of their wretched ancestors.' She paused, her face hardening at the edges. 'The second Fall is coming.'

She looked me in the eyes, something sharing between us. Something that no one else could feel. We were the two that had chosen this fate for our people, and any retribution would belong to us. We could no longer pretend this wasn't life or death.

The Khat wasn't just coming with an army.

He was coming to burn us all alive.

Chapter Seven

I wiped the sweat from my forehead with a strip of boilweed, kneading the damp fibres between my fingers.

Spout, I thought.

It was funny to consider this older, more wearied sweat. Growing up, I'd perspired when most other Jadans didn't waste a drop. Fear, dread and a flaw in my body wrung me out like damp fabric. For that I should have been dead. I never sweat enough to tip me over the edge, but it was enough to draw attention of my superiors, and one thing I've learned about the sands is that vipers always go for whatever skin is exposed.

Nobles teased me about the sweat, and pushed me, and made me drink foul things like spoiled milk too see if it would leak out of my forehead. They drew unusable signs on my eyelids, the ink dripping down and stinging my vision for the rest of the day. The Nobles called me Spout because I leaked. Because I was defective. Broken.

In a way they were right.

I was broken.

And I used to think broken always meant bad. But I grew up and learned more about the nature of things. I learned that some terrible systems worked just as intended, but could only do harm. Like the wool hat of the Vicaress. Like the things I'd found in Ka'in's tinkershop. Like the Khatdom itself.

And when an evil piece of tinkering worked well, its perfect gears and oiled parts churning hate and pain into the world, it demanded breaking. And the only way to destroy something like that was by the hands of someone who understood the cracks.

I'd been working for days now in the Sanctuary tinkershop, only stopping for a few meagre hours of sleep each night, subsisting on the figs and orangefruit that Cam brought. I ate, but had no taste for food. I could recognize the sweet juices of the orangefruit flesh, the tough pulp of the luscious figs, but it all dried to ash in my mouth.

There was only one thing that mattered.

Flight.

I wiped the sweat on my shirt and set my hammer back on the anvil. The Sanctuary tinkershop had every material and tool I wanted to work with, so my lack of answers was only due to my own incompetence.

Slumping into my chair, I took a swig from my water skin. I'd been pounding down a new fan blade for nearly an hour, hoping to discover a smelting that would produce a lighter metal. But even if I could, it wouldn't make a difference. My glider was too heavy, and pushing wind downward wasn't nearly enough to get the platform to rise off the ground; let alone to lift someone riding on top.

The clay urn of Charged Water – I preferred not to think of it as Wraithwater unless I had to – held the last of the abbs, which I'd dissolved inside days ago. The urn gave off considerable energy, enough where I had to wear double-thick gloves when even standing next to it; but the tinkering wasn't close to enough.

I emptied the rest of my waterskin into my stomach. The

Coldmaker stared at me from the corner of the tinkershop. The lid was open, taunting.

After all the weeks of being in the City of David's Fall, we'd still had no luck finding a Frost. I had a team of Street Jadans searching the abandoned Manors inside and out. Shilah had assembled a team of Builders checking for secret panels in the empty Cry Temples. For the first time since the Great Drought, Jadans could wander wherever we'd like within David's Fall, but the fleeing Nobles had made sure to empty the place of any Frosts – if there were even any here to begin with. And since the Cry Patches here hadn't gotten any Cold since the days of King David himself, there was no chance of finding a Frost by accident.

I looked at the hammer, considering taking another few cracks just to get my frustration out, but instead turned to the book of paintings on the nearby table. I'd been studying it earlier, having put if off to the side so as not to get my sweat on any of the brittle pages. The library had plenty of scrolls and volumes related to the Fall. Ka'in's collection was as complete as any I'd seen, and it was obvious that he was quite proud of the city's history.

The tome in my hands now depicted violent recreations of the events at the Southern cliffs. I flipped back to the page I'd been lamenting over: an image of black-skinned demons shoving Jadans over the edge. The sands above and below the cliffs were on fire. Scorched bones from the Jadan bodies littered the fires, faceless and rotting, crawling with scarabs.

The text accompanying the current drawing was in the common tongue. I wasn't as good at reading as I would have liked – the Nobles reserved a lot of words and terms for themselves – but I could surmise the general feel of the passage. It was pretty much the same as all of the passages, adding up to a single narrative.

During the Drought, many Jadans disregarded the Khat's

Gospels and fled to this city – Ziah, as it was known then – to escape the fate of becoming slaves. So when the time came, the Crier cursed Ziah, letting his brother Sun destroy those who hid within the city walls. The city began to heat up slowly, letting the Jadans boil over, eventually becoming so unbearable that everyone had to jump to their deaths.

This was known as the Fall.

I flipped through the pages. The answer was here in these pages, even if I couldn't yet see it. It was between the words. Under the spine. Beneath the pages.

What do Jadans need?

There was one aspect of the whole scenario which I found most intriguing. The First Khat had set the land on fire – using the mythical substance known as 'Desert' – but the land had also gone back to normal after the Fall. Most likely, the city's return was either because Desert had limited power, or that the Khat had taken it back after performing his terrible trick. These were my first, most obvious guesses. There was also a chance that the First Khat had tinkerers who'd discovered some alchemy to stop the effect, which I prayed was not the case.

What do Jadans need?

Flight.

A Frost.

Answers.

If Desert was a real thing it would answer so many mysteries; about the city, about the Great Drought. But there had never been any proof of its existence. If Desert was real, it was even rarer and more secret than Frosts.

'If you're taking a break,' Leah said from behind me, giving me a start, 'might I suggest some music?'

I'd forgotten she was with me in the tinkershop. I spun in my chair, finding her with her sewing needles idly in hand. The boilweed sheet she had been working on was even better work than the Opened Eye flag she'd sewn, this one about twice the size of a large sleeping blanket. I'd asked for the final cloth to be as large as she could make it, and Leah didn't seem to mind the task. She did however insist on doing all the work in here with me.

'Thanks,' I said, my heart rate calming. 'I guess I wouldn't mind music.'

Leah beamed as she dropped the needles and picked up her harp. She wore gold ribbons in her luscious hair, which was fluffy and thick. I couldn't tell for sure, but I suspected she'd begun to wipe orangefruit peels on the back of her neck. I got a whiff every time she watched me work over my shoulder.

'What do you want to hear?' she asked, setting the instrument between her thighs.

'I want you to make something up,' I said, looking away from her muscled legs and wiping a new sheen of sweat from my forehead. 'Maybe I can feed off of your creativity. I'm certainly not having much luck of my own.'

She flexed her fingers. Then she began caressing two of the strings, plucking out a few gentle notes. Her face furrowed with disappointment. She bit her bottom lip, which was so plump that I had to look away. I'd thought about asking her to do her stitching work elsewhere, so I wouldn't be distracted by her smooth skin and curious eyes, but her presence had an inspirational effect. I wanted to impress her. I wanted to become the Inventor who she believed me to be.

Shilah and I had created this wonderful, world-changing invention that could actually *make* Cold. I thought it had been a sign from the Crier. It was supposed to float our people to freedom on a tide of hope. It was supposed to motivate the Nobles to throw down their weapons and titles, helping us recreate paradise.

The Khat's forces had arrived last night.

Our city was surrounded, with the gates barred and armies at our doorstep. Moans of fear could be heard throughout the moat, although they clashed with the rallies of hope. Most of the Flock really did see Shilah and I as Meshua, although at best, the Coldmaker now seemed like a happy accident. My fingers were numb to new ideas.

'It's not in tune with itself,' Leah said of her harp, tightening the string. 'That's more important than anything else.'

She began to play a few scales, up and down, but they weren't straight paths. The notes were punctuated by quick flurries. The melody was frantic. My heart quickened with the pace of her fingers and then slowed as she brought the notes to rest.

I was enraptured, letting myself be lulled away in the story of her song. A little distance from the problem might help. I could visualize the path she was taking me along. She took long strolls through the alleyways, relaxed and whimsical, but every few corners she would crouch low and sprint across the hot stones, as if pursued by taskmasters.

I closed my eyes and jumped with her from note to note.

How to fly?

If we could fly, we could rise up and gather the Cold in the stars ourselves. We could end the Drought in a way the Khat would never expect.

I'd been tinkering with the Sand Glider design that Leroi had come up back in the Tavor Manor. His was a slab of wood that had special blades at the back to push air, powered by a Cold Charge. In theory it was capable of riding the sands, although Leroi could never get it to work, because the Charge wasn't strong enough. I thought the Wraithwater might do the trick, so much so that I could put the fan blades facing downwards and push my way to the sky. I built a model, but was having no luck with my 'Air Glider', so far, successful only in keeping the slab firmly on the stone floor while blowing all sorts of scrolls and trinkets around the vast tinkershop.

Despair was setting in heavy.

Besides the how of actually flying, there was also no telling how high into the sky the Cold waited. For all I knew there wouldn't even be any air up there. Even if I succeeded in finding a way up, there was a possibility I would suffocate while trying to breathe thick black darkness.

Every idea I was coming up with was as trivial as the last.

I'd thought about a giant catapult that could launch me towards the stars, but that was quickly abandoned. Not only was it impractical, but dangerous. I'd never get high enough to reach Cold, and even with Leah's ensuing Sky Sheet, I'd most likely come down hard enough to break all of my bones. It would never work by a long shot.

I'd looked to the extinct birds of the past, staring at pictures and diagrams in the books, wondering over how wings might have worked. I had learned the hard way that my arms were too weak and my body too heavy to fly in such a way. I'd experimented with tinkered wings, thankfully when Leah wasn't there, as I was glad no one had witnessed that particular humiliation.

I thought about the Fire-powders that the Vicaress had shot into the air when she'd cornered our Coldmarch group at the River Singe. She'd used the powders to call her Hookmen from a distance. The red streaks had climbed into the night like whips of oil and flame, but the sizzling streaks didn't seem anywhere near strong enough to carry a person.

Impossible.

The music was lovely, my thoughts anything but.

Leah stopped playing at once, the flowery melody wilting.

'Sorry for interrupting,' Cam said, sliding open the proper door. 'That was really pretty. I immediately regret coming in, but there's something you need to see, Micah.'

I let out a long sigh. 'More armies?'

Cam nodded. 'These from the Glasslands, I think. All their spears are glinting like crazy.'

'But no sign of the Khat yet?'

Cam shook his head. 'At least no sign of his chariot. He could be hiding—'

'Then it can wait,'I said.

'But—'

'Is Shilah up there?'I asked.

'Yes, but she wanted to see you. To plan together.'

I looked over at Leah and gave her a go-ahead motion. She began playing the harp again without hesitation.

'This *is* the plan,' I said, getting up and gesturing to the frame of the useless Air Glider. In essence it was only a platform of thin wood, the clay urn, and two cages on the sides where the blades would sit. But there was another piece, a piece that couldn't be seen that weighed everything down. I wanted to smash the invention against the wall. 'I don't know any other plan.'

Cam nodded, biting his bottom lip.

'What?' I asked.

'Nothing.'

'Please tell me you have some ideas. Some secret that the High Nobles have been hiding since the Great Drought?'

Cam scratched at his chin which had gone gold with stubble. His eyes went over to Leah, whose hands caressed the harp like a mother lovingly braiding a child's hair. Leah expertly plucked, not looking at the strings. Her eyes were focused on me. Large and inquisitive and lovely.

Cam leaned in and whispered. 'Better be careful, pal.'

My stomach clenched and I snapped my fingers. 'Ideas. Ideas.'

Cam sucked his cheek. 'I can check the library for any clues again.'

'No. We've already been over those texts, and there was nothing about flying.'

Cam eyed the shelf that used to hold the tinkershop books. I'd burned most of them, as the bulk of the pages were filled with designs that would only be useful in rebuilding Ka'in's torture machines.

'You feel trapped?' Cam asked.

I gave him an incredulous look. 'You don't? There are more armies showing up every day and the gates are all barred closed. We're actually under siege.'

Cam shook his head. 'I'm hopeful. More hopeful than scared at least.'

'Don't go telling me you believe in me,' I said. 'That you're not scared because you trust that I'll figure a way out.'

Cam pretended to lock his lips with an invisible key.

'No,' I said. 'Tell me that.'

'Well it's true.'

I flexed my bronze fingers. 'I've never wanted to figure anything out so badly. Not even the Coldmaker. We actually need to fly, or else we die. The Coldmaker wasn't life or death.'

'Of course it was.' Cam shrugged.

'How so?'

Cam went over to the Air Glider, running his hand across the wooden platform. He stretched his fingers out to touch the clay urn in the middle.

'In so many ways. Especially my life. Hey, this is better than Leroi's,' he said. 'The old man would have been mighty proud of you.'

'For failing?'

Cam ran his hand across one of the cages. I'd wrapped the copper wires around the outside bars, filtering them into the abb-Charged water. I'd already fit in most of the new wind-blades in the metal cage, but I hadn't bothered with building railings on the upper platform yet. I never expected the machine to get off the ground.

'For a brilliant Inventor, sometimes you can be Taskmaster dumb,' Cam flicked the metal with his fingernail. 'Maybe it's a balance thing. You have to say stupid things sometimes in order to save up for the really smart ideas. It's probably why one day I'm going to say something so profound that Shilah's head will—' Cam cut himself off, his eyes going wide. 'Anyway. You would have told me you'd failed on the Coldmaker, up until the very second it proved itself a miracle. In fact, I remember you saying just that.' He gestured to the top of the urn. 'May I?'

I went to the cage and fitted the new blade in place, screwing it down. Once the blade was snug in its casing, I closed the cage and gestured for Cam to start it.

Cam flipped the lever on the side of the urn. Inside, the dividing rubber slid out of place and the spring-loaded gears dipped the copper wire into the solution. The giant blades began to whirr. They picked up speed inside the cage, forcing air downwards and sending out a smattering of dust. The wooden platform rocked from side to side slightly, the blades loud and frantic, but it wasn't nearly enough to get any lift.

Cam turned the lever off.

Leah stared with wide eyes and then went back to playing her harp, the song coming back to life.

Cam bent down to examine the blades.

'The clay container has the last of the Charged Water,' I said. 'So there's no way to get any more power. Until we find a Frost, that is.'

'And you've tried putting in tears?' Cam asked. 'That was the secret to the last big invention. I bet you Jadan tears are always the secret. It's poetic. World *Crier* and all.'

I offered him a warm smile. His head was at least in the right place. I was lucky to have a real friend by my side.

'I've tried tears,' I said with a sigh. 'And blood. Spit. Extra Chills. Every coloured salt. Powdered glass from the Shocklands. I tried fruit and green leaves and sugar. I doubled the salt. I—'

'Did you try a *mixture* of Jadan tears? From more than one Jadan?' Cam asked, running his hand along the cage. 'If . . . in case the Crier is more present in a group.'

'Hmm.' I felt a small trickle of hope. 'No I guess I haven't.'

Cam nodded. 'Come on. We'll get some onions on the way to the balcony and maybe we can get the Five to shed us a few vials.'

'Dunes wouldn't even need onions,' I said with a smile. 'He'd cry a whole vial if I asked him.'

'It's a plan.'

I closed the book, making sure Leah wouldn't have to witness any of the paintings. 'And seeing the arriving armies might help spur me some ideas. Maybe if I stare at the Southern cliff for a while. At the place where we'll all have to jump if I fail.'

Cam turned, a sad look in his eyes.

'I meant it in a hopeful way,' I said.

'It came out a bit gloomy.'

'It's reality,' I said, swallowing hard. 'I just feel so weighed down. Since Abb. Since killing all those Nobles and . . . burying them in the sands. It's like a slab of stone on my back, and I'm laying on broken glass.'

'I can help with that,' Leah whispered, only looking at her strings. 'I would make you feel better.'

I coughed, trying to focus on the problem at hand.

Cam came over and put a hand over my shoulder.

'I'll help too,' he said.

He pretended to push an invisible slab off of me, his face straining. His arms slapped across my back as he succeeded in removing the imaginary burden and he gave a dramatic sigh, wiping his hands of what would be dust.

'Better?' he asked with a smirk.

I smiled. 'Actually, yes.'

'What's that thing you used to say?' he asked.

I cocked my head. 'What? Family?'

Cam's eyes were alight. I couldn't understand how or why. He'd been outside watching the Khat's armies more than I had, spending so much time with Shilah and helping her keep the Flock calm. He saw what was surrounding the city, clawing at our walls and foaming at the mouth.

'The thing,' Cam said. 'The thing that your father said when he took you out to the dunes. With the bucket.'

Had I really shared that memory with him? I didn't remember telling anyone. The moment was too precious, too delicate, so much so that even speaking of it threatened to make it alter in any way.

I could still see my father at the banks of the River Kiln, hurling fistfuls of sand out of the bucket he'd made me carry across the dunes. With each toss he told me about a different lie the Nobles made us carry around, the things that held our people down. I'd been dripping with sweat, close to death, too empty to carry on, and ended up learning the most important lesson I'd ever learned.

'Drop the Bucket,' I whispered.

My father had gifted me the saying. It meant that words can kill just as quickly as thirst. It meant that I should search for truth, not for answers. It meant that the first, deepest and only freedom our people have left is to choose what to believe.

But the choice was everything.

'Drop the Bucket,' I said again, this time even quieter.

'That.' Cam nodded. 'But I meant the other thing.'

'What do Jadans need?' I whispered.

Cam clapped me on the shoulder and led me over to the broken Coldmaker. I had a hard time looking inside, the spot where the Frost should have been empty now.

My chest rippled with loss. With hard truth.

The machine didn't actually make Cold. It just redistributed the Cold from the Frost. Or extracted it. Even if I didn't understand the mechanics, the Invention made it very clear that it didn't create something out of nothing. It seemed to me that the whole machine was just an illusion. Yet it had served a purpose.

'Say it again,' Cam prodded.

'What do Jadans need?'

'This,' Cam said, jabbing a finger towards the bronze Opened Eye that I'd chiselled into the lid. 'They needed this and it came. Through your hands.'

'But it doesn't even work.'

'But it did work, and it will again you fool!' Cam said. 'You asked the question. This was the answer. It was exactly what Jadans needed.' He turned his finger upwards. 'The Coldmaker started the rebellion. The Wraiths continued the rebellion. And now the Jadans need something else to finish the rebellion. We've had periods of failure along the way, but they were just cracks in the road, not the road itself.'

'Flight,' I said, with a sigh. 'We need to fly so we can gather the Cold up there ourselves. That's what Jadans need. We've already been over that, and I don't know what else to—'

Cam bopped me on the head with his fist, just as Shilah had.

I scowled. Then I laughed.

Cam shrugged. 'I thought that might be your idea button. Anyway, correct me if I'm wrong, but it wasn't a Coldmaker you were trying to invent back in Leroi's tinkershop, right?'

I gave a begrudging nod. 'I was trying to make a Cold-finder. The Coldmaker was an accident.'

'Mhmm. And the Charged Water wasn't intended for torturing Nobles at first either? It was to power inventions, right? Also an accident?'

'Right.'

'That's reality, Spout. Perhaps it's "happy accidents" that the Jadans need. You might come across something that doesn't look like flight, but will end up sending us straight to the stars. You just keep pushing, keep trying, and I think the Crier will provide something unexpected.'

Emotions welled up in my chest. This was something we never talked about, although we should have. 'You believe in the World Crier. You actually believe.'

Leah's music became dreamy. I didn't look back in case she took that as a cue to stop playing.

Cam gave me an obvious sort of look. 'Of course I do! How could I not?'

'Because of all the slavery and death and pain. Because of how unfair everything is. Because of the armies surrounding us and only getting bigger. Because of all the bad in the world.' I let out a long sigh. 'If the Crier had any power at all, how could He let all of this happen?'

Cam twitched his lips.

'Here's how I see it,' he said softly. 'All the paintings, all the busts, all the images of the World Crier as an actual person, whether Noble or Jadan, I think – I don't think it's supposed to be literal. Put aside the Cold falling into the Patches and the Great Drought, I see the World Crier in a different sort of way. As an Idea more than a being. You of all people should know how much power an Idea holds. And as far as all the bad in the world, I don't think it's so much that things are flooded with bad, it's just that things are missing good. Just like the ancient Cry Patches across the world, and mountain tops, and boiling rivers are missing Cold. Does that make sense?'

I raised an eyebrow.

'Okay,' Cam said, waving it away and going to the nearest table, where I had my meagre rations. 'I'll put it in tinker-terms.'

He picked up my waterskin and held it over a cup. 'Like this. The inside of the cup is dry, right?'

'Right.'

Cam shook his head. 'Dry is just a made up word to describe missing water. It's not that it's dry, it's just that the inside of the cup isn't wet. Wet is the real thing. The thing that matters.' He poured a bit of water into the cup. 'It's not the emptiness that's real, it's what the object is empty of.'

'The Khat's Priests taught you this?'

'Shivers and Frosts, no!' Cam said with a chuckle. 'High Noble or not, the Priests would toss me in the Pyramid pits if they heard me talking like this. They believe in very black and white decrees. The Sun versus the Crier. Worthy versus unworthy.'

'They'd toss you in the pits for helping a Jadan capture a city.'

'Exactly my point! It's because they've abandoned the Crier. They've pushed Him out of their hearts. All the spite and anger and hate, those are the marks of His absence. That's the emptiness. And the First Khat must have found a way to push the Crier out of the land, but that doesn't mean the Crier doesn't exist. That He doesn't still have real power.'

The music became choppy and then disappeared.

They put it in the ground, I thought. Just like Old Man Gum had said over and over in my barracks. They put Desert in the ground, gaining control, but losing everything that mattered.

Cam slid his finger around the rim of the glass. 'The World Crier is like the water. The essence that matters. And even if He's sometimes missing, even when it feels like everything is dry and will be dry forever, we can still know that He's real. That He exists.'

'But how?'

'How?' Cam asked, his brow furrowed. 'Haven't you ever laughed or loved so hard that you cried?'

I thought about it. 'Yes. I guess I have.'

'Boom. World Crier.' He clapped my shoulder. 'What other proof do you need?'

'Cam,' I said after a breath.

'Yeah, Spout?'

'That profound thing that you've been saving for?' My heart squeezed, accepting a different hard truth. It stung. It burned. It made me feel lonelier than I had in a long time. But it was also so damn beautiful. 'I wish Shilah had heard it.'

Cam turned back to the urn and touched his fingers lightly to the clay.

'It's okay,' he said. 'That one was for you.'

'For us,'I said. 'Family.'

Shilah surveyed the land from the balcony, holding the special Stinger that I'd tinkered for her. What made it different was that the end of the weapon had a braid of rubber bowstring which could be looped around her wrist in battle. I'd offered to use camel leather for the loop, having uncovered a few strips in the tinkershop, but Shilah refused so violently that I thought she might use the Stinger on me.

I'd added the braid to the weapon not because of the practicality, but because it matched Shilah's hair. Her braid had become a mark of distinction, with the Flock always whispering about the blade she kept hidden in her locks. There were wild speculations, always shifting and changing. They said that the metal was always cold. That the blade had been melted down from King David's old staff. That it had been mined out of the Great Divide, right under the spot where the Giant Frost had fallen and cracked open the land. I'd even heard it said that Shilah's blade was etched with the very same words which caused the Crier to weep the world.

It was just an ordinary blade, small and sleek, but I would never have dreamed of taking their stories away. The older

I'd gotten, the more I realized that it wasn't so much the world that gave rise to stories, but rather the other way around.

The 'Khatdom' wasn't real; it was just a story that the Nobles enforced with whips, pain, fear and history. The Gospels and Decrees were stories, all with very real consequences. The idea that Abb was my 'father' was just a story, since there was no actual blood relation; yet it was this forced and imaginary bond that had shaped me completely. Every Invention of mine had started out as nothing more than a notion in my head, of what might be.

Even the Crier Himself was just a story as far as I knew.

Perhaps such a story is what Jadans need.

I looked out across the landscape surrounding our city, trying not to buckle beneath the sight.

It had taken weeks for the Noble armies to amass in full, but finally the entire City of David's Fall was surrounded. Thousands of enemy Nobles. They were stocked with gleaming armour and spears, and their tents and encampments stretched as far as the horizon would allow.

Makeshift markets had already been erected on the fringes. Caravans had been immobilized and opened for business. Pedlars and merchants were selling goods with feverish excitement to all the High Nobles who'd come to witness the spectacle. Thousands of pale faces smirked beneath vibrant parasols.

It was curious how commerce had been the first thing to thrive here, in the face of an impending slaughter. How prepared the merchants were for such a moment. They toted things like parasols with Closed Eyes, exotic fruits and thin sun skirts for surviving the long wait while the land boiled us alive. Purified prayer water was hawked by Priests, Sobek meat was roasted on spits and all sorts of other luxuries were enjoyed in preparation for the show.

Dunes and the Five had been surveying the incoming hordes, looking closely for overturned land, especially on our side of the walls. So far they'd found no signs of digging; of things being put in the ground. We hardly knew anything about Desert, and Old Man Gum's warning was the only thing we had to go on. I was actually hoping the Five might find a freshly buried Desert, because even though it would be poisoning the land, at least we would understand the Khat's tactic and possibly be able to put up a fight.

Because if we were wrong, and the Desert could be used some other way, we stood no chance.

The gates to the city had all been sealed shut from the other side. The Khat was allowing no one in or out. And although most of the Jadans inside the city still believed in our cause, there was a faction that sat by the walls and wailed for release.

A slight but steady stream of our people abandoned the Flock with each day, realizing what was about to befall the city. They foresaw death and decided to join up with the crestfallen. They pounded their fists against the sealed doorways, screaming about their unworthiness until their voices broke, apologizing and begging the Khat not to be sent to the black. The doors remained sealed. There would be no way out. The Khat would make an example of us all.

It made me question whether the Khat had allowed us to take the Sanctuary in the first place, to rally his armies over a dramatic cause. It was possible that the Nobles we'd discovered in the Sanctuary had been willingly sacrificed, as the Khat knew it would make for a spectacle. A better story.

By now, rumour would have got out about the Jadans who could make Ice. About 'Meshua'. And even though we were sealed off from the rest of the Khatdom, Jadans and Nobles alike would have heard about us all the way back in Paphos. There would be talks of rebellion stirring even in the furthest reaches of the Khatdom, like the Shocklands and the Hotland Delta. Two golden abbs were out there somewhere in the pockets of my Jadan kin, along with stories of what they could do, and chances were word was spreading. Such powerful rumours were a new enemy that the Khat wouldn't be able to simply whip or lie into submission.

But with something as glorious as a second Fall, he could end it all in a single strike.

One final Cleansing.

Not only our rebellion, but future rebellions. This would prove that the 'divinity' of the Khats was still intact, and would lead to another eight hundred years of torment and servitude. Any hope of things changing would die along with our secrets.

The Coldmaker would be destroyed. Knowledge of how it worked would be destroyed. And even if there was another Jadan who stumbled across the secret for Ice generations in the future, he or she would remember the second Fall and abandon the pursuit. They'd probably turn themselves over to the taskmasters just for entertaining such a blasphemous thought.

I almost envied the Khat's genius manoeuvring.

'There are more Khatfists and soldiers showing up every hour,' Shilah said, her words solemn.

'Yes,' I said. 'Who wouldn't want to see us Jadan scum burn? The whole Khatdom is going to have eyes here. So just imagine if we succeed.'

'*When* we succeed,' Cam coughed into his palm.

'When we succeed,' I said. 'Then things will change.'

Shilah lifted the Stinger and swept the blades towards the massive Noble crowds, searching for a particular enemy. Here on the top plateau, we were too high up and too far away from the gates to be able to make out individual faces within the crowd of thousands. But one figure stood out wherever she lurked. Shilah swooped through the armies and eventually honed in on the black-clad figure. She hovered near the Khat's tent, holding up a pike with a golden Closed Eye at the tip.

The Vicaress of David's Fall.

'What do you think she's thinking?' Shilah asked. 'She obviously knows we killed the Vicaress of Paphos.'

'They were second cousins,' Cam said.

'Is that right?' I asked.

'Yes,' Cam said. 'And they were close.'

Shilah kept the tip of the Stinger pinned on the dark figure, following her through the bustling crowd. This Vicaress was not nearly as graceful as the one I'd known, walking with a limp and a hunched back. Nobles were bowing to her regardless, and she was giving out scrolls to whoever showed supplication. My teeth probably would have broken from clenching if I knew what was written on those parchments.

'Soon the Vicaress of Belisk is going to mourn both of them,' Shilah said. 'And then the Vicaress of Marlea is going to mourn all three. And so on and so on until every one of the Khat's entire High Noble family is dead.'

Cam jerked, his cough real this time.

'In his immediate family,' Shilah corrected, swinging her Stinger around and pointing it at Cam playfully. 'Some of you High Nobles have earned your place at my side.'

Cam help up his hands defensively and then caressed his cheek. 'Phew. Be a travesty if such beauty ended here.'

My stomach knotted. I surveyed the outer lands. Their outer perimeters continued to bulge deeper into the sands. 'Still no sign of the Khat himself, though.'

'He'll want to make it dramatic,' Cam said. 'He'll probably wait until all his favourite, most vicious relatives are here before he shows.'

'How many more can there be?' I asked under my breath,

estimating at least five thousand bodies surrounding us. This was including the Jadans who had been brought along from other cities. A large group had been tasked with building a stage, the purpose of which I was not eager to find out.

A flicker of fear crossed Shilah's face. She quickly composed herself.

'It doesn't matter,' she said. 'Because we know what to expect. And they don't know that we know.'

'And if the Khat just decides to break open the gates and flood the city?' I asked. 'He can kill us all with a few hundred swords.'

'Then he'll have lost the bigger battle,' Shilah said. 'In a sense. He'll have to admit he doesn't have the Crier's divine powers on his side and he can't make the city burn. The minute he enters the city, he'll have proven that there is no second "Fall", because a Fall entails us all killing ourselves when we can't take the heat. So the more Nobles who show up the better. Even if we die, they'll be forced to look that lie in the face.'

I nodded. 'You know what, you're right. I bet he didn't plan for that.'

Cam prodded me with an elbow. 'See. Happy accidents.'

Just then, drums pounded in the distance.

They were low and droning, and it wasn't the first time they'd been sounded. We hadn't figured out their meaning, but Shilah was convinced that they were purely for intimidation. I wasn't so sure.

The groups of Jadans camping around the Sanctuary reacted the same as they had during the last bout of drumming. They whispered and trembled and looked up to us for leadership, their faces distraught with terror. Children screamed and older Jadans tried to calm them down. Hope left the air after each thunderous beat.

I had no more Ice.

Nothing to give except promises so hollow that they could be cracked open and admired for their staggering emptiness.

Breathing became difficult.

It's what the Khat wanted. I was losing my composure.

The Sun was in a fine mood. Its fiery tongues explored my body, tasting my dismay.

The drums echoed off the buildings and temples and barracks of the city, loud even up on our top plateau. The notes gathered into an ear-rattling thrum, reminding us that we were trapped in every direction. Reminding us there was no escape.

The ranks of Noble shoppers and spectators cheered as the drums suddenly halted. Then they went about spending their Cold. Merrily they tried on jewellery and bit into ripe Khatmelons. Dozens of easels had been set up close to the walls, artists waiting with wet brushes, eager to capture the moment on canvas.

'Any sign of Ka'in?' Cam asked.

'Nothing yet,' I said.

'He'll probably try to make his entrance as dramatic as the Khat,' Cam said, clearly perturbed. 'Ka'in's probably the bastard behind that stage.'

'What do you think it's for?' I asked, heart in my throat.

We went silent for a while, listening to the absence of drums.

'You been holding up okay?' I asked Shilah. 'I know I've kind of left you alone in command.'

She and Cam exchanged a glance.

It was full of answers.

She nodded. 'It's okay, Micah. And your work is more important. The Flock is scared of course, but they're trying to stay calm. Ellia and Ellcia are building us one hell of a reputation, too. And of course Leah's been cooing about you as if she's seen the Crier's blood in your veins.'

Heat shot into my cheeks and another long silence settled in.

'How's the tinkering coming?' Shilah asked, a smirk on her lips. 'Any breakthroughs?'

Cam went tense.

I paused and then shook my head.

'Want me to help come up with some ideas?' Shilah asked, putting her hand on the back of my neck. 'Don't forget we're still a team.'

A tear formed at the corner of my eye. I dabbed at the wetness with my bronze pinky.

'Yes,' I said. 'Yes, I would like that. Cam had a good idea to try, but I can use as many ideas as you have.'

She squeezed and then let go, her fingers dragging across my numbers.

'Consider it done.' She snuck Cam a secret wink that unfortunately I could see. 'And don't worry. We'll have plenty of time. The Khat has one play here, and it's going to fail.'

'I hope you're right,' I said.

'She's right,' Cam said. 'High Nobles are arrogant. Not me of course, but as a general rule they are. And the Khat is the Highest Noble. He won't expect us to know anything. Especially not about Desert.'

'If it's even a real thing,' I said.

Whips cracked. Shouting began in the distance.

I couldn't tell which side of the wall was screaming.

Chapter Eight

'Cam knows what the Khat looks like,' Shilah whispered. 'I think.'

I shifted back and forth on my stomach, the white stone tiles on the roof still blistering from the day's heat.

'I don't think he does,' I said. 'He's never mentioned it to me, at least.'

Shilah didn't fidget. She remained flat on her stomach and chest, her eyes focused. Her braid sat heavy against the roof, pulled down by an unnatural weight, the outline of a blade sheathed in locks.

There were a few flash explosives in my boilweed bag – the kind Leroi had used to help us escape the Tavor manor – which would allow us a getaway if need be. Although Leroi never showed me the exact proportions for the weapons, I'd watched him tinker enough of them to know the basic ingredients.

Essence of Yitzhun and crushed Golem Grease were rare, but Dunes found me some in one of the apothecaries. Since the Nobles had abandoned the city, I'd been able to raid any shops I'd like, and I would have bet that my wares had now become more impressive than any tinkershop in the Khatdom.

Ironic that for the first time in my life I had access to unlimited tinkering materials, but still couldn't find the answer to Flight.

'You don't think he looks like Cam, do you?' Shilah asked.

'No way,' I said. 'I've heard that evil poxes the skin. Which means that the Khat's face probably looks like melted candlewax.'

'Evil poxes the skin, huh?' Shilah gave me a funny look. 'What about the Vicaress of Paphos? Some said she was the most beautiful Noble in the Khatdom.'

'Fair point. But she eventually got poxed by five hooked blades in the chest.'

Shilah reached over and scratched her fingers through my hair. 'Never thought we'd grow up to be doing this, did you? Trying to defend a city against the Khat himself.'

'No. No I did not.' I cleared my throat. 'Do you want to talk about Cam?'

Shilah turned forward again, watching the stage. The flames around the perimeter glowed a deep red. The kindling would have had to been sprinkled with murr-thorn to get such a menacing colour.

'What about Cam?' Shilah asked.

'You know what.'

'I hardly think now is the time, Micah.'

'I'm not angry or anything.'

'I said—'

'Seriously, I'm not upset. I thought I might be at first. Maybe not angry, but sad, or lonely even, but I'm past that. I just want you to be happy. And obviously I see the appeal in Cam.' I paused, making sure I sounded sincere. 'I want you happy and alive.'

Shilah let out a long sigh. The expressionless mask tumbled away with the deep breath. Her shoulders went slack, and suddenly her back loosened to match my own.

'I don't know when it happened,' she said, blindly feeling for my hand. She eventually found my fingers and gave them a gentle squeeze.

I squeezed back. It was a relief to hear her admit the truth. It was also a relief for me to admit it.

'I'm just happy to have you both in my life,' I said. 'At times like this, you appreciate the things that matter.'

Her hand went towards my cheek. She had to roll awkwardly to make contact, but eventually her palm went flat on my face. Her skin was throbbing with the roof's heat. I flinched.

'Sorry,' she said with a quiet laugh.

'No it's fine.' I smiled, taking her fingers and pressing them tighter. 'It's good.'

Horns sounded. The night's entertainment was about to begin.

The Khat had arrived this morning, his chariot was one I hadn't seen before. It was expansive and heavy, nearly crushing the two dozen Jadans backs on which it arrived. The bejewelled base and white tent top were big enough to shelter half of my original barracks.

The Nobles had exploded with awe and jubilation. They chanted and bowed and dropped to their knees, fraying their expensive silk garb. They waved freshly purchased copies of the Khat's Gospels – bound in tanned camel leather – while shouting choice verses from the pages. They wore smiles the size of the Great Divide, dripping with conceit.

Shilah and I had been watching the development throughout the day from different vantage points, taking in the spectacle. With the arrival of the Khat, the Nobles had become feverish in their expectations.

Closed Eye necklaces were waved. Chills were set on pedestals and kissed. Communal swimming pools were dug out and lined in clay, with the Nobles luxuriating within a mixture of floral potions and dissolved Shivers, wasting Cold and shouting about what a day to be alive.

The Nobles hadn't brought too many Jadans with them, perhaps a hundred in total, but their dark skin was easily visible. Taskmasters kept dragging groups of them on top of the stage, still alive. Then they would laugh as they hurled our kin face first into dead-carts waiting below, piled high with rotting corpses.

Chants of 'Fall' erupted near the stage while the horrified Jadans scrambled off the carts and desperately tried to rub away the blood and ichor. Many vomited, although none was given any boilweed with which to clean themselves up. The Nobles laughed and ate camel cheese. I couldn't imagine what was being done to the Domestic Jadans in private.

The Khat had yet to come out of his chariot, and the anticipation had only grown throughout the day, the armies and High Nobles gathering tighter around him, confident in his divinity.

In a similar way, the Flock had become even more reverent of Shilah and I. They gathered around the Sanctuary, hundreds strong, and offered gifts and songs and dances created in our honour. They chanted 'Meshua' into the endless hours of night, thanking us for preemptively saving them, unfazed by anything other than their own irrational optimism.

The 'Beggars' had a different outlook.

That was the name Shilah had given the faction of Jadans who huddled by the front gates of the city. They beat their fists, shouting their apologies to the Nobles on the other side. The gates remained barred regardless of their pleas, and the Nobles hurled spoiled food and rocks over the walls at them. There weren't as many Beggars as the Flock, but their numbers were still great.

Night had fallen, and Shilah and I had made our way down to the bottom plateau in secrecy. We'd shrouded ourselves in cloaks and Khatberry juice, finding a Cry Temple near the gates to hunch down on top of. We were supposed to be back in the Sanctuary, having promised Dunes and the Five that we wouldn't come out at night without their protection, but we couldn't stay away.

A black tent had been erected on the outskirts of the armies. The Vicaress had been seen dragging Jadan children inside the tent, cuffed and chained, brought in from the surrounding cities with the caravans. The Vicaress was going to use the poor kids for some grand display tonight. Whether it be by blade, or fire, or wool hat, she was about to send another message to Shilah and I.

Shilah squeezed my hand again. The sound of horns doubled.

'We could go back and keep tinkering,' she said. 'We don't have to stay and watch.'

'Of course we do.'

She nodded, heaviness falling on both of our shoulders. I was going to make it a point of performing a Jadan burial for those children. We wouldn't have their bodies, but hopefully I could float a few seeds and songs into the black on their behalf.

'I'm glad it's just me and you,' Shilah said. 'I don't think anyone else would understand.'

A figure strutted up the stairs to the stage. He opened his arms wide for the buzzing crowd. Thousands cheered. Swathes of Nobles fawned like he was the Khat.

His face was covered entirely by a mask, a long beak protruding from the portion around his mouth. His eyes were covered by mesh netting, with a velvet casing wrapping around his hair. The mutilated skin at his neck and along his arms gave his identity away. I hoped the scars burned.

The Vicaress arrived next.

She walked with jerky movements, stiff and unsure. She

reminded me of a clay statue halfway between moulded and dry. Her eyes were as dull as sand. They barely caught the fire from her dagger, the same kind all the Vicaresses carried. Deadly metal wreathed in flame.

She lurched her way onto stage and the crowd gave a respectful cheer. She waved for quiet and then gestured to the taskmasters in front of the black tent. A part of me wished the heat within the fabric had been too much to bear, and the children were already gone. It might have been a mercy.

'You going to be okay?' Shilah whispered.

'Yes,' I lied.

'I'm right here. I'm still with you.'

One of the taskmasters handed the Vicaress a cone clearly made of Glassland Purple – which amplified sounds – and she set it to her lips. It allowed her to speak much louder, but did nothing for the stuttering. 'We are h-here to w-witness t-truth! We are here to w-watch j-justice! Praise be-be the K-Khat!'

'Praise be the Khat!' the massive crowd answered.

The voices at the outskirts were delayed, proving the vastness of the armies. The Nobles of each city stuck together, their different fashions apparent, with those of Paphos getting the closest spots to the stage. It struck me as significant that Nobles, who had everything they could possibly want, still found ways to posture over each other.

Shilah's hand returned to my back, and I was glad for her comfort. Then I realized that she was reaching into the boil-weed bag, scavenging for a flash explosive.

'You shouldn't,' I said. 'We're too far away from the stage, and if we attack them first, the Khat can justify storming—'

She cut me off, putting a finger to her lips. 'In case it's really bad.'

'Unbearably bad,' I whispered. 'Then yes. We can use them.'

She nodded. 'Unbearably bad. And if so you'll throw one too?'

'Right at Ka'in's mask.'

After a few moments, shrouded figures began walking on stage. They all wore ominous beak masks as well, and each had a different High Noble Crest embroidered on their robe. They were silent and held long metal rods in their hands. The rods were rounded at the ends, not sharp. They were for bashing instead of stabbing, and I wished I could have somehow snuck the Jadan children some Grassland Dream. They should have been numb for this.

Once the stage was fully lined, Ka'in took off his mask, strutting over to the Vicaress. His mutilated face became visible in her flame.

Gasps filtered through the Noble ranks.

Ka'in took the purple cone, his voice instantly loud enough to for Shilah and I to hear clearly.

'Beautiful Nobles!' he shouted. The burned skin of his face was glossed over with salve, making his skin appear to ooze as he spoke. 'Honoured sons and daughters! My fellow chosen! Welcome to the event of the centuries! A little of this, a lot of that, and even more of that. Praise be the Khat!'

The crowd echoed, 'Praise be the Khat,' although it came out quiet and unsure, clearly still reeling from his disfiguration.

'The Second Fall!' Ka'in shouted, a wet rattle in his throat clogging up the words. 'When the evil in the World Cried comes crumbling down. Did you even think you'd live to see such wonder? What a beautiful even-ing.' He rested the mask on the top of his head, the beak casting a shadow over his grotesque nose. 'This is indeed my face. Can we all see?'

Ka'in walked to the front of the stage. He gestured impatiently for the Vicaress to accompany him, and she stumbled forward, one stiff foot at a time. Firelight from her blade added to the horror of his face.

Ka'in tossed the mask aside and then slapped the glass cone, eliciting a high shriek to get everyone's attention. 'Can we see!'

The crowd murmured.

Ka'in's face turned murderous and pinched with rage. All the burned skin contracted, like his mouth had become a sinkhole. His eyes went darker than when he'd been wearing the mask.

'CAN WE SEE?'

The crowd finally assented with a loud bark.

Ka'in laughed, long and high. It was a cackle more than anything else. The cone distorted the sound to an eerie texture that made me press my palm harder against the hot stone.

'The Khatdom has gathered,' Ka'in continued. 'Lovely skin from Paphos and Belisk and the Glasslands. Mirrlah. Marlea. All those sky cities. The Hotland Delta, and even some folks from the Shocklands! Ba-zow! And a very special welcome to the Khatmonks from the southern Cry Temple there in the back. Bow low, old holies!'

The Khatmonks didn't flinch. Dressed in beige robes, their faces were hooded, blank in the dim light of torches. They kept rigid, hands stuck in a prayer position.

Ka'in shrugged and made a dismissive gesture. 'Anyway. What a special night! I am Ka'in of House Erridian and this is, welcome to, behold the Second Fall. The despicable Jadans have once again spat on our mercy. They saw our mercy and they said no, we don't wan't *that* mercy! Take our ungrateful spit! They said we don't believe in your Crier. We don't believe in your Khat! We're going to take the Cold for ourselves and burn your face, Ka'in! CAN WE SEE?'

The crowd bristled, waving necklaces at the city.

'They did this to me?' Ka'in gasped, pointing to his face. 'Sunspawn. The purveyors of all that is evil and greedy. So here we gather once again, ready to show them why exactly their kind is unworthy. The Khat is talking with the Crier right now! Seriously! Right this second! Listen. He is asking our Creator to once again show these Jadans why they are unworthy. Can we hear?'

A hush fell over the land.

Ka'in's face went soft and he began swaying from foot to foot. 'My brothers and sisters and lovers and future lovers. How lucky is our generation, to feel the glow of the Crier's love? New Ziah will burn and we shall bask in the cleansing light. Just watch. New Ziah will burn. And then the nasty, evil, plague of Jadans will Fall.'

Ka'in turned around and signalled the other Nobles on stage. They removed their masks, and Shilah and I both gasped, recognizing one of them instantly.

The crest on his robe should have given it away sooner.

Lord Tavor beamed, holding two rounded rods just like the rest of the High Nobles. He lorded over the crowd even from the back of the stage, sneering and standing tall. The similarities between father and son were uncanny. Cam had the same eye-wrinkles. The same golden hair. The same strong chin and fair skin.

'Not a word of this to Cam,' Shilah said. 'He doesn't need to know.'

'Agreed.'

Ka'in held his hands up for quiet. 'The Khat has agreed to let me start this very special occasion with a something also special!' Ka'in shouted. 'Would you like that? A demonstration of what exquisiteness our Noble people can coax out of a dark world?'

This was not going to be pleasant.

The only thing I could hope for was that it was over quickly.

Ka'in reached into his pocket and unfolded a different mask. This one had a shock of golden hair fastened to the back. The streaks of paint at the cheeks were colourful and happy, with expressive eyebrows painted over bright eyes. Somehow it was even more unsettling than the mask with the beak.

The Vicaress signalled over to the tent, and the taskmasters began ushering the Jadan children through the flap. They couldn't have been more than five or six years old, all of them dressed in crisp slave uniforms. Chattering and smiling, they were unaware that their lives were about to end, which made my heart shatter.

They rushed up the stairs of the stage without any sort of prodding, and lined up in rows behind the Vicaress. The girls had their hair done up and their faces scrubbed clean, Rose of Gilead petals decorating their hair.

They looked so happy.

'Are we ready?' Ka'in shouted into the cone, through mask lips painted vivid red. 'Can we hear?'

'You okay?' I whispered.

Shilah said nothing, her own mask returning.

I took a flash explosive of my own out of the bag, feeling its weight in my palm.

Only if it's unbearable, I reminded myself. You can't give the Nobles reason to storm the city.

I never thought myself capable of sitting idly and watching Jadan children get slaughtered. Watching Matty die had provided more than enough of that for a lifetime. Yet here I was. I had to let some Jadan children die in order to save the Jadan children in our Flock.

This world was much more complicated than expected.

Lord Tavor's eyes gleamed with a sick hunger.

The Vicaress staggered down the rows, her dagger high and flickering. She bent over and whispered a few things to the different children, who reached out and touched her silk sleeve.

'The prayer,' Shilah whispered. 'I think you should say it.'

I nodded, willing it up from my chest. '*Shemma hares lahyim criyah Meshua ris yim slochim.*'

Shilah's hand found mine once more, and we waited for the nightmare to begin.

'Are we ready?' Ka'in shouted to the teeming masses.

A booming cheer resounded.

'Here we have a new generation of Jadan children,' Ka'in shouted, gesturing to the group. 'Good Jadan children that know their place. Good Jadan children that are going to give us a good gift.'

I clenched my jaw so tight my teeth felt like they were going to shatter.

Ka'in gestured to the other High Nobles who stepped up behind the rows of children and lifted their metal rods high.

Then the children began to sing.

Here are we
Here are we
At the Fall
At the Fall
He can see
He can see
At the Fall
At the Fall
Eyes are Closed
Eyes are Closed
At the Fall
At the Fall
And He chose
And He chose
Let them Fall
Let them Fall

The High Nobles hit the metal rods together with resonant tings, all in rhythm. The sound was somehow lovely and soothing. Everything appeared rehearsed, and my jaw dropped.

What was this?

The children swayed in a coordinated dance as they chanted. The Vicaress jerked her blade through the air, matching the sway of the notes. Her thin lips were pulled wide in a smile that appeared oddly genuine.

> They will learn
> They will learn
> At the Fall
> At the Fall
> It's their turn
> It's their turn
> At the Fall
> At the Fall
> They will yearn
> They will yearn
> At the Fall
> At the Fall
> Let them burn
> Let them burn
> Let them Fall
> Let them Fall

The children ended their song with bows and fancy twirls. The High Nobles on stage clanged their rods with hearty approbation. They cheered and yelled, and the children broke ranks, each going over and kneeling before a respective High Noble. I thought this might be where the killing would happen, but the Nobles began pulling candied figs and sweet breads from their pockets. The kids reached up and received treats and Wisps, and they giggled and stuffed gem candy into their cheeks. They laughed and bowed and then rushed off the stage, shooting towards the black tent.

Most of the Nobles in the crowd seemed just as confused as Shilah and I.

'What in the Sun-damn blazes was that?' Shilah asked.

'I don't know, I thought . . . I thought.'

'Me too.'

Once the Jadan children were all safely back inside the tent, Ka'in threw off the colourful mask, revealing the marred skin and singed scalp of his true self.

'A tingly song! Makes you feel all tingly!' Ka'in said, clacking his teeth. 'Written just for you beautiful Nobles. You see, this just goes to show that we truly are deserved of our title. Even when the Jadans inside of New Ziah spit at the Crier and kneel before the Sun, and curse our mercy, we are shined and refined. They are ungrateful. Unworthy. Beneath us!'

'Damn right they are!' someone shouted.

'But the *good* Jadan children will breed a cleaner slave race,' Ka'in continued. 'They will know their place!' He picked up two of the rods, clanged them a few times for no apparent reason, and then went back to his cone.

'We reward those who are loyal to the Khatdom!' Ka'in shouted, the clatter in his throat more apparent than ever. 'Those Jadan children are the future gatherers of the Khat's Cold. They're the future weavers and builders and cooks and Domestics.' Ka'in gave a happy shiver. 'Such fun. They will know their place!'

The crowd grumbled a bit, but a good portion nodded their agreement.

'Praise be the Khat!' A few of them shouted. 'Praise be his mercy!'

'And the good children will tell their good children will

tell their tiny good children all about what happened here at the Second Fall!' Ka'in exclaimed. 'They will share stories about how loyalty is rewarded. About how the faithless are destroyed!'

Ka'in grabbed his bird mask and dusted it off before returning to the spotlight.

'Speaking of the faithless,' Ka'in said. 'There are those in New Ziah who clamour against the walls and beg for a way out every hour, every day. You have heard them. Wah, wah! We're sorry! We have sinned but we don't deserve punishment!'

The High Nobles on stage retrieved the beaked masks at their feet, strapping them back over their faces. They picked up the musical rods and crossed them over their chests. This also looked rehearsed.

'Over the next few weeks,' Ka'in said, his voice getting grave and serious, 'the Crier will allow his brother Sun into the very land itself, and you will see with your own eyes the city of New Ziah burning. No one will be allowed in or out. The land will become so unbearable that all those dirty, sinful Jadans will have no choice but to jump off the southern cliff and die. Our people soar like the birds of old, and they plummet like stones.' Ka'in bobbed his head. 'Okay, I lied. We did let *some* of those whining Jadans out. But for a purpose. What say we get the festivities started a little early?'

Ka'in held up an open hand and signalled to some unseen faction.

Then the sound of rattling chains.

A long group of Jadans was led towards the stage, bound at the ankles and wrists. I recognized a lot of faces; Beggars who chose not to join the Flock. They had boilweed shoved in their mouths so they couldn't make any sound.

Ka'in strapped his mask over his face and pretended to

kiss the Vicaress's face with a few pecks. Then he took the fiery blade from her hand.

I couldn't watch.

A large hand grabbed my ankle.

I stifled my shout, my heart leaping into my throat as I turned.

'Apologies,' Dunes said, keeping low and flat on his stomach. 'But you two shouldn't be here. I can't protect you if I don't know where you are.'

'Sorry,' I whispered, swallowing hard. 'We had to watch.'

'Sorry, Dunes,' Shilah said. 'It was my decision to come.'

'Neither of you have to explain, it's just that I wish I could have told you sooner. We found one.'

My body gave a worse start than when he'd grabbed my leg. 'You did?'

Dunes nodded, his chin bobbing against the hot tiles.

'It's real?' I asked.

'Yes,' Dunes said. 'And it's as terrible as we feared.'

Shilah and I exchanged a glance.

'Where?' I asked. 'Where did you find one?'

Dunes shuffled backwards and gestured for us to follow. 'They put it in the ground.'

Chapter Nine

'So this is the answer.' Cam leaned in and indulged in a long sniff. His eyes rolled back. His bottom lip trembled. 'The answer to all the mysteries of the Great Drought and the Crier and everything. And to think, I've never seen a picture of this stuff, or a mention, or anything at all in any of the books I've ever read.'

'Does that surprise you?' Samsah asked, leaning his large body against the cave wall. The dim light from the Sinai made his square face seem solemn and serious, everything about him reeking of caution.

'No. No surprise.' Cam shook his head, wrinkling his nose and sniffing again. 'It makes everything seem more real.'

'Issit real?' Ellcia asked.

'Issit, Micah?' Ellia whispered, glancing from behind her sister's shoulder.

'Yes,' I said, muffled by the strip of boilweed over my mouth. I waved my hand over the top of the table and felt the surging heat. 'Very real.'

I'd called the meeting in my old tinkershop, back in the cave, only inviting the most trusted members of the Flock. I didn't want to chance bringing the weapon of the enemy into the Sanctuary. There were too many innocent Jadans there.

A few leftover tinkering remnants remained in the cave, including stacks of clean boilweed. Anyone not wearing breathing protection had to stay behind a line I'd painted around the table, at the spot where the trace of heat ended. I'd demanded five minutes alone with the stuff to make sure it wasn't poisonous, breathing it in with the utmost hesitation. When I was still standing after the allotted time, I'd let the others into the cave.

I still felt nauseous and sweaty, but that was probably more from the reputation than the thing itself. Dunes had carried it from the bottom plateau back through the tunnels of the Coldmarch. He seemed relatively unharmed, which gave me hope that we weren't all in danger of keeling over dead any moment.

Shilah had tears in the corners of her eyes. I hadn't seen her so emotional since the discovery of the Coldmaker; when she'd taken me in her arms and kissed me. But this time she didn't weep with celebration. This was much more sombre. This was from the pain of being right all along.

They put it in the ground.

Desert.

It was real, and now we had a piece of our own.

'Here is the reason our people were made slaves,' Shilah said, stabbing a finger towards the table, but careful not to cross the line. 'This is how the Sun-damn Khat stole the world. Now we have actual, absolute proof. Dunes, you're a hero.'

Dunes didn't break rank. He remained completely still. The only sign of pride was a darkening of his cheeks.

I checked the tension on the boilweed strips to make sure the Desert was still strapped down. The ropes fastened on top kept cooking down into wilted mush, and I'd already had to change the boilweed out three times. My audience was too precious. And there was no telling how caustic or explosive an impact might be if the Desert hit the stone floor without padding. I'd ringed the table with the thickest boilweed I had just in case the thing escaped, but I wasn't sure if it would be enough. We were all blind in a sense; our eyes closed to what this thing could do.

It was roughly the same size as the Frost, the opposite in every other respect. It was hot to the touch, and its sheen was a sickening orange that oozed and squirmed. It reeked of death, and vibrated with a tiny, sickening sound that I could feel in my ears, like a shriek deep beneath the land. The noise could have been my imagination, but I didn't think so.

Like the Frost, the Desert also had a strange pattern at its core, but this one seemed to steal light instead of giving it off. Three parallel lines scarred the centre of the orb. The spaces between the lines appeared to be sinking, almost like they might swallow our fingers whole if we tried to touch its surface.

Split sat in a chair, tugging at his wan cheeks. His mumbles were getting more gruesome the longer he stared at the bubbling orange surface, the colour only slightly quelled by the boilweed wraps. 'Boil the skin off my arms. This is the curse.'

Het remained in line with the Five, but as opposed to Dunes, Het wasn't able to keep still, his fingers cycling through every ward he knew.

The Five stood at attention in the corner, while the rest of us were circled up around the table, keeping somewhat of a safe distance. Standing too close meant getting struck with a terrible heat and an equally terrible smell.

I couldn't believe I had a piece of Desert in my possession. We were likely the first Jadans in the history of the Khatdom to bear witness to the sickening material.

I stepped further ftom the table, taking off the mask and clearing my throat. 'Thoughts?'

'This proves once again that you're Meshua,' Leah said, her hands grabbing fistfuls of her shirt at her side. It was a nervous habit, but I almost asked her to stop. The motion unintentionally – I hoped – tugged down the cloth at her neckline, and I couldn't deal with any more heat.

'The Crier obviously wanted you to have the weapon of the enemy,' Leah said. 'This way you could study it. And then destroy it with your bare hands.'

Shilah rolled her eyes.

'Shilah,' I said. 'Thoughts?'

'I have many thoughts,' she said, her voice heating up. 'First thought. We show the Desert to every Jadan in the city. We march them in here and show them the lie that killed our people. Then we strap it to the end of a pike and wave it across the walls to show the Khat and Ka'in and the Vicaress that they don't scare us and that—'

I held up my hand to stop her.

'Yes?' she asked, visibly boiling.

'We can't do that. Think about it.'

'I have,' Shilah said, her knuckles tight around the handle of her Stinger.

'If this is truly what we think it is—'

'Sun-damned Desert,' Split chimed in, swallowing hard. 'What else could this foul shit be?'

'Yes, Desert,' I said. 'We have to consider all of our options and, more importantly, all of the consequences.'

Ellia slipped to her knees, turning away from the table and placing her forehead against the ground. Ellcia grabbed her sister by the shoulder and hurled her back to her feet. 'Get up, priss,' she whispered. 'Time fur praying latah.'

'I wassun't praying,' she whispered. 'My head was hot. I wanted to cool it off.'

'Dunes found the Desert buried in the ground on the second plateau,' I said. 'The soil and sand was freshly upturned, which is exactly what Shilah said we should look for. So good thinking on that, Shilah. It means the Khat snuck someone inside the city walls to plant it. There's heat coming off it, and probably other poisons, so I'm guessing maybe it makes the land sick and the ground dies?'

'Micah, this is everything we've been waiting for,' Shilah said. 'This is how we get our people to fight back. We expose the truth of the Drought.' She turned to Ellia and Ellcia. 'Tell me, girls. If you were seeing this for the first time, wouldn't you feel inspired to fight?'

The sisters nodded in unison.

'Maybe that plan would work,' I said. 'But we could also take a book out of the Khat's page. He's much better at manipulation than we are.'

Shilah crossed her arms, the Stinger blade catching some of the Sinai light. 'We don't want to manipulate our own people, Micah.'

'Not manipulate in a bad way. But . . . like how Cam did with the Jadan kids and the promises. That was smart manipulation,' I said, giving Cam a wink and a nod. 'And it was for good.'

'So what are you suggesting?' Samsah asked.

'We make it a story that works for us,' I said. 'If we go and show the Desert, then the Khat could easily say that the Desert rained upon us from the sky, and it was proof that the Crier wants us gone. There's no proof to trace the Desert back to the Khat.'

'Dammit,' Shilah said. 'You're right.'

Leah came to my side, bunching the cloth at her waist even tighter in her fist.

I cleared my throat. 'So what we need to do is keep things very secret. Because if we keep the Desert out of the ground, then the land won't heat up, right?'

'We hope,' Split croaked.

'And if the land doesn't heat up, that means the Khat will send more Desert inside,' Shilah said quickly. 'And put more of it in the ground.'

I nodded. 'And if we keep finding them, and keeping them out of the ground, then there's no second Fall and the Khat loses. And *that's* how we control the story.'

'So we have to find any Desert he sends in,' Shilah said. 'We have to have different teams on the lookout all the time.'

'You all,' I said to the Five. 'I want to know what you think.'

'We are released?' Kasroot asked nervously.

'Released,' I said with a sigh. 'Although I'm in no way your master, and you can do what you like.'

Dunes came to me and knelt so hard he must have bruised a knee. 'Put me in charge of this, Meshua. I won't fail you. I won't sleep until every piece of Desert is found. I'll make sure every plateau is covered. You can trust me.'

I nodded. 'I already trust you. Completely.'

Dunes took a deep, satisfied breath. He turned to Shilah next. 'Put me in charge of this, Meshua. I won't fail you. I won't sleep until—'

Shilah cut him off with a gesture, a wry smile on her lips. 'Done. Just keep me informed on what you're doing. I trust you completely, too.'

Jia wrapped Shilah and I in a hug with one scoop of his large arms, shaking us profusely. 'You brilliant, wonderful, beautiful souls. I can't believe I'm alive to see this moment. Desert. This will change everything!'

Jia released us, his words not helping. I knew his feelings came out of a place of love and respect, but I didn't need the extra pressure. The presence of the Desert alone was making me uneasy enough.

Jia pulled out two vials of honey from one of the folds in his robe. 'I was saving these for a moment like this.'

Shilah and I accepted the gift, knowing Jia wouldn't take no for an answer.

Cleave said nothing. His eyes said everything.

Eventually everyone settled at the rim of the line, staring in at the Desert. The boilweed strips were already looking feeble and I would have to find a more suitable substance to keep the stuff secure in the future. Especially if we were planning on finding more.

Cam sniffed again, pressing his nose to the line and giving an uneasy smile. 'Is it just me, or is anyone else addicted to the smell?'

Shilah raised an eyebrow. 'It smells like baked dung.'

'I'll have to bake more dung,' Cam said with a laugh and then stopped short mid-chuckle. 'Wait, are you being serious? It smells like . . . gem candy and lilacs.'

Shilah paused. 'Cam, it smells awful.'

'Very bad,' Ellcia blurted.

'Terrible,' Dunes agreed.

'Like a taskmaster foot after stomping around in a bucket of fermented fungus,' Kasroot said with a shudder. 'I'm going to have to drink soap to get it out of the back of my throat.'

I nodded. 'I'd say that's about right.'

Cam put a finger to his nostril, confused.

Split sighed. 'Don't worry, Camlish. I smell it too.'

'You do?' Shilah asked. 'Smell what?'

Split sank back into his chair. 'Different than how Cam described.' He cleared his throat, looking a bit embarrassed. 'But it smells wonderful; enticing to say the least.'

Silence filled the room as everyone made the connection.

'Everyone clear out and get some air,' I said. 'In case the Desert has fumes and can make you sick. Get clean air and drink plenty of Cold water. We've been exposed more than enough.'

Shilah squeezed between Leah and I, threading her arm

through mine. Leah looked ready to bite her in the throat, but stepped aside.

'We'll meet you at the Sanctuary,' Shilah announced. 'Everyone is dismissed.'

The tinkershop began to empty, with Split and Cam slinking off to the side, whispering to each other. Leah went to say something to me, but then gave a demure nod and followed the others out.

'Dunes,' I called out. 'Can you bring me ink and some glass vials? And plenty of Cold. And,' I tapped my bottom lip, 'the Coldmaker.'

Dunes gave an excited nod and then rushed into the tunnel.

'You too,' I said to Shilah, patting her arm. 'Go get some air.'

'No,' Shilah said. 'I'm here for you, and you're not going to push me away. Micah, it's Desert! It proves everything we needed to know. It's another miracle.'

I smiled and then pulled her into a hug, her body warm against mine. I breathed her in.

'I'm not pushing you away,' I said. 'I just need some time. You go take command and help Dunes make the teams that will search for the Desert. You're better at that. I'll do what I'm good at.'

Shilah leaned back and putting her hands on my cheeks, pressing gently. 'Meshua is two, remember?'

I nodded and took off my gloves, threading my hands in her hair. She gave me a curious look, but didn't look offended. I found the braid in the back and worked out the knife, careful not to slice away any of her locks.

'I'll wash it,' I said, gesturing to the sacred pool. 'But I need a good blade to work with.'

'What are you planning on doing?' Shilah said.

I turned to the Desert, looking into its glowing centre. It slithered over with heat, already nearly burning through the boilweed strips. The small patch of Adaam Grass in the back of the cavern looked dimmer, like it was sickly. A part of me wanted to flee and have the Five seal the tunnels behind us with heavy stones.

But there was no turning away.

The Khat had fired the first arrow.

Now it was time to shoot one back.

Chapter Ten

Three days later I had started to descend into madness.

'Okay,' I mumbled into the boilweed mask. 'Time for you to scream for mercy.'

I held the burning candle over the first bucket, dripping wax all over the surface of the Desert inside. I tried to pour on the shape of the Opened Eye, although the splatter was difficult to control.

I waited, propped up on my toes.

No response.

I shrugged, used to these letdowns. The Desert in the first bucket, Blue Eyes, was just as tough and merciless as the Vicaress I'd named it after.

The Five had unearthed four pieces of Desert at this point, and each one had proven to be as resilient as the last. Three out of four pieces of Desert taunted me from their own individual buckets. The last one remained in one of my ongoing tub experiments. So far the tub results made me want to pull my hair out, making it impossible to sleep more than an hour at a time.

'How about a little of this then,' I said into the bucket, picking up the vial of Sobek poison. 'Have a taste.'

I poured the lizard venom on Blue Eyes, making sure to coat as much as I could. I waited for a hiss or a change in colour, or a dissolution into the belly of the object, but the venom just careened down the sides and pooled at the bottom, bubbling from the heat.

I picked up a piece of metal from the fire, one that I'd forged with an Opened Eye. I heated the tip and tried to brand the top of the second piece of Desert, the one called Thoth.

I knew from various attempts that the heated metal wouldn't affect the Desert, as the pieces had all proven immune to both sharp objects and temperature. Fire did nothing. Cold did nothing. But stabbing at the stuff with a fiery brand was satisfying, and since I was the only one around, I indulged myself.

I'd recently sprinkled my boilweed mask with powdered Draft, and my breath tingled. I made sure to coat the inner lining of the mask as often as possible.

Looking around the Coldmarch tinkershop, I appraised all the scribbles and carvings from my past kin. They were easy to find scratched into the walls between any pillars of pink salt. The Jadans here before me had been courageous enough to seek out Langria, desperate to believe in something bigger than themselves.

Unyielding, irrational hope.

Something I desperately needed.

I ran my fingers across the word Meshua, carved nicely into the stone. It looked like my handwriting. It *was* my handwriting. I must have carved it at some point, but was too tired to remember. My eyes burned from the lack of sleep.

I couldn't afford to waste time. I needed to figure out how it worked. For all I knew, the Khat had an unlimited supply of Desert. It was also possible that putting the Desert in the ground was only the beginning. Planting it could have even been a decoy for other, unstoppable attacks that were on their way.

I grabbed my Claw Staff from the table and snapped open the teeth. Reaching into the next bucket, I snapped the grip around the third piece of Desert, which I'd dubbed 'Ka'in'. Raising the Desert was like trying to lift a small child, but I muscled it over to the Charged clay urn and dipped it inside. The room sizzled, and I caught some of the steam in a few upside-down beakers.

Even with the boilweed mask, I made sure not to breath as I collected the steam. My gloves were triple-thick, but I could still feel the intense heat.

After the beakers – made of Glassland White – were thoroughly coated, I dropped Ka'in back into its bucket and immediately corked the glass. Then I spun the beakers and placed the bottoms in a Cold bath. The steam cooled, pooling in the bottom of the beakers, and I brought the containers to my work table.

Then I picked out a few random vials from the tinkering cabinet I'd restocked. I hoped that one of them might be the key to negating the Desert's effect. So far I was getting absolutely nothing in the way of a cure. I'd tried pouring blood and tears on the Desert, along with my own sweat. None got any reaction. Over the last few days I'd tinkered with pretty much every substance I could think of. Love balms, groan salve, powered scarab, Dybbuk grease, orangefruit juice, pulped lizard eyes, and even some pulverized fossils from extinct creatures.

Unlike my accidental success with the Frost, nothing spurred any meaningful reaction. No happy accidents.

I looked to the corner of the room, appraising my only ongoing tub experiments. It was the only tinkering so far that gave me any answers, all of which centring around how doomed the world truly was.

Samsah and Cam had helped me build two custom metal tubs lined with lead, and Shilah had helped me with the plants. Inside the first tub, I had put layers of earth from the Sanctuary garden, exactly as the land might have naturally been found before the Great Drought. Dark soil – which had to constantly be kept alive with Cold water – sat and the bottom, and rocks were layered on top of that. Last was a slew of different plants placed on top. I wanted to put in a few beetles and Skinkmanders in for the sake of being realistic, but even with ways for the creatures to crawl out, Shilah was adamant about me not tinkering with anything that could feel pain.

Once everything had been ready, I'd cored out a hole in the centre and buried a piece of Desert – this one named the Khat – in the bottom.

The carnage had come all too quickly.

The land in the tub heated up and changed colours, going from light beige to a sickening orange which was similar to the Desert's own colour. The plants on top smouldered, close to catching flame, and then wilted black.

After a few days left on its own, everything in the tub was ashen and sandy and decimated. I'd placed a gloved hand on the soil periodically, always wincing from the evil heat. It was a terrible thing to witness the fate our ancient world had suffered, setting my stomach to constant knots and my eyes to tears.

Yesterday I'd dug up the Khat from the tub to examine the thing, finding the piece had lost none of its lustre or potency. I'd put it back in its bucket and then grated Wisps and Drafts into the tub, practically drowning the land with Cold water. Nothing brought the land back to the original vibrant green, with the plants remaining ashen and stiff. The Desert had been removed, but everything was determined to remain dead.

The second tub I'd filled with brown and sandy earth that Dunes had dug up from the first plateau. Since the land of this city had already been killed eight hundred years ago, I wanted to see what further damage a new piece of Desert might inflict. I'd buried the Khat in the bottom of that tub, desperately hoping that already dead land might be immune to heating up.

I was sorely mistaken.

If anything, the second tub got even hotter than the first. The temperature had become blistering, as if the Sun itself was down in the tinkershop with me.

The tubs told me that the Desert that the First Khat had planted around the world – pieces we had no way of finding – might still be active, continuing to infect the land. And that there might not be a cure.

I'd left the Desert in the bottom of the second tub to remind me what I was up against. If the Khat succeeded at planting Desert that we couldn't find, then we would all suffer a horrible death, forced to jump off the cliff. The Nobles below would give ecstatic cheers below. We could of course find a way to kill ourselves besides jumping off the cliffs, but suicides in any way would still be a victory for the Khat. There was no room for mistakes.

I picked out a vial filled with Essence of Rah, the contents vibrant yellow. I'd tried to get a reaction with the Rah yesterday and failed, but I wanted to see what might happen if I first mixed the powder with the honey that Jia had given me. Sweet and bright felt like a lucky combination.

Suddenly my tinkered chimes rang out from walls of the tinkershop.

I hadn't wanted to put anyone else in danger while I was experimenting, so I'd tinkered a series of bells in the main tunnel for visitors to announce themselves. It was the same kind of system I'm rigged up in my first barracks, but this time instead of being used to wake Jadans up, it was used to keep us alive.

I yanked the handle on my end of the rope three times.

After a moment, the Five stormed into the tinkershop. Dunes led the charge. The bucket in his arms caused straining in his massive shoulder. They lined up in front of me, all dropping into the bow they insisted on doing.

'Meshua,' they said one by one; all accept Cleave, who had yet to speak.

'Another piece of Desert,' I sighed. 'I guess that makes five times you've now saved the city. Excellent work, my friends. As always.'

They maintained in rigid stances, although pride lifted their chests.

'Released,' I said with another sigh.

Kasroot stumbled backwards from the Desert as far as he could, taking out some vials of perfume and dabbing the liquid all over his arms. A look of pure disgust thinned out his face.

'I'm impossibly glad that you didn't explode yourself today,' Jia said, his voice annoyingly bubbly.

'Thanks, Jia. Me too.'

Dunes craned his face backwards so he could look at the giant sheet above us, emotion spilling into his face. 'The Crier has been watching over you, Meshua.'

I tilted my head up as well, staring. Leah had done a fantastic job with the construction. The fabric was dozens of sleeping blankets wide, held up on pikes and strung across a large swath of the tinkershop. She'd worked on it day and night. The stitching was so tight it rivalled the skill of my father. She had also decorated the bottom in a large Open Eye, done up with colourful yarn. The yarn – dyed red with alder – reminded me of her thick hair, which might have been deliberate.

'And how goes the inventing?' Dunes asked, his eyes eager.

In the hope that an answer might come if I wasn't focused on the problem at hand, I'd been creating a storm of useless trinkets. Crank fans which spun on their own. Sinais which shifted lenses and changed colours. A toy caravan cart with a fin at the bottom, winding through a circular groove I'd carved into the cave floor.

All a bunch of nonsense, serving no other purpose than to stave of the despair.

I shook my head, peering into the new bucket Dunes had brought. This piece of Desert was the same size as the others, with the same sickening glow.

This one would be called 'Lord Tavor'.

'Nothing today, Dunes,' I said. 'I'm stumped. I can't seem to break it.'

'What if,' Jia said, already chewing on something, 'we put the Desert in the ground outside of the walls?'

My whole body went stiff. Everything in my mind shifted at once.

'What did you say?' I asked quietly.

Jia shrugged, picking a piece of food out of his back teeth. 'You were saying before that if we show everyone we have the Desert inside, they might think we brought it upon ourselves. But what if we put the Desert in the ground outside the walls?'

I paused, dropping the pestle in my hand. Then I rushed over to Jia, wrapping my arms around him as best I could. He smelled like dirt, sunlight and gem candy.

'Jia,' I said. 'Yes. I love it.'

Jia hugged me back, laughing deeply and lifting me off my feet. 'I save all the best ideas and food for you, Meshua!'

He let me go and I stepped backwards. I was having trouble closing my jaw. He was on to something. Perhaps I'd been making things too complicated for myself with all of this tinkering. My heart pounded, the floodgates open.

Dunes remained kneeling, his voice distant. 'That is quite the idea.'

I started pacing the tinkershop.

'And if we can heat up the land outside,' I said, 'Then the armies will have to disperse. Yes. Okay. I like it. We can space all five pieces out outside the walls to make sure the whole place is covered. We have to tell Shilah immediately, she's going to be so excited. Jia, start tonight. I'm putting you in charge of figuring out how to sneak past the armies undetected and take—'

'Apologies for interrupting,' Dunes said, slowly rising to his feet, his chin tucked against his large chest. 'But won't using the Desert in that way make us as bad as the Khat? We don't even know the extent of how it will affect the land inside the walls.'

I gritted my teeth and whipped around at Dunes. 'Just because it wasn't your idea, don't be so quick to dismiss it. I never took you for the jealous type.'

Dunes folded into himself, looking ashamed.

My heart clenched. I hadn't meant to snap at him like that. Stress was rotting away at my insides. I had to make sure to keep an eye on the decay.

'I'm so sorry, Dunes,' I said. 'I haven't been sleeping much. You're right. I shouldn't be so quick to do something drastic. Can you bring me Shilah and Cam so we can discuss all of this?'

'Of course.' Dunes kept his head down, his tone formal. 'By your command.'

'I'm sorry,' I said again, going over and offering an apologetic touch. I had to stretch my arm quite a bit to reach the corded muscle of his shoulder. 'I'm lucky to have you around.'

'You never have to apologize to me,' Dunes said, not meeting my eyes. 'I shall get them at once.'

'What would you like the rest of us to do?' Het asked,

running his fingers over a warding string he removed from his pocket. There were at least four Open Eyes painted on the beads.

'What do you want to do?' I asked. 'You've earned anything.'

Kasroot shuddered, looking at the new Desert. 'I want to bathe,' he said. 'The curse is all over my skin. I can feel it.'

'I want to keep searching,' Het said. 'More Desert must be out there somewhere.'

Cleave gave a slow, agreeable nod.

'Released,' I said. 'You've have my appreciation.'

They bowed and began to dissipate, running almost soundlessly over the cool stone. I wanted to call after Dunes to apologize again, but he was already back in the tunnel, in front of the other Five, moving faster than I'd ever seen him go.

I picked up the new bucket and put it with the others. Then I sat back in my chair and stared at the line of orange glow, flames licking at the hollowness in my chest.

Jia's idea proved I'd been focusing too much on the defensive.

I kept thinking of our people as victims, which was what the Khat wanted. He made sure our people understood we were weak, binding our feet and telling us we could never stand. I kept thinking I needed to tinker with the Desert, when the pieces inherently held terrible amounts of power.

Power to deceive. Power to destroy.

And now their power was mine.

Cam rubbed at his elbow with a rip of boilweed, trying to get his arm clean. Normally his skin was as fair as a sandviper egg, but since he'd been off digging with the teams, he'd been consistently stained. His fingernails were chipped, with dark earth trapped underneath, and his long hair was held back with rope. No longer silky and golden, his shoulder-length locks had become encrusted with sweat and dirt, darkening all of his features.

He'd never looked more like my brother.

'You know what I think,' Cam said.

'Hmm?' I said, staring at the bucket.

'I think it's such an awesome idea that Jia deserves a song and a statue. Perhaps even a city named after him once all of this is over.' Cam gave me a wry smirk. 'Speaking of, the "Camlands" are still in consideration, right? I don't need anything big, either, just a city with a view.'

Shilah sighed, but her face was alight. 'Once we save the land we want to keep it alive, not bore it back to death.'

Cam waved the dirty scrap of boilweed over his head like a flag. 'The Camlands anthem will be the sounds of pure laughter.'

Shilah finally let out a chuckle, nudging Cam with her elbow, which was just as muddy as his skin. Their dirt matched, as if they'd been off digging together in the same spot.

The five pieces of Desert were all back in their buckets, lined up on a table. I'd laid glass slabs overtop them to keep them stifled.

Jia's idea had become intoxicating, and I was in a rare mood. Images of taskmasters wrapping boilweed over their feet while they rushed across the burning land filled me with a dark joy. Breaking the Khat's siege would be a blow to every one of his claims.

'By the way,' Cam said with a mocking smirk, 'Leah is still waiting outside the tunnels. She brought a meal and blanket with her.'

I swallowed hard. 'I told her this needs to be just us three today.'

'She looks prepared to wait it out,' Cam said.

Shilah put a hand on my shoulder. 'How right you were

to keep it private, Micah.' Shilah said. 'We need to focus and think this through, like you said. If we got the land to heat up outside the walls, couldn't the Khat simply claim that the Crier missed his mark?'

My stomach began to rumble. Not only was I hungry, but I desperately wanted not to have to question this plan. It was the only advantage we had, and I was tired of second guessing. Life had been much simpler when I only knew what I was told.

A part of me wanted to ignore any need for discussion and just go ahead with the attack. To begin the Noble Fall. To purge my mind of the agonizing cloud of indecision.

'Or,' Shilah said, bobbing her head back and forth with a sigh, 'he could say that the Sun got in the way. Or that we made a deal with the Sun. Or that having Jadans interspersed throughout their army drew the heat away from the city. And if he said that, well he could justify killing all the Jadans out there. Including—'

I slammed my hand on the table, the glass rattling on the buckets, the Desert shaking against the metal.

'DAMMIT!'

Shilah's face immediately softened with concern. 'It's okay, Spout. This isn't the end.'

'It's anything but okay,' I said. 'Because you're right. Anything we do or say, the Khat can twist. The Khats have been doing it for eight hundred years. They're smarter than us. And crueller than us. And they're Sun-damn going to win. Shilah, we figured out how to make Cold, and still they're going to win.'

A heavy silence fell between the three of us.

'They won't,' Shilah said. 'It's just that we can't use their tactics against them. We need our own.'

'And what would you have me do?' I snarled, curling my fists under the table. 'I don't have any Frosts. Or abbs. The

Coldmaker is dead. So is Leroi. And the Khat keeps planting the damn Desert in our city. And one of them will surely slip past us soon. What weapon do we have? We have nothing.'

'Spout,' Cam said, 'we'll find a—'

'No, Camlish,' I said, firing out of my seat and kicking it over. I turned my back to them both, my whole body seizing up. Every breath was poison. Hate pulsed through my veins. 'You grew up High Noble in a manor full of food and Cold and slaves. You got anything you wanted. I've watched my people die at the hands of Nobles in the most terrible ways since I was a little boy. I can't calm down, because now I've gotten us all killed. Every Jadan in this city will die unless I figure out another miracle. So just shut up. How could you possibly understand any of this?'

'Micah Ben-Abb!' Shilah hissed. 'Turn around.'

I wanted to hit him. I wanted to hit her.

Something terrible was burning me up from the inside.

'Micah!' she yelled.

I spun around, my arms trembling at my sides. I couldn't look either of them in the face. I could only stare up at Leah's sheet, at the giant Opened Eye that meant less as the days progressed. I needed a Fist. I was just about to wave two knuckles at the sheet when Shilah slammed her hand on the table, the sound even louder than mine.

'Apologize to Cam,' Shilah said. Her back was as rigid as a blade. 'Right now.'

I kept silent. Rage boiled my chest, and I wanted to flip over the table. To let the Desert win already. To end it all.

'I mean it,' Shilah said, this time her words infuriatingly calm. 'Now.'

I tried. I tried to calm down, to look them in the eyes; but it was like trying to look directly into the Sun. My insides squirmed and my throat clamped up, unable to find the words. My tongue went numb in protest.

'I'm sorry,' I forced out at last, exhausted.

I immediately began to feel better. But Cam looked like he'd just been put under the Vicaress's wool hat.

Shilah had every right to take my head and slam it against the wall.

'I'm sorry,' I said again.

It took Cam a moment to speak. He looked stunned, like the wind had been kicked out of his chest.

'I didn't get anything I wanted,' Cam said.

I picked up my chair and slumped back down, folding my arms on the table and laying my chin on my wrist. 'I know.'

'It wasn't easy believing the things I did,' Cam said, dabbing at the corner of his eye. 'I had to watch your people die too.'

Shilah went over and put an arm around Cam's shoulder.

'I know,' I said, slumping. I couldn't remember ever feeling so heavy.

Cam swallowed hard. 'I prayed every day that things would change. I had to watch my family act like monsters,' Cam said. 'They had the same blood as me, but felt nothing like I felt. I prayed that I could convince them to – none of my prayers ever meant a thing. Until I met a brilliant Jadan Inventor who I could actually believe in. Until I finally understood that the world could be made right.'

Shilah squeezed his shoulder.

'And whatever you say,' Cam said, 'I'll still believe in you with all of my heart, Micah. I always will.'

A tear dropped down his cheek.

The light inside the buckets changed slightly. I wouldn't have noticed, but the glass coverings intensified the effect.

'Cam,' I gasped, lifting my head off my arms. 'I don't—'

'You never have to apologize to me,' Cam said.

'Cam,' I said, pointing a trembling finger at his face. 'Your tears.'

Cam sniffed, brushing it away. 'I know. I was being weak.'

Another tear formed at the corner of his eye, and the orange light reflected in the glass got a shade lighter.

I hopped out of my chair again, rushing around the table. Shilah looked confused, ready to jump between Cam and I in case I was having a breakdown, but I went right to my empty vials in the cabinet. I grabbed one and hurried to Cam's side, before the effect dissipated.

'May I?' I asked gently, my heart thumping.

Cam looked perplexed. 'May you what?'

'Have them,' I said. 'Your tears.'

Cam gave a slow, confused nod.

I put the vial against his cheek and gathered the drop of moisture. It was only two or three, but I had to know. I went to slide the glass off the nearest Desert, when I stopped myself, barely able to steady my hand.

I grabbed three boilweed masks and passed them out as fast as I could. 'Put these on. Hurry.'

'Micah,' Shilah said. 'You don't think . . .'

'Mask,' I said, strapping mine over my face. They did the same.

Time slowed to a crawl as I slid the glass covering and let a single tear fall. The chamber itself held its breath as the bead descended.

I leaned over the bucket so I could see inside.

Nothing.

The Desert remained impervious.

'Damn,' I cursed into the mask. 'I thought that—'

The exploding heat was worse than anything I'd ever felt in my life. I whipped my head back so fast that my neck spasmed. The orange light of the Desert turned blinding yellow, fierce enough to melt the salt pillars.

The three us stumbled back from the table as the effect continued to grow. Heat shot up from the bucket, the light inside sickening.

Cam's face lit with ecstasy. His eyelids closed and began fluttering. His whole body shook, his expression ecstatic.

'Cam!' I shouted through the mask, but he'd been transported somewhere else entirely. It was as if he was trapped in a dream.

The Desert continued to react. The air above the table became opaque. I had a feeling we were about to be swallowed, burned to ash in the blink of an eye. The heat was nearly unbearable.

Cam's body continued to spasm.

'Cam!' Shilah shouted, her jaw set with pain as she tried to shake him awake. 'Camlish!'

I went to grab Cam as well when I noticed something startling.

Leah's boilweed sheet above us was moving. The whole thing was floating towards the cave ceiling. The Eye in the centre of the fabric billowed into itself, the lid shutting as it buckled.

The four heavy metal pikes it had been suspended across lifted as well, still attached to the sheet. It wasn't like the explosive force of flamepowders, but rather it lifted with the steady motion of a stone slab being pulled across wooden rollers. Powerful. Heavy. Moving as if imbued with a force of its own.

The boilweed sheet continued to rise, the sickening orange below making a light spectacle of the salt pillars. My stomach clenched; I was close to vomiting because of the smell. Eventually the sheet reached the ceiling, pressing into the stone roof so firmly it was like it had been sewn into the rocks. The pikes dangled beneath.

Cam collapsed in the direction of the table, and Shilah wrenched him backwards so hard that he tumbled into her arms. He let out a terrible gasp and then a series of frantic wheezes. His arms reached for the table, his fingers twisting in different directions, desperate.

Cam gasped. His eyes were far away, hazy with sensation. His mouth was open, and I thought I heard him pant the word 'more'.

Shilah slapped his cheek hard, wrenching him tighter against his body. He began to blink wildly, coming to.

I pressed my mask tighter over my lips and held my breath. The boilweed sheet above began to sizzle and wither, dropping charred flecks back down towards the fiery bucket beneath it. The Opened Eye made of yarn burned into nonexistence, the smouldering blackness from the heat beginning to spread to the edges of the sheet. It was being eaten up.

'Oh,' I said. I rushed around the table and wrapped my arms around Cam and Shilah as best I could, pushing frantically to get them out of the way. 'Move!' I shouted, managing to wrench them a few steps back. 'We have to—'

The pikes fell.

I shoved my friends backwards, every muscle in my legs and shoulders practically ripping out of place. One of the pikes landed right where Cam's leg had been, smashing against the ground with terrible force. The clang was deafening. One pike landed on my small vial cabinet next to the table, smashing the dozen glass containers to bits, powders and liquid flinging everywhere. I tried to remember if there was Pinion's acid in there. I pushed again, Shilah's legs kicking up as we collapsed, the three of us landing another step away. One pike landed harmlessly against the stone floor, but the last one landed sideways on the buckets, shattering the glass coverings. The buckets rattled but fortunately stayed in place.

But now that the Deserts were free, they began to react further to the air, their lights growing and heat blazing deeper into the room. The metal buckets kept the heat rising towards the ceiling, otherwise it would have washed over us and chewed up our skin.

'Come on!' I yelled, pulling Cam and Shilah towards the tunnels.

We weren't safe in the chamber or in the tunnel. There was no telling how long the reaction would last, if it was poisonous, and if it would get worse. A part of me worried that I'd accidentally begun the Second Fall.

Shilah nodded, her mask still tight on her face, and together we pulled Cam back onto his wobbly feet. His face still flushed with a dark pleasure. We wrenched him towards the tunnels, but he resisted, his body bucking and his arms grasping back towards the spilled Desert. His eyes were closed again, and blood had begun to drip from his nose. Tears spilled down his face, uncontrollably. He looked worse now that the other pieces had been released, drowning in emotions. He tried to push my arm away and nearly knocked my brronze fingers off, pain shooting up my arm. Shilah wrenched him harder, grabbing him by the midsection and hugging him tightly.

'More,' Cam gasped, bucking.

We needed to get him out of there. Together, Shilah and I pulled him into the tunnel, his whole body working against us. But the further away we got, the less he resisted. I looked back, expecting to see flames and fire spirits crawling along the stone in our wake, ready to devour, but the glow remained localized in the tinkershop.

Leah was waiting in the tunnel, pacing nervously next to her harp. She had a blanket spread out, with a Sinai and all sorts of foods spread across the top.

'Thank the Crier,' Leah said, coming over to us. She went straight for me, putting a hand on my cheek, ignoring Cam completely. 'Are you hurt, Meshua? I heard a noise but I know you asked me to wait out here. Did something—'

'Your water,' Shilah gasped, whipping off her mask and pointing to the blanket, a snarl in her voice. 'Give us your water.'

Leah's eyes narrowed, her hand pressing tighter against my skin.

'Please,' I said. 'We don't know what's happened to him.'

'Of course,' Leah said, letting go and grabbing the water-skin. She popped in all the Wisps she had in her pocket and shook the container violently.

Shilah went to the floor and set Cam on his back, angled up so his shoulder blades rested on her knees. She wiped away the blood under his nose with her bare fingers, depositing it on her pants. Cam mumbled a few things, breathing too heavy, as if he were unable to properly fill his lungs. Leah handed over the water and Shilah grabbed it without pause. She held the spout to Cam's lips and tilted, letting the cool water splash down his throat. Cam spit it up at first, but eventually began to drink, sucking desperately. Shilah splashed the water on his face after a slew of heavy gulps, washing away the blood and lingering heat.

I paced nervously, cursing my curiosity. If anything happened to Cam I'd never forgive myself.

'Come on,' Shilah urged, rubbing Cam's chest. 'You're okay. Come back to me. You're okay.'

Cam finally opened his eyes. He looked back and forth frantically, confusion and shame sharing an equal portion of his face.

Shilah choked out a sob of relief and kissed his forehead, letting her lips linger. Her relief resonated in my heart.

Cam wiggled some more, looking mortified.

Leah came over to me, resting a hand on my waist. 'Are you okay?'

'I'm fine,' I said.

'What happened?' Cam asked, trying to sit up.

Shilah kept him pressed against her knees, her palm flat on his chest, continuing to rub. 'Relax.'

'I've never felt anything like that,' Cam said, swallowing

hard and squirming some more. 'It's like I didn't have any control at all. Seriously. Everything that happened was out of my control.'

Tears continued to spill out of the corners of his eyes.

Cam pointed to his face. 'See, I'm not doing these tears.'

He seemed fine; like his normal self. I breathed relief.

And my mind began to put together the truth.

Shilah looked up at me. Something dangerous exchanged between us. This was a true partnership, because she didn't judge me for where my mind was heading. Instantly our eyes were knitting something, the needle of an idea passing back and forth.

'Shivers and shit pebbles,' Cam said, his arms slumping by his sides. 'I don't belong here. I'm dangerous—'

Shilah slapped him without mercy.

'Never say that again,' Shilah said.

Cam smiled, his cheek blossoming red. 'Shivers and shit pebbles? I thought it had a ring.'

Shilah rolled her eyes.

My eyes were somewhere else. The new Idea was already consuming me.

'Leah,' I said, pulling her aside. My heart thundered.

She lit up, looking at my hands on her arm. 'Yes. What do you want to do?'

'How are your hands?'

Leah raised an eyebrow. Her face was full of delight.

'For stitching,' I clarified, feeling my throat go stiff. 'Just stitching.'

Leah sighed. 'Good as can be.'

'Excellent,' I said. 'Because we have work to do.'

Chapter Eleven

The painting wall was up in a matter of hours, built under the cover of night. Hundreds of frames had been stacked on top of each other, held together with boilweed rope and stabilized with long poles at their backs. They made a giant circular curtain, the faces in the frames all facing inward.

The Builders had created the wall with a feverish energy at my request, quickly erecting the circle of frames as high as they could go. Ellcia and Ellia had given over all the portraits in the Sanctuary, which meant the Builders had enough materials with which to span the wall quite high. It was a sight to behold, but mostly from the inside. The Domestics had painted the back of the frames beige, also at my request.

I'd had it built near the Southern cliff, specifically because of a large, heavy boulder there. I had a feeling the rock was practically immovable, and Dunes and the Five had already proven my assumption correct. Even Cleave couldn't make the stone budge. The Builders put up the wall with the boulder in the centre, leaving plenty of space for tinkering material. They'd also made sure there wasn't so much as a crack between the frames, through which the rising Sun might peek.

Our Idea had been kept a complete secret.

I hoped that when the Sun rose, the Nobles would only see the beige colour of dead land.

I hoped the spirits of those depicted in the paintings had moved on from the black, but if any of them were still lingering, I wished for their songs to guide my hands. Jadan needed – indeed I needed – something bigger than myself.

Shilah and I both strapped on my boilweed gloves, ready to go through the flap and start tinkering inside the wall.

'The Khat still hasn't come out of his tent,' Shilah said.

'I'm sure he's getting nervous. Two weeks they've been sieging with no Fall.'

Shilah put an elbow on my shoulder, running her hand along the beige back of one of the frames. 'You did good.'

'I feel like I've done nothing compared to you,' I said. 'Look how organized everyone is. You're a damn good leader. The Flock is a damn good army.'

Shilah shrugged, but pride flushed her cheeks. 'It's a team effort, partner.'

'You think this is finally the answer we've been waiting for?' I asked, trying not to let my voice break.

'Why. Are you nervous?'

I thought about it. 'Maybe a little. But not about the Idea, or the tinkering.'

'Because you think Cam is hurting,' she said. 'And because you think that if you succeed, and that if Cam's Noble tears end up being secret to flight, that he'll be devastated to know his kind is deeply linked to the Desert. And you think it will drive a rift between you two.'

My heart squeezed. She could read me almost as well as my father had been able to. 'It's scary how right you can be.'

Shilah's fingers went to the back of my neck, tracing my numbers. 'Love fills in all rifts. And Cam loves you more than anyone else in the World Cried.'

'I don't know about anyone else,' I muttered.

She ignored my remark. 'You have to understand that it's himself that he needs to accept. We can call Cam family as much as we want, but until he looks at his reflection and sees past the colour of his hair and skin, he's vulnerable. The Khat has built his empire on assuring the world that Jadans are physically different than Nobles, and the effect of the Desert furthered the argument. It's just one more thing for Cam to feel guilty about, so we have to give him time,' Shilah said. 'He'll be back. Same thing happened after the inked Cold in Leroi's tinkershop, remember?'

'I remember.'

We paused, watching the night sky. I quickly found the stars that made up Great Gale and let myself enjoy the slight breeze across the plateau.

'You really have had some great ideas,' Shilah said.

'Thanks.'

'And this one is absolutely, brilliantly mad.'

I laughed. 'As I get older, I think that might be what it takes to be a real Inventor.'

Shilah nodded to the boilweed curtain built into the frames to let people in and out, reminding me of the one in my home barracks when I was younger. This seemed fitting somehow.

'The Nobles will never see it coming,' Shilah said.

She took two fingers and gently touched each of my eyelids.

It looked like a warding gesture Het would make, but this one felt very intimate. I pressed my hand over hers, remembering her touch.

'All the stuff is inside?' Shilah asked.

I nodded. 'Just about.'

A large portion of the Flock had gathered to be near our tinkering, collectively chanting 'Meshua'. Spirits were lifting in the city, and the Beggars had been dwindling in numbers, many of their members having returned to us. The Nobles had been besieging us for weeks, and still there had been no Second Fall. Dunes and the Five had found every piece of Desert planted so far, and the city was as cool as could be expected.

We had the Khat backed into a corner, and everyone could see his iron grip beginning to tremble.

Trying to calm my nerves, I kept thinking about Matty. I could almost see my little friend sitting cross-legged in the black all this time, watching over me from so far away. His small hands would be holding a melon that tasted like starlight, and he'd be laughing at his vision come to life. It had been his Idea all along.

Flight.

I took out the small vial of Noble tears that Split had eagerly offered after hearing our discovery. He hadn't taken the Desert effect to be a slight like Cam had, but rather he saw it as an opportunity for justice.

'So what's the Flock thinking?' I asked. 'About all of this.'

Shilah looked around. 'Well, word has been spreading about a Firepox plague spreading through the Noble armies out there. Which is great. And the Khat keeps claiming the Fall is going to happen any day, but the land hasn't changed at all. So I think the Flock knows there's something important happening here. Plus, there's more of us than ever.'

Samsah finished bringing the last of the hamsa wood behind the curtain, giving me a solemn nod before letting the flap close. Hamsa was light, springy and resistant to burning, which made it the perfect material.

'It's time,' Shilah said.

I beckoned for Leah, who was waiting with the other Domestics. She had the stitched-up boilweed lumped in her arms. I told her she could leave the new sheet inside the curtain, but she insisted on carrying it at all times. She couldn't have looked more pleased. Other Domestics at her back gave me flirtatious little waves as Leah sauntered over to where Shilah and I were standing, hips swaying wildly.

'I can't believe you're letting me be a part of this,' Leah said. 'I'm so honoured, Meshua.'

'I trust you,' I said. 'You've proven yourself countless times.'

Leah gave me a smouldering look, enough to shame Desert to ash.

Shilah sighed, beckoning for Ellia and Ellcia, who joined the group, still cackling as they surveyed the back of the frames. I didn't find anything funny about the wall of paintings, but I was merely an Inventor; I did not pretend to understand women.

'Dunes!' I called out into the crowd. 'We're ready!'

A cough from behind me.

I spun to find the big man already at my back, kneeling in the sand.

'By your command,' he whispered.

'How long have you been there?' I asked.

'I've just arrived, Meshua. For you, I have vowed to move like a jaguar.'

'What's a jaguar?' I asked.

'It was an animal from before the Drought,' Shilah chimed. 'They were supposed to be very beautiful.'

'And fast,' Dunes said. 'And fierce. And loyal. And intelligent. And—'

'Is the Desert inside already?' I asked, pointing inside the wall. I hated to cut Dunes off, but my hands were itching to tinker. They hadn't felt so restless since I'd first gotten to Leroi's shop.

'Yes, Meshua.'

I smiled, turning to Shilah. 'Any speeches?'

She paused, taking out the map her mother had given her and tapping on the city where we stood. 'The City of the Jadans' Rise. Not New Ziah.'

I smiled, my hands hot inside the boilweed gloves. 'Perfect.'
'Wait!'

We spun towards the noise, and found Cam careening across the plain, pushing himself through the throngs of Jadans. His eyes were puffy and his face was red, and he looked like he'd run all the way from the bottom plateau. A glass vial was in his hand, which he held above the crowd.

Shilah gave me a nudge with her elbow, a smug look on her face.

Stopping at the edge of our little group, Cam hunched over and put his hands on his knees, breathing heavy. 'I have' – gasp – 'Some.'

Shilah went over and put a hand on Cam's back, giving me a wink. 'Some what?'

Cam sucked in a heavy breath and stood straight, holding the vial.

'Sorry it took me so long,' he said, not meeting my eyes. 'I figured they'd be purer if I cried them alone. But here you go, one vial of pure Noble tears.'

'Cam,' I said.

Cam swallowed hard, still bent over. 'Micah.'

'I love you,' I said.

Shilah leaded down and kissed Cam on the cheek. 'So do I, dummy.'

Even in the dark, I could see Cam go strawberry red.

'We weren't going to start without you,' Shilah said.

'Camlish Tavuh,' Ellcia said.

'Yeah?'

'You aint nuh man-priss. Yoose family.'

Cam let his hand fall by his side, overwhelmed.

'Right?' Ellcia asked her sister.

'Nuh man-priss at all,' Ellia answered.

Dunes stood up, but kept hunched in a bow. 'The only Noble I've ever been proud to serve.'

'Thanks,' Cam said, staring at his feet.

'Hold on!' a hurried voice called.

We all turned collectively in the other direction.

Split excused his way through the crowd, Picka bleating at his side. The dwarf camel nuzzled a few children as she passed, and then bit at their pockets, the little Jadans squealing with delight.

'Micah, Shilah, hold on!' Split called, pushing through the crowd, which was still chanting 'Meshua'. Split also had a little glass vial in hand, filled to the top with clear liquid. Shilah put her face against Picka's snout, ruffling the hair on her neck.

'I missed you, girl,' Shilah said. 'You are the most beautiful camel in the whole World Cried, big or small, yes you are.'

Picka purred with delight.

'Picka wanted to wish you luck,' Split said. 'And I wanted to bring you these.' He handed over a few vials of tears. 'And this.'

Reaching under his shirt, he pulled out a necklace. On the end was an ugly hunk of metallic rock that looked like it had melted and then been left to cool back into place. The hue was different to anything I knew; it trapped all sorts of colours in the stone.

'It belonged to my wife and then my daughter,' he said. 'They both loved camels more than anything else. It's why I got Picka in the first place.'

I glanced over the necklace. Funny how the mind could make out shapes only after it knew what to look for. I could now see the jewellery was indeed shaped like a camel.

'Thank you,' I said. 'But why are you giving it to me?'

Split backed away with a bow. 'Because the rock it was made from once fell from the sky. So I figured it may bring you luck up there. Maybe it'll let whatever, or whoever, you find know that you rise in peace.'

'Thank you, Split.'

'There are days where I feel nothing but despair, knowing that such big hearts and born into a world designed to break them.' Split gave me a gentle nod. 'This is not one of those days.'

'I couldn't have asked for a better—'

Just then Picka let out a sad bleat.

Split sighed. 'I told you I'd find you some food in a moment, you silly beast. You just ruined a nice moment!'

Picka answered with a waggle of her black tongue.

Split sighed and then kicked some sand at Cam's feet. 'You feeling better?'

Cam nodded, his cheeks deep with colour.

Split pointed to the other glass vial in my hand. 'You cry some as well?'

'Went through half a dozen onions,' Cam said. 'You?'

Split scoffed. 'A real man doesn't need onions to cry, boy.' He put his hand around Cam and nodded towards the crowd. 'Now let's go get a good view.'

'Probably not going to be much to view,' I said. 'Tonight's just the beginning steps. We don't even know if it's going to be strong enough.'

Split gave an over-exaggerated wink and then gesture to the crowd of chanting Jadans, hope flush in their faces. 'Of course.'

Cam bit his lip. He was sweating. 'I was hoping I could be in there while you work, Spout.'

Shilah and I exchanged a look, remembering the mess that had happened in the cave the last time Cam was around the active Desert.

Cam took out another vial and two strips of boilweed from his pocket. He uncapped the vial – releasing the familiar scent of rosemusk – and poured some liquid on the boilweed strips before stuffing them up his nostrils.

'See,' Cam said, nasally and high pitched. 'Impenetrable.'

I laughed. 'Of course you can be in there with us, Cam. Just—'

Cam cut me off with a wave of his hand. 'I'll stand at the very edge by the boilweed curtain. And of course, first sign of anything weird, Dunes can toss me outside.' Cam lowered his head. 'I just want to be with you while you do it.'

'Good, because I can't do it without you,' I said, putting my arm around him, leading him inside. 'Now let's figure out if it can be even done.'

The first step was working out how to harness the heat.

The events in the Coldmarch cave had proven that, against Desert, boilweed would get eaten away faster than fine cheese at a High Noble banquet. Desert's heat clearly had power to lift heavy things, but I had to figure out a way to keep the force from destroying something once it was in the air, otherwise whatever was up there – including me – would come careening out of the sky and end up parchment-flat on the stone below.

I thought about creating some sort of giant, upside-down metal basin to catch the heat, but the weight of such a thing would be staggering; also I needed the container to be flexible enough to expand and contract along with the fluctuating heat. Rigorous metal wouldn't let me know when the Desert's effect was dissipating. I'd need to know when to pour on more Noble tears.

Shilah and I had returned to the Coldmarch tinkershop earlier, and after stepping around broken glass and ashen boilweed, we found that the Desert pieces had gone back to normal. Since the Desert hadn't been able to burn through the steel bucket, yet the ceiling had been charred to a black crisp, I was able to assume that the brunt of the heat rises.

And so, with the crowd of Jadans chanting outside, and the sky full of stars overhead, my tinkering began.

As we worked, Cam sat against the wall, nose stuffed up, giving me continuous nods of approval. Whenever Shilah and I poured tears on the Desert, Cam's eyes would go red. He became a bit squirmy, but he seemed to be in control of himself. We let him stay.

To me, the burning Desert smelled like the most vile thing in existence. I copied Cam's rosemusk idea, stuffing my nose and passing out potent nose plugs for each of my assistants.

We pushed things over the burning buckets to observe the strength of the heat, keeping the test objects tethered to rope. The current was able to lift a large rubber ball, an over-ripe Khatmelon, and even a few sand shoes, but they all burned to their crispy cores in a matter of moments.

I missed this sort of creation.

The kind with purpose; which led you along, even when your feet were tired and your eyes could no longer see the way. The kind that convinces you you're not separate from the materials. The kind that leaves you feeling like, if the Crier was real, then He was probably the *act* of Creation itself.

Hours passed in a trance.

The group hardly spoke after I told everyone what I needed; which was useful considering I made everyone wear Cold-sprinkled masks while inside the walls. We couldn't talk easily, but glances and body language told us everything we needed to know. It was like Flight was in there with us, whispering into our ears and guiding our hands. Leading our eyes. Dancing our fingers.

Samsah built us a beautiful dome-sail using the hamsa wood. The dome he constructed could flex and sway as easily as a Marlean Teardancer. Leah cut and shaped the boilweed sheet to go around the dome, lining it with the waxy fabric which I'd piled in the corner. I got the idea because the waxy paper had worked so well in my Cold Wrap, which felt like a lifetime ago, as a barrier between the Desert heat and boil-weed sail. The waxy fabric was practically impenetrable to the Sun, and we'd discovered that it was immune to the Desert heat as well.

Leah used the Glue of the Dunai to keep the sail together instead of stitching, which would have given the heat tiny cracks in which to lick the boilweed. I hadn't told her to do that, and only after did I realize what a wonderful idea it had been. Dunes and Samsah built the base of the craft out of hard rubber and the rest of the hamsa, making it large enough to carry a few bodies.

My job was to tame the Desert.

I borrowed a lot of the caging designs from the Coldmaker, specifically the compartment which held Jadan tears. I fastened new gears and levers which would spin out a droplet of Noble tears on command, and send it falling onto the Desert. I had to use Golemclay for the container vials, where otherwise I would have used glass, but the mechanics were rather similar. I double-walled the steel bucket in which the Desert sat, shaping it to funnel the heat outward and spread into the pliable dome-sail evenly before escaping through the small hole in the top. I barred the Desert in with heavy steel so it wouldn't shift.

I figured I'd need to be able to control my direction while hovering in the sky, and so I'd stripped a fan blade from my Air Glider and positioned it horizontal instead of vertical. I attached it to this new craft on a pivot bearing so I could swing it in three different directions. I also stocked the base of the craft with two oars, just in case the night sky could be paddled like a river.

I barely needed to think. The Idea did the thinking for me.

And in a matter of hours, the craft was very nearly complete.

I only had to put on the final touches.

This came in the form of painting a feather onto the side of the base.

Unlike the literal descriptions I'd used in the past, like with my 'Claw Staff' and 'Rope Shoes', this Invention's name would be imbued with more meaning.

I stepped back and appraised the craft.

Alder paint dripped off the end of my brush. A tear dripped down my cheek, carrying memories.

Matty.

This craft would be called a Matty.

It was a gorgeous piece of tinkering. The base was spacious and sleek, the Desert was safely sequestered, the railing was steady. And the dome-sail looked ready to do battle with the heat, and quite possibly to win.

Shilah came to my side, putting a hand on my shoulder. 'This is a big moment. One of the most important in the history of the World Cried. We did it.'

'We don't even know if it's going to work,' I said.

She paused, nodded and then punched me in the arm.

I laughed, rubbing the stinging spot. 'You're right,' I said. 'It's a big deal.'

Shilah bit her bottom lip, rubbing at the visible portion of the burn scars on her chest. I still winced every time she touched them, but she seemed unbothered. 'I wish I could see the Khat's face when he sees this. You ready?'

I nodded, tossing Dunes the anchor rope. He caught it and in one smooth motion began fastening it around the immovable boulder. I checked my forehead for sweat, and even though I'd been around the impossible heat of the Desert for some time now, and my breath had been stifled by a boilweed mask, I found no moisture. My forehead was as dry as dust.

Cam stood up and came to my side, his eyes glossy.

'Here it is,' he said. 'The beginning of the end of the Drought. I'm so honoured to be by your side, my friends.'

He still had the plugs in his nose, so the tone ended up coming out less serious than he intended. Shilah chuckled, pinching her nose and matching his tone. 'We're the honoured ones.'

Cam laughed and poked at her stomach. She angled away, giggling.

My heart swelled with something lovely, their happiness somehow spilling over to me. This was a bit surprising, but not at all unwelcome. I gave Dunes a nod as he tied off the rope. I stepped into the craft.

'Okay everyone, step back,' I said. 'Masks on.'

I pulled the camel necklace around my neck and rubbed it in my fingers for luck. Then I examined the structure of the Matty; everything felt tight and in place and ready.

Shilah came up and leaned over the railing, lowering her voice. She was now carrying a canvas bag which I didn't recognize, holding something heavy and square. 'You sure you don't want to test it without a rider first?'

I shook my head, swallowing my fear.

'I knew you wouldn't.' She reached in and squeezed my bronze fingers. Then with a small umph she lifted in the bag and put it next to me. I peeked in and found the Coldmaker.

But it had been altered.

Instead of just the bronze Opened Eye etched on top, there were words painted in alder red, spanning the entire golden surface. They were drawn on in all different styles and sizes, dozens of them, clearly coming from different hands.

I read each one, getting more choked up by the second.

All of my friends had written their names on the Coldmaker.

'For luck,' Shilah said. 'We all believe in you.'

I nodded, my chest glowing. All around me were faces filled with hope and pride.

Shilah drew two fingers down her cheek, then backed away. 'We'll see you on the other side.'

I took a deep breath, putting on my protective glasses, which I'd tinkered to be airtight against my face. I was glad I was already wearing my boilweed mask over my mouth, as it disguised a loud sob of happiness.

This was going to work.

Even against impossible odds, surrounded by all of the armies in the Khatdom, and plotted against by the Khat himself, we could do anything. I could feel the World Crier around me, taking the shape of the people I love.

We'd created the Matty together, after all.

I flipped the lever and let the first Noble tear fall.

Violent orange blasted from the bucket and flared against my glasses. I huddled towards the railing, with my hand on the Glider lever, ready to start up the blades. Heat began to rise from the bucket, filling out the dome above. The hamsa wood stretched and bulged, groaning, almost as if it were annoyed.

The dome-sail plumed outward, going taut, catching all the terrible heat. There was a light whistling sound as the heat funnelled through the small hole in the top of the sail, escaping upwards instead of spilling back down and burning me to bones.

There was a gentle lurch.

And I began to fly.

I let out a furious bellow of excitement, which was muffled by the mask. Still, I was sure that all of my enemies down on the plains below could hear my war cry. I was sure the Flock could hear my victory. The Matty kept rising, the speed picking up as the heat sizzled skyward into the sail. I imagined it was trying to return to the Sun from whence it came.

Eventually the dome-sail rose past the top of the painting wall, peeking over the edge. Then I was above it completely.

The Flock pointed and shouted with glee. They knelt and

bowed and wept and shouted 'Meshua!' as they took in the Matty in all its glory.

Once again we had done the impossible.

The Matty halted suddenly, the rope underneath going taut against the boulder. I almost shouted for Dunes to cut me loose so I could keep rising, could keep howling for the whole world to hear. I wanted to fly over my people. I wanted to bless all the Jadans in the city with life and hope, and the thing in which our history had been sorely lacking.

Wonder.

I stood tall, ripping off my mask and shouting my happiness with all the power in my lungs. My echoes of victory washed across all the plateaus. I danced around the bucket. I sang the Jadans' Anthem until my voice cracked. I kissed the Coldmaker, careful not to smudge any of the names. I lifted my arms towards the sky, empty air above and beneath.

'Yes!' I screamed, heat on my tongue. 'I'm here!'

Soon enough I began to cough, having breathed in too much of the Desert fumes. I had to get back to the mission. I put my mask on and went to the fan cage, flipping the copper wire down into the Charged urn. The blades began to whirr, pushing wind and propelling the Matty sideways.

I pivoted the fan all the way to the right, and I began to swing around, circling around the perimeter of the painting wall, taut against the rope. I tested all the different directions, able to actually control my direction. The Flock made so much noise that I could feel the earth laughing through the rope. My Jadan kin waved flags with Opened Eyes and bronze fingers.

'Yes!' I shouted.

Even above the roaring glider blades and the bubbling Desert, I could hear my friends in the tinkershop below, yelling with excitement.

After a while the effect on the Desert began to dissipate,

and the Matty drifted slowly back towards the land. I touched down with grace and poise, and hopped out of the base, going right to Shilah and wrapping her in my arms. I laughed wildly and held her tight. She laughed along with me, her fingers catching in my hair.

Cam came over and joined us in the hug, the three of us falling deep into something grander than ourselves. We could feel the rivers of history parting. We could hear the songs of our ancestors.

The Drought was almost over.

Chapter Twelve

From up here, the massive sand dunes below looked like fingernails.

The caravan roads were barely discernible, mere cracks in the land.

The Khat's vast armies reminded me of tiny beetles circling around a city the size of an orangefruit, the once high walls now so puny that they could be toppled by a few well-aimed pebbles. The blazing lights of the enemy fires were barely specks of light, like Adaam Grass spread too thin.

Once again it had become difficult to breathe, only this time for a better reason.

My laughter was the nervous kind, the sky air escaping my lips in wispy clouds, but I was prepared. I gathered the coat around my shoulders and pressed the hat down around my ears – I'd found both items in Ka'in's personal cabinet of ancient artefacts, both made of heavy wool – to keep from shaking. I couldn't help but think about how such things have such vastly different uses depending on the circumstances.

I surveyed the expansive land, settled with patches of blackness far vaster than any city. Out there were empty sands that could swallow the River Singe whole. And there were patterns across the dank dunes, the outlines faint and constantly shifting. It was like the land was painting something I'd have to live hundreds of years to see completed. To see its message written in starlight and sand.

I tried to hold hope as I ventured higher and higher into the night sky. I envisioned tossing my fear over the side to keep the Matty light. The stars kept their distance above as always, taunting me, moving away at the same speed I approached. I was determined to meet them nonetheless.

My knuckles creaked as I gripped the railing and looked further over the edge, trying to figure how high I'd gone compared to the last three untethered trips. I was now so high that I worried that the world might leave without me. I picked up my Claw Staff and waved it into the empty air above me, stretching for the stars.

'Come on!' I yelled. 'I'm here! Right here! Give me something!'

The Crier didn't answer.

I kept rising.

My first time taking the Matty off rope, two nights prior, I'd only used a single Noble tear. Just the one drop alone proved more powerful than expected, lifting me a thousand hands high at least; so high that my scream might not have touched down for days, had I fallen over the edge.

The invention had lifted with such vigour that I'd had to lay flat on the bottom of the base and close my eyes in terror, praying that the Matty wouldn't tip. I'd tied the harness rope so tight around my waist that I'd left bruises. When I'd finally worked up the courage to look over the railing, seeing the plateaus below reduced to the size of a garden, everything had nearly gone black.

The second night I'd chanced two tears. I'd gone the same

distance upwards as before on the first, and once I had felt
the Matty begin to descend, I let another drop out of the vial.
I soared even higher, at incredible speeds, hanging in the sky
for hours. The exhilaration was more intense than feeling
Ice. I'd been dizzy with elation and sick with happiness. The
wind had brought the Matty away from the topmost plateau
of the city, shooting me out over the deadlands, but the glider
blades put me back where I started. The Matty had been
surprisingly easy to manoeuvre, the fan powerful and precise,
and as the Desert calmed, I was able to land softly outside of
the painting wall, the Flock greeting me like I was the Crier
Himself.

Shilah and Cam greeted me as equals, which I much
preferred.

Shilah had then told me about what had gone on at the
walls while I was up there flying. Ka'in had allowed a large
portion of the remaining Beggars out of the city walls and
then brought them on stage for a 'freedom ceremony'. In an
obvious turn, he branded each of their necks with a circle
– representing the Sun, so the heat knew where to attack –
and then tossed the Jadans back inside the walls, having
whipped them bloody. He gave them no salve for their wounds
and no hope for escape.

Shilah had done her duty as 'Meshua'. She took in our
new family members and showed them nothing but peace
and kindness. She gave them salve. They weren't ready for
hope, but they at least accepted the medicine.

The Five found a dozen new pieces of Desert buried inside
the walls the following morning. The Khat was getting
desperate. And so on the third rise I'd dropped five tears on
the Desert.

I had to find the Cold in the sky. Even a single Frost would
have done for now.

I kept my mask pressed tight and launched so high that

my lungs began to freeze. Breath started leaving my lips in white clouds, and it had reminded me of the kind of Cold my body had endured on the Ice raft while crossing the Singe. My limbs went stiff and numb. I ended up having to huddle next to the Desert bucket to keep my teeth from chattering, breathing in the putrid heat as I waited for the Matty to descend. The headache from the fumes had lasted all night.

Tonight was my fourth rise.

I had just released the seventh Noble tear.

The land beneath me was impossibly far, enough to make me question if it was even real anymore. The City of the Jadans' Rise was off to my distant right, the Matty having drifted dangerously away, so much so that I wondered if I was closer to Marlea than I was to my Flock. I gathered the wool coat around me, staving off the shivers, beginning to worry. I wasn't worried about falling, or about going too high, or because it would take me quite some time to glide my way back.

I still hadn't found any Cold up here.

I was nearer to the World Crier than any Jadan had ever been before, but the air gave me nothing back for my efforts. The night sky was chilled to a terrifying degree, but I couldn't take the air back down with me. I needed some physical pieces to bring home. I needed more than that. I needed a Frost. Yet all around me was only empty sky and distant light.

I gritted my teeth and went higher.

Eleven tears.

Twelve tears.

Fifteen tears.

I rose so high that I began to go painfully lightheaded, my legs too wobbly to keep me upright. I doubled the rope around my waist. The Matty began to shake and rattle. Each breath became a struggle. My lungs felt like they had crystallized over with Ice. My skin went pale, my arms matching the hamsa wood. I waved the Claw Staff around wildly, anger stiffening my shoulder.

Sixteen tears.

'Come on!' I yelled, although I barely had enough air to get out a squeak. 'I'm here. This is what you wanted, right! This is why you showed me the way up!'

I bared my teeth and turned up the glider blades as fast as they would go, the copper wire dipping all the way into the Charged water. The blades sped up with a thunderous roar and the Matty was propelled sideways with a heavy lurch.

I looped the rope around my forearm as well and chanced leaning my back over the railing; this way I could look up past the dome-sail and into the heavens.

There were far more stars up here than I'd ever seen before. I had to believe that some of them were Frosts, but I wasn't getting any closer.

'I'm here!' I shouted, gasping for air. Breathing was painfully Cold this far into the sky. My lips felt as brittle as overcooked clay. 'What more can I do!'

I screamed and waved my Claw Staff and let out three more of Cam's tears onto the Desert at once. The Matty shot upwards so fast that it threw me down onto the floor before I knew what was happening. I was pinned. The dome-sail creaked and groaned, threatening to burst a seam. I wrenched myself to my feet, heat spilling across my face and desperation overcoming me.

'Damn it! I've done everything you wanted! Give me something!'

My Claw Staff dropped over the railing, cascading silently into the night. The loss didn't feel like an accident. I began grasping out into the open air with my bare hands, stretching as far as the rope would allow. My palms swung through the darkness, clasping for anything at all. I didn't even need a

Frost anymore. A single Wisp would do it. A single Wisp would make me cry with belief.

'I'm here!' I shouted. The glider blades were deafening. The heat of the Desert was searing, getting more intense by the second. 'I'm right here! You said you needed me! I'm here!'

My shoulder muscles burned as I reached out past the railing.

'Help me! Give me something!'

But there was no answer.

Only empty air and Cold darkness.

The Crier had abandoned me.

Heat exploded at my back. I fell over the railing. There was a terrible wrenching pain in my stomach and waist.

And then nothing.

I woke to a mouthful of sand.

Wincing against the harsh light, I scrambled to get my bearings. I tried to move and then realized a rope was digging into my waist. I quickly scrambled at the knot and sucked in a heavy breath once I was free. I rubbed my forehead, a splitting headache cracking my skull from ear to ear. It was so light everywhere. Impossibly light. The light and heat were scratching my eyelids, trying to blind me. At first I thought I might have somehow landed inside of a star. I spat, cleaning out my gritty cheeks, and then rubbed the crusty blood from under my nose. After a few surreal moments, my dreams tailing away, I realized that I was only back on land and that it was morning.

I was outside of the Matty, exposed to an angry Sun. I scrambled back to the base under the shade of the dome-sail, which was sagging, the hamsa wood leaning to one side. I scrambled into the shadow and curled up, taking long slow breaths and trying to work out what had happened.

From the way I'd landed outside of the craft, I must have gone unconscious, dangling beneath the Matty as it descended. If I hadn't had the rope around me, I would have been dead.

I coughed. The back of my throat tasted like burnt ash.

Too many tears, I thought. I have to be more careful next time.

I lifted my shirt and found the angriest bruise ringing my waist. It was chaffed a deep brown, almost black.

I checked the storage container tucked under the glider blades, trying to remember if I'd stocked anything besides Cold. I didn't remember packing any rations, but in the compartment I found two full waterskins, dark bread, honey and some candied figs. No groan salve, but the food was better than nothing. The rations spoke of Jia's touch, and I would have to thank him profusely.

I quickly sucked down an entire waterskin, gulping desperately to try and get rid of the taste of death and heat. Then I popped a candied fig in my cheek and let the sugar dissolve slowly.

I got to my knees and looked out over the railing of the Matty, my eyes having to adjust. Sand stretched as far as I could see – which wasn't far, as I seemed to have landed between two high dunes. I had no indication of where I'd ended up. Strangely enough, however, the sand was redder than what I was used to; perhaps a shade more vibrant.

The candied fig was a blessing against my throat, and I closed my eyes, concentrating on the sweetness.

I was alive.

The Matty was relatively intact.

And I had some food and water.

I couldn't have drifted too far from the city walls, so I tossed on my boilweed mask and prepared to rise once again. Shilah and Cam would be worried sick about me, so I had to push through my headache and get back. I checked the dome-sail for rips or tears, but miraculously everything was intact.

I flipped the gear on and stepped back from the bucket.

Nothing happened.

I frowned, tapping at the side of my contraption, hoping nothing had been knocked out of place. I had no idea how harsh the landing had been.

I turned the gear switch back and forth, but the Desert remained calm.

Undoing the latch, I peered inside.

My heart sank.

I checked my pockets for the extra tear vials and found them empty as well. They must have tipped out when I fell over the railing.

I checked the patch of sand where I'd landed and then rushed back to the storage compartment, tossing aside the food and waterskins, looking desperately for some backup tears.

I searched through every inch, but found nothing. I swallowed hard, still tasting sand and fire. If I couldn't fly, it would be a long, terrible journey home. Since I was outside of the walls, I would have to sneak past thousands of angry and suspicious Nobles, not to mention figure a way through the sealed gates. My only hope was that the Khat's armies still hadn't discovered the Coldmarch entrance into the city, which was under the red Closed Eye statue. If I could make it to the secret entrance, I could get back inside.

I took the Coldmaker out of its bag and gave it a kiss, careful not to smudge any of the alder names.

'Sorry,' I said, my voice feeling frail and weak, 'but you're too heavy. I'll come back for you soon, I promise.'

I wrapped the Coldmaker in my wool coat and buried it next to the Matty. Then I gathered my rations into the bag. I still had a few Drafts that I'd been using to grate into my mask, so I knew I'd be okay as long as I could keep the Sun at an arm's length for a while. I stopped to give the side of the Matty a kiss too, right on the feather.

Then I scrambled to the top of the nearest dune.

I found myself in the middle of a collection of dunes, each one higher than the next. I couldn't see the city walls anywhere, nor the ring of the Khat's armies, and I tried not to panic. The Sun was rising, and at least I could keep track of my direction.

I sighed, turning South.

Even if I hadn't landed due North of the city, South was my best chance at finding my way back. I'd either run into the Singe, a caravan or a Pedlar. South of the city, towards Paphos, always has more signs of life.

I steadied my nerves and began walking.

The reddish sands were piled high like regular dunes, but these were springier and denser than what I was used to. I expected to sink up to my ankles, but I could walk almost as well as if I'd had rope shoes on.

I walked for an unnerving amount of time, the sands at last smoothing into solid land and spilling me out between high rock formations I didn't recognize. The sprawling cliffs offered a fantastic amount of shade, and I stepped into the shadows with a grateful sigh. Taking a swig of water, I rounded through a passageway in the rocks and came across something ever more curious.

'Huh,' I whispered to myself.

The land was alive and growing.

Beneath my feet was lovely soil, brown and dark, with round bushes sprouting up everywhere. The bushes were only about waist height, but there were little green berries growing within the thorny leaves.

Wooden puppets, suspended by poles, loomed around the garden. They were built to look like Jadans. Their wooden feet moved along with the slight wind, their dancing shoes gently scraping the soil. Jadan dolls in a garden struck me as rather out of place. I didn't recognize the green fruit on the bushes either, and I wondered if I'd perhaps landed in Marlea; that I'd stumbled upon a High Noble garden.

Some of the bushes provided home for strange beetles the size of Wisps. Yellow carapaces, plump legs and wide incisors meant they looked like no beetles with which I was familiar. They munched on the fruit, letting me know it was probably safe to eat.

Wasting no time, I plucked a few of the green berries and chomped them into a fine pulp. The taste reminded me of Khatmelon, but this was sweeter and didn't leave the chalky aftertaste. I chewed harder, letting out an unintentional groan of pleasure. I plucked an entire bush clean, stowing the bounty in my bag. My journey home would be dangerous, but it would at least be tasty.

I started plucking the next bush clean, when I was startled by a noise.

I jumped to my feet as someone wandered into the garden. He looked to be around my age, although he was taller and more stretched out. His shirt was wrapped around his waist, and the skin of his chest and arms was much lighter than mine. He was clearly Jadan; although he looked rather well taken care of for a slave. He didn't have the pampered look of Domestic, but he was also free of scarring, with most of his skin clear and smooth.

He also carried death.

'You have a scorpion on you!' I shouted.

The boy blinked, looking rather shocked. He didn't seem surprised at the scorpion, however, which was as fat as my palm and resting on his shoulder. The deadly creature's tail was erect and tense, preparing to sting.

'Yes,' the boy said, calmly and slowly, his eyes narrowing.

He had an odd accent. 'Why are you speaking in the enemy tongue?'

'Kill it!' I said, moving towards him, trying to figure what I could use to swat the scorpion away. 'You need me to kill it?'

All of a sudden the boy had a knife in his hand, moving even quicker than Shilah. But he didn't turn the blade on the creature.

He pointed it at me.

'Don't you dare!' he snarled.

'I'll help you!' I said. 'I'll kill it. Look, it's about to sting you!'

'This my friend, Zizi,' the boy said, nodding to his shoulder, where the scorpion waited, its tail deadly and poised. 'You kill him, you die. Now stop moving!'

I halted, putting my hands over my head.

'What are you doing in the knuckleberry patch?' the young man asked. 'Sett put you up to this? She still trying to get my growing secrets?'

'Who's Sett?' I asked. 'What's a knuckleberry?'

He gave me an incredulous look. 'What's a knuckleberry?'

'You sure you don't need help with that scorpion?'

The boy prodded the inside of his cheek with his tongue. 'Turn around, spy. Slowly.'

'I'm not—'

'Turn around,' the boy barked, his voice rather commanding for a Jadan.

I slowly turned, letting him see that I was unarmed.

'Crier below,' the boy said. 'You've got numbers on your neck.'

'Yes,' I said turning around, echoing his confusion. 'Don't you?'

'But it was closed ten years ago,' he said to himself. A flash of panic ran through the boy's eyes. He waved the blade. 'Get on your stomach!'

'I'm not your enemy,' I said, waving my bronze fingers. 'Haven't you heard of the boy with these before? Mesh—'

'On your stomach now,' he said. 'Or I have Zizi sting you. And it won't be pleasant. Zizi's got a mean streak when it comes to spies.'

The scorpion wiggled its tail, which came dangerously close to stinging the boy's neck.

'Spies?' I asked.

'On your stomach!'

'Okay, okay.'

I got down and pressed my face into the lush dirt. It didn't smell like the soil in Paphos or the Sanctuary gardens. I was breathing in something new.

The boy's shadow straddled me and there was a ripping sound. I peeked, and saw him cutting up his shirt with the knife. Then he bent down and tied my wrists behind my back, using an impressive knot which Leroi had never taught me. I gave an experimental tug and found I was trapped.

'Huh,' he said, prodding my tattoo.

'Whose garden is this?' I asked.

'Don't play dumb,' the boy said. 'Now get up.'

I did as I was told, the knife tip pressing against my back. I was more scared of the scorpion than the knife, however. The hissing was right behind my ear.

'How did you get all the way through?' the boy asked. 'How did you get to this side of everything? No one has done that before.'

'What are you talking about?' I asked. 'My name is Micah. I've been—'

'Micah,' the boy said with a deep laugh. 'That's a nice touch.'

'That's my name. I'm from Paphos originally, but—'

'Course you're from Paphos,' he said. 'I told you not to play dumb. I know the Khat doesn't make his spies dumb.

And I especially know you're not dumb because you got so far. No other spies have ever gotten so much as through Hulcum's Pass.' The boy sighed. 'Sett's going to be mighty disappointed.'

Then things went dark as he fit the rest of the shirt over my head, making it a blindfold. He grabbed my arm and then led me forward.

'Walk,' he said. 'I promise I won't hurt you. That's not my job. I just grow things.'

We trudged onward, and I let myself be led, praying the scorpion kept its distance. I remained quiet, trying to figure out a plan. I had clearly stumbled into a High Noble manor, as the High Nobles are the ones always worried about spies – Lord Tavor had been worried enough to task Leroi with creating batches of dreadful anklets. But if the High Nobles here were worried about spies, it was probably because they had a Frost. Which meant that if I could keep from being stabbed or stung, this could end up working in my favour.

'I'm not a spy,' I said after a while. 'I flew here.'

The boy laughed again. Zizi hissed.

'Funny,' he said, leading me along. 'You're good at lying, and I imagine we could have had a few great laughs together, especially since I miss the common tongue. Too bad.'

'What's your name?' I asked.

'Eliezah,' he said. 'But they call me Shaman Eli.'

Shaman Eli? I thought. I'd heard that name before. But I couldn't remember where.

I stayed quiet and tried to work up a plan, thinking of ways I might be able to talk myself out of captivity. We kept walking, my mind spinning faster than glider blades. Eventually the springy earth turned to stone beneath my feet.

'I like you, spy,' Shaman Eli said. 'Enjoy this while you can. You're the first outsider to see in ten years.'

He lifted off my blindfold.

My knees went weak.

I'd been stung by the scorpion. I was seeing things. This couldn't be real.

The land at my feet split into a giant canyon, the biggest I'd ever seen. I knew right away this was the Great Divide. The missing land stretched out to both sides, seemingly going on forever. It curved and dipped and spun as it expanded into the rock, uneven and craggy. Only the wind would be able to navigate such devastating terrain. Its scale was so devastating that it made my mind flinch.

And then I looked straight down towards the bottom of the canyon, and my world nearly collapsed.

Past the beautiful stone archways, detailed monuments, and old buildings carved right into the stone were distant pockets of green. The colour was lost in shadows – I had to squint to make it out – but it was still intense, with trees and bushes and flowers bursting with life, far more vibrant than any High Noble garden I'd seen; all being tended to by Jadans in strange hats. The base of the canyon was straight out of the past; it looked like it had been preserved from before the Great Drought.

Everything else above it, however, had succumbed to the same disease as the rest of the world. There was plenty of sand and dust and empty stretches of rock the higher the Divide climbed. Hundreds of structures rose from the emptiness, looking like they might have once been beautiful, but had been left to become rubble.

But what really made my knees go weak, what made my mouth go dry, were the warriors.

Jadan warriors.

Everywhere I looked, Jadans were training for battle. Brown and black skin glistened with sweat under a harsh Sun. Even from the high vantage point, I could hear the grunts and cries of struggle. There were swords clanging everywhere, arrows flying, bodies wrestling and a number of other foreign weapons being rehearsed.

Different sections of the canyon appeared to be reserved for different types of fighting, with a single Jadan marching around each patch holding an Opened Eye flag and barking orders at those locked in combat. The flag bearers were louder and shouted with more fervour than any taskmasters I'd ever heard. The fighting Jadans looked hardened and scarred, even downright mean. Jadan men and women alike were practising the warring arts. I couldn't process what I was seeing.

'What is this place?' I gasped.

'You're funny, spy. I'll plead with Sett to make your death swift.' He clapped me on the back and began leading me down the stairs, his grip gentle yet unyielding. 'Welcome to Langria.'

PART THREE

Chapter Thirteen

In the land of the free, I never expected to end up in chains.

The room in which I was locked was dark and old, the air stifling. A few hours must have passed since Eli had left me here, and I would have wagered the leaders of Langria were making me wait on purpose. My anticipation had been built, and my fear had successfully clouded the room. The metal restraints on my wrists, ankles and neck were cool to the touch, but burned with the heat of my indignation.

The Flock was at the mercy of my absence. Shilah would keep things stable, but I feared the Khat could still ignite the Second Fall at any moment. I needed to get out of this room and plead my situation to whoever was in charge. I needed to fly home as soon as possible.

The Jadans of Langria were our long-lost family. They were living proof that the Crier hadn't abandoned our people, and that the Khatdom was in fact a lie. Accidentally flying as North as North goes and finding this place could be the monumental discovery that would change Jadan minds across the world. Knowledge of the free lands might have even been the happy accident I was supposed to find.

Yet I'd been thrown in chains and promised death.

My skin already held angry rashes from all my squirming, but the chains were well forged. I wasn't going anywhere.

A day earlier I'd commanded a city.

Hours ago I'd held dominion over the skies.

Now I was a slave again.

Parading me through the scowls and two-knuckle gestures of the fighters, Shaman Eli had led me into the canyonside, blindfolded me once more and taken me straight to this cell. He'd locked me inside, taking away my bronze fingers just in case I had any 'spy weapons' hidden inside. His touch had been kind and gentle, making sure the shackles weren't cutting off my circulation and that I could breathe, yet his mastery was absolute. He gave me a friendly pat on the shoulder and told me all about how I would be tortured.

There was no cruelty or malice in his words, just assurance. He was sharing the horrific details out of kindness. Fear was its own kind of torture, and his matter-of-fact explanation did in fact take away some of the looming sting.

Not enough, but some.

'They will work on your fingers first, since they're the most sensitive,' was his warning. 'Tell them everything you know after the first cuts. Sett's interrogators are trained from birth for the job. They can spot lies in the way your body moves almost as well as they can hear them. If you empty yourself of all your truth up front, there's no more need to go cutting. They will give you sweet death and only a little suffering.'

I'd tried to plea with Eli, to tell him who I was, but he only ever held up a gentle hand at my interjections. Zizi hissed whenever Eli's shoulder moved, waving its stinger in my direction. Quickly enough I'd realized that the scorpion had been de-barbed.

'Please don't speak,' he'd said. 'I'm on your side and the

side of mercy for now. But anything you let slip might make me change my mind.'

After a few attempts at explanation I'd resigned to silence. Eli gave me another pat on the shoulder, a sad nod, and eventually left me alone with my thoughts.

My friends would never know where I'd died.

I pulled at the shackles once again, splitting the skin on my wrists.

I had nothing better to do. The pain at least kept the dread and panic at bay.

I coughed out another lungful of hot, dusty air. The room was lit up by the streaming Sunlight from the single window. The beam was thin, terrible and directed straight at my forehead. The heat was uncomfortable, but a part of me was glad I couldn't move my head too much, otherwise I'd be able to study all the nasty stains on the stone floor and wall. I caught glimpses of some red, some brown. Careening along the wall near my head were chalky white scrapes from desperate fingernails.

I closed my eyes and prayed.

Not to the World Crier.

I prayed to Shilah.

She had once told me that I needed to have faith in something, even if it wasn't in the divine. She told me that otherwise life was too messy to ever make clean decisions. I still had my fair share of doubts about the Crier, especially in His ability to help in any way, and so now most of my faith ended up in my partner. It was a decision I was okay with.

Even if my life was to end here, I prayed that Shilah would build another Matty and find the Frosts herself. So she could be the true Meshua our people needed.

I prayed that she would find strength in Cam.

I prayed for her happiness and courage.

I prayed that she wouldn't miss me too much.

I closed my eyes and lost myself to her posture.

The doors to the cell opened.

Two burly Jadans walked in and took position at either side of the doorway. Their forearms were carved up with chaotic battle scars rather than straight-line whip scars, and from the smoothness of their cheeks I would have guessed they had never learned to smile. They stared at me as if I had yellow hair and the Khat's face.

And then someone even worse walked in.

I could tell by the way this Jadan walked that she was the one in charge. Slowly, but with purpose, as if she had all the time in the World Cried to get answers out of me. Her dark face was crowned with a head of short grey hair, and even though her eyes were dull in colour, they sparkled with intelligence and cunning. Usually Jadan women this old had been all but eaten up and spat out by the Nobles, but she carried herself like she'd done the chewing.

She held an ominous wooden box in one hand and a circular disc in her other. I tried to figure out how sharp the edges of the disc might be, and how they would be used on my soft flesh to extract answers.

The woman turned to the guards and said something in a language that sounded a bit like Ancient Jadan. It was less throaty and had shorter words, but still had an eerie similarity. I was stunned to hear such language used so casually.

The guards filed out of the cell and shut the door behind them.

The new woman strutted up to me and held out the metal disc of torture. There was a click of switch and the pop of a spring. I winced, expecting pain.

Instead, the back of the circle shot outwards, a latticework stand expanding. Thin metal that had been tucked behind the circle folded out intricately and eventually locked into a small tower of sorts.

It looked like a chair.

The woman confirmed my suspicions by placing the legs on the ground and sitting on the top. Her gray hair blocked the beam of Sunlight, offering me a bit of mercy.

Her chair was an interesting bit of tinkering. I tried to cock my head to study the spring-work, but the chains on my neck kept me from doing so.

'Congratulation,' the woman said, her voice rounded at the edges, her tongue unhurried. 'You made yourself further than any other spy in eight hundred years. It was only a time matter before Khats finally sent cunning one.'

She was clunky in the common tongue, and from the disgust in her eyes I could tell that she wasn't thrilled to use the language.

'I'm not a spy,' I said, speaking slowly and trying to look harmless.

The woman nodded, giving me a go-ahead look. 'You hear whispers of Coldmarch and decide you make it North on your own. You stealed Cold and hide in caravans. You braved sands merciless. Look at numbers on your neck. You're revolutionary. Down with the Khat. You put yourself at mercy, and swear to the undying Crier that you pledge life entirely to free people of Langria.'

I paused, my tongue feeling heavy. 'Huh?'

'Is next part of your speech,' she said. 'Is like Khats have had same scribe for eight hundred years. Every speech is changed bit, but all have the same inner guts. Did I get right?'

I tried to sit as upright as I could, which didn't amount to much.

'My name is Micah,' I said. 'And I—'

'Meshua!' the woman said with honey tones, clapping a

hand against her knee. 'The saviour is finally arrived! And right age, too.' Her face lit with something close to humour. 'Bold new words for scribes. My compliments to Khat. Now how did you get to far side of Langria undetected. How did you get past warriors in Dagon?'

'What's Dagon?'

She gave me an impatient look.

I tried not to sigh. I had to sound like a leader in my own right. I tried to speak like she walked, unhurried and clear. 'Like I said. My name is Micah, and I am in charge of the free Jadans at the City of David's Fall. Right now my people are besieged – surrounded there by the Khat and thousands of soldiers, and I have been looking for ways to fight back. I have invented . . .'

I trailed off, trying to think of the best way to explain my predicament to someone who thought I was a liar and didn't quite speak my language.

'I can make Cold,' I said. 'And I have discovered the secret to flight.'

'Of course have!' she said, biting her bottom lip to keep from bursting out laughing. 'You are Meshua! You come with miracles to fix world.'

I sighed. I wasn't helping my case. 'I didn't intend to come here, but now that I have, I think it might have been for a reason. My people need your help. Our people need your help.'

She leaned in, the chair creaking. Her eyes were like Wraiths, ready to erupt with the slightest touch. 'Is right?'

'That's right,' I said, dredging up every bit of confidence left inside me.

Her palm was poised on the eerie wooden box on her lap, almost as if her fingers were decided whether or not I should be tortured. 'I can be seeing why Shaman Eli took liking for you. He's sucker for mystery.'

'My friends are in danger,' I said, my face going fiery hot. I rattled my chains. 'And they need me to go back to them. I can't stay here. Please. We need your help.'

She took her time to respond, tapping her feet against the ground to a rhythm I couldn't hear, matching it with her fingers on the box. Her thumb played with the latch to open the thing, and my stomach clenched up tight thinking about what sort of blades or broken glass she was about to stick in me.

'I need you be seeing from my perspective,' she said. 'Is it right? Perspective?'

I nodded.

'I like what you is having to say.' She spoke slowly and with regret, as if dredging up the words from a place she didn't like visiting. 'I like clever tongue and new speech. Is interesting you say City of David's Fall is where half of soldiers went, and I is glad to be knowing this. But best lies always come bits of truth. The Khat has victory before because of good lies. And so you can't be having special treatments. Because I need not bits of truth, I need all truth.' She opened the latch on the wooden box, keeping the lid raised so that the contents were hidden from me. Her hand swept through her torture materials. 'I need know how you be getting to other side of Langria. No spy ever make it so far, and I need know what Khat knows. Never in my whole line of Melekah has happened a spy break through. Close, but never through.'

'I didn't break through,' I said. 'I flew here.'

She nodded, still picking through the box's contents. 'Mhmm.'

'Flight,' I said, feeling desperate and afraid. I still couldn't get my head around the fact that I was in the legendary Langria about to be tortured to death. 'Flying. Like a bird. Flying in the air.'

'Yes,' she snorted, still distracted. 'Bird Meesh-Dahm. Now be patient. Your truth coming.'

She began tapping her feet again on the stone floor, humming a foreign melody.

'I'm not a spy,' I pleaded. 'Please. You have to believe me. What can I do to prove it to you?'

She gave me a helpless nod, a sad look in her eyes.

'I can tell you how the Khat destroyed the world!' I cried, nearly a shout. 'I know the secret to how he took away the Cold.'

'Yes.' She seemed completely unmoved, letting out a sigh. 'He be using Desert. Other spies have bargain with this too. We know Desert.'

'You do?'

'Yes,' she said, giving another sad nod. 'They put in ground.'

The door behind her opened and another Jadan woman walked in. This one was younger than the one sitting in the chair, but not by much. She seemed harder around the edges. She wore glass eyewear, tinted red, but even behind it her eyes were wild and untamed. She wore a red uniform that reminded me of the one Jadanmaster Gramble used to wear on the days of the Procession.

A surge of dread boiled my heart.

The women exchanged a few words in their odd language. The newcomer tossed out the word 'Sett' at the woman in the chair that made me think it was a name. Their conversation was detailed and complex, spinning between them like a spider's web. The grey-haired woman, presumably Sett, gestured to a few parts of my body. She started with my hands, probably instructing the newcomer where I should be dissected.

Then Sett kissed the red-clad woman on the cheek, letting her lips linger. There was passion behind the kiss, Sett's hand reaching behind the other woman's head and nesting in her wavy hair. The romantic gesture seemed out of place preceding the moments where I was about to start screaming for mercy.

Sett pulled herself from the embrace and went for the door.

The newcomer's eyes dug into me with anger and hatred. She had a sleek face but wide-set eyes behind the glasses. She was looking through me, at all the tender bits that she was planning on eviscerating.

I wasn't so much afraid of the pain as the fact that I would not get back to my friends. I'd been tortured before; I could handle torture. But those tortures were when I was a Street Jadan, with nothing more than my own life hanging in the balance. Now I had an entire city of innocent Jadans depending on me to figure a way back. I couldn't let my people suffer more than I would.

'Wait!' I shouted.

Sett began to close the door behind her.

I took a deep breath.

I held one left truth to reveal.

'*Shemma hares lahyim criyah Meshua ris yim slochim,*' I shouted.

The woman in red buckled at the knees.

Sett paused, a tremor going through her body before she stormed back through the room. Her posture was much less sure this time. She swept past her torturer friend and knelt down in front of me, her rapid thoughts apparent.

'How you know these words?' Sett asked. 'Khat never know.'

She was still relatively calm, but there was fear in her tone.

'I was on the Coldmarch,' I said. 'I'm not a spy. Please, I'll tell you everything. Just let me go. I'll show you how I got here.'

'How. You know. These words.'

She was almost snarling at this point.

'My father taught them to me,' I said with defiance. 'His name was Abb and he was the best Jadan I've ever known.'

Sett put her hands under my chin. She didn't strangle me, but rather pressed her fingers up, as if feeling for a secret lever.

'Tell me you not being a spy,' she said.

'I'm not a spy,' I said.

Her concentration was intimidating. She pressed her fingers up into my throat further, her gaze boring into mine.

After a long moment she sighed, giving another sad nod. 'I'm just no good enough with tongue of enemy. Sinniah, you use tools now.'

'I am Micah from Paphos,' I said, leaning forward as much as I could. 'I swear to the Crier that—'

Sett cut me off, her face growing curious as she looked down my shirt. She reached under the fabric, pulling out my necklace.

Her face gave a heavy start as the little camel came into the light.

'Where you get this?' she gasped. Her hand was shaking.

'A friend gave it to me,' I said.

'What friend?'

'His name is Split the Pedlar, he was my Shepherd for the Coldmarch.'

Sett ripped the necklace off me in one pull, standing up and slamming the lid of the wooden box. She hurled herself towards Sinniah and once again they began speaking rapidly in the foreign language, both of them gesturing wildly. I couldn't tell, but it seemed like the Sinniah was trying to convince Sett that the necklace was a trick. Sett's tone turned harsh as they delved into deeper and more impassioned arguments.

Eventually Sinniah stormed out – there was no kiss this time – and slammed the door behind her. Sett grabbed the box, let out a long sigh and then went to follow her.

'Wait!' I called. 'I can prove everything!'

Sett turned to face me, flush with pain. 'You stay here, bird.'

I couldn't move if I'd wanted to.

Before I had time to answer she was gone.

After an agonizing wait, Sett returned with two new people.

One of them I recognized as Shaman Eli.

The other was a girl a little older than me, her skin quite fair for a Jadan and her hair long and straight. She had a large bump in her nose and her ears were too large for her face, but the most standout feature was a certain smugness. She stood as if the ground under her feet were unworthy of her delicate frame.

Sett returned to her tinkered stool, opening the wooden box once again.

'Please,' I said, my throat parched and lips cracked. The relentless Sun had stripped me of most of my water, and sweat stung my eyes. 'I'm not lying.'

Sett gestured over one shoulder and then the other. 'Shaman Eli and Lop were some of last who came on Coldmarch. They speak best tongue of enemy. I want to be making sure I don't misunderstand anything.' She turned to Eli. 'Is right? "Misunderstand"?'

Eli nodded, an excited look on his face. He had a shirt on this time, but Zizi the scorpion was still on his shoulder. I seemed to be the only one in the cell who thought the presence of such a creature was odd.

'Also, I am Sett,' she said. 'Melekah of Langria.'

I tried to bow my head but couldn't.

'It's an honour,' I said. 'I didn't think Langria was actually real.'

Sett's face furrowed with confusion. 'You say you fly here. Like bird.'

'Yes,' I said.

'And you know sacred words.'

'*Shemma hares lahyim*—'

Sett waved me quiet. 'Is not needed to repeat.'

Lop's hands quivered at her sides, giving me a scrutinizing look.

'And you have necklace,' Sett said.

I cracked a helpless smile, my head cloudy with Sunlight. 'Actually you have my necklace.'

'Tell Lop and Shaman Eli speech you being tell me,' Sett said, unamused.

I gathered my breath. I was ravenous and parched, but I was finally getting somewhere.

I told them everything I possibly could.

Sett waited patiently on her stool, listening to Eli relay my story in the foreign language, the ominous box in her lap. She fiddled with the latch, her thumb slowing down as my tale progressed. Thankfully she blocked the beam of Sunlight for the duration of my story and I got a reprieve from the heat.

I told them everything from the Coldmaker to the Matty, and then sat back and waited. I kept my mouth closed. Liars rambled, and keeping my tongue still would help my case.

Sett opened the torture box. I tried not to flinch.

She reached inside and pulled out the camel necklace, holding it in front of me.

'Who this belong to?' she asked.

'Split,' I said. 'Split the Pedlar.'

Eli said something in the language I decided was Langrian, but Sett stopped him by reaching back with an annoyed wave. She peered deeper into my eyes.

I swallowed hard, taking a different approach. 'It belongs to Langria?'

Sett's sharp inhale grew into a long sigh. She got up from her stool and gave Lop a dissatisfied gesture.

Panic flooded my chest. My chains felt tighter and I couldn't breathe. I didn't know how else to get out of this. I'd told them everything I knew, all of it true.

I closed my eyes and tried to summon anything that might prove who I was; anything that would keep the blades out of the precious fingers I had left. The back of my mind must have had information that the Khat could never possibly know. I leapt into memory, desperately grasping.

And then it hit me.

'Anyah,' I said. 'She was Split's daughter. And her mother was Lizah. They were captured by Hookmen and murdered.'

Sett turned slowly to Eli, her face going pale. 'Murdered. This is same as Luchtach, right?'

Eli swallowed hard and then nodded, his hand stroking the scorpion's back.

Sett's knees buckled and she walked over to the wall and rested her forehead against the stone, muttering something under her breath. Eli and Lop exchanged a horrified look.

'You knew them?' I asked, the realization dawning on me. I wished I could shift out of the Sunlight so I could see Sett better.

Sett nodded. She pulled herself back to her feet, leaving a wet spot behind on the stone.

'Yes,' she said. 'Lizah is being my sister. She leave Langria when younger. I not know she being murder. I has feeling, but I not know.'

A lump formed in my throat.

'I'm sorry,' I said.

Sett turned to Eli and spoke a long string of Langrian, not pausing, everything coming out in one desperate burst. After that she made a hurried gesture towards me.

Eli came over and began unlocking my chains. Lop looked unsure, keeping towards the back of the room.

'Sett wants you to know,' Eli said hurriedly, digging a key

into the manacle around my neck first, 'that she is willing to trust you. That she will let you go, but that if you are a spy for the Khat and end up bringing the downfall of Langria, then her spirit will wait for you in the black and spend all of eternity making sure you never find your Frost.'

I nodded, relief sweeping me as my neck was unchained and I could slump out of the Sunlight. 'I would expect nothing less.'

Eli gave me a wink as he undid my wrists. 'I found your cart.'

'Hmm?'

'The flying cart,' he said. 'With the feather on the side.'

I smiled, a blister on my lips cracking. 'Oh. I call it a Matty.'

'Matty,' Eli repeated with satisfaction. 'It's beautiful. I couldn't figure out how it works. But I showed it to Sett and she believes you. She was very impressed. She makes things too.' Eli helped me to my feet, clapping me on the shoulder. 'If you really are Meshua, you came at the right time.'

Sett reached into the torture box.

I expected a blade, but she came out with a crystal cup and a Wisp. She cooled the drink and then removed a fistful of green knuckleberries.

'Shaman Eli say you like these,' Sett said. 'Eat. Drink. You show us flying and prove you are who you say.'

I took the water without her having to ask twice and gulped it all down. The single Wisp dissolved inside felt like a full abb after all this, and my insides thundered with satisfaction.

I wiped my mouth, the back of my hand tingling with relief.

'I can't anymore,' I said. 'Fly.'

Lop poked Eli on the shoulder and gave him a told-you-so kind of look.

'Why you no can fly?' Sett asked. 'You say you is Meshua.'

'I said I was Micah.' I shrugged. 'But I need a Noble tear for the invention to work. I don't have any left.'

'Noble.' Sett touched a finger under her eye, a question in her expression. 'Tear?'

'Yes,' I said, heart in my throat. 'Can you get me one?'

Sett paused and then let out a dark laugh.

'Maybe you is belonging in Langria, bird.'

Chapter Fourteen

'It looks empty out there,' I said.

'Is always looking empty.'

'Because of what's happening where I came from? Did the soldiers leave to go join the Khat and the rest of his armies?'

'Many, yes. But that is being new. Is always looking empty because the Asham are no fools.' Sett paused, considering her words. 'They is fools, but they fools who is being trained in war.'

I'd picked up that Asham was the Langrian word for Noble.

I was happy to adjust.

'How many Asham are usually out there?' I asked.

'Ten of five. Ten of six. Now are only four of one.'

'Really?'

I scanned the dunes and trenches, looking for any signs of life. I couldn't make out so much as a single sandviper. The wind was unimpeded as it swept across the rocky trenches and high dunes, making white sand tumble across the craggy landscape.

Sett and I had come here by a series of long tunnels, all naturally lit by Adaam Grass. I wished so badly that Shilah was here by my side. Even if she was falling for Cam, she would always be my partner in things like this.

The walk underground had taken about half an hour, and the Sun felt scorching after my being protected by such velvety darkness. Nasty heat now burrowed into the top of my head as I studied the lands at the South edge of the Great Divide.

Sett told me that this was where the bulk of the battles took place.

The Dagon.

Here the terrain finally showed a bit of mercy, but the warriors did not. The plains angled downwards, the only spot into the valley not cluttered with massive, blade-sharp rock faces, and so naturally it had become the site of most of the clashes. The sands and rocks in the Dagon looked peaceful and serene at the moment, but Sett had assured me those plains had been witness to more death than anywhere in the entire Khatdom, including the Southern Cliff of David's Fall. Sett told me that if I had a big shovel and dug deep enough, I'd find enough bones to build a bridge across the Singe.

I took in more of the planes, readjusting the Farsight over my face.

Sett's invention, the Farsight, was amazing, granting my eyes a temporary vision that was almost unfair. I could see everything so closely through the lens. If I'd had one of these back home, I could have looked out from the top plateau and been able to see inside of the Khat's tent.

Sett had come from a long line of inventors. The Melekah – the leaders of Langria – were expected to be the most creative members of their society. Even though Langria was constantly at war, the free Jadans saw greater power in the mind than the fist. Only the most imaginative minds in Langria stayed in positions of power. Some Melekah chose the art of tactics, and some chose music and sculpting; but most of the time the leaders fell into a life of tinkering. The Farsight was one of Sett's mother's designs, allowing the user to see much further and more clearly than normal, using a system of mirrors and refracted glass. It was against inventions such as these that the Khat's armies had been losing for the last eight centuries.

Sett put her hand on the side of the Farsight and gently guided my vision.

We were standing on the place Sett translated as the Ridge, towards the middle of the Great Divide. The bulk of Langria was at our backs, with all sorts of terrain and warriors protecting the rest of the distance.

'One Asham face painted like rock,' Sett told me.

It took me a moment to pick out what she was referring to, but I found one rock with cracks in the shape of ears. There was a flash of white, which I processed as the blinking of eyes. The outline of the enemy face took shape, painted to look like the rest of the rock. He was peeking out from behind a clump of other large stones, and besides the single blink, the enemy remained completely still.

'Wow,' I gasped. 'I would never have—'

Sett nudged the Farsight, dragging my view to the left. My attention was brought to the side of a boulder, which led into a channel between two cliff faces.

'See blade?' she asked.

I had to focus, but this target was more obvious. At waist height hung a slice of silver that didn't fit with the surroundings.

'Yes,' I said.

'Asham hiding there behind rock. And here too.'

She moved the Farsight again, this time further into the Dagon, towards the dunes. I still couldn't understand how she could spot the enemies without the Farsight. My view settled on a trench in the land, long and curvy and black, big enough to hide a caravan cart.

'Two in hole,' Sett said.

'I don't see them.'

'Don't look bodies inside. Look Meesh-Dahm above.'

'Meesh. Dahm?'

'Yes. Is . . .'

Her pause was long, but again she seemed unhurried.

'Colourness. Aliveness. Blood Spirit.' Her words were powerful and clear, but she didn't seem satisfied with any of her choices.

'Energy,' she finally said, sounding somewhat satisfied.

I paused. 'How can I see their energy?'

Sett tilted the Farsight lens up just a nudge.

'Out there in Dagon, Sun is all-place, is right? Eats through air no problems.'

'Sure.'

'And Sun is being evil. Sun is tainting all air we breathe.'

'Yes.'

'Meesh-Dahm fight Sun. Lots of Meesh-Dahm in Cold, and two Asham down there just be drinking Cold. Look above trench. Air is not so evil, see?'

I squinted hard, trying to make out what she could possibly mean. I held my breath to keep the Farsight from shaking. For quite a while nothing jumped out. The cut in the land looked like any other, the air above it just as ordinary.

And then I saw it.

The difference was so small that I never would have thought to search for such a thing. But now that Sett had pointed it out, I couldn't believe I'd never thought to look for such a reaction before. The Inventor in me hung his head, embarrassed.

There was a stillness above the trench.

The air was at peace.

The phenomenon was happening only in two spots, and the calm streaks were situated a few paces away from each other. The negation of the effect between the spots only made the sensation itself more apparent.

Intense heat rose from the sands, visibly making its way into the sky to be with its maker, Sun. I'd grown used to such a basic thing, as it was the nature of heat itself, rising heaviest in the places where there was nothing to get in its way: like in the empty dunes, or along stretches of black stone. The watery effect reminded me of an artist with too much paint on the brush, dragging a stroke from the ground upwards. But in the case of these two spots above the trench, it looked like the brush had two gaps in its bristles. Now that I knew what to look for, the absence of the heat was a complete giveaway that something was different within the shadows below. Sett was right; two Asham must have been using Cold down there for the heat to be missing in such a way.

'I see it,' I said. 'That's incredible. How did you figure that out?'

'Was needed.'

And that's all she said about the matter.

My mind stretched around its own corners, deciding what such an effect could mean in regards to Cold. And what it might inspire in any of my future inventions. I'd already been working hard to keep my focus – I'd been itching like mad to see the insides of the Farsight – and this new discovery only made my fingers more frantic.

'Now pick Asham,' she said.

Sett's face was severe and serious, and I was in complete awe. She was like a hero out of the old stories Shilah and I used to tell in Leroi's tinkershop. Not only was this woman confident and strong, but she had a special kind of mind.

She was the Inventor I'd been waiting my whole life to meet.

'Pick Asham for what?' I asked.

'For tear. Which one you want us steal?'

'I guess the Asham with the painted face would probably be the easiest. He's closest, and he's alone.'

Sett nodded and then pulled out two other contraptions from her pocket. The devices were boxy and sleek. The face of each was made of Glassland Silver, which was incredibly rare and valuable. It was the only kind of glass that could bend. Sett's invention had one lever protruding near her thumb and one rising near her pinky. Sett quickly fit her palms through the straps on the back, pulling them tight.

'What are those?' I asked.

She pushed the lever by her thumb. A black cap slid over the glass, blocking the shine. When she let the lever loose, the cap snapped off, revealing the shiny surface once again.

'For talk,' she explained. 'Over distance.'

She clipped the thumb lever on and off in rhythm. Then she used her pinky, which made the glass dent like a bowl. Angling her palm to catch some Sun, she reflecting it to the ground near my feet. The light was in a single tiny spot, burning bright and focused.

'Wow,' I said. 'Genius. What are they called?'

She answered something throaty and short.

I nodded, pretending to understand.

I wanted to know everything. I wanted to learn the entire history of Langria; to scour over every ancient stone in every hidden chamber, to see all the inventions and art that the Langrians had crafted over eight hundred years of free thinking. But I couldn't. There was no time. Here I was in the greatest kept secret in the entire World Cried, a place full of wonder that was begging to be explored, and I had to leave as fast as possible.

Shilah needed me.

Or maybe I needed her.

Even if Shilah kept finding ways to delay the Second Fall,

digging up every piece of Desert that the Khat's spies planted, the Asham armies wouldn't rest until every Jadan inside was dead. They'd burn the entire Flock by hand if it came to that. I was old enough to know that trouble wasn't just going to slink away, head hung in defeat.

I had to get back.

And I had to bring a miracle.

Sett angled the light into the Dagon, clicking the levers and going through a flurry of signals. The light was less focused after having travelled all that way, and it had expanded to the size of a ripe Khatmelon.

I was aware that Sett was rather busy, but for some reason a question burned out off my lips before I could stop it.

'What's the Langrian word for Khatmelon?' I asked.

'What is Khatmelon? I do not know this word. We give the ruiner of world no name tribute here.'

'Little red fruit with green spots.' I approximated the size with my hands. 'About this – never mind.'

Moving only her wrist, Sett dragged the spot of light across the distant stones. It shot over to where the painted face was hiding. She circled his face with enough distance that the Asham seemed completely unaware of his being spotted.

Three Jadan women appeared out of nowhere. They moved so fast I could barely believe they weren't a mirage. Firing across the rocks like whips, they made the Five seem as slow as crystallized honey. The women wore black clothing, and their skin was dark as night, refusing to glisten in the harsh Sunlight.

'On skin is called "Chossek" powder,' Sett said, reading my mind. 'Mix of ash and Wisp and Dybbuk grease. Hard to see.'

'They're like shadows.'

Sett shook her head with a coy smirk. 'Shadows common. Everything have shadow,' Sett said. 'Sinniah more special than shadows.'

'That's Sinniah out there?'

Sett nodded, dragging two fingers down her cheek. I was taken aback to see the forbidden gesture made by someone who'd never had reason to abandon it.

I returned to the Farsight, frantically trying to follow the Jadan warriors across the expanse of Dagon. I was just able to make out their long spears.

'Aren't you worried?' I asked, lump in my throat.

Sett laughed deeply. 'More worry if Sinniah lost taste for glory.'

I twisted the knob on top of the Farsight, bringing the view wider. Sinniah and her two warrior women approached the Asham from the rear. The kept low as they slunk across the rocks, spears above their heads poised to strike. They reminded me of Zizi, but with their Stingers still attached. Rope was coiled on each of their hips. I recognized Sinniah as the warrior in front; mostly from the ferocity in her expression. She signalled to the other two women with a twist of her closed fist, and at once the two women flipped their spears around to the blunt side. They closed in on the waiting Asham, flanking from the sides. Sinniah approached from the top.

'So beautiful,' Sett said. 'I being luckiest Jadan in Langria.'

I sucked in a breath as the three warriors closed in. Scanning the nearby plains for any sign of another enemy, I found only stillness.

Sinniah crept to the top of the rock. The Asham face below her didn't show any signs of suspicion. Sinniah raised her spear and then thrust down with the butt end. The strike landed with incredible precision right in the middle of the Asham's skull.

The enemy crumbled.

Without hesitation, the other warriors were at his side. They took the rope off their hips and began binding the Asham's ankles. They wrenched his arms behind his back and bound him at the wrists. Moving without error, it was like their every motion had been practised a thousand times. Sinniah remained on top of the rock, crouched low and swivelling her neck from side to side. She kept the pointed end of the spear out this time, guiding her vision. I noticed a lever on the shaft that she kept her thumb over.

'It's not just a spear is it?' I asked.

Sinniah pocketed her mirror contraptions and shook her head. 'Spring tight inside. End of spear open up and shoot poison arrow, Asham never have chance.'

'Incredible,' I said, smirking.

'You are maker too,' Sett said with a smile. 'We be learning from each other. Come now. Sinniah taking Asham to my chamber.'

Sett motioned back towards Langria. The series of tunnels would be dark and cool, but I wasn't quite ready to get back underground.

I still had to ask the question.

I'd been so frantic about getting the tear that I'd pushed aside the bigger issue. Getting back to my friends didn't mean we'd win. It felt like the entire World Cried depended on Sett's answer to this question – at the very least the entire Flock depended on the answer – and until now I'd been too nervous to bring it up. I didn't know what I'd do if she said no.

'Sett,' I said gently.

She gave me a slow nod.

I took a deep breath. My voice came out quiet and weak. 'Can I have a Frost to bring back with me?'

Sett paused.

I tried not to shake with anticipation.

She cocked her head, her eyebrows furrowed.

'What is Frost?'

I choked out a nervous laugh.

'The biggest Cold,' I said, using my hands to approximate

the size. Then I drew the three-line symbol against my chest, the lines that glowed at the core of every Frost. 'You do have Frosts here, right? The Cold with the most . . .' I paused, trying to recall the words correctly. 'Meesh-Dahm.'

'Ah,' Sett nodded, tracing the symbol. 'Yes. Crier Tear. Is called "Khol" in our tongue.'

'Khol,' I said, starting to get excited. 'Yes. I need a Khol to make my other machine work. And I can teach you its secret if you let me have one Khol.'

Sett gave me a sad look. 'We have Khol once.'

I swallowed hard, hoping that her meaning was lost in translation.

'What do you mean, had one *once*?'

'At beginning,' Sett said. 'Khol making Langria what is.'

The air felt thick, making it difficult to speak.

'You don't have any more?'

'Khol only fall in Paphos now,' she said with a dismissive shake of her head.

A part of me shattered and died.

All of a sudden the Sun was a hundred times hotter.

The land under my feet became sharp and uneven.

I began to sweat.

'I don't understand,' I said, gesturing wildly back at the green valley. At the river running through the bottom of Langria. At all the chambers and buildings and tunnels and all the mysteries of this legendary place. 'But this is Langria. This is supposed to be the answer to everything. The Crier still gives you Cold here. Don't you have a Cry Patch? I don't understand!'

Sett put a hand on my shoulder.

'I sorry,' she said. 'We have no Khol.'

Fiery tears formed at the corners of my eyes.

It felt like I just doomed my entire Flock. Shilah, Cam, Split, the Five: none of them stood a chance.

I'd failed.

'Come,' Sett said 'Is time.'

'Time for what?'

'If you Meshua,' she said. 'If you wanting to help Jadans. Is time you learning real history of our people.'

Chapter Fifteen

Langria was not what I'd expected.

This was supposed to be the place full of forests and fruit and freedom songs. A land where I might dig my hands into rich soil and come away with a feeling of abundance. It was supposed to be blanketed by a sky where love reigned supreme, making Sun seem insignificant, where Jadan runaways would be welcomed with opened arms and abundant Cold.

Yet Langria was anything but paradise.

This was a place of despair.

On the way back, Sett had taken me on a detour out of the tunnels so I could better understand these lands. We climbed crude stairs by light of her lantern for what felt like an eternity, exiting onto a shelf of rock that she called Pass of Arron. The pass let out on the Southern side of the valley, looking North. The position was high and unobstructed, which allowed us a view of most of Langria.

Langria was much smaller than I initially had gathered looking at it from above. The occupied part consisted mostly of hooded buildings, dilapidated carvings, and scattered patches of green, all tucked against the bottom of the lowest portion of the Great Divide. The green sections were rather small and shy, huddling close to the river. There were still plenty of fruit trees and red flowers in the gardens, all being tended to by Jadans wearing wide-brimmed hats, but even hidden in shadow, I could see the worry on their faces. They had buckets of Cold at their feet, but the buckets were barely filled halfway, the rations made up entirely of Wisps.

I searched around the rest of the Divide, finding that the amount of green life trailed off severely in each direction. Langria existed in a small, protected section of the Divide, where the river bent out from the mountainous cliff faces and then returned back under.

Above the city were sections of rock that had dried into sections, like they had once held gardens that could no longer be sustained. The dead portion of the valley was much larger than the alive portion, and it gave the appearance that Langria had been shrinking into itself, dying for a long time.

Along the patches of emptiness, the new deadlands, warriors continued to hone their skills. They struggled with swords and bows, practising with fury, their wiry muscles flexing and moving. Their skin wasn't as dark as the Jadans back home, but they wore the same familiar pain I saw my whole life.

Hunger and loss.

Watching the warriors, grief overtook my heart. Ellia and Ellcia had been on to something when they said Langria wasn't real.

Sett handed me the Farsight.

'What happened here?' I asked, pointing to all the dead land leading down to Langria. 'It looks like there should be more. More gardens, more life.'

'Spy happen.'

'Hmm?'

'Langria proud nation. A hundred of eight years freedom. Langria survive on mostly what is "Wisp" in the common tongue, and yet we survive. Khat no break us. And then ten year ago be coming a spy here. Spy put Desert in ground, and many of us dead. We still get Wisp from above, but many tree go black. River angry.'

I felt my mouth go dry. 'Ten years ago, you said?'

Sett nodded.

'The spy came through the Coldmarch,' I said. 'Didn't they? They Khat was able to sneak someone in disguised as a runaway. That's why the Coldmarch was shut down.'

Sett said nothing, only looking out on her domain with sadness.

'I—'

'Khat no win through war,' she said. 'Had to deceive.'

Rage grew in my chest. I imagined that until recently the whole valley was filled with lush plants. With children laughing and playing games on the shore of the river where they could jump right in.

But because of a betrayal, the land had been stripped down to its bones. It had been made feeble and frail.

'Where did the spy plant the Desert?' I asked.

'No one be knowing exactly,' she said. 'Some be saying she only planting half of Desert, because half her heart still for Jadankind.'

My mind began spinning as fast as it ever had, thinking about my experiments with the Desert. Just like with the Frost – or Khol – I hadn't been able to break the Desert in any way. It resisted both hammer and blade and water. I wondered how this spy could have found its weakness and broken it in half.

'But you still get Cold here?' I asked. 'You still have a Cry Patch?'

Sett gestured to the top of the Divide, the North side, where I had touched down. The place where the sands were reddish and springy.

'Yes,' she said. 'We still be getting Wisps, but not near as many as before. Langria be dying since Desert.'

I looked through the Farsight, glancing up to the top of the Divide.

'Tell me everything,' I said.

'Yes,' she said. 'I have Shaman Eli give story in tongue of enemy. I need you understand. We go in moment, for now you look at Khol-flowers.'

'Khol-flowers?'

'Spirit of Jadan people,' Sett said, gesturing for me to use the Farsight.

I put it to my eyes and once again she guided my vision. I was swept from a scene where two Jadan women were practising with spears, across the thin river, to a spot near what might be a Cry Temple. The building was made of ironstone, and looked strong enough to withstand an attack from any army. A giant Opened Eye was carved into the top of the entrance.

'Inside the building?' I asked.

'No.'

Sett pushed the Farsight down just a nudge, setting me in front of the temple.

There was a small garden.

And it was growing a single kind of flower.

One I recognized instantly.

'Alder,' I said. 'They're alder flowers.'

'In tongue of enemy yes, alder.'

I felt like my legs were starting to give. Things were starting to fall into place, and memories of the Coldmarch came rushing back.

The garden was surrounded by a ring of gifts. There were flowers and flutes and woodcarvings just to name a few. The soil in which the flowers sat was the most alive that I'd ever seen, darker than my skin.

'That's why alder is the sign of the Coldmarch,' I said.

'Yes. And used to grow much larger patch than that, back before spy and Desert. Spirit of Jadan people cling final breath.'

Three Jadan men kneeled at the edge of the garden, planting Wisps into the soil.

'Are they trying to grow them back?' I asked. 'Those men?'

'No. Nothing really help after Desert. They pay tribute to Adaam.'

'Adaam, like the Adaam Grass?'

'Yes. You is learning all.'

Three large chimes rang through Langria and all the fighting stopped at once. The skirmishing Jadans threw down their weapons and gave one another small gestures of respect. Some grabbed wrists. Some hugged. Some drew two fingers down their cheeks.

Then they began to disappear.

In a matter of moments almost all of the barren lands were emptied.

'Where'd they go?' I asked.

'Tunnels. Not enough Cold anymore to be in Sun all time, so have to strength in darkness. Then training under ground. You come now.'

I took one last look at the alder flowers and gave the Farsight back to Sett. We retreated into the tunnels and took a long staircase back down.

'Most Langria is tunnels,' Sett said. 'Free Jadans very good at make tunnels.'

I nodded, thinking about all the stretches of Coldmarch that had involved tunnels. We took the stairs in silence for a while and then emptied into a long chamber, the ceiling so low that we had to hunch. I couldn't make out her expression from the dim light of the Adaam grass, but I could tell that Sett had a strange energy about her. I kept a safe distance and used the quiet to think.

Why did Langria still have a Cold patch, when the rest of the world dried up?

Why did the Desert destroy only *some* of Langria?

How much more time could my friends hold out?

The tunnel eventually led us to an open chamber, and my head felt like it might burst. My fingers itched to tinker, but that was just normal.

We stood in the doorway to the room, watching people crowded around a well. They were dropping buckets into a hole. As they pulled them back up they chanted a song in unison, clapping their tired hands. They looked exhausted, pushed right up to their limits.

Still they sang.

The melody was simple, yet intoxicating. It reminded me of Moussa, my other closest friend while growing up in the barracks. He loved music almost as much as I loved inventing, and we'd secretly share any scraps of melodies overheard on the streets. He was the best singer in the barracks. I hadn't seen him since he'd been tortured by the Vicaress, forced to give information on my whereabouts. I had no idea if he was still alive, or if he was now singing in the black. My chest squeezed. I wanted to pause and listen to the new song, but Sett nodded for me to follow her.

'Tell me about Second Fall,' Sett said.

I filled her in on everything left to tell as we passed through the tunnels. Sett had to hunch as we walked, as she was nearly a head taller than me, and her gray hair brushed the ceiling. The tunnel walls were smooth and precise, but I still felt like we were being watched.

She was patient as I finished telling about the Desert they'd buried, waiting to speak until the end.

'Yes,' she finally said. 'They try planting Desert in Dagon all time. We find lots of Desert here too.'

'Damn them.'

Sett laughed. 'Yes. Also, how you learn fly? Why Asham let you become Maker in Paphos? Isn't they making you slave in Paphos?'

'Not all Asham are bad. One of my closest friends is—'

Sett spat to the side. 'All Asham poison.'

'I wouldn't be alive if not for *this* Asham. His name is Camlish and he's risked his life for me many times. He's actually helping us inside the city, going against his own people.'

Sett huffed. 'Trust me. All Asham poison. Come from first Khat.'

We didn't speak for a while after that.

At last we stopped in front of a chamber where Sinniah and the warriors were waiting. The Asham was crumpled on the floor in front of them. I almost couldn't make the warriors out, since the room was dark and they were still covered in Chossek powder. Shaman Eli and Lop were holding hands in the corner, whispering quietly.

Sett touched two fingers to her lips and then pressed them towards Sinniah. Sinniah returned the gesture, and then they began speaking rapidly in Langrian. This exchange didn't have the cadence of an argument, although the tone was cautious, especially on Sinniah's end.

Sinniah bowed.

Sett gestured to Shaman Eli, who gave Lop a kiss on the cheek and then followed us out into the tunnel.

'Nice pick,' Eli said, gesturing back to the chamber. 'This Noble looks like he's got lots of tears.'

'What did they say?' I asked him under my breath, keeping a bit of distance back from Sett. This was not hard, as she moved almost as swiftly as Sinniah.

Shaman Eli shook his head. 'Don't worry. It's good things. They trust you for now.'

I raised an eyebrow. 'For now?'

Eli shrugged, and I noticed that thankfully Zizi was nowhere to be seen. 'There are some words that don't translate.'

'Fair enough. Good to see you, by the way.'

Eli clapped me on the shoulder. 'You going to teach me how to fly, Meshua? I think it will very much impress Lop if I fly.'

I smiled, trying to keep up with Sett's pace. 'If I can get back to my friends again, I'll teach you everything you want to know. Also, I'm not Meshua.'

Eli winked. 'Of course not. You just fly around wherever you want and make Cold. Regular Jadan through and through.'

I shook my head, but I had nothing with which to refute him.

'I learned all about Meshua from Split the Pedlar,' he said. 'Split was my Shepherd for the second leg of the Coldmarch.'

'That's how I know your name!' I said. 'From Split. He mentioned you.'

Eli put his hand over his chest. 'You've heard of me before? That will very much impress Lop. Can I tell her this?'

I shrugged. 'I don't mind. But just don't call me Mesh—'

I stopped myself as Sett had led us to a huge cavern.

Immediately I knew this place was important. There were oil lanterns glowing everywhere, illuminating things far better than Adaam Grass could have. The ceiling was high and held up with stone arches, all carved with Jadan faces. Each face had a single braid detailed into the stone.

There was a clear path through the cavern on which to walk, while the rest of the floor was adorned in small, detailed scenes from Jadan history. Some pictures were done with paint, some with coloured stones, but all of them were painstakingly detailed. They depicted stars and animals and forests. More than anything else there were scenes of battle.

In the middle of the chamber stood a large cabinet that had

its doors wide open. In the centre, suspended on a bar of steel, was a huge scroll that must have weighed the same as a small child. The top of the scroll was adorned with an Opened Eye cap that kept the whole scroll tight, and a large necklace rested against the body, hanging on a rope of gold. The dangling pendant was shaped like the three lines – two upright, one lying across their tops – that shone in the centre of a Khol.

The place was a giant dome, perfectly round, split in half by a red alder line. One side of the room held hundreds of weapons, pinned to the walls on stands and nails. There were axes and bows and daggers; but there were also weapons that I didn't recognize. Things with springs and gears that threatened to cut a hole through any besieging army.

All of the weapons had a tiny scroll underneath, resting on a protruding dowel. The size of the scrolls varied from a single loop to the size of my wrist.

The other side of the room had hundreds of leaves preserved between sheets of glass. The leaves sat on shelves with plaques underneath. The leaves varied greatly as well, in shape, colour and size.

A large word had been painted on top of each side of the room, written in what had to be Langrian.

'What do they say?' I asked Eli, pointing to the headings.

He first gestured to the weapons wall. 'To Kill.'

Then he pointed to the leaf wall. 'To Live.'

'Like in Coldmarch tunnels under Mama Jana's' – "Lost" and "Saved."'

'Mama Jana!' Eli exclaimed. 'I remember her having great fingernails.'

I gave a small laugh, awed by the room. 'Yes, she did.'

'Is she still alive?'

I paused, swallowing hard. 'I hope so.'

Sett said something long and potent in Langrian, pointing to the weapons.

'The weapons are of fallen warriors,' Eli relayed. 'When a Langrian is killed in battle we put the weapon to rest for at least seven days. It is believed that if the weapon is used again quickly, the original warrior's spirit might have to wait in the black. Many children choose to use the weapons of their ancestors when they are of age. The scrolls beneath have all the great deeds and honours that different weapons have acquired in their lifetime.'

Sett swung her arm and gestured to the leaves.

Eli straightened up, puffing out his chest with pride. 'But not all Langrians are warriors. This other wall is dedicated to life. Whenever a new garden is successfully formed, the grower gets to put a leaf from their harvest on the wall. There used to be new gardens all the time, back before the spy maimed our land. Now there are hardly any new gardens. But guess who has gotten to put three leafs on the wall in the last year alone?'

I raised an eyebrow. 'Is that why they call you Shaman Eli?'

Eli smiled widely. He was missing a few teeth in the back and one in the front, but otherwise he had pink and healthy gums.

Sett gestured to the large scroll in the centre of the room. 'Sit together. Here.'

The three of us settled in front of the shrine.

'Big history written in scroll,' Sett said. 'I give you only small history as you is being in hurry to get back friends.'

'Thank you,' I said.

Then Sett told me of Langria, pausing enough between sentences so Eli could translate.

'The first thing you must know about is Adaam and Vivus. They were two young boys from Paphos, neighbours, growing up together before the Great Drought. They used to run, play and explore the woods together when they were very young.

Adaam liked music and singing; he was a sweet boy. Vivus did not like these things. He preferred cruelty and power. As the years progressed they drifted apart. Adaam watched Vivus begin to do more and more terrible things. Stealing. Hurting those weaker than him. Forcing the young girls to try things they did not want to try. Adaam once stumbled across Vivus skinning a lamb alive in the woods behind their houses, boilweed shoved in the poor creature's mouth to keep it from bleating. The death was not for food or ritual, and afterwards Vivus tossed the dead lamb into the forest to rot. Adaam knew Vivus just wanted to watch the creature suffer. Adaam saw it all from the beginning.

'Unfortunately Vivus found his way into a position of power. He became a soldier of the King's law and lied his way up in status. He accused many innocents of terrible crimes. There was never any proof of course, but Vivus would say they were performing rituals to Sun and practising unholy things with fire. The King of Paphos trusted Vivus, and so he handed out punishment accordingly, which meant lashings and death. The people of Paphos began to fear Vivus greatly and trembled at the sound of his name.

'Adaam on the other hand had become a simple singer, with no power except that of his voice, and so he watched helpless and afraid as Vivus rose through the ranks. When every one of the King's descendants died mysterious deaths, followed by the King himself – who was found hanging on the end of a rope – no one dared question Vivus. And since there was no one else to challenge him, Vivus took the throne. He reigned for a while with an iron fist, but Vivus did not stay in Paphos. He had grander aspirations. He wanted to be the first King of every land, and left with a small group of close advisors to travel the World Cried and understand what was out there. Vivus left one of his closest generals in power in Paphos, a woman nearly as terrible as himself, and set out.

'A year or so later after Vivus left,' Sett and then Eli continued, 'is when the world began to die. City by city the Patches became barren and the land heated to terrible temperatures. Forests died in flashes of ash and fire. Rivers began to boil. Grass was overtaken by sand and rock. And many, many died. Hundreds of thousands perished in terror and anguish, with refugees flooding Paphos, where Cold still fell. Vivus eventually returned with his Gospels, calling himself "The Khat". He claimed to have the answers to why everything was dying and how to save it. And when Ziah fell, the world dropped to its knees. Every Jadan – the word just meant people back then – had to accept a life in chains if they wanted to live. They also had to give up their Khol. Since Khol were Meesh-Dahm in essence, kept on display in the Cry Temples for all to admire, the Khat made them illegal, and had his Priests and taskmasters bring them all to the Pyramid.

'But Adaam knew Vivus for what he was: a liar and a thief. He did not trust a word of what the Khat had to say. He figured the Khat must have found Evil in some corner of the world, and that he was responsible for all this death and chaos.

'And so Adaam gathered a group. A small group. Six families. Not to fight, but to run away and try and preserve the Jadan way of life. Adaam believed with his whole heart that there still must be somewhere in the world where Cold was still Cried. Before Adaam left, he sent word to Vivus that he had written an Anthem for him. One so beautiful that the slaves would sing it gladly throughout all the ages of his rule. Vivus was happy to accept, and he sent for his old friend to give a grand performance of this masterpiece. But while the Pyramid was busy setting everything up, Adaam found a Khol and stole it, sneaking away into the night. Then he took the very first Flock and left the city. Off to find a new pasture in a dead world.'

I finally remembered to breathe.

Eli tried to parallel Sett's emotion, but his tone paled in comparison.

'Adaam could have gone in any direction, but chose to go North. I don't know if you know this, but Cold almost always falls at an angle, from North to South.'

I nodded. The Patch Jadans had made mention of this characteristic before, telling me the best technique was to dig at an angle to find the existing holes. I was too young to have worked in the Patches, so I had never experienced it myself.

'So Adaam went North and the pass was hard. The Flock barely had enough food and Cold to get by, but they were resilient. And they had the wind of belief at their backs. They passed the husks of once-great cities, now burned to ash and rubble. For weeks they travelled by starlight, under a sky that used to bless the whole land, but now only blessed a tyrant and a liar.

'Two children died on the first Coldmarch. The familes gave them a proper burial and then had to move on. The terrain was terrible; they found no Cold anywhere. Soon they were all on the brink of death. They pushed North as far as they could go, but eventually they began to run low on food and Cold. Dozens of vultures circled them, for there were still birds then. The birds too were desperate, clinging to a life without Cold. Adaam and the Flock desperately pressed on, the Khol their only source of hope, until they ran into a massive split in the land: the place they decreed to be the 'Great Divide'. The Flock took refuge in the Great Divide to try and get away from the Sun. For days they pushed through the nightmare terrain, but things were getting desperate.

'Then one night at Sunset Adaam set out alone. The Flock was all but dead. They had no food or Cold left, only the

Khol. Adaam kept pushing North, taking the Khol with him, tears in his eyes for his people. He called out to the Crier, begging for a sign, for anything. Eventually he came to a boiling river, and his heart was shattered. He couldn't go any further and he was to the point of death. And so he dropped to his knees and wept.

'He took out the Khol and said his final prayer.' Sett paused, switching to the common tongue. 'I believe you be knowing it, Micah.'

'*Shemma hares lahyim criyah Meshua ris yim slochim,*' I said.

It was hard to speak. I was shocked, finally understanding the history of the words.

Sett nodded and then continued the story.

'And then Adaam pressed the Khol against his face and in that moment the Crier spoke. The spirit of the Crier swept inside him, bringing Meesh-Dahm—' Eli stopped translating. 'Meesh-Dahm is like . . .'

'Energy,' I said.

'Yes,' Eli exclaimed. 'How'd you know that?'

My heart pounded. I felt like a part of me had always known this story. The story, but not the ending. Everything inside of me clenched with awe and anticipation.

'What happened?' I asked.

'The Crier told Adaam to make Langria. He said Adaam could *make* Cold fall. Our Creator just needed to know where to Cry. And so Adaam put the Khol in the ground by the river and that night—'

I leapt to my feet, opening my arms wide. My chest felt like it was about to burst from revelation.

'HE PUT IT IN THE GROUND!' I shouted.

Sett already had a dagger out. 'What?'

I began to dance. I couldn't keep still. I did the same dance my father used to do. It made me smile so wide my cheeks could have smashed through the walls of the cavern.

'HE PUT IT IN THE GROUND!' I shouted, hopping from foot to foot. 'He put it in the ground. He put it in the ground.'

'Yes,' Sett said. 'He put in ground. Now hush and be still, I finish story.'

I threw my head back and howled with delight. I could feel the Crier in me too. This was my moment. This was what my whole life was leading up to. The Coldmaker. The Flock. The Matty. It was all bringing me here, to this spot, to this story, so all the pieces could finally fall into place.

Sinniah and her warriors leapt into the cavern with their spears out. Sett waved them back.

'Tell me, Micah,' Sett said. 'What you be doing?'

I leaned over to catch my breath, putting a hand over my chest. My heart was thumping so loud that any of my Ancestors waiting in the black would be able to hear my joy.

I had found the message.

I knew how to save the World Cried.

'Let me guess,' I said, finding it hard to speak, as my blood was rushing. 'That night, Cold began to fall on top of the Divide. And the river cooled because the land cooled, and so Adaam was able to swim across safely. With the last of his strength he climbed the mountain, to the North side, and found a new Cry Patch. The Flock survived and called it a miracle and together they started Langria!'

Sett looked confused.

Eli translated my words. It was surreal to hear my message take on the form of such old and powerful sounds. I suddenly felt connected to these people. They were my family too. We were all one Flock.

And I'd save them all.

I ached for Shilah and Cam to be at my side. To share this discovery.

'Yes,' Sett said slowly. 'So you *do* be knowing story?'

I laughed, continuing to dance. My elation rang through the

chamber, and I could hear a bright future reverberating off every weapon and every leaf on the wall. A new age rang with my laughter.

'They're seeds,' I said, aghast that I was finally speaking the answer after all this time. 'Khol. They're seeds for Cry Patches! They let the Crier know where to cry. They're seeds!'

'Slow down,' Sett says. 'I want understand.'

Everything started falling into place.

Answers to all the ancient mysteries rained down into my mind from all sides.

Adaam planted the Khol down in the valley.

Which made the land come alive.

And a new Cry Patch was formed.

Langria got Cold on the North side, up on the top of the Divide. It fell in the red sands up high, which meant that the Cold was probably headed towards the spot where the Khol was planted. But the rising land got in the way. The Cold struck the ground before it could reach down into the valley itself. It was also probably why they only got Wisps.

And it now made sense why the Khat continued to demand all the Khol come to him, under penalty of death. He must have known that Khol was the only way to fight Desert. To make new Cry Patches.

The seed idea also kept in line with all my experiments in the tubs.

The Desert took away life.

The Khol would restore it.

It was so simple I laughed; it was so beautiful I cried.

I started pacing the walkway, tears staining my cheeks. I was too excited to stand still. I remembered what Cam had said about the Crier, about feeling such powerful waves of love and connection that tears came into being.

If it was true, then the Crier was here.

He'd always been here.

'This is it,' I said. 'This is how we end the Great Drought. We plant Khol in the ground and it takes away the effect of the Desert. We put it in the ground, and Cold begins to fall again. Old Man Gum wasn't talking about Desert back then. He was talking about Frosts. Khol. THEY PUT IT IN THE GROUND!'

'Meshua,' Sett said. 'Too fast.'

I almost couldn't handle the emotions. I was seeing things in an entirely new light.

'Khol make new Cry Patches,' I said. 'They must be seeds. The Crier was giving us a way back all to Him all this time. And the stories about the Khol in the black bringing us home. It all makes sense!'

Sett sighed. 'Yes. This being thought of before. But no matter. Khol all destroyed. Is broken idea.'

It didn't bother me that my Idea wasn't the first of its kind. Even if they'd thought of it before, they hadn't been able to act on it.

But I could.

'The Khat has plenty of Khol in the Pyramid,' I said. 'I'd bet my life on it.'

'Is no matter,' Sett said, giving a sad shake of her head.

Then she began speaking rapid Langrian. Eli helped out.

'Sett says we'll never make there. Paphos has too many Noble – Asham. The numbers make it impossible. There are two hundred and eight Jadans in Langria. There are ten thousand Asham in Paphos.'

'No there aren't,' I said with a laugh.

Sett cocked her head.

'Most Asham have gone to the City of David's Fall. Thousands of them, with more arriving every day to watch. I bet the Pyramid is practically unguarded.'

'But City of David's Fall on way to Paphos,' Sett said. 'We be caught. We no be having numbers to fight through.'

'We don't need numbers,' I said. 'You said other spies have tried to plant Desert in Langria before, right?'

Sett nodded.

'Please tell me you still have them.'

'The spies?' Eli asked.

I shook my head. 'The Desert.'

Eli spat on the ground and then realized he'd hit one of the paintings. He bent down to wipe the moisture away, and Sinniah shot him an irritated look.

'Why would we keep that poison here?' Eli asked.

Sett sighed, letting her head fall. 'We have. I do keep Desert.'

I raised an eyebrow.

'So not to fall back in enemy hand,' Sett explained. 'I keep locked away.'

'How many of them do you have?' I asked.

'Eight.'

'Good,' I said. 'And Sett.'

'Yes?'

'You're an Inventor. I imagine you have created lots of weapons. Powerful weapons. And a tinkershop – a shop for making.'

Sett smiled, my plan starting to settle behind her eyes. 'Yes.'

'Show me.'

She motioned for me to follow.

As we exited the chamber, I pulled Eli aside. Zizi wasn't anywhere on his body, so I felt comfortable wrapping my arm around his shoulder.

Eli's face was frozen in shock, and I could tell he was having trouble processing the plan.

'I have one more question for you,' I said.

'Meshua,' he answered under his breath. 'You really are Meshua.'

'Actually that's what my question is about. What does Meshua actually mean? What's the translation in the common tongue?'

Eli's lips worked soundlessly as we trailed behind Sett and the warriors. Sett and Sinniah were conversing in rapid Langrian, keeping their voices low.

'Eli,' I said.

'Hmm?'

'What does it mean?'

'It's like . . . in the prophecies it means, "The split in the sky, through which Cold will once again be Cried, returning to the land and the Jadan people".' Eli paused, biting his bottom lip.

'That's quite a long translation for one simple word.'

'Oh, you want the literal translation?' he asked.

'Yes. If you know it.'

'It means "opening",' Eli tapped his lip. 'Or more precisely, it means "spout".'

And that's when I knew it was all real.

I laughed like never before, with tears running down my chin and neck. And just like with the dance, I realized it was my father's laugh.

And I could hear him laughing along.

Chapter Sixteen

The Langria tinkershop was the real paradise.

We'd had to go down quite a few tunnels and carved staircases to get here, as it was kept at a distance from the bulk of Langria. Sett said it was both for the noise and in case there were any accidents.

I could see why.

The whole place was alive with preparation. It was as large as the Coldmarch cave under Jadans' Rise, but this one wasn't mostly empty stone and sleeping space. Sett's tinkershop didn't have to worry about watchful Asham, or a sparseness of materials. It was uninhabited and served a singular purpose.

To create weapons of war.

When we arrived the place was in full swing. The sounds of tinkering filling the space, echoing with power and purpose. Clanging metals. Grinding wood. Squealing glass. There were ten or so Jadans working inside, so focused on their tasks that barely any of them noticed our arrival. A few wore boilweed strips over their mouths to protect them from heat and fumes. They presided over glass containers filled with bubbling concoctions, smouldering and grey, one swallow probably able to send even Slab Hagan to the black. Smiths pounded out weapons in smelting chambers, resulting smoke pouring up a series of small tunnels dug into the stone above. Bronze and iron weapons were being heated down and pounded sharp. There were spears and axes and arrowheads.

There were also small cages filled with animals. Skinkmanders hissed about behind bars of iron. Sobek lizards stuck to the sides of enclosures. Sandvipers slithered in the bottom of glass tubs, their tongues flickering through the holes in the top. One container was filled with water and enclosed a small population of slimy creatures that I recognized as Hotland Newts. I'd only ever seen the tadpole versions in person, and I hadn't imagined the adults would have so many fingers.

Along the edges of the room were dozens of Cold Bellows. Piles of Wisps waited in buckets beside them. It was nice to see that the Langrians used the same Bellows design that I did; the kind with the spin top and grating gears. It reminded me of the one I'd fixed for Mama Jana, making me feel less out of place.

Sett clapped her hands and called something out in Langrian.

All the tinkershop workers stopped at once, turning to Sett. The ones that weren't holding blazing hot metal or dangerous mixtures made the gesture of two fingers down the cheek. Everyone else bowed.

Sett pointed to me and said a few more things I couldn't understand. But from the reaction from the tinkershop workers, she might have been saying: 'Don't kill this stranger. He's with me.'

'This is called the Battle Room,' Eli whispered to me, looking a bit uncomfortable.

The workers started up again, although a few eyed me suspiciously; I got an especially nasty snarl from a broad-shouldered woman smelting an axe.

Sett gestured around the place. 'This being reason we hold off Asham for a hundred years of eight.'

'It's incredible,' I said. My fingers absently clutched the fabric of my shirt, flexing the bronze fingers Eli had given back. I wanted to grab tools and start tinkering, but I had to repress my instincts. I was a guest here.

'Tell me plan,' Sett said.

I glanced around the tinkershop, taking it all in. This would be more than enough. I'd already spotted hamsa wood and boilweed and plenty of metal. I hoped they had the waxy paper.

'Where did you get all of this?' I asked. 'It can't all be found in Langria?'

'Shepherds having once bring things with them,' Sett said. 'As gifts and tribute. Is enough for plan?'

'Yes,' I said. 'I hope.'

Eli smiled, pulling out a wad of some dried leaf and stuffing it under his lip. 'You have a lot of hope I think. This is probably a good trait in a saviour.'

'I'm not a saviour,' I said, although 'Spout' kept echoing in my head.

Eli shrugged, his eyes going soft. 'Well, could you be our saviour, please? Langria's had a few rough years and it's about time we had one.'

I felt a swell in my chest.

'I can try.'

Eli cracked his knuckles. 'Good. Because if I was the one to find the saviour, then I think Lop will be most impressed.'

I gestured towards Sinniah and her warriors, asking Sett: 'How's their tongue of the enemy?'

'Is enough,' Sinniah answered for herself.

I nodded, turning to the warriors behind us. 'We're going to need a lot more Asham tears, please. I need you and your warriors to bring back as many Asham as you can.'

Sett stepped in between us, moving faster than I'd ever seen. Her eyes were ablaze.

'Just because I say you no spy, you are no Melekah! You give no orders here, boy!'

Sett's voice was seething and the muscles in her neck were coiled tight.

I bowed my head, falling into my old slave stance. I grew terribly afraid and mortified.

'You're right,' I said. 'I'm sorry. I'm so sorry. I shouldn't have presumed—'

Sett took a step forward, bending down to look me in the eyes. Her teeth were bared and she looked like she might strike me.

I cowed, flinching into myself.

Sett growled something Langrian, loud enough for the rest of the Battle Room to hear. Her eyes were like diamonds and her words like steel.

The workers halted their tinkering.

There was a heavy pause.

And then Sinniah began cackling at my back, the other warriors following suit. Then the whole room was rippling with laughter. Sett sputtered for a moment and then joined in. Smiling wildly, she stepped away, running her hand through Sinniah's hair, whispering something into her ear. Then she grabbed Sinniah's hand and kissed her knuckles.

Sinniah's face flushed and in return she ran her hand through Sett's hair, which was much thinner and grey. Sinniah nodded to the warriors and the group took their leave.

I turned to Eli and whispered. 'What just happened?'

Sett gestured for me to come closer, her face still alight. But I saw something else in her face. I think there was some truth in her words. 'Just joke. Free Jadans being good with joke. Now come, tell me plan.'

'I'm sorry again—'

Sett waved me quiet. 'You bird. I wanted see if you show claws or lay egg.'

My cheeks steamed with embarrassment.

'Talons,' Lop said, stepping in. 'They're called "talons" in the common tongue. For birds.'

Lop flashed me a curious look. Eli stepped closer to her, putting his hand around her waist.

Sett nodded. 'Yes, is right.'

'So the plan,' I said. 'First we—'

I was cut off by a group of warriors storming the Battle Room. I thought it was a dark cloud at first, since they still all had Chossek powder covering their skin; it turned out to be a group of five men and woman. They were bloody and torn up, gasping for air, but still stood tall.

The older woman up front – who was shorter than the rest and completely bald – barked something in Langrian, holding two knuckles in triumph. She had eyes that could make a taskmaster drop his whip and run for the dunes.

The Battle Room cheered. Other new arrivals at the bald woman's back stormed into the room and went straight for a barrels full of arrows, loading up their slings. The bald woman gave Sett a respectful nod and asked something, her eyes flashing to me. Sett nodded and drew two fingers down her cheek. The short woman gave me a swift bow and disappeared into another tunnel, this one guarded over the entrance by a statue of a creature I didn't recognize. The animal had a fearsome face with triangle ears and a sleek body; sort of like one of the Khat's hounds if it had been stretched out.

'Rivvy and her sect have a group of Asham cornered,' Eli explained, still possessively clutching Lop. Zizi had returned to the grower's shoulder, although from where it had scuttled I couldn't say. 'They have taken two of their numbers already, and the others have been driven into a ravine where they can't climb out.'

'Yes,' Sett said. 'Is glory today. Come, Meshua, we talk in Clock Chamber.'

Sett maintained the saviour term with a bit of playfulness, which I much preferred to all the heaviness my Flock heaped upon the words. She led us down the same tunnel the short woman had disappeared, and I took in the animal statue as we passed.

'What is it?' I asked.

'Is called "Jaguar",' Sett explained, rubbing a fist against her chest. 'Is in my Meesh-Dahm.'

So that's a jaguar, I thought, wondering if Dunes actually knew what they looked like. Then I shot Eli a perplexed look as we swept down the smooth clay tunnel.

'Meesh-Dahm?' I asked him. 'But what do jaguars have to do with Cold?'

'The Jaguars disappeared after the Great Drought,' Eli explained. 'Along with hundreds of other animals. In Langria, we believe that the missing animals and plants will return when Cold returns. For now, the world is too hot, so they have retreated inside of us, in our Meesh-Dahm where there is Cold. We keep their spirits alive inside of ours.'

'How does Sett know that she has the Jaguar?' I whispered.

Eli thought about it for a second. 'Have you ever seen your mind?'

I shook my head. 'I don't think that's possible.'

'But you know you have one,' Eli said with a point of his finger.

'Yes, but that's also because everyone has one.'

'Yes, but you have an Inventor's mind. Not like everyone. Just like I have a grower's mind. And neither of us has seen those things inside of us, but we know they are there.'

I big my lower lip, following the logic. 'I guess.'

Eli shrugged. 'Sett has the spirit of the Jaguar inside of her, and it's where she gets patience and leadership.'

'So is Zizi in your Meesh-Dahm?' I asked.

Eli laughed, rubbing the barbless Stinger of the Scorpion.

I shuddered. I could almost feel the little thing crawling down my shirt.

'No way,' Eli said. 'Zizi is just my friend. I don't have any animals in my Meesh-Dahm. I have the Willow.'

'What's the Willow?'

'It was a beautiful tree that stood all along the banks of the Singe, back before the rivers began to boil. It had long branches and was thin and smooth, and it bent like a dancer in the wind. They called it the "Weeping Tree".'

I conjured up an image and felt a strange pang of longing, even though I'd never seen or heard of a Willow before. Something about Eli's description resonated.

'I hope I can see it one day,' I said.

Lop narrowed her eyes at me, finally speaking up. 'Are you really Meshua?'

'Of course he is,' Eli said. 'And don't forget who found him. And saved him.'

'I thought you tied him up and threatened his life,' Lop said. 'Because you thought he was a spy.'

Eli shot me a panicked look, shaking his head.

'That's not true,' I agreed. 'He was kind and gentle and made me feel most welcome. I would have been lost and probably wandered the sands forever without his help.'

Lop gave Eli an impressed look.

When she wasn't looking, Eli snuck me a thankful nod.

'What's in your Meesh-Dahm, Lop?' I asked.

'Rabbit,' she said.

'What's a rabbit?' I asked.

'The most beautiful and smartest of all the animals,' Eli said, quick to jump in. 'Rabbits were treasured almost as much as Cold.'

Lop rolled her eyes, but she thrust her chest out a bit and

found a new spring in her gate. Eli grabbed her hand and squeezed.

'I wonder if I have anything in my Meesh-Dahm,' I said.

Eli and Lop exchanged a perplexed glance at my side.

'What?' I asked.

'I thought you knew,' Eli said. 'Sett has been telling you.'

'Telling me what?'

'You're the first Jadan ever to fly. You very clearly have an animal spirit in your Meesh-Dahm.'

'I do?'

Eli gave me an obvious sort of nod. 'Bird.'

I conjured up an image of a single feather made of metal and string; a present I had once given to Matty, who had been obsessed with birds.

Then I touched the spot on my wrist beneath my thumb.

We reached the end of the tunnel, our group spilling into a new chamber, which was arguably more impressive than the Battle Room. The bald warrior named Rivvy was racing out of the chamber just as we arrived. Sett waved our group to the side so we wouldn't be in the way. Rivvy was concentrating deeply, holding a long metal box with both hands. She moved swiftly, yet the box didn't tilt at all. She whispered something to me as we passed, and I didn't understand the words, but the tone was respectful.

'This where I be making . . .' Sett's words trailed off as she gestured around the wild chamber. 'This where I wander the . . . Eli, what is "Deeyoneh" in tongue of enemy?'

'Imagination.'

'Yes,' Sett said. 'Imagination. Is right.'

The first thing I noticed about the Clock Chamber – besides the cacophony of tinkering materials and overflowing display cases – was the giant Khatclock in the back. They won't call it a Khatclock here, I thought.

It was like all the ones on the Coldmarch, only this model was ten times larger. The face took up the entire back wall of the chamber and was done up with a red alder Opened Eye.

I stepped in the chamber. My eyes went watery with wonder and I had to blink. It was too much to try and take in all at once.

Hundreds of hourglasses were keeping track of time, coming in all different sizes. Some were gear-controlled to flip over on their own when the sand ran light. Some had clearly been due to flip for some time, the sand heavy and settled on the bottom. One hourglass swung on the end of an incredibly slow-moving pendulum.

I didn't spot any Cold-charge urns, but the room was far too full of things to understand at a glance. There were vertical gardens of wicked-looking plants growing in the dark corners. There were locked cabinets, bound in chains. There were more kinds of tools than Leroi had had in his shop. I also spotted a section of the room with highly detailed inventions straight out of the Ancient shops, like music boxes and wind-up toys.

Long ladders made of knotted rope hung off the ceiling of the chamber, leading to higher shelves cut into the stone. The shelves all had their own tinkering materials and cabinets.

And weapons.

There were so many weapons.

There were also weapons on stands, on tables and in chests. A lot of the weapons looked familiar in design, but with something small altered. I spilled over with speculations on how everything worked, my imagination straining.

Sett stepped in front of me, blocking my view.

'You telling plan first,' she said. 'Then you see my making.'

I gave an absent nod, flexing my bronze fingers.

Then I told her what I had in mind.

Sett had Eli translate a few words that she didn't understand, and after I was finished she gave an agreeable bow. She
immediately commanded Eli and Lop to start gathering the
materials that I'd requested.

Then she began to explain some of her most beloved
inventions.

The first was a kind of sword.

The blade portion was long, sharp and sleek, but there was
an extended piece attached to the end. The addition
was about the third of the size of the rest of the blade. The
offshoot metal rested flush with the end of the sword, held
in place by an odd-looking disc.

Sett picked up the blade and held it out horizontally.
Unlocking the disc, she motioned with her wrist like she was
turning a crank. The extra piece of metal spun on the end
like a wheel, giving the sword a surprise extension.

'Is hard to block,' Sett said, taking a regular sword off a
rack and putting it in my hands. She had me hold the blade
up and out like I was defending an attack.

'Lean body back,' she gestured.

I nodded, holding my arm steady and tilting away.

'More,' she commanded.

I obliged.

'Even more,' Sett huffed. 'You want be keeping nose, don't
you?'

I strained to keep the blade as far from my body as possible.

Then she sliced downward. I kept my arm stiff and blocked
the blow. The additional piece of metal continued onward
over my sword, nearly gouging a line down the middle of
my face.

'Is help,' Sett said. 'No good for kill strike but take many
Asham eyes. They no expect it keep coming.'

'We should bring those,' I said with a nod. Blood rushed
through my veins. 'Definitely.'

Next Sett led me to a table laid out with arrows, vials of materials and metal boxes like the one Rivvy had carried out. The arrows weren't ordinary arrows. They had bulky glass triangle casings on the ends that were hinged open and empty.

'These favourites for Langrian warriors,' Sett said. 'We make now.'

She picked up one of the vials. It housed hundreds of tiny black needle-things submerged in a viscous liquid.

'Skinkmander stingers,' Sett said, shaking a portion of the stingers into the hollow arrowhead. 'Stingers be growing back, so no kill animal. We no kill animal if no have to. Animals being sacred in Langria.'

'And the solution the stingers are in?'

'Eliezah!' Sett shouted over my shoulder. *'Chellek shesh "solution" eschut luh?'*

Langrian was such a beautiful language. I ached to know more. I wanted to speak with the free Jadans in their own tongue; to feel a part of the place.

'Mechtuk!' Eli shouted back, grabbing armfuls of boilweed.

'Yes,' Sett said. 'Solution is from Sobek lizard. Poison.'

I nodded. A charge of dark excitement ran through my body.

Sett picked up a small pouch made of a thin rubber substance and very carefully added in a few drops of what looked like Milk of the Dunai. Then she tied off the pouch and laid it inside the triangle casing, closing the glass arrowhead with precision.

'Is for boom,' Sett said, gesturing with her hands. 'Even if arrow miss Asham, it boom with stinger and poison. Take many Asham lives. Is good.'

'Let's make as many of those as we can,' I said, lust for battle stirring in my veins. I hadn't felt those sorts of hungers since using the Wraiths.

Then Sett brought me to a table with a few inventions that

were round and flat and almost looked like Open Eyes, ringed in blades. Sett grabbed a steel rod and pressed the tip against the metal circle in the centre.

The whole thing snapped together like a biting jaw.

'For Asham feet,' Sett explained. 'We place in Dagon under sand and very good pain for enemy. We use for your plan?'

I swallowed, my mouth tasting heavy of anticipation. The term 'Foot Fangs' popped into my head. 'Can't hurt.'

The rest of the wares only got more impressive.

My favourite invention was a heavy spring-propelled hook loaded into the body of a spear. She said the spear could shoot the hook up forty paces, carrying a rope behind it. Eli didn't miss the chance to tell me he'd grown a lot of the plant fibre used to make the rope.

'Is being for scale rocks and cliffs,' Sett said, aiming the hook towards one of the high cutouts of stone. 'When in Dagon, if Asham being trap us, we escape.'

She aimed and pressed the button on the side of the spear. The hook arced onto one of the outcroppings above us, skittering into the hole. Sett yanked the rope back and then twisted her wrist, which made the sharp metal grab on some surface above.

She let the spear go. It dangled in the air before her. Then she pulled it tight to show the sturdiness.

'Is good,' she said.

My lips split into a wide smile. 'So where is the Desert?'

Sett clapped her hands. 'Eliezah! Sullop!'

Eli and Lop stopped their gathering and sped over to Sett, who said something in Langrian, sending them back into the tunnel.

'Where are they going?' I asked.

Sett put a hand on her stomach. 'I being hungry. Send for food.'

I didn't realize it until then. I'd been too distracted by all
the fantastic creations, but I too was famished.

'So where is the Desert?' I said. 'We can probably get to
work.'

Sett gave me an eager nod. 'Come. Is close.'

She beckoned for me to follow through the room, leading
me to the giant Khatclock in the back.

'This Adaamclock of Coldmarch,' she said. 'Is very important
of Langria.'

'It doesn't work,' I said, pointing to the hands.

'Is not for measure time, like hourglass or gear clock. Is
for secrets.'

'Secrets?'

'Yes. If ever Asham breach Langria, place for Melekah hide.
Very strong metal walls inside, no able break out or in. Is
once be having food and Cold and water inside. Can live for
long time in secrets.'

'But not anymore?'

Sett shook her head sadly. 'After spy plant Desert, many
of us die, and no able to save food or Cold. Starving and too
much Sun everywhere.'

She reached under her shirt and removed a rusted key.
Then she slid open a hidden section of the clock's pupil and
fit the key in to a small slot.

'Now place for me hide Desert,' she said. 'So no spy can
get. I have only key in or out.'

Then she grabbed the two large clock hands and heaved
them up. They seemed heavy in her hands, and I tried to help,
but she waved me back. She struggled to get them to turn, but
eventually they spun upwards with a series of clicks. She had
to stand on her toes to get the hands to point all the way up.

The clock hands fell into position with a muffled thump.
A latch behind the face made a sound. Sett grit her teeth and
pulled the door open, revealing the chamber within.

It was smaller than I expected. It would only be able to hide ten or so bodies comfortably. The terrible heat hit me immediately.

A giant steel crate sat in the middle of the space, the lid closed and latched.

I coughed. The air was foul and boiling over with heat. And the Desert smell had the same distinct odour I was familiar with.

'Is bad,' Sett said. 'Very secret. Much metal walls.'

'And you said there's eight pieces of Desert inside?'

'Yes.'

'Good,' I said. 'We need to bring them all too.'

Sett nodded, putting a hand on her lower back, her face turning into a grimace. 'I hurt back. You bring crate out and we begin plan making.'

I paused. The crate looked quite heavy, and I thought maybe I should find a proper mask and gloves before I got too close.

'Alone?'

'Yes,' Sett said, urgency in her eyes. 'Is not heavy. You bring.'

The heat made my skin sweat and crawl. I stepped into the dark space and a sense of suffocation took over. The metal walls were too close together. Panic rippled in my chest.

'You know what,' I said, turning around. 'I think—'

The clock face slammed, closing me in.

There was the distant scrape of a key into a lock.

'HEY!' I yelled, slamming my palm against the metal. 'SETT!'

The heat inside the chamber was almost worse than being out in the Sun. It was already burning me from the inside.

I tried not to breathe, but my lungs were desperate. The pressure and pain quickly rose. The chamber was all black. My terror echoed.

I could feel the Desert behind me, calling for my death.

I scrambled around the back of the clock for a latch. My palms eventually touched a small hole that was meant for a key. My bronze fingers screeched as I frantically clawed at the opening. I felt around for anything else, praying there was some other release.

I couldn't get out.

And I couldn't hold my breath any longer.

My chest burned like hot coals.

I started to see colours behind my eyes, molten reds and sickness greens.

The pressure was too much. I opened my mouth and sucked in a lung full of poisoned air. I choked and screamed for help. I cried out to Eli and Lop. I cried out to Shilah and Cam. I cried out in vain.

I was going to die alone, in this foul place of silence and heat and death.

I'd failed Shilah as a partner.

I failed Cam as a friend.

I failed Abb as a son.

I slumped against the metal and counted my final breaths.

Chapter Seventeen

The Desert fumes had killed me.

I was falling out of my body, heading towards a terrible light. I was being sent to Sun to be punished for my sins. For failing to save my people. Everything around me was bright and hot and my eyes wouldn't work right. My ears were stuffed with heat and I couldn't hear; there would be no songs of my Ancestors. My Khol was burning somewhere in the black, knowing its owner would never track it down.

And then my mouth tasted a clean breath.

My whole body shuddered with relief.

I was out of the space, Sett looming over me.

How long had I been inside? The colours and sounds of the Clock Chamber were so vibrant I had to close my eyes. I sucked down the clear, cool air with the kind of release I'd never felt before, although my throat had nearly pinched closed from fear. I gasped. I wheezed. My limbs felt rubbery and stiff at the same time.

Sett grabbed me by the throat and lifted me to my feet. She was much stronger than she had let on before. Her face was filled with calm fury, and she whipped out a dagger, pressing it against my forehead. Pain shot through to the back of my skull as she drew blood. Then she loosened her hand, allowing me a small moment to fill my lungs.

Before I could get much, two fingers were shoved under my chin, just like she'd done before. No one else was in the chamber around us, and even if I was able to scream for help, I wouldn't get any. Sett was Melekah. Her decisions would be law.

'Why you here?' she asked between her teeth. Her face was diamond at the edges, but boilweed soft in her eyes. Her hands were trembling. I couldn't tell why.

'I don't—'

She jabbed the blade deeper into my forehead, a small whimper coming to her throat instead of mine. I held back my scream. The pressure was extraordinary and pain cleansed my mind of any thoughts.

She snarled this time. Her fingers were pressing hard enough under my chin that sharper fingernails would have emerged through my mouth.

'Why. You. Here?' she snarled.

I was barely able to make the words. I gasped: 'It was an accident.'

'You sneak in Langria and ask where Desert. This is thing spy be doing. You is spy and you being lied to me.'

'No,' I said, wincing against her blade. I couldn't get away. 'I swear, I'm not a spy!'

'What is Khat's plan?'

'I don't know!'

The blade went deeper and a flash of white light cracked through my head.

'How you get in?'

Blood spilled down my forehead and I could only see red. 'I flew! Fly!'

'Who you are?'

'Huh?'

She spun the blade around and struck me in the side of the head with the handle. My world cracked.

'Who you are!' she screamed.

'I'm Jadan like you, trying to help!' I couldn't think clearly; I didn't know what she wanted from me. 'I'm Micah from Paphos.'

I couldn't see her face clearly through the bloody haze, but I could have sworn she'd begun to whimper.

'You spy,' she cried. 'You have be spy.'

'I'm not!'

She hit me again, but there wasn't much force behind it this time.

'Who you are?'

'My name's Micah! I'm just a Jadan!'

'Who you are!'

A surge of passion rushed through me. The word came out before I could think too long on the matter. It was time to stop running. I had to embrace the possibility. The Crier had done everything to keep me alive. To bring me here. To show me all the secrets. It was time.

'MESHUA!' I screamed. 'I'm Meshua!'

Sett's fingers pressed harder than ever. She paused, trembling, concentrating with all her being.

She released me, stumbling backwards. She dropped her blade. Beads of my blood splattered against the stone at my feet.

'Is true,' she gasped. 'You no lie.'

I collapsed to the floor, crawling away. I needed to be away from the smell of the Desert. I needed to get away from the place I'd been ready to die.

'It's true,' I choked out.

There was a long pause as I wrenched my body across the floor.

'I'm sorry. I had being sure.' Sett remained stoic, but her

blank face was shattering. 'Why World Crier sending you after all this time? So many pain. So many suffer. Why Drought end *now* of all times?'

I paused, collapsing on my stomach. I'd been drained of all my fight.

'Because it can.' I closed my eyes. The cool stone felt wonderful against the side of my face. 'Because it finally can.'

Sett returned to my side with water and Wisps. She rolled me over and dragged my upper body into her lap, as if I were a small child. I didn't struggle. She wiped my forehead with fresh boilweed. She cleaned my cheeks and neck.

'I sorry,' she whispered. 'Fear only way sometimes to truth.'

'I understand,' I said, my chest heaving up and down. 'I would have done the same thing. I did ask for Desert and Asham to be brought into Langria. I understand.'

'Yes, and now I'm being sure, I get them for you. Desert and Asham.'

My body trembled. I couldn't help it.

'You able get up?' she asked.

I checked, finding some strength back in my legs. The cool water had taken away some of the fire in the back of my throat, but it was still present.

She helped me to my feet and headed for one of the locked cabinets. The chains came away easily in her touch, and they coiled neatly at the base. Sett took a long breath before opening the doors. I couldn't see what was inside, as her back was in the way, but it was clear she was taking time with a decision.

Her hands returned holding an old cloth. The beige fabric looked so worn I thought it might twist apart with the slightest pressure. Sett held the cloth more carefully than she did the glass-tipped arrows.

This must have been quite the weapon.

She peeled back the fabric layers with care. One by one, the strips were removed, revealing a final layer. Sett kept undoing the folds, but there was nothing inside, making me think it was the ancient garment itself she wanted to show me.

And then a dull brown bead appeared in the folds.

I almost laughed, wondering if the buildup had been one of her jokes.

'That's a Wisp,' I said matter-of-factly.

'Yes,' Sett said, staring intently. 'Is right. A Wisp.'

I paused.

'Yes,' I said again, feeling out of sorts. 'It's a Wisp.'

'This is first Wisp of Langria,' Sett said. 'Very sacred. Very holy.'

My whole body stiffened. 'The *first* Wisp?'

Sett nodded. 'When Adaam climb up top of Great Divide. This first Wisp he find in new Cry Patch. He save as blessing. Is being passed down from Melekah to Melekah since beginning.'

She held it out further. I almost felt afraid to touch such a relic.

'It's beautiful,' I said, keeping my hands at my side.

In truth it looked like every other Wisp I'd ever seen, but now that I understood its place, it made my eyes water. I was looking at the history of our people. The story of our survival. It was fascinating that the same thing could be so different depending on context. Cold was life itself, yet too much of it at once could burn the skin black. A piece of Desert was death in the ground, but the secret to flight in the sky; possibly even the secret to our salvation. As with myself, perhaps Meshua had always been inside, waiting, shifting, and I just had to figure out where to open.

'You have it,' Sett said.

'I have what?'

Sett folded the cloth back over itself, trapping the Wisp back in the deep folds. She knelt down in front of me, on both feet, and placed the shroud at my feet.

'You are Meshua,' she said with severity. 'You be having everything.'

'No, I couldn't possibly—'

'You be having everything.' Sett dipped her forehead against the ground. 'I being your warrior. I being council. I being lover if you is needing that. I serve anything you is needing.'

'I—' My tongue was as heavy as a barrel of figs. I was more uncomfortable now than when I'd been in the Desert chamber. 'I—'

'I belong you, body and Meesh-Dahm,' Sett said. 'What you command, Meshua? You is wanting pleasure? Sinniah understand. She pleasure too if you wishing. My body is being older, but I having wisdom and pleasure for you.'

Sett remained on her knees, but her hand ran tenderly up my ankle.

'Um. Thank you,' my throat went too dry. It was as if I hadn't had a drink of water in years. 'But I can't possibly . . .'

And then Sett snorted out a laugh.

And then the whole room began to giggle.

The laughter erupted from behind inventions and in dark corners. I couldn't see where the sounds were coming from.

I spun around, Sett's hand falling from my leg.

Sett's laughter grew. Suddenly the whole room was abuzz with laughter, coming from all the cracks.

'I don't – what is happening?' I asked, stumbling back.

Sett bit her bottom lip. Her face was bright and trembling. 'Is joke. Free Jadans good at jokes.'

Her laughter burst out again. She slapped her palm against the floor.

And then a huge portion of the Langrian army revealed

themselves, practically appearing out of thin air. Their cheers and laughter were deafening as they rose from behind chests and stepped out of shadows. There were at least fifty warriors clapping their hands and whistling, the noise shifting to appreciation.

More figures spilled in from the tunnel, whooping and beating their chests. Some waved Opened Eye flags. Eli and Lop were near the front of the crowd and they raced in, holding hands, impossibly broad smiles on their faces. Sinniah was in the corner, buckled over and gasping for air, slapping her hand against her knee.

I'd never been more confused. All I could do was blink and stare.

Sett rose to her feet holding the sacred cloth. She clapped a hand against my shoulder and then pinched my cheek.

'Welcome Meshua,' she shouted over the din, stepping aside with a small bow. 'You family now.'

All at once the free Jadans began to swarm me, talking of 'Meshua'. They shook my hand and kissed my cheeks. They offered weapons and food and Wisps. Some of them bowed, some of them cried, but all of them seemed genuinely happy. I'd never experienced anything like this reception; not even with the Flock. It was more elated than reverent, which I much preferred.

A thin Jadan man came to me. He had a burn scar covering the lower portion of his face and was missing a hand. He touched my shoulder with a stump of wrist, smiling brightly. He wore his wounds with confidence.

These truly were warriors.

The Langrians continued to swarm me, trying to speak in the common tongue. I understood some of it, but most of their accents were too heavy or their words too disjointed for me to follow. I nodded politely and smiled.

Eli came over and handed me some knuckleberries, his face

wrinkled from laughter. Sett handed me back the camel necklace and then turned to the crowd, gesturing for order.

The celebrations quieted and Sett clamoured something in
Langrian and then put the Wisp back in the cabinet, locking
it up. The warriors began to form ranks, order quickly restored
out of the chaos. Sett shook her head, picking up one of her
spears.

'That's not really the first Wisp,' I said quietly, putting the
necklace back on. 'Is it?'

Sett clapped her hands and called out a burst of throaty
Langrian. The warriors answered by swiftly marching out
of the room. Three of them stopped at the tinkering table
with the glass arrows. Others grabbed a few Spin Swords
and crossbows, looking back with grateful nods or gestures
of encouragement; both at Sett and myself.

Sinniah came over and stroked Sett's hair, whispering something into her ear. Sett blushed like a child, colour rushing
to her already dark cheeks, and then she laughed again. She
flashed me a wink.

I gave Sett an embarrassed smile. 'You got me.'

'Warriors came while you trapped. I already being know
how long stay inside clock and live. I went longer for my
test. You okay. And people of Langria see your truth in fear.
They believe you Meshua now.'

My throat was tight with emotion. I couldn't speak.

'Sinniah capture Asham for you,' Sett said. 'She promise
many tears.'

Sinniah gave a serious nod at her side. The severity returned
to the woman's face – the same as when I first met her – her
eyes wild and lips thin.

'We start making your plan,' Sett continued, gesturing to
the tinkershop. 'You and me. Two makers.'

I held up my hands. They were slick with sweat and dirt
and dried blood; and not just my own. The free Jadans had

welcomed me as one of them. They were counting on me to make good on my word and bring them a miracle. To make Langria *real*. Not just a war-torn city clinging to life, but the place it was always supposed to be.

And it wasn't only Langria.

If I could get enough Khol, I could plant Cry Patches for all the cities in the world. The seeds of hope would return to the world, and once again the Jadans would know their worth. I flexed my bronze fingers, relishing the sound of creaking metal.

'Let's get started.'

Chapter Eighteen

Sett's tinkering recourses were far vaster than I'd expected.

Over the years the free Jadans had acquired every material I could think of, whether through the Coldmarch gifts, spoils from the Dagon or returning with raiding parties who'd pillaged the nearest caravan posts. Langrian steel was stout, their waxy fabric strong and their hamsa wood free of scarab damage.

Sett's tinkerers had been working with skill and passion for hours now, trying to match the dimensions of my original Matty and succeeding. We'd set up another open-air workspace, the sky at our disposal, and each time one of the pieces came together my heart sang a bit louder, calling out to my friends.

Four half-formed dome-sails now swayed in the hard Langrian wind. The expanse looking over the alder flowers was wide and empty, and Sett told me that Great Gale chose to dance across these lands all night, twirling sand and dust like the hem of a dress. I was glad to see the Crier's Sister here, bringing sweet memories on her breath. I wasn't as far away from home as I thought. Here was the same lovely wind, playing in the same lovely starlight.

Sett had sent a few of her stronger warriors to retrieve the original Matty down from the Cry Patch earlier in the night, and I was surprised that none of the sail had ripped on its way down. It was ready again to conquer the sky. It was also ready to be copied.

The Langrian workers tinkered in unison by my side. I barely had to repeat any requests, and some I don't remember giving at all. They were precise, fluid and together in their making. Sett averred that I was a natural leader, keeping everyone focused and moving, but I didn't feel like I had much to do with the momentum. It was almost as if some unseen force was guided them onwards.

I thought my biggest problem was going to be getting a strong enough Cold Charge for all of the new glider blades, but the free Jadans had more Cold than expected. Sett brought out a stockpile of Drafts and Shivers they'd gathered from their enemies over the years. The sieging Asham often carried big Cold with them, to keep alive during their extended time in the Dagon. Funny that they ended up bringing life to their enemies, gifting them the kind of Cold that Langrians would normally be without.

Sett only had two Chills in the chest, but I didn't worry too much. A lesser Charge meant we'd travel to Paphos slower than what was ideal, but with all the Frosts we'd find in the Pyramid, I'd be able to return to my friends in Jadans' Rise with speed and salvation.

Just a little longer.

I smiled as I took an empty urn and started the new batch of Cold Charge. I took the leftover solution from the original Matty – the liquid still crackled with pain when I dipped in my finger – and then I added all the salt and Cold that the Langrians could afford.

Although most Jadans on the rock face were there to tinker and cheer us on, a handful of onlookers mourned the loss of their big Cold. They paced the outskirts of the plain with dread on their faces. I couldn't understand what they were saying to each other, but I knew it wasn't complimentary.

I was experienced enough to know I couldn't convince everyone of my dream; still I wanted to tread lightly. These brave Langrians had been defending their homeland with blood and lives for eight hundred years. It was expected they should be wary of an outsider, especially after what happened with the spy. Their rejection was disheartening, but their grumbling would soon end. They just needed to see me fly.

I looked up at the night sky, ready to be up there once again.

When the Cold Charge was ready, I took one of the Asham tear vials that Sinniah had supplied. She'd managed to fill six vials to the brim. I didn't ask her methods for extraction and she didn't tell me.

This was war.

I quickly went to work on a small addition to the original Matty, adding a sliding cover over the Desert. This would hopefully allow me to descend without having to wait for the tear effect to wear out. If Sett and I were going to raid the Pyramid with any sort of secrecy, we'd need precision.

Then I put on a boilweed mask and stepped into the craft. But before I rose, I decided to test the glider blades. They started up as I flipped the lever, and though the new Charge was clearly weaker than the original, still the blades turned fast and strong. This elicited impressed looks from the Langrians at the fringe.

And then, heart in my throat, I let a single Asham tear fall.

The Desert fumed to life.

The metal bucket spat up terrible heat and hate and fumes. The dome-sail was ready, catching it all and billowing outward.

I tried to keep a stoic face as my Matty rose, showing the free Jadans that I wasn't scared.

There was a collective gasp from below. I smiled beneath my mask.

It felt wonderful to shoot in the air once again. I didn't realize how much I missed flying. My chest rang out with freedom.

Rising a decent distance from the ground – so I wouldn't knock into any buildings or statues – I lowered the copper rod deeper into the Cold Charge, spinning the blades and speeding across the sky. The directional lever was a bit tight, creaking with sand as I swung it around, but it still turned the Matty back and forth. I did a loop over the crowd and then spun the tiller the other way.

I wanted to give the Langrians a show. To give them a story.

I let another few tears fall and raced upwards towards the stars. I threw my head back and howled into the boilweed mask. I told myself I'd only allow a few minutes of bliss, and then I'd have to return to land. The other Mattys had to be finished. It was good for Sett's tinkerers to see what we were building, but I couldn't indulge my senses.

My friends were still in terrible danger.

If they were still alive at all.

I nudged the new steel covering slightly over the Desert holder and I began to descend. Then I removed the Cold Charge from the fan blades, and the Matty calmed. I looked over the side railing to see how far I'd risen.

I was already past the top of the valley. I could see the entirety of Langria, and the Dagon, brushed in shadow. The land was silvery and dark, with small pricks of light from place to place reminding me of dying Adaam Grass. There was too little life smeared over too much rock.

The Great Divide was vast, making me feel insignificant,

continuing as far as I could see. It only seemed to get more dangerous and deeper the further it went along. It was so large that it might have encircled the entire World Cried. It echoed with secrets and whispering of things much bigger and more ancient than myself.

I leaned over the railing so I could see past the dome-sail above me. The night sky was gorgeous and clear. Cold swirled between the stars above, and now I finally knew the way to call them down. To plant a Khol in the ground. The Crier had always been up there, blind and bound, yet desperate to help.

What a glorious revelation.

All I had to do was get into the Khat's Pyramid.

I pushed the steel cap tighter over the Desert. The fumes weren't so terrible with the cap on, and so I took off my mask, breathing the night air as I drifted downward. The Matty struck the rockface below harder than I would have liked, but nothing important jarred loose, most of the rattles coming from my teeth.

The Langrians cheered as I landed, every one of them.

Sett raced over to the Matty, putting her hands on the railing.

'What do you think?' I asked.

'Is good,' she whispered, her expression full of awe. 'Is very good.'

'Are you ready to go up with me?' I asked. 'I need to see how these things fly with two bodies.'

Sinniah called something from behind, but Sett waved her off, stepping over the railing and onto the craft. I handed Sett one of the boilweed masks, and she strapped it over her mouth. I hooked an anchoring rope around her belt.

Her eyes were flush with excitement.

I let a tear fall.

*　　*　　*

Soon we had four Mattys built and ready to fly.

My craft was the only one with a feather painted on the side, but other than that, all four were nearly identical. Because of the Langrian workers' skill, the crafts had come together more swiftly than I had thought possible.

The Asham would probably be able to spot our crafts from their side of the Dagon, and I could only imagine what they would think as we soared past, but I didn't care. Even if they sent word back to Paphos by the fastest camel in the Khatdom, we'd beat them by days.

I put down my hammer and let out a long breath. 'And now to pick the riders.'

Sett laid a hand on my shoulder. 'I having them picked out before we start.'

I looked at her and raised an eyebrow. 'How'd you know we'd run out of materials after four Mattys?'

She gave me an obvious sort of look. 'Because I Melekah. I know how much in Langria.' She squeezed my shoulder. 'And who in Langria.'

I tried to give a cool nod, but I was rather impressed. She'd been able to pick out exactly what went into the original Matty just by looking at it, and then match those figures against her own materials. That's something even Leroi wouldn't have been able to do.

'Who'd you have in mind?' I asked.

Sett turned to the crowd and barked something throaty. Warriors began lining up in front of the crafts. All of them were women.

The first to step up to me was Rivvy, the short, bald woman from earlier. She bowed, her head going as low as my knee.

'Rivvy you having met,' Sett said. 'Fierce as can be. Baboon in Meesh-Dahm.'

Rivvy pounded her chest and showed her teeth, which were large and well taken care of. She said something in

Langrian and then went away to pick at the chests of weapons that were fully stocked. She went for a large, spiked hammer which was almost as tall as she was.

'What's a baboon?' I asked Sett.

Sett shrugged. 'None idea. Rivvy says name coming in dream.'

The next woman to step up had frayed hair and a round face. There was a nervous look about her, her movements twitchy and quick. Her eyes had a bulging, constantly surprised expression. She bowed, not nearly as low as Rivvy, keeping her eyes trained on my face.

'This Zeekah,' Sett said. 'Zeekah having best ears in Langria. She hear Asham even move as slow as stone.'

'Meshua,' Zeekah said, the word coming out as a nasally spurt.

I bowed back. 'What animal do you have in your Meesh-Dahm, Zeekah?'

Zeekah shot a fearful look to Sett, who translated my words into Langrian. Zeekah listened intently, and then spread her hands on the sides of her head, wiggling her fingers and sticking out her tongue.

'Loonchin,' Sett explained.

'Ah,' I said and then shrugged. 'No idea.'

Lop cleared her throat from the side of us. 'Loonchin were furry creatures with split tongues that lived in the tallest grasses. They would lick fallen Wisps and then wrap their tongue around the grass, moving up and down. Apparently the Cold friction would make lovely mating songs.'

I smiled. I would have liked to have seen a Loonchin.

The next warrior didn't have much bulk to her, but her forearms were like cudgels, dark and frightfully hard. She moved with all the grace of a broken piece of pottery, the anger in her eyes just as loud. She wasn't any taller than I was, but she commanded attention.

'Bear,' the warrior said, introducing herself and bowing. 'I be your blade, Meshua.'

There was a grunt from a select group within the crowd, beating fists against their chest and stomping their feet. Bear turned, and with her fingers shaped like claws slapped her forearms together, her wrists making a fierce knocking sound.

'They all having bear inside them,' Sett explained, gesturing.

'Your name is just Bear?' I asked.

'Is Meesh-Dahm,' Bear said, turning around with a snarl and going for the weapons chest. 'I needing no other name.'

Sett beckoned me closer and whispered in my ear. She was trying to hold back a laugh but not doing a very good job. 'Bear is named "Anyuzzeh'leqquk" when born. This mean "gentle kiss of wind". Bear change name as fast as being allowed.'

Then came a stunning woman. One of the loveliest I'd ever seen. Her stride alone made me want to melt. She had long, dark hair – even thicker than Leah's – and lips that could have commanded all the Taskmasters in Paphos to jump straight into the Singe.

'This Gullesh,' Sett said. 'She best arrow shot in—'

Sett cut herself off, stepping up to Gullesh and grabbing her by the neck. Gullesh squirmed, but Sett held her tightly, adjusting her fingers and looking deep into Gullesh's eyes. After a few breaths Sett eventually let the warrior go, spitting on the ground at her feet. They exchanged a few harsh words. Gullesh slunk away, head hung low.

'What happened?' I asked.

'Droughtweed in eyes,' Sett said, wrinkling her nose in disgust. 'We take other instead.'

Sett pointed to one of the tinkerers instead of a warrior. This woman gave a slow nod and made her way into the line. Her robes were full of stains and grease, and she had a sadness in her eyes that made me look away.

'Is good meet,' the tinkerer said with a bow. Her voice dripped with melancholy.

I bowed back. 'What's your name?'

'Ellora'.

'She one of finest makers in Langria,' Sett said.

I nodded as Ellora gave a second bow and excused herself, going to a Matty instead of the weapon box. She ran a hand over the railing, her face despondent.

'Does she not want to go?' I whispered.

'She not want do anything much,' Sett said. 'Is okay. Is good for her.'

'What's her Meesh-Dahm animal?' I asked.

Sett shook her head, giving me a look that said to leave it alone.

The last warrior to come up introduced herself as Tully. She was all elbows and knees, but her face sang of mischief. Tully claimed to have 'fox' in her Meesh-Dahm. I didn't know what a fox was, but I liked her immediately.

And so the warriors were decided.

We practised flying for a few hours. Two riders to a Matty. I examined the dome-sails and tear mechanisms after each short rise, and found everything stable. Surprisingly, the Langrians weren't nearly as intimidated by flying as I would have thought, proficient almost on the first rise. The only one who was squeamish about flying was Zeekah, but I was getting a feeling that squeamish was her natural state. The Langrians took to the sky like they belonged there, like they'd been flying for years. A small part of me was jealous, but mostly I was just grateful to have extraordinary warriors to fight by my side. They quickly proved they didn't need much practice, which was good, because we didn't have time to waste.

We paired up, each standing in front of our crafts, stocked up with weapons and rations.

Sett and I.

Sinniah and Bear.

Zeekah and Ellora.

Rivvy and Tully.

The Langrians left in the crowd gathered around the Mattys. They cheered and waved and cried with one another.

Sett turned to them and sang with all of her heart.

I couldn't understand the words, but instinctively I knew it was a freedom song. It made me miss home more than ever, and by the end there was more than one kind of tear in my eye.

Sinniah came over and gave Sett a passionate kiss, digging her hands into Sett's gray hair. The clamouring from the crowd grew louder. The other chosen warriors said goodbye to their families – some with kisses, some with playful punches on the arm – and we climbed into our Mattys.

There was barely space for Sett and I in our Matty, between all of the weapons and supplies we'd packed, and I hoped we hadn't weighed down the craft too much. I strapped on my boilweed mask and carefully opened the lips of the Coldmaker bag. I put my hands on the bronze eye, and then touched each of my friends' names.

'You can do the honours,' I said to Sett, taking my hand out and gesturing to the tear lever.

Sett shook her head, putting on her boilweed mask and eyewear. 'No. As one.'

Sett took my fingers and we dropped a tear together. The Matty struggled at first, the dome-sail groaning, but finally the craft took off. Sett laughed, the orange glow of the Desert reflected in the glass over her eyes.

The other Mattys rose as well, three spots of light appearing below. I heard distant cries of excitement. Heat spilled through the small holes in the top of their sails. Even though Sun was gone for the night, the heat still went up, trying to find its maker. The bond between fire and Sun must have been nearly unbreakable, the same being true of the Crier and his Cold.

Sett let out another Asham tear from the vial and wrenched us higher, the Matty climbing high above the Divide. I looked North and my jaw dropped.

The Crying.

Cold was falling into the Langrian's Cry Patch.

The Wisps were barely apparent, their streaks dull and nearly indiscernible, but the fact that they existed at all made me want to follow them down and kiss the red sands upon which they landed. If we had more time, I might have done just that.

'Is beautiful,' Sett said through her mask, coming to my side. 'Is so beautiful.'

The Wisps caught just a hint of starlight as they fell. They were real. Tangible. Adaam had put the Khol in the ground, and now the Cold knew where to fall.

'Do you believe in the Crier?' I asked.

'Hmm?'

I took off my mask, deciding to deal with a few fumes for the moment. The questions in my heart burned brighter than any Desert.

'Do you believe in the Crier?' I asked Sett again.

Sett looked away from the other Mattys, swinging her attention back to me. Her eyebrow had raised.

'Believe?' she asked. She took off her mask and cleared her throat.

'Yes,' I said. 'Do you think he's real?'

Sett shivered. 'Sorry. I being very excited. Why you ask such thing?'

I pointed out at the falling Wisps. There were only a handful of brown streaks falling to the land, barely discernible. I tried to make my words as simple and clear for her to understand. Considering the subject, this was both impossibly difficult and surprisingly easy.

'Desert takes away Meesh-dahm in the land,' I said. 'Khol puts Meesh-Dahm back in. The Cold from the sky is attracted to Meesh-Dahm, and that's how it knows where to fall.'

Sett nodded.

'So couldn't it all be just a natural effect?'

'Natural. Effect,' Sett repeated slowly.

I felt frustrated, trying to think of how I could use my hands to explain. 'Natural effect means, when—'

She waved me off. 'I understand. Go on. Speaking slowly please.'

I felt rather emotional. Speaking slow was going to be a challenge. Lonely thoughts scraped at a foundation I wasn't ready to lose.

'So if there is a clear cause and effect with Khol,' I blathered, 'it could all just be natural. Like how magnets find metal. How fire turns things to ash. How Golemstone reacts with the Milk of the Dunai. It would even make more sense that way. Because if the Crier was real, then why was he unable to stop the First Khat? If he was real, couldn't he have protected us from all of this pain and suffering? The truth could be that the world is simply a combination of materials and that we're all Sun-damn tinkering alone.'

As I finished, my throat burned with fear and indignation. The Desert fumes didn't help. My whole face was on fire.

Sett blinked for a while, saying nothing. I realized I hadn't spoken slowly enough, and passion had certainly distorted my words. I took a deep breath, turning away from the Desert. 'Let me try again—'

Sett held up a finger. 'I understand.'

And then she went quiet. She gave me another blank stare

for a while, like she went somewhere and left her body behind. It quickly became uncomfortable, and I coughed, both from the heat and impatience.

Sett moved, her hand going straight on top of the Coldmaker bag.

'You make this,' she said.

I nodded.

She cleared out a space next to the machine, pushing it aside, along with some weapons and food.

'You sit,' she said.

I pointed to the glider blades. 'But we need to go South.'

'We have small more time to rise,' she said. 'Sit. This important.'

I glanced over the railing, making sure the other Mattys were still on course. Then I sat. It was much cooler in the bottom of the craft, the Desert fumes absent, and the edge was taken from my mood.

Sett opened the lips of the bag. 'You are maker, yes?'

I nodded. 'We say "Inventor" in the common tongue, but yes.'

Sett snorted. 'Is maker. You maker.' She tapped the bronze lid. 'This Cold-*maker*.'

'It is.'

'And it no work now.' She smiled. 'Missing Khol.'

I nodded.

'Is natural effect.'

'Yes.'

'But you sitting right there!' she exclaimed with a laugh, opening her palms towards me. 'If just natural effect, you fix! Fix now, please.'

'I'm trying. We're headed to the Pyramid to get—'

She grabbed my wrist and brought my bronze fingers to the lid. 'Look you same colour. Very connect. You fix. Now.'

'I'm trying—'

'Fix!'

'I can't.'

'Why not! You maker!'

'I'm not all-powerful or divine. I'm just a Jadan.'

'So why World Crier must be all-powerful and divine?'

'Because he made the world.'

She tapped the box. 'You make this. You can't fix by only you. But you still love Coldmaker? You proud of make.'

The bronze lid felt wonderful against my palm. 'I do. I am.'

'And you want with whole heart to fix Coldmaker.' She laughed. 'You fly to Langria for finding answer you need. Very big adventure. And still Coldmaker not work. Does that mean *you* not real?'

I pressed my teeth together tightly, trying to hold back. Tears stung my eyes.

'And now you fly to Paphos,' she said. 'With free Jadans. To break in Pyramid and find Khol, which being a very difficult idea. Deadly also. This show you very much want bring life to Coldmaker.' Sett placed her hand flat on lid next to mine. 'But machine still broken. For *now*.'

'For now,' I whispered.

She stood up and helped me up to the railing beside her. We'd risen high enough that the air had begun to grow Cold. I dipped the copper wire from the glider blade into the charge and started them turning. The Matty picked up pace and after a moment we began making our way South.

'This why I know Crier is being real,' Sett called over the rumble of blades. 'Even if He make Jadans, make whole world and sky and stars and Khol, it not meaning that he get to do any power he wanting. There always being rules we can't breaking. Especially biggest rule for makers.'

'What's the biggest rule?'

She gestured over the railing to the other Mattys, they too

now pushing South. The three crafts followed in our wake, defying the winds and pull of the ground. They were a splendid sight, especially with the Wisps falling at their backs.

'When you maker, you always needing help,' Sett called. 'But when you maker, you never being alone.'

Chapter Nineteen

Steering the Matty away from my friends nearly broke me.

I had dozens of good reasons to return to Jadans' Rise, but unfortunately, I had an even better reason to stay away.

We couldn't risk being seen. If the Khat or any of his sieging army spotted us flying through the air, towards Paphos, he'd send warriors and Khatfists and taskmasters back in our wake.

The Pyramid would never again go unguarded.

I was desperate to steer the Matty right to the top plateau and shout for my friends until my throat bled. I wanted to wake up every enemy in the camp with my yelling. I wanted to thunder my presence until Cam and Shilah were again in my arms.

But I wasn't a child anymore. I was a leader.

And being a leader meant sometimes accepting the hard choices.

Sett and I passed the city by a wide margin, away from any of the Khat's roads. There could have still been Asham arriving to see the Second Fall, and we had to keep a distance.

Heart in my throat, I watched the city fade through the Farsight.

The walls were still being sieged, which flooded me with relief. If the Asham were still outside, it meant that there hadn't yet been a Fall. I hadn't yet failed my people. Shilah continued to thwart the Khat in my absence, and I felt a heavy wave of pride.

Sett put a hand on my shoulder, smiling over her mask. I nodded back.

We checked our supplies and prepped the weapons in silence.

Paphos was smaller than I remembered.

All the different parts of the city seemed to have shrunk. The walls around the Garden Quarters, which in my mind were once the size of the Great Divide, now looked laughably breachable. The Cry Temples, with roofs too high for a younger me to climb, now looked like caravan carts without the wheels. I used to think the Market Quarters here were so vast that they must have sold everything in the World Cried, but now the few streets looked measly and sparse. The biggest thing about the city, besides the Pyramid, appeared to be the slave barracks on the outskirts. I never realized how many of us there were, how much space we commanded.

I hadn't been gone from Paphos that long, and it was possible that the city looked reduced because I was approaching it from unthinkable heights, but I had a feeling the difference was in me rather than the place.

It hadn't been just the streets and temples and barracks of the city that had served as my walls. Rather it was the system itself. The ruthless culture. The terrible lies. A lifetime of being tortured by the Sun and still living in darkness.

We'd been flying all night, taking turns resting and navigating. The Sun would be up in a few hours. The Crying had ended, and we didn't need to worry about any falling Cold taking out our sails, but I wished I could have witnessed the phenomenon here as well. To see Drafts and Shivers and Chills falling, and maybe even a Frost, all from above. It might have given me a hint as to how high up the Cold came from.

All four Mattys had crossed the Singe and were now heading straight for the Pyramid. I tried not to think about a specific Jadan barracks off near the eastern dunes. I certainly did not look in that direction.

I turned my body away as well as my eyes. The memories were too painful.

I nudged the cap tighter over the Desert, and the Matty began to descend. The other Mattys did the same. Our caravan of the sky drifted downward as one.

Sett's face was a beacon of hope, casting one of the brightest smiles I'd ever seen. She rubbed her arms. Her hair looked less grey and her face looked younger. Her wrinkles had even smoothed.

'I never be thinking air could be so Cold up there,' Sett said. 'Is the second best thing I've ever felt.'

'What's the first?'

She winked. 'One day you find out. But not from me.'

I laughed. 'Just think, when we get the Khol, the whole world can be just as Cold and wonderful. The Sun will be powerless.'

Sett smiled even brighter, brushing against the railing.

'This Paphos,' she said, looking out over the different quarters.

I couldn't tell if it was a question or a statement.

Far below were the rooftops I used to crawl. The streets I used to bleed upon. The alleyways where my back had tasted whips and my feet raced across hot stone, running for my life.

Now everything down there seemed weak. Fragile.

How had I ever really thought this was everything to know?

How could I have been so blind?

I began to envision planting Khol in the deadlands at our back. Of turning the dunes into vast new Cry Patches. Of making Jadan houses of worship, where we could sing our songs, the ones we would write. Of digging Jadan swimming pools in which to laugh. And planting Jadan gardens where we could grow knuckleberries as big as our fists.

I could feel our return to grace.

I could feel our chains crushing to dust beneath my fingers.

Bloodlust flooded my heart. I went to take a deep breath, but stopped myself. I wanted to feel the aggression. The hate.

The Khat had stolen everything. His line had hoarded the seeds to paradise and lied about the plague they'd forced into the land. The Pyramid would likely be empty, but I hoped some vile Asham was foolish enough to try and stand in our way.

Sett came to my side.

'I knowing that look,' she said. 'Is blood hunger.'

'You going to tell me we should pray for peace instead?'

'Yes, always pray for peace.' Sett made a fist. 'But always prepare for battle.'

'I'll remember that.'

The Matty continued to drop. Sett adjusted the blades to line us up with the Pyramid.

'You know what "Meshua" mean?' she asked.

'Spout,' I said under my breath.

She laughed. 'Shaman Eli tell you this?'

'Yes.'

'He not tell full truth. Spout is empty thing. Spout only be important when something meaning pouring through.'

'And what am I supposed to pour through? Peace?'

Sett shook her head. 'Peace beautiful. One of best things in life. But just like spout, is empty thing. Peace only being important when allows something meaning pouring through.'

I smiled, nudging my foot against the Coldmaker.

'Cold?'

She shook her head, turning around to look at the closest Matty, the one carrying Sinniah. It was dropping quickly, tightening the gap between us.

'One day you know,' Sett said. 'And I be proud seeing different look in you eye.'

It didn't take long to reach the Pyramid.

The Monument Quarters had plenty of impressive buildings, even other small pyramids honouring later Khats, but the First Khat's Pyramid was truly a sight to behold. A massive tribute to all that was unholy in the world. The stone tip loomed over the city, like the presence of the Khat himself. The steep sides were slick and smooth, the stones having been mortared tight and well maintained over eight centuries. This was thanks to the labour and deaths of countless Jadans.

But the Pyramid had a glaring weakness.

Something the Khat never would have had to worry about until now.

Balconies.

The platforms with ornate railings were visible even from our height. There was one balcony each side of the Pyramid, which allowed the Khats to look out over all of the lands they'd killed. And they were big enough to hold groups. The current Khat often held banquets and celebrations on the balconies, the High Nobles and Priests consuming fine foods and drink, while far below were the cracks of whips and thumps of Jadan bodies being tossed into the dunes.

Sett and I had discussed the plan with the other warriors before we left. Each Matty was to head for a different balcony. I didn't know if they'd be big enough to land the Mattys on, but at least we could use them as a way in.

I aimed for the North balcony.

The other Mattys began to split off behind us and head around to their marks.

We had to angle just right, and descend with perfect timing, so I took over from Sett at the blades because I'd had more practice landing the craft.

I smiled beneath my mask, thinking of my father.

Drop the bucket.

We were going faster than intended. I needed to concentrate. I nudged the covering off the Desert to slow us down. The Matty buckled upwards, but it wasn't quite enough.

We were dropping too fast and the angle was wrong. The craft shook, the dome-sail wanting one thing while momentum wanted another.

We were going to miss the balcony.

I went back to release another Noble tear, with the plan of spinning the craft around and coming in for another landing, when there was the sound of a metal spring and the flash of rope.

The end of Sett's spear shot across the gap, the hook expertly grabbing the railing of the balcony.

I nodded and then slid the covering off the Desert to give us a bit more lift. Sett propped the spear under the railing so it would catch. The Matty rose quickly and then stopped abruptly as the rope went taut. The railing groaned, threatening to break, and Sett grabbed the spear for extra support. The muscles in her arms flexed with deep lines, and I was impressed by how she handled the strain.

I closed the cap on the Desert. She pulled on the rope. Together we brought the Matty down to the balcony, which looked just big enough to fit the craft. Slowly we descended, the dome-sail creaking as the fumes and heat died out. I spun the glider blades faster to push the craft over the flat surface below, the craft pivoting, and as if practised, we touched down gently.

I snapped the Desert cap, threw off my mask and put a hand on Sett's shoulder.

'We make a good team.'

'This exciting,' she whispered in my ear. 'Thank you finding Langria.'

I looked down the side of the Pyramid, immediately getting a sense of unease. We were far closer to the ground now than when flying, but standing on something solid somehow made it feel like a longer way to fall. The sloping stones looked hungry, ready to break every bone in my body on the roll down.

I took out the Farsight. There wasn't much light to go by, but I didn't see too much movement down by any of the many Pyramid gates. Then I touched the lid of the Coldmaker. The bronze was Cold.

'Next time I see you,' I said to the machine, 'I'll have you working.'

A gust of wind caressed my cheeks. I faced the stars and smiled. Maybe it was an empty thing to do, but maybe not. Sometimes hope is everything.

Sett loaded up with one of every kind of weapon we brought. Then she attached pouches of the Chossek powder to her belt, for darkening our skin. She gave me a nod, her expression ready and focused.

I touched my lips and then held them out towards the sands.

I decided to bring a crossbow. That left me a hand free, and I grabbed an oil lantern, keeping it dark for now. I wished it was a Sinai, so I could adjust the light, and I told myself I would show Sett my design if we made it out of this alive.

'Okay,' I said, gesturing to the balcony door. 'Lets just hope the others landed without issue.'

Sett tightened her grip over the sword with the rotating end, which I decided to call a 'Swing Sword'.

'They did,' she said. 'Is sure. We meet them inside.'

'From the rumours,' I said. 'The Khat keeps the Khol down at the very bottom chambers, behind all sorts of defenses. Guards. Hounds. Traps. We need to be ready for anything, and be fast. If we don't get out before the Sun rises, someone will surely look up at the Pyramid and see the Mattys.'

Sett nodded and we left the craft behind. The balcony door was unlocked.

We entered a dark room with a stale smell, but with Cold lingering in the air. The whole Pyramid was likely constantly cooled at all times, and I ground my teeth thinking about how much Meesh-Dahm was being wasted on lifeless rock.

Sett took the lantern and lit the fire, slowly feeding it oil.

'Khol,' she said matter-of-factly. 'Right over there.'

I dropped to my knees, nearly dropping the lantern.

I gasped. 'Tears above, it is a Khol!'

It was right in front of us, sitting on a pedestal in the middle of the room. A bed of silks were folded underneath, carefully arranged so they wouldn't obstruct the three lines at the Khol's centre.

We were saved.

I gasped, dropping my supplies and rushing over.

At first I thought it must be a trick; that guards were waiting in the dark corners of the room, running their thumbs across their sharp blades as we rushed into their trap. But there was no one else in the lavish room. Just us and the Khol.

Sett rushed at my side, victory sounds on her lips. They were almost growls.

'I can't,' I said, reaching out and my hands on the Khol. 'I can't believe that – DAMN IT!'

Sett jumped into a defensive stance. Her blade was up before I could finish shouting. 'What is it, Meshua?'

Damn the Khat.

Damn them all.

'It's fake,' I seethed.

My palms were flat and tight around the curved sides of the Khol, trembling from anger.

'What you meaning?' Sett asked, pointing her blade at the dark corners of the room. 'I never being seen Khol before, but from scrolls and carvings—'

I picked up the imposter Khol and smashed it against the ground.

The sphere smashed into a thousand glittering pieces. The crash made me cringe, but thankfully the sound was more delicate than violent, like the ringing of small bells. I couldn't tell what the fake Khol was made of, but it was utterly convincing.

The jagged shards spread across the floor, scattering beneath golden-gilded chairs and fancy glass statuettes.

'Real Khol are Cold to the touch,' I said, clenching my teeth. 'And a real Khol doesn't shatter.'

Sett nodded.

Then it truly dawned on me how difficult this mission would be. We had no idea what we were getting ourselves in to. The Pyramid was going to be a different world entirely, one with which none of us were familiar.

A door across the room flew opened.

Sett turned, blade ready.

I ducked, going back for my crossbow.

Zeekah and Bear shot into the room. Zeekah wielded two short whips with blades at the end, ready to slice through the air. Bear lumbered through with her huge spiked hammer, the weapon above her head. They both relaxed when they saw that Sett and I were the source of the crash. Bear pointed the hammer at a patch of the shards. For reasons beyond me, she didn't topple over from weight of the weapon.

Sett said something in Langrian. There was a bite of reproach in her tone. Bear started to answer but Sett shook her head.

'Common tongue from now,' Sett said. 'So Meshua understand.'

Bear swallowed hard, looking like she'd just tasted a scorpion. 'No break things, Meshua. We need being shadow and dreams.'

Bear's common tongue was much worse than Sett's. Her words sounded like they were covered in sand and ground under a boot.

'Sorry,' I said. 'I'll be better. But I doubt anyone's here anyway.'

Zeekah's head jerked, her ear perking up. 'Coming.'

Four more figures stormed into the extravagant chamber. It took me a moment to register that the dark bodies were the rest of the Langrian warriors. They all arrived covered in Chossek, with weapons at the ready.

I felt soured by the fake Khol, but having these fighters around me made things much more bearable. The Khat would have his traps, but he wouldn't be expecting a force like ours. Sinniah stepped over the shards without care, putting her forehead against Sett's.

'What happen?' Sinniah asked.

'Khol not real,' Sett announced. 'Real Khol is having Cold touch.'

The warriors around the room nodded, taking in the information.

Zeekah wrinkled her nose. 'Paphos smell of poison.'

Sett spat on the ground. 'All Asham poison.'

'Come,' Sinniah said. 'I think seeing way down.'

We filed out of the room, and the hallway split into four directions. Ellora kept at the back, looking sullen and mournful. Everyone else was poised and buzzing for battle.

Fighting was probably like breathing to the Langrians, and Ellora was the only one who didn't seem like she belonged.

The warriors positioned themselves so I'd be in the middle of the pack. I wanted to be at the front where the danger was, but they were all much faster on their feet and I didn't have a choice. Bear was the closest warrior to me, her giant hammer raised with menace.

One of the hallways slanted downwards. That would be our path.

'That one,' I said quietly, pointing. 'On the right.'

Sett and Sinniah stormed down the hallway without hesitation, weapons at the ready. I followed behind trying to keep my crossbow tip from skewering any ankles.

The tunnel thinned out, so much that we had to file through one at a time.

The walls were even cooler here, smooth and tight. I felt the weight of all the stone around me, enough to shallow my breathing and cripple my speed. The Langrians reacted differently, moving through the tunnel like it was leading them to a banquet instead of deeper into an enemy fortress.

We swept along without speaking. Sett made small hand signals as the tunnel rounded corners and became stairs. Sinniah relayed the commands back with Bear whispering things to me like 'soft your step' and 'low your face' as rough translations. The warriors moved as one, with me carried by their force.

The Pyramid apparently wasn't all sprawling chambers, but more of a solid piece with spaces carved out through. The Inventor in me knew a design like this would be easier to keep standing over time. The nervous side of me felt trapped by the oppressive amount of stone. There wouldn't be any quick ways of escaping, should trouble arise.

Bear and I rounded another corner and found Sett pressed with her ear against a doorway, her thumb rubbing the hilt of her Swing Sword. We gathered tight in a group, and Sett made a few hand signals for us to stop and be quiet. Bear pressed her lips against my ear, giving me a start.

'Two Asham,' Bear whispered. Her breath was thick with heat, voice barely discernible. 'Sett and Sinniah being first. You stay. No follow.'

Sett and Sinniah fell into another kiss. Their lips pressed against each other with feverish desperation, yet silently. I imagined their feelings for each other were intensified constantly by battle, never knowing if they'd make it out alive.

I understood the sentiment. My heart ached to be home.

The warriors smeared some of the Chossek powder on their skin, offering some for me as well. I smoothed a single layer over my arms and face to be polite, although my skin was already darker than theirs. I probably didn't need it, but it made me feel like a part of the group.

Sett and Sinniah picked up their weapons. Sett loosened the disc on her Spin Sword. Sinniah took a glass Javelin off her back, the weapon veined with something black and smoky down the middle.

Sett snuffed the lantern and handed me the weapons bag. Then she stalked through the door like a silent wraith, keeping tight to the left wall. Sinniah was right at her back. Through the closing gap, I could see the distant image of the two Asham standing in the middle of the next hallway. One of them carried a Sinai, the dim glow not quite reaching the walls. Their conversation continued like nothing was wrong, clearly unaware that death came at them from the shadows.

Bear caught the door before it shut completely. We all watched through the crack.

'Bastard still hasn't broken yet,' one of the Asham said. 'Can you believe that?'

'He will. Left him with enough to put down a whole Jadan

barracks, didn't we? Damn traitor will go weak soon enough. Did you spit in his food?'

'Always,' the other Asham said with a cackle. 'And more than just spit this time. Made it real Jadan-like for him.'

'Delicious.'

'That's what the bastard gets for keeping us from seeing the Fall. Biggest celebration in our lifetimes and we're stuck here playing Domestic. It's lizard dung.'

'You're telling me. But you know how it is: can't trust a Jadan to do Noble work.'

One of the Asham was holding a tray with food balanced on top. The other was tapping something out of a vial into his palm. I could just make out the outline of Sett and Sinniah slinking through the darkness against the wall. They moved without a single sound; for a moment I couldn't tell if the twisting shadows in the shapes of warriors were real or imagined.

The Asham with the vial brought his hand to his nose and sniffed deeply. 'We'll have our own celebration. How much do you want before we hit the stables?'

'My own stash.'

They both laughed.

A sword and Javelin were raised.

Before Bear could stop me, I burst through the door, waving my crossbow.

'Wait!' I shouted.

The Asham spilled his tray, gruel splattering over from a cracked bowl and splashing on his fancy shoes.

'Shit,' the Asham said, shaking his leg. 'Shit.'

'Who's there?' The other vial Asham asked, waving the Sinai in my direction. His hair was dirty yellow, not quite as vibrant as Cam's.

'I'm trying to help you,' I said. 'Don't move.'

The Asham with the tray narrowed his eyes. His gaze went down to my ankle.

'Holy blood,' he said. 'That's a damn Jadan, that is. What are you doing with a weapon, slave?'

'No anklet on it either,' the Asham with the vial said, his tone delighted. He ran his finger under his nose, giving a single sniff. 'Oh, boy, are you in trouble.'

Sett and Sinniah stepped up behind them. They had each taken out a sleek dagger. The tip of each blade found and pricked into a fair-skinned throat, poised to sink deep. The Asham froze in shock.

'Don't kill them,' I called out. Something had been off about their conversation. I needed to know more. 'These Asham can tell us things.'

The Asham with the vial sniffed again. Now that I was closer I could tell that it was Grassland Dream he'd been taking.

'Oh, I get it,' he said. 'This is an uprising. How droll!'

His friend didn't seem to find this as funny. 'It's an insult to the Crier.' He gasped as Sinniah's blade dug out a trickle of red. 'It's high blasphemy!'

'Obviously,' the one under the Grassland Dream said. 'Which makes it even more delicious. Taking arms against High Nobility. In the Pyramid. What a story! This is wonderful, Philip. Our friends will come back from the Fall thinking they have all the best stories and—'

'This Asham poison words,' Sett said in a lazy manner. 'I kill now?'

I held up my hand, getting closer.

'Just hold on,' I said. 'No killing yet.'

'Killing?' the Dream Asham cackled, his eyes red. 'This just keeps getting better. You think the Crier will allow you to kill his High Priests in the most holy place. You will be struck with fire and plague before you even load that crossbow, you little—'

Sett jammed the dagger all the way into the Asham's neck

and then ripped the blade through the front of his throat, cutting through cartilage and gristle. A voiceless gasp spurted from the Asham's severed wind pipe.

Sett let the body fall. She spat into his dirty yellow hair as he spasmed to death, trying to plug his leak. Noble blood fountained into the spilled gruel at his feet.

'You is so beautiful,' Sinniah said to Sett, pursing her lips. 'Do killing mine now. I watch.'

Sett bowed and then gestured to the other captive, giving me a wink. 'We kill now too.'

It wasn't a question. I didn't have time to object.

Set grabbed her Spin Sword, did a manoeuvre with her wrist to get the end piece turning, and then flashed the sword through the air. The end piece expertly sped with its rotation, slicing the front of the other Asham's throat.

The second body collapsed.

Their blood mixed on the stone floor, and Sinniah spat into the resulting puddle.

'Why did you kill them both?' I gasped.

'Is for luck,' Sett explained, calmly locking the disc tight back on her sword so it wouldn't spin. She seemed bored. 'All Asham poison.'

'But they could have told us where the Khol were.'

Sett shook her head and then made a gesture with her hand like a mouth opening and closing. 'No. They just . . . *sliyom*.'

'*Sliyom* means lie,' Ellora explained from behind me.

I spun. The rest of the Langrians had filtered into the room without a sound. I was thoroughly impressed at their stealth. Now I understood how these Asham had been taken by complete surprise.

'Thank you, Ellora,' Sett said. 'They just lie.'

I started to speak and then stopped myself, taking a frustrated breath instead.

'You're probably right,' I said, feeling a surge of anger.

Sett shrugged. 'We try again next one we find.'

One of the Asham was still wiggling at our feet. Bear stepped up and raised her giant hammer.

I turned away, scanning the room, my stomach clenching. When the pounding sound was over, I stepped away from the river of blood.

'They were talking about a prisoner,' I said.

'Many prisoners in Paphos,' Sett said, picking up the Sinai and giving it a look of appreciation. 'All prisoners in Paphos. No time for one. You knowing what this make is?'

I nodded, holding out my hand. 'I do. I'll handle it.'

It wasn't the killing that had bothered me. Something about the Asham conversation wasn't sitting right.

Sett took her weapons bag and wandered to the far side of the room, sweeping the rest of the chamber. There was a single locked door off to the side, and three tunnels out of the place. Only one of the tunnels dipped at an angle downward. I nodded and and we took that one with speed.

After making it around the first corner, I stopped myself.

Returning went against all of my better instincts, but I couldn't help it. Something had hooked into my mind. I had to know for sure.

'Hold on,' I said, letting out a sigh. 'I'm going back.'

Bear stepped in my way, giving Sett a questioning look.

'I just need to see,' I said, ducking beneath her spiked weapon with a speed that surprised myself. None of the others tried to stop me, although Sett started calling my name. Ellora stepped aside, giving me a sad smile as I skirted around her and fled back to the bloody room.

I set the Sinai next to the fallen Asham. I tried not to think about all the fluids coating my arms as I searched their pockets. Eventually I found a large steel key and a smaller brass one that seemed painfully familiar. I shot over to the locked door before the warriors could talk me out of my madness.

The bigger key fit the lock. The door swung open.

I stepped inside, steeling myself for an attack. The Asham could have been guarding some ancient beast for all I knew, like a Firegog or a Sand Golem. Such things were possible in a place this old; a place with this many secrets.

I brought the Sinai in the room, surprised to find all sorts of poisons stacked from floor to ceiling. The room was stocked with crystal bottles of ale, coming in all shapes and sizes. There were also bowls of Grassland Dream everywhere, packed to the rim, the powder nearly spilling over. There were three Droughtweed pipes on a small table, ready to be smoked. Next to them were little brown button-looking plants in a bowl, a pestle sitting at the ready.

Two pale legs stuck out from the shadows.

They were dirty, the skin fair and sallow. And on one was a terrible invention. One that I knew all too well.

An anklet.

The same kind that Leroi had been ordered to make for every Jadan in the Tavor Manor. The type that had Pinion's acid inside. The type that would burn through the wearer's leg if the anklet wasn't wound by a small brass key – the kind now in my possession – every few hours.

I swung the light forward, heart in my throat.

And then I saw the man's face.

I lost breath. I lost words.

In my life I had created Cold and flown to Langria, but it was this face that shattered all of my notions of what was possible.

He shied away from the light, putting a hand in front of his face.

'Just leave the food, dammit. No Erridian bastard is going to get the satisfaction of watching me break.'

I began to shake.

His voice was the same low, gritty tone from my past; full of sadness and longing; dripping with ideas. A sob wracked my chest.

It couldn't be him.

I wasn't ready to hope for such things.

'Leroi?' I whispered, my voice cracking.

His hand slowly came away from his face, revealing the same speckled goatee I had once known. His haunted eyes blinked over and over. His hair was no longer slicked back, but the same grey. He went silent.

'It's me,' I said, choking. 'It's Spout.'

Leroi slowly gathered his leg back, hiding the anklet. His arms began to quiver. He looked through me, unfocused. I couldn't tell how deeply they'd broken him, and for a moment I wasn't even sure if he'd remember me.

Then there was a smile. Blood ran down his gums and he was missing a few teeth, but his smile was glowing.

'Of course it is,' Leroi whispered.

I could barely speak. 'You're alive.'

Leroi paused. He wiped at his face, tears spilling.

'You should be in Langria, Spout,' he croaked.

'I was.' I laughed. 'But now I'm glad I'm here.'

Leroi's face passed through a flurry of emotions. Clearly I was the last person in the entire World Cried he expected to walk into his cell. He eyed the crossbow I was holding and weapons strapped on my belt, his expression getting more confused by the moment.

He looked so feeble.

His arms were sticks; his chest was sunken.

But his eyes were clear.

'Cam and Shilah are okay,' I said. 'They're in Jadans' Rise – the City of David's Fall. But we don't call it that anymore.'

Leroi went to say something, and then his expression dropped. 'The Second Fall. But that—'

I reached out my hand.

He stared at my bronze fingers, and then slowly took my hand. His grip was so weak, his fingers thin and spindly. I helped him to his feet, and although he was a head taller than me, he seemed so feeble that I thought I'd have to carry him in my arms.

'Has it been that long?' he asked, his hand going to my arm and then my shoulder, checking if I was real. 'You've filled out. I thought you were a guard at first.'

Heat stung my cheeks. 'I have a lot to tell you.'

'What happened to your hand?' The last of the haze drained from his face, and was replaced with concern. 'What are you doing in the Pyramid? How did you get all the way up here? I thought—'

I wrapped him in a hug, making sure not to squeeze too tight. I didn't want to break anything in his bony frame. He smelled awful, like he'd been sleeping in a dead-cart. I couldn't care less, searching out his familiar scent within the foulness. He paused and then squeezed back, his cheek going to my hair. His warmth and odour were both welcome.

It was better than finding a Khol.

'I missed you,' I said.

He didn't say anything. I could tell he was too choked up.

Releasing him, I picked up the Sinai and crossbow, trying to stand tall like Shilah; to show him how far I've come.

I knew I couldn't have my father back.

But I would settle for my teacher.

'I'm going to tell you everything,' I said. 'But right now we have to move.'

'What's going on, Spout?'

'We need Kho – Frosts. As many as we can get. Leroi, they're seeds!'

'What do you mean, seeds?'

I pulled out the smaller brass key and fit it into the anklet. I turned it the opposite way of the winding, and the contraption came off with a satisfying click.

'Frosts make Cry Patches,' I said. 'Plant them in the ground and Cold knows where to fall. It's the secret to ending the Great Drought.'

'I—' Leroi swallowed hard 'but I don't – how—'

'I'll tell you everything. I have so many stories!' I laughed, grabbing his arm. His elbow felt like the knob of a hammer. 'I've learned so many things that I can teach you. But right now you need to answer two questions for me.'

Leroi nodded, wiping more tears away. He was clearly overwhelmed, but his eyes weren't glazed over in the way I'd known. He'd resisted the drink or any of the other poisons.

A lump welled in my throat. Leroi was a High Noble, a Tavor even, and yet here he was. Tortured and tempted, bound and locked away in a small closet. No one was safe from the Khat's terror.

'How many Frosts does the Khat have here?' I took a deep breath. 'And do you know where they are?'

Whispers came from behind me, back out in the chamber.

Leroi kicked aside the anklet, looking over my shoulder. 'From what I understand, the Khat has more Frosts than we can count. But he keeps them in the deep chambers under the Pyramid, and there are traps down there. I know some of the secrets, but I haven't been past a certain point. And even if most of the Nobles here have gone to see the Second Fall, I imagine we would need a small army if we were going to escape with any.' His eyes narrowed. 'Is there someone out there with you?'

I cracked a smile and ran two fingers down my cheek.

Chapter Twenty

I shared as much news with everyone as best as I could as we rushed through the hallways.

Who Leroi was to me; what he'd done; who the Langrians were to me; how we'd all gotten to the Pyramid; The Coldmaker; The Mattys.

Who put what in the ground.

It was all one big jumble of emotion. My words came out messy and stunted. My head wrenched back and forth to try and remember who knew what, and what still needed to be said.

I was happy.

I was excited.

I was almost whole.

Leroi guided us along the right paths, his puny legs barely able to stand. His kneecaps were swollen and bulging, as red as Sobek bites, and he had a smattering of Firepox on his elbows.

Leroi couldn't stop staring. At both me and the Langrians. His face was in constant disbelief.

There was no sign of enemies, although there was plenty of tension.

At first Rivvy and Tully looked at Leroi like they wanted to grind him into sand, but I explained that Leroi was a 'maker' as well; that he'd taught me everything I knew; that he alone was responsible for my survival. I told them that Leroi had sacrificed himself to allow me and my friends to escape the Tavor manor. Soon enough the Langrians softened up, and even Ellora finally proved she was capable of a smile. She ended up hovering closest to Leroi as we ran.

'To the right,' Leroi called out, the walls clearly funnelling into a long chamber. 'We're getting close to the bottom levels.'

The warriors moved in silence, their weapons ready.

'You should see Sett's tinkershop in Langria,' I said to Leroi.

He coughed, looking into his palm with a grimace and then hiding it from view. 'Course I should. I think I'd like that more than most things.'

'Can you believe it's happening?' I asked, almost giddy. I was so full of energy I could probably fly back to my friends without the Matty. 'That we're going to end the Drought. Me and you, back together. With Langrian warriors.'

Leroi took a deep breath, emotion darkening his features.

'What?' I asked.

'Frosts are seeds,' he said, his gaze distant. 'How could we not have known?'

I shrugged. 'It's no one's fault but the Khat's.'

We filtered into a new chamber. The centre passage through the room was clear, but each side of the walkway was stacked with thousands of glass bottles and vials. The containers were all different sizes, but filled with the same black, gritty substance.

'Scrolls and books,' Leroi explained, waving us through. 'All burned to ash and stuffed in glass. Anything from before the Drought and after. Anything that had to do with Jadan history. They were destroyed and put on display.'

My stomach knotted at all the loss. All those stories and wisdom wasted. 'Why would they save the ash?'

Leroi grunted and squeezed his hands into fists.

Sinniah instinctively – at least I hoped it was only instinct – raised her Javelin at Leroi, but Sett waved her down.

'Because sometimes pain isn't enough,' Leroi said. 'Sometimes they just have to twist the blade.'

Towards the end of the chamber the glass containers became larger, more like tubs, each labelled. Inside were shocks of hair clinging to what looked like old camel leather, scattered with more black ash.

Leroi shook his head. 'You don't need to know about those.'

The group slowed as Sinniah stopped, making a hand gesture. Sett tried to urge her onward, but Sinniah stubbornly tapped on one of the glass displays with her sword.

'Is scalps,' she said.

Leroi's face fell. 'Yes.'

'Of Jadan,' Sinniah growled. 'These Jadan scalp. Very old.'

Leroi looked down at his ankle; the skin there was rubbed red and raw from the anklet.

Sinniah snarled. 'All Asham poison.'

I pointed to Leroi. 'He had nothing to do with this.'

Sinniah snarled, but Zeekah came up and put a hand on her shoulder.

'This isn't the time for judgment,' I said. 'Like it or not we've always needed Asham help, and Asham deeyoneh. What about your Marcheyes and Shepherds? Not all Asham are poison. Some Asham are family.'

Sett gave me an impressed look.

Leroi blinked, visibly stunned.

'What?' I asked.

'I don't know half of those words,' Leroi said. 'But I can tell you've grown up.'

'I can see a lot of truth now. And I see what matters,' I

said, giving a dismissive wave of my crossbow. 'Now show us the way, Leroi. We need to find those Frosts and get them into the ground.'

Sett bowed to me. 'Young wisdom.'

Sinniah's scowl deepened, but then it broke into an appreciative smile.

'Meshua,' she said.

The next chamber was filled entirely with flames.

The tunnel fed directly into the fires, with no way through. We'd either have to turn back, or get burned alive.

Sett rubbed her hands over the threshold to the chamber.

'What are you looking for?' I asked.

'Switch or button,' Sett said. 'Must being way kill flame.'

'I go through,' Bear said, pounding a fist against her chest. 'I fastest.'

Tully rapped her knuckles against Bear's forehead. 'You not so fast, cub.'

Bear prodded Tully in the chest with the handle of her hammer. Tully chuckled with delight.

Sett continued to look for a secret, running her hands along the ground of the tunnel. Flames licked at her knuckles. 'Is right, Bear. But this too much fire and steps. I find the secret button.'

I braced myself against the deadly inferno. The flames were everywhere. They lasted the entire chamber, and the room was far too long to chance running through.

Leroi shook his head. 'The Khat calls this the Chamber of Eternal Flame. And as far as I know, the fire never ends. We can't get through.'

Sett made a dismissive sound. 'For maker, you sure talking dumb. No fire last forever. Need something to feed.'

Leroi laughed, which turned into a nasty cough. 'Okay, what I mean is, there's no way to stop the fires from here.

It's probably all controlled from underneath, a machine that feeds up smokeless oil. But it's never turned off, and there's only one way to the deeper layers. *Through* this room.'

Sett stood up, crossing her hands across her chest.

Leroi's bottom gums were bleeding. I wondered when was the last time he had a proper meal, or any Cold water.

'Did she understand?' Leroi whispered. 'Should I speak—'

'I understand!' Sett hissed. 'Do you?'

He smiled. 'I like her.'

Ellora leaned against the tunnel wall, muttering to herself.

'This room is the Khat's way of proving his divinity,' Leroi said, a bit of mischief behind his eyes. 'Only those made entirely of Cold can pass through the room. The Worthy. He claims that the Crier chooses who gets to live and die, and that the Khat is his instrument. He apparently touches his Priests and says a prayer, and then they can walk through as well.'

Sett and Sinniah gave each other a look. Bear stepped up to the door frame, the charred stone lined with soot.

'I can make,' Bear said, preparing to leap into the room. 'I so fast.'

I almost shouted at her to stop. It would be certain death.

But before I could, Sett put a hand on Bear's arm. 'No. You never get through. Too far.'

I stepped up to the frame, looking over Bear's shoulder. There had to be a trick. The Khat had been proven a liar over and over, and there was no way he had enough Cold in him to resist flames. Even with access to all of those Frosts, there had to be a secret, especially if Priests could pass as well.

I skirted around Bear. Sett went to stop me, but I halted right at the threshold. The heat of the flames gnawed at my face, and I nearly flinched backwards. I steeled myself, knowing if I could handle the heat from the Desert, I could handle this. I leaned in as far as pain would allow, and looked up into the ceiling. It was stained black, charred from a life-time of being roasted from below.

But the shading was not even.

The whole top of the chamber was charred to some degree, but there were certain places where the stone was consider-ably less dark. There were flames beneath the clear spots as well, but they didn't seem to be spitting up any soot. It reminded me of Sett's revelation about Meesh-Dahm in the Dagon, when the Asham were hiding below in the trench.

I gave Leroi a curious look, my mind putting everything together.

'Mirrors,' I said at last. 'Right?'

Leroi narrowed his eyes, surveying the room and then grabbed me by the shoulders. 'Bless your mind, Spout.'

'You obviously taught me well.' I pointed into the chamber, turning to the Langrians. 'They're mirrors. There's a path through, but it looks like the whole room is on fire because of reflections.'

Bear nodded. 'Yes. Is obvious.'

'Not to you.' Tully slapped her in the back of the head, retreating quickly as Bear growled and raised her hammer.

Sett tapped her bottom lip, appraising the chamber. 'Is right. Is clever.'

'The line of Khats have been cruel and soulless, but they know how to keep their reputation.' Leroi nodded, but his enthusiasm began to wane. 'There's a problem, however. I've never been through the room myself. And even with the mirrors, the room is still blistering hot and we'd need to know the exact path across.'

Sett leaned in, cupping a hand over her mouth. 'What is "reputation"?'

I thought about it for a second. 'The story of your deeds.'

Sett held up her sword. 'Well Langria have reputation too. If path through, we take.'

Leroi stepped in front. 'We really should think this through—'

'I have an idea,' I said, the words coming to my lips before the plan was formed. I gestured for Sett's hook invention and the bag of Chossek powder on her hip. She handed them over with a probing look.

The powder was good for darkening things. I just hoped it was sticky.

I balanced the bag on top of the hook, opening the lips. Then I aimed the spear towards the ceiling at the centre of the room.

I steadied my breath and fired.

The bag was quick to slip to the side, the hook shooting out without it, smacking the ceiling and dropping into the fires. Most of the powder stayed in the bag, which landed harmlessly by my feet. A little bit of it clouded against one mirror that was off to the right, however, the surface tilted to show the flames but not catch our reflections.

'Crap,' I said, reeling back the rope. It scraped the hook through the flames but eventually it caught on a mirror I couldn't see. I tugged, but the hook was caught, and the rope instantly began to crack and sizzle, burning to ash.

'Good starting, Meshua,' Bear said, rubbing a fist against her chest. 'We finish.'

She patted me on the head and pushed me aside. Then she picked up the Chossek powder and handed the bag to Tully. She stared at the stained mirror closest to us and then commanded something in Langrian. Tully's smile turned wicked.

'What did she say?' Leroi asked.

Sett twitched her lips. 'She saying "You throw. I destroy".'

Bear drew back her giant hammer and barrelled into the room. She swung the weapon fast, obliterating the first mirror.

Tully was at her back. She howled wildly, throwing the

Chossek powder over Bear's shoulder. The cloud spread out and stained the next mirror, a pace to the left.

Bear cocked her arms back again – with Tully ducking to the side like it was a practised move – and she attacked the second mirror with such force that I could feel the shattering all the way back in the tunnel.

The shards burst outwards into the flames, glittering orange and white and blue, but the reflections on the ground were minimal. Bear hopped along the safe path as best she could, Tully tossing out the powder, smashing a third and fourth mirror, until Bear screamed a command and they retreated back to the group.

Taking refuge in the tunnel, Tully brushed the heat off Bear's skin.

The rest of the Langrians cheered gleefully.

'Crier above,' Leroi said. 'Are you hurt?'

Ellora came up to Leroi and put a hand on his shoulder. 'They Langria warriors. Made of fury. They friends with pain. We all friends with pain.'

Leroi stared at Ellora's fingers. I hoped he wouldn't buckle under the weight.

Rivvy reached for the Chossek powder. 'You rest, Bear. Zeekah and I going next.'

Zeekah's eyes lit up with fear; still she nodded.

Bear shook her head and filled her lungs. She looked to Tully, both of them growling, and together they stormed back into the room. Their war cry seemed loud enough to scare some of the flames back.

They ran across the mirror shards, which showed the safe passage. Then they broke more mirrors in front of them, bashing halfway through the room. Their cries burned my ears. Tully kept tossing the powder out wildly over Bear's shoulder, spotting the next mirrors. The mace-hammer flashed wildly. I thought I could smell burning hair and skin.

Eventually they made it to the other side of the room.

Bear collapsed as soon as she stepped into the following tunnel.

I was nearly sick with guilt, but in their wake was a clear trail of mirror shards. The flames were still menacing, hungrily licking the empty spaces, but we had our path.

Sett made a hand signal and the Langrians stormed through without thinking, following the trail. I followed behind Rivvy, the shards of broken mirrors crunching under my sandals. The room was the hottest thing I'd ever felt, the air stifling and toxic, and I had no idea how Tully and Bear had handled it for so long.

We made it across to the other side in a flash. The heat was terrible, but the flames themselves remained just out of reach.

Sett was already kneeling next to Bear. She tossed a Wisp into a waterskin and tilted it to Bear's lips, which were angry and charred. Tully was hunched over her knees, coughing out Chossek powder. Bear didn't seem responsive to the water, but Sett continued to pour life on her lips and face. Bears' arms had blistered. I couldn't look at the skin on her knuckles, which was burned to a crisp and bloody. There were also shards of mirror sticking out of her wrists.

Sett massaged Bear's cheek, whispering a prayer. I recognized the words and said the second half with her.

'Is she alive?' I asked.

Sett continued to hum.

Ellora and Leroi made their way through the fiery room last. Ellora had Leroi's arm draped over her shoulder, helping him along. My heart felt like it was getting attacked from all different angles.

Sinniah gave up her waterskin next, dissolving in a few Wisps. Sett shook it up and began pouring it onto Bear's arms. Sett's hum deepened in cadence as she worked, beautiful and forlorn.

Bear's body shuddered, her eyes slowly opening. Her jaw was clenched, and she gestured with only her fingers for the waterskin to go to her lips. Sett obliged, and Bear sucked down the rest of the water. Her body shook with pain as she drank. I couldn't watch. Bear's burns were terrible. Her eyes found mine. She gave me a victorious nod.

I nodded back.

Bear said something in Langrian to Sett, and Sett's hand went to Bear's chest, rubbing the spot over her heart.

Zeekah was closest beside me. I asked her: 'What did Bear say?'

'Death not catch me yet,' Zeekah translated. 'I being too fast.'

'You stay here,' Sett said to Bear, helping her against the cool stone wall of the tunnel. She snapped her fingers at Rivvy, who handed over her waterskin and Wisps next, placing them next to Bear. 'We find you on way back.'

Bear looked like she was going to argue, but her body collapsed against the wall, clenching in pain.

'Be wind,' she said.

Sett went over to Tully next, who waved her away. Tully had gotten crispy at the edges, but her injuries weren't nearly as severe as Bear's.

'I'm sorry,' I said, kneeling before Bear.

Bear laughed like my apology was the funniest thing in the world.

Her eyes closed.

The warriors continued on.

The tunnel was relentless in its twisting. My sense of direction was quickly dismantled. The floor was steep and slick, but the air was cooler down here. I dragged my fingers along the walls, my skin tingling beneath the sensation.

We had to be getting close.

There were noises in the distance. Strange sounds I didn't recognize.

'What do you think is down here?' I asked the group.

'I've heard rumours,' Leroi said. 'But I don't want to believe them.'

'Why not?'

A shudder ran through Leroi's body, his legs struggling to carry him forward. I wondered how long he must have been made to sit in that room, the poisons offering a tempting escape. Yet he refrained. I still had so much to learn from him.

Leroi shook his head.

Ellora was at his side, looking ready to catch him should he fall. Sett was leading the charge of the warriors, sword out in case any Asham felt like surprising us. Tully's cough wasn't going away, but she kept it stifled and maintained pace.

The tunnel filtered into a long hallway, the walls widening. In the distance was an abrupt end to our passage.

A single Sinai sat in the centre of the hallway, illuminating the walls.

Detailed paintings had been done on the stone itself, floor to ceiling. The light was too dim from where we were standing to make out the shapes and colours, but Sett shot into the hallway with her oil lantern above her head. She swung it from wall to wall. Her face opened up with awe.

The pictures were of animals.

Hundreds of them.

Colourful depictions showed vast plains, teeming with life. I didn't recognize most of the animals, but I didn't expect to. A whole section was dedicated to an open sky, with birds soaring through thick white clouds, their feathers wide and glorious. There were forests of flowers, and impossibly tall trees, all flooded with colour.

A large patch was also dedicated to water animals, showing fish that I'd never seen before. Some fish lit up like Adaam Grass. Others were striped and long.

It was enough to wonder over for days. The paintings were magnificent, but there was no door anywhere. My stomach clenched, thinking we must have picked the wrong passage, although I hadn't seen any others.

The strangest part of the room, however, were the odd sounds.

They were distant and full of fear. Some were high pitched and squeaky like a rusty wheel. Others low and menacing. I pressed my ear to the animal pictures on the walls, wondering from where the sounds could possibly be coming.

Zeekah's head cocked from side to side. 'I be hearing . . . I be hear – Loonchin?' She shook her head and then went straight for a painting of high grasses. There were funny-looking creatures leaping over the green blades, their tongues long and split at the centre. Zeekah frantically tapped her finger against the painting, her cheeks filling with colour. 'Is Loonchin!'

'Yes,' Leroi said absently. His eyes narrowed as he scanned the walls.

The rest of the warriors began to search for their own Meesh-Dahm animal pictures on the walls. Rivvy found her baboon, which turned out to be a hairy creature with a long face and fierce fangs. Tully found her fox, which was poking up from a hole in a kind of grass that was impossibly green. Sinniah searched across the plains portion of the wall, eventually settling on a beautiful beast I didn't recognize. This one was orange and had black stripes. Tully pointed out a bear, which was blocky, black and menacing.

'Bear be jealous,' Tully said with a sigh.

Sett reached out to the forest portion, finding her Jaguar. She touched the painting and then put two fingers to her lips.

Ellora swallowed hard. Sett came over and gave Ellora a reassuring squeeze on her hand.

'Ellora no longer have animal in Meesh-Dahm,' Sett told me. 'Is gone.'

'Why'd it leave?' I asked.

Zeekah's eyes nearly popped out of her head. Ellora appeared to crumble under my question.

'Sorry,' I said. 'I didn't mean to—'

Sett gave the room a placating gesture.

Ellora nodded, as if saying it was okay. She kept her eyes off the walls.

'Ellora being lost her daughter,' Sett said. 'She go playing too far in Dagon. Asham snatch her up. And so no more Meesh-Dahm. Leave with heart.'

Sett spoke calmly, but I could tell that the loss stung her as well.

Leroi's lips thinned. He took a step closer to Ellora, looking like he wanted to reach out and comfort her. Ellora met his eyes.

Then there was a brash, shrill sort of sound.

It was like a horn blast, but this had more body to it. Less hollow and deeper.

I narrowed my eyes, trying to find any sort of cracks that might betray a door. If there were any, then the paintings were doing a fantastic job of hiding the evidence. The whole wall was one smooth piece.

Zeekah dropped to her stomach.

I ducked as well, but then I realized that she was just putting her ear to the ground. No one was attacking.

'Down here,' Zeekah said, rubbing her ear on the floor. 'This way through. I never be hearing sound like these before.'

Sett bit her bottom lip. She tapped the floor with her sword, trying to find any sort of way in. Eventually she found a single crack, which Zeekah crawled towards. Sett wiggled her blade inside the crack, trying to pry it open, but it didn't budge.

If there was a way to open the floor, it wasn't through force.

Then the sound of footsteps. Coming from the tunnel behind us.

I'd been too distracted by the mysterious moans and wails to notice. The feet were moving fast and loud, almost a panicked run.

Sett and Sinniah looked at each other with a grin.

'Is good,' Sett said to me with a grin. 'We get answer now.'

An Asham came rushing around the corner, clutching a golden staff in his hands. The staff wasn't so much of a weapon as a talisman, gleaming with jewels and fine metal. There was also a Draft at the end, painted with a Closed Eye. The Asham was wearing a long hat with a Closed Eye on top. On anyone else, the hat would have scraped the ceiling, but the Asham was unnaturally short. His face was pinched and long, like a knife blade, but there were also pouches of flesh around his jowls.

He didn't seem to be scared of us. Instead, his face trembled with rage. He pointed the staff at us.

'Slaves,' he snarled. 'How dare you do this? The Khat has shown your kind life and mercy. And you dare take up arms to—' The tiny man stopped himself, letting out a frustrated huff. 'Leroi Tavor! What in the Crier's name are you doing out of your cell? And with these traitorous blasphemers!'

'This is Nad the second,' Leroi explained to me, bringing his voice down and gesturing to the new Asham. 'One of the Khat's High Priests. He's not on our side. He's an ass.'

Nad the Second's face went alder red. 'Any Jadan to take arms against the Crier will have their souls banished. They shall be tortured in the black forever.' Thin lips flung spit across the room. 'It is the duty of the Nobility to—'

Sett seemed unconcerned. She yawned at his threats.

'How we get through floor?' Sett asked him, interrupting, pointing to the crease in the floor. 'Tell us. You no lie or we killing you.'

Nad the Second's face pinched so tightly that I thought it might collapse into itself. His bloodshot eyes flashed around the room and his face shook with rage.

'If you slaves think I would ever allow you—'

Sett spoke to Sinniah in Langrian. Sinniah nodded, saying something back.

'And you dare speak unholy tongues in the sacred Pyramid?' the Priest seethed, his lips cracking into an evil grin. 'You have no idea what is going to befall you—'

Sinniah hurled her Javelin.

The sleek weapon soared through the air and went straight through Nad's left eye. The glass outer layer of the Javelin shattered on impact, the shards exploding into the Priest's skull. The smoky metal layer beneath the glass carried onward by momentum. It sliced through the back of Nad's head, clearing the other side.

The Priest was dead before he even had a chance to shriek. His body fell against the stone, but his head couldn't make it quite flat, as the bloody metal pole sticking out the back of his skull kept his neck propped up.

Rivvy growled. Tully clapped her hands gently.

I turned to Sinniah with wide eyes. It all happened so fast.

'Don't be worrying.' Sett winked at me. 'We know way now.'

'You do?' I swallowed hard. 'How?'

Sett gestured two fingers towards her eyes and then at one section of the wall. 'Asham give away secret with his looking. Asham very stupid and small.'

Sinniah walked over to the fallen Asham. She gathered spit in her cheeks and then unleased it on his body. Leroi gave me a questioning look as Sinniah did it again. Leroi looked a bit horrified, but sort of relieved.

'It's for luck,' I said with a shrug. 'The spit.'

Sinniah licked her lips. 'All Asham poison.'

'What's an Asham?' Leroi asked.

I pretended not to hear him.

Sett went to a section of the wall, stepping up to a painting I hadn't noticed before. It was of a well made of grey bricks, and at the bottom was a Khol. There were no animals around the well, and it looked rather out of place now that Sett was pointing it out.

Sett crouched down. She pressed the Khol at the bottom of the painting with two fingers.

The Cold buckled into the wall.

There was a clicking of gears and grinding sound of large slabs of stone, moving somewhere beneath us.

The floor began to open at the seams.

The sounds below instantly doubled in volume. Now I could hear new low growls as well as high-pitched squeaks.

The space widened enough for two bodies to fit through and then stopped.

Sinniah went over and kissed Sett's knuckles. Sett returned the affection with a smouldering look.

The exotic sounds kept intensifying, coming up in spurts of chattering and growls.

'Leroi,' I said, 'what's down there?'

He leaned over the dark staircase. 'I always hoped.'

'Monsters?' I asked.

Leroi swallowed hard. 'Far from it, Micah. Far from it.'

Tully handed Sinniah one of the small spears strapped on her back. Sinniah took the weapon, judging the weight. Her face arrived at an unsatisfied pout, but then led the charge down the stairs. She didn't stop to think, moving with full speed. Sett watched her go, eyes full of love and admiration.

Rivvy and Tully followed next.

I looked at Leroi, his face as pale as bone.

'Do you want to stay behind?' I asked.

Leroi coughed into his hand. Red splashed into his palm. He gave me a weak smile and then pointing to the skin on his knees.

'Just a bit of Firepox,' Leroi said. 'Don't worry. I'll be okay.'

'You sure?'

He looked over at Ellora.

'I think I'd die rather than miss this,' Leroi said, giving my shoulder a squeeze and then stepping down the stairs. I followed behind, the rest of the warriors at my back. The staircase was long and blissfully cool. It felt like we were walking on Ice, the stone beneath us wonderful to the touch. It was odd however, that the tunnel was stale and full of fear. The air had a thick texture, reminding me of how Picka's fur smelled after it had been shed. It made my nose wrinkle.

About halfway down, I glanced over my shoulder and found Sett at the top of the staircase, digging through her weapons bag.

'What are you doing?' I asked, the warriors rushing past me.

Sett pulled the toothed contraption that I decided to call a 'Foot Fang' out of the bag, wrenching the side apart. She set the invention in the middle of the third step down, lost in shadow.

'In case more Asham follow,' Sett said with a laugh, coming down to meet me along the stairs.

Together we followed the warriors. The air turned even cooler as we descended. Ahead of us, the rest of our group had already reached the bottom. Now there were all sorts of gasps mixing in with the unrecognizable sounds.

Sett and I hurried down.

Ellora was on her knees, touching the ground and praying. Tully had dropped her whips, the blades harmlessly at rest.

Sinniah and Rivvy were crying, which was something I also never thought I'd see. Sett stumbled as we joined the group, nearly tripping and falling as she took everything in.

We'd stepped into the past.

The room was nearly deafening with their calls.

Animals.

Real animals.

The cages and stables and pits stretched down the entire chamber.

The whole place stunk, but the air was cooled so deeply my skin had already begun to shiver. The room was vast, larger than the Coldmarch caves. Maybe five times as big. There were dozens of Sinais lining the rows of animal cages, casting light on things that didn't still exist.

I stumbled along, trying to make sense of what I was seeing.

The floor was almost painfully Cold. My heart yearned for Shilah; for her to be here by my side witnessing this. A true miracle.

'Crier above,' I said, everything about me stiffening with shock. 'He saved the animals. He's been keeping them alive all this time.'

'He didn't save them,' Sett said, her upper lip trembling in anger. 'He – he tortured them. He killed their families. He—'

She stopped. The anger faded. She took it all in as her face filled with serenity.

I understood.

Dozens upon dozens of different kinds of animals spread throughout the chamber, caged, but very much alive. On my right was an enclosure with mounds of dirt piled high. There were crusty pillars in the centre of the mounds, with small snouts poking out of dark holes. Wiry whiskers tasted the air.

Next was a cage with a stone floor, a group of plump creatures sprawled on their bellies. Bristles covered their hides, huddling in the shadows, they trembled and tried to escape our presence.

On my other side was a deep pool, filled with water. Spiny faces bobbed on the surface, long and toothy. Their skin was pebbled and green. They were the same creatures at the edge of the waters in the painting upstairs. Their large, curious eyes followed the group as we walked.

For once, the Langrians were just as shaken as I was.

Rivvy was sobbing uncontrollably. Tully had an arm around Rivvy's shoulder, but Tully wasn't faring much better. Her normally mischievous expression was now completely severe.

We moved as one, coming to a deeper cage than the rest, which spanned back a few dozen paces. On the other side of thick iron bars were four monstrous creatures lying in the shadows, their hide white and smooth like armour. They had sad eyes, large and rimmed red. Three horns rose from each of their heads. The smallest of the group had one of its horns broken in half.

'Rhinoceros,' Sett gasped.

We kept moving, everyone else too astonished to speak.

Sett's hand went to her chest. Her fingers clenched as if she were in deep pain.

The chamber was much vaster than I first realized.

There were beasts that I recognized from books. Horses. They were lined in stables, braying and snorting bursts of cloudy air from their long faces. Their legs were almost as feeble as Leroi's, but their haunches looked powerful.

There were furry animals in other cages; and animals with black carapace; and animals that made sounds I'd never heard.

Our formation broke, with different warriors drifting to

different animals. The whole place was a mess of cages, with so much wonder to behold.

Flat faces were pressed against the bars closest to me. Their fuzzy beige heads came to waist height, and their tapered ears curled out of the bars, angled and twitching in rhythm to our footsteps.

There was a huge glass enclosure filled halfway up with water, the depths visible through the glass. A Cold white mist rose off the top. Vibrant fins of all sizes cut across my vision, graceful and sleek. Sett put her palm to the glass, her hand shaking.

Then a breathtaking animal, furry and curious, swam up to the edge, coming straight to Sett's hand. It pawed at her with nub fingers; its head was the size of her palm.

'Is so beautiful,' Sett whispered.

Sinniah came to her side, pressing her palm up to the glass as well. 'I know this animal. This called "otter".'

Three more otter creatures appeared from the depths, rotating and circling their kin. There was a splash into a surface of the water, back where we couldn't see, and soon enough a handful of tiny versions joined the dance at the glass, trying to catch the attention of our group.

'Children,' Ellora sighed. 'Is otter children.'

Zeekah giggled, following the tiny otters in their play.

Rivvy still hadn't stopped crying, but as she moved onto the next cage her weeping exploded into a heavy wave of sobs.

'What is?' Sinniah asked her.

Rivvy stumbled into one of the offshoot paths, pressing her forehead against more metal bars. Slowly, an animal waddled from the back of the cage, its fur frizzy and wild. The creature walked with its weight on its hind legs. It looked harmless enough, with a flat head the shape of a long hammer. Its eyes were incredibly sad.

'Baboon,' Rivvy gasped, rubbing her chest and then putting her hand into the cage. 'Is my Meesh-Dahm.'

Sett went to say something, but then stopped herself.

The baboon sniffed Rivvy's hand. I could see the tips of impressive fangs peeking over its dark lips, but it didn't bite. Instead it made a soft cooing sound.

Then another baboon shot out of the back of the cage, snarling and snapping its teeth wildly. This one had blue on its nose, and even though it seemed as fierce as a sandviper, it was quite a beautiful creature. The baboon was nearly as tall as Rivvy.

Rivvy pulled her hand out of the cage, laughing and then beating her hand against her chest. She playfully bared her teeth as well. 'Baboon.'

I turned to Sett, but she was no longer by my side. She'd been called to another cage, this one large and brick. The iron bars in front had been scarred by something sharp.

Sett nearly collapsed.

Pacing the concrete floor was the most stunning animal yet. It had a long, powerful tail, and circular patterns on gorgeous orange fur. It let out a feral growl that I could feel in the back of my skull. Behind it slept a smaller version of the same creature, tiny children nudging at its belly.

'Jaguar,' Sett gasped.

I was speechless.

Zeekah's head swivelled in a different direction, as if she'd been struck a heavy blow. Her ear perked up and her already wide eyes opened to the point of horror.

'Please,' Zeekah whispered. 'Oh please.'

She kept her ear thrust out and scampered along, following a strange sound. I hadn't noticed this one in the din of all the others. It was small and wistful.

Zeekah was desperate, racing, letting her ear guide her.

Eventually she stopped and fell to one knee.

'Loonchin!' she cried, tears spilling down her face. 'Is most beautiful Loonchin!'

I swept up beside her. The Loonchin was a heartbreaking sight.

This cage had a soil floor, but only a few strands of long grass poking up from the centre. Entwined in the grass was a skinny animal. It had bony shoulders and was rubbing its split tongue up and down one of the green blades, producing a long-drawn-out song. The sound was pure sorrow. There was a Draft at the creature's side, but otherwise it was alone in the enclosure.

Zeekah reached into the bars, but the creature only gave her a sad look, continuing to cry out through music.

'She's the only one here,' a new voice said.

The whole group spun, raising their weapons.

A strange boy stood behind us.

He couldn't have been older than seven, clearly High Noble. His skin was the fairest I'd ever seen, his hair so yellow that it was verging on white. He had a sweet face, but there was something off about it. His eyes were a little too close together, and his tongue seemed too big for his mouth. There was also a smattering of red scarring near his left ear.

He held no weapons. Only a bucket that was segmented inside, each compartment holding different kinds of food.

'She's sad,' the boy said, holding the bucket up. 'Want to feed her?'

Sett had her sword raised. I made a swift gesture for her to lower the blade.

I knelt down in front of the boy, offering a calm smile.

The boy continued to hold out the food, looking unconcerned that a group of Jadan warriors stood in front of him, armed from ankles to neck.

'Who are you?' I asked.

'Do *you* want to feed her?' The boy asked me, reaching

into the bucket and grabbing something that looked like ground figs. He wouldn't meet my eyes. 'She's very good.'

'Who are you?'

He paused, tilting his head like I'd just asked him the colour of the Sun.

'I'm the Khat.'

Chapter Twenty-one

The boy tossed a handful of food into the cage for the Loonchin.

The creature ignored the food, its attention going back to the Draft instead. It dragged its tongue across the Cold, leaving a thin scar across the brown surface, and then once again fit its forked tongue around the grass. Rubbing up and down, the lonely song continued.

'I love animals,' the boy said. 'They're my best friends.'

I looked at Leroi, my face locked in surprise. Leroi seemed just as confused, turning his palms up and shaking his head.

The boy put his tongue against the iron bar and giggled. He walked to the next enclosure, which had a group of small green slimy animals grouped in a murky puddle, their throats puffing out. The boy took a pinch of grittier food from one of the bucket slots and tossed it in, wiping his palm on his dirty shirt. The green animals hopped to the food with powerful back legs, muddy water splashing up from behind.

Sinniah slowly took a dagger off her belt, pointing it at the boy's back.

'No,' I hissed to her. 'He's just a kid.'

'He says he's Khat,' Sinniah said, blood in her eyes. 'If this Khat—'

'Leroi, what do you know about this?' I asked.

Leroi started blubbering. 'I don't – there were never any – I didn't know any rumours—'

The boy began skipping down the cages, tossing food past bars and over panes of glass. He seemed to have forgotten we were there. He giggled with his throws, laughing and smiling at the animals.

'The Crier's might upon his name,' the boy began singing. 'Worthy of the Cold. Dynasty forever, service for your soul!'

The boy stopped, glancing back at me. He had a confused look, as if he were seeing me for the first time.

'I like your skin and hair,' the boy said. 'Can I touch you?'

I nodded, hunching down. The boy gently set down his bucket and side-stepped towards me. Reaching out his small fingers, he traced the skin on my arm and then touched my hair.

'Oh. That's great,' the boy said, giggling. 'I like it.'

'What do you mean, you're the Khat?' I asked him.

'My daddy went up in the sky last year,' the boy said, digging his fingers into the roots of my hair. His stubby nose wrinkled in curiosity. 'So I'm the Khat now. Nad says so.'

I turned to Leroi. His expression was distant.

'The Khat died?' I whispered to Leroi, mostly just moving my mouth.

Leroi's face was still. 'I don't know. There was no word—'

'Do you know where is Nad?' the boy asked, gently, his fingers moving to the numbers tattooed on the back of my neck. 'Hey. What kind of animal are you?'

'We not animals,' Sinniah hissed. 'We Jadans, you little monst—'

I waved Sinniah away. Obviously the boy didn't mean any harm.

The little Khat nodded. 'Daddy used to tell me about Jadans.'

'What did he say?'

The boy swallowed hard, shaking his head. His face flushed with fear as he looked down at his bucket, not making eye contact with anyone.

'I'm Micah,' I said. 'What's your name?'

'Vivus,' the boy answered, still rather tense. 'I'm the Khat now, but I wish I had a brother, though. I asked daddy, but daddy said no.'

I looked to Leroi to make sense of this.

Leroi stroked his goatee, which had grown long and haggard. He more mumbled to himself than me. 'I guess it's possible. I haven't actually seen the Khat in a long time.'

'Okay, Vivus,' I said. 'If your daddy is up in the sky now, do you know who is at the City of David's Fall? They say the Khat is there.'

The boy shook his head and then went back to pick up the food. He gestured to the next cage. 'I have to feed them. Do you want to feed them with me?'

Sett watched the boy through incredulous eyes. The other warriors wore conflicted expressions. Fingers ran over blades. Hands squeezed handles. The only Langrian who wasn't overtly considering killing this child and ending the line of tyrants was Ellora. She appeared worried and sombre, leaning on her elbow so it would brush Leroi.

I stepped in between the boy and the warriors.

The Khat or not, he was just a child. If I let any harm come to him, I was poison.

'Absolutely, I want to feed them with you,' I said. 'But Vivus, I need to ask you something. I'm looking for a Frost. Do you know if there are any Frosts down here with the animals?'

The boy wouldn't meet my eyes as he spoke.

'Yes,' he said. 'I have a Frost. I *am* the Khat, you know.'

He made it sound like he just had a single Frost, but at least it held a ring of hope.

'It's for the animals, though,' the little Khat said.

'Where is it?' I asked.

The boy laughed, rubbing his stomach.

'I don't understand,' I said.

He grabbed my hand and began pulling me down the rows of cages. The warriors parted, their hands behind their backs. I could only imagine the plans they were conceiving.

'Blessed be their master' – the little Khat had begun singing – 'who keeps them from the sands. His holiness the Khat.'

I recognized what he was singing as the Khat's Anthem. I'd been made to sing that song every day of my life as a Street Jadan. Being led through a chamber full of extinct animals with the very Asham the song was about was a little too much for me to take.

The world had surprised me yet again. How little truth I actually knew.

I spotted at least a dozen other species in the cages we passed. Young animals huddled beneath their parents, appraising us with big, fearful eyes.

The little Khat kept up his pace. His palm was sweaty against mine. Over my shoulder I saw the warriors following us closely. They kept in battle formation.

Many of the animals hooted and chittered and howled as we passed.

Soon we came to a section of the room proving to be the loudest of them all. The corner was stocked with dozens of cages, all of them with a spindly metal mesh for covering. The spaces between the bars were so tight that thoughts would probably have to fold themselves in half to pass through. But noise seemed to be having little trouble escaping; if only the same could be said for the creatures inside.

Chattering and chirps filtered through the cages, only getting louder at our approach. These were truly desperate sounds. Not like the other animals, who seemed merely unhappy to be in the cages, the animals in this section of the chamber knew they didn't belong down here. Their screams proved the stranglehold wickedness maintained over a merciless world.

Birds.

Dozens of them flitting from one side of their cage to the other.

They looked just like Matty's sculpture had predicted. They had tiny beaks, thin legs and small eyes like beads on fancy bracelets.

And feathers. So many feathers.

Angry reds, deep blues and yellows so bright they hurt my eyes. The birds tried to stretch their wings as they hopped from perch to perch inside the cages, grinding their beautiful feathers against the bars. The bottoms of the cages were lined with shredded fluff, white dung and broken dreams. These magnificent creatures had been stripped of their gift. These were chains I knew quite well.

The little Khat led me right up to the stacks, holding my hand. I nearly fainted once again. It was too much.

My hand went to my chest. My heart was an echo of the despair, too sensitive to their pain. Too sensitive to the loss of their potential. Perhaps there really was a bird hiding in my Meesh-Dahm, pecking at my ribs and yelling for me to do something.

The little Khat picked up a different food container sitting in front of the cages. This one had tiny seeds and grains. He took a handful from the mix and scattered the food into the cages. The birds ignored it, still uselessly trying to squeeze through the metal. They knew it was impossible, yet still they tried, snapping at each other, pushing each other down, turning the anger inward.

One bird remained at the bottom of its cage. Above, the other birds scrambled and fluttered, but this bird was calm and still. Its wings were tucked around its body, smooth and without fraying. Feathers the colour of alder made it appear darker than the other birds. It had a long curved beak, which it rested against its body.

The bird stared right at me.

Something moved in my Meesh-Dahm.

'Why is that one at the bottom, Vivus?' I asked, rubbing my fist over my heart.

The little Khat threw another handful of seed into the cages, ignoring me. The food got stuck in feathers and he giggled as he watched the birds peck it off their bodies. He went to throw another batch, but I gently placed my bronze fingers on his wrist.

'Vivus,' I said, 'why is that one at the bottom?'

Again he wouldn't meet my eyes. 'What one?'

'The red one.'

'That's a ibis. She's broke.'

'Broke?'

The little Khat held out his arms, flapping them. But he left a crook in his elbow, letting that arm struggle. Then he threw in more seed, gently striking the birds.

I locked eyes again with the ibis. I couldn't tell at first, but now I could see that its left wing didn't look right. For some reason, it struck me as one of the saddest things I'd ever seen. Not only was she in a cage, but she wouldn't be able to fly, even if she were free.

The ibis stared at me calmly. Its chest rose and fell with small breaths.

'Meshua,' Sett called from behind. 'Is beautiful bird, but . . .'

I swallowed, tearing myself away from the cage. Then I put my hand on the little Khat's shoulder. 'Vivus, what about the Frost?'

The little Khat sighed and grabbed my hand again. He led me on through the chamber, the warriors keeping close behind. They kept getting distracted by all the cages, and so their movements were not nearly as smooth.

Eventually the little Khat led me around a bend and the room opened up.

'This is the animal well,' he said proudly.

At the end of the path was an impressive well. Instead of of normal red brick, this was built with solid gold. The sleek sheen caught the light of a half-dozen Sinais placed around the well's perimeter, glowing impressively bright.

A Closed Eye rested on a pike next to the well. It too was made of gold.

The warriors began to close in on the little Khat from all sides. Sinniah had her spear pointed at the base of his spine. I waved them off. Sinniah's eyes narrowed, dark thoughts clear in her expression.

The little Khat tugged me closer to the water. A golden stool waited next to the well, and the boy kicked off his muddy sandals before stepping up.

'Look,' he said, pointing down over the rim.

I stepped closer and peered inside. The water was dark, but at the very bottom I could just make out a soft golden glow. I thought at first it might be the reflection from the well itself, but after my eyes adjusted I could see the distinct three-line symbol of a Khol, although it was quite faint and distant.

Hope and despair grabbed me at the same time.

One Frost. Only one, but it was better than nothing.

'Down there,' the little Khat whispered conspiratorially, covering his mouth.

'What's it doing down there?' I asked.

The little Khat reached up to the Closed Eye on the pike and flipped open the lid. Inside was a golden bowl in place of the pupil. The bowl came away with a long golden chain. The little Khat lowered it down into the water. The chain moved slowly, obviously balanced with weights beneath.

The warriors began to advance again, but I halted them with a scathing look.

The little Khat drew up the bucket full of water, giggling at the whirring sound the chain made. He put the golden bowl on the rim and scooped up some water in his palm.

'For you to drink,' he said sweetly. 'Micah.'

His palms were dirty. Still I didn't hesitate, bringing my lips down and tasting the water.

Cold.

Not the Coldest thing I'd ever felt – not like water with abbs and Ice inside – but a different sort of Cold. A deeper, purer sensation. My lips and tongue tingled, but not from the temperature, and not from going numb. It was the opposite in fact. They tingled with life; with memory; with potential.

I nearly fainted.

I wasn't prepared.

Something inside of me was being shaken loose, roused from a nightmare. A soft joke from my father. A touch of comfort felt in an otherwise lonely room.

The little Khat emptied the rest of the bowl into my face, tossing it with glee.

My whole upper body exploded with life.

The boy laughed. 'It's good, right!'

I gasped, speechless as the water dripped under my shirt. It felt like old scars were being smoothed back to skin. I looked under the cloth to see if that was the case, but the scars were still there. The sensation was all in my mind.

'I don't—' I choked. 'How?'

The little Khat grabbed my hand again. He looked up at me with big, soulful eyes. 'I like you. Will you be my friend?'

'Yes,' I said, still shaken. My teeth began to chatter. 'Do you want to meet everyone else? They can be your friends too, if you want.'

The boy looked afraid at first, but eventually nodded.

I called out to the warriors. Thankfully they dropped their weapons before I had to ask. They came up and introduced themselves. The boy didn't reach out to touch any of them, but he seemed open to their presence now that they were unarmed. Sinniah was not pleased, but Sett kept a hand on her lower back, which seemed to do the trick. The little Khat nodded and smiled at his feet, blushing as he repeated each of their names.

Leroi was last to come up. The boy relaxed, staring at his fair skin.

'Vivus,' I said, 'can my friends try the water?'

The boy began picking his nose; then he nodded.

One by one, the Langrians touched a finger into the bowl and then brought it to their lips. Their faces lit. They weren't alone in the feeling.

'I don't understand,' I whispered to Leroi. 'I didn't think Frosts dissolve in water.'

Leroi tapped his lip, which was dry and close to bleeding. 'Maybe they do very slowly. Or maybe they can give the water Cold just by their nature.'

'Meesh-Dahm,' Sett said with confidence.

My mind was swimming, scrutinizing the inner-workings of the Coldmaker. How much did I really know about Cold at all?

There would be time to explore the questions later. Right now the only thing that mattered was getting that single Khol into the ground. Planting it in Jadans' Rise and creating a new Cry Patch. I didn't see any more Khol anyway – fake or otherwise – but at least we had a start.

'Vivus,' I asked. 'We need to borrow the Frost.'

Vivus shook his head. 'Oh, no. It's for the animals. You can't have it. Daddy said that it keeps the animals alive. They need it.'

'Meesh-Dahm,' Sett whispered, looking around at the cages.

I paused, trying to think of what to do. We could just take the Khol, as there was really not much the little Khat could do to stop us. And a single new Cry Patch might be enough to at least stop the Second Fall.

I could jump into the well, swim to the bottom and save my people.

I steeled myself.

I would never let any harm come to the boy, but I couldn't spare his feelings. This was war.

The little Khat slipped back into his sandals, looking like he might run.

'There could be alarm,' Sinniah said, raising her spear. 'We can't let—'

I had to make a decision quickly. Every moment's delay was a chance for an Asham Priest to stumble across Bear, or the dead guards, or Nad. We had to get the Khol and get the Mattys back into the sky.

'I—'

The little Khat slid the stool up the Closed Eye pike. He carefully took his sandals off again and stepped on top. Putting the bowl in place beneath the lid, he closed the lid and then began to twist the whole eye. The boy's soft hands struggled, but soon the pole rotated. Gears and pulleys made themselves known with sounds beneath the stone.

'Is alarm,' Rivvy gasped, looking around.

Zeekah covered her ears.

'No,' I said, my heart thundering. 'I don't think so.'

The little Khat finished twisting the eye, locking it in place.

The floor began to open.

Around the cages and down the rows of cages, discs of stone rolled to the side. Waves of impossible Cold flooded the chamber.

The animal sound got louder. The warriors jerked their attention to the spots in the floor opening up, their hands instinctively grasping for weapons.

The little Khat tugged my hand.

'But you can have any of those,' he said. 'They're *mine*.'

I looked around the chamber, too astonished to speak.

The secret holes were all lined in steel and rimmed in thin layers of Ice. Mist drifted out of their shadows.

Because of Khol.

Hundreds of them.

They were packed together tightly in each space. There were more Khol than I could fathom. Enough Khol to put the world back to how it was before the Drought a dozen times over. The golden Cold pulsed with relief, as if glad to be released from their cells.

My jaw dropped.

My heart leapt.

Now I understood why the chamber was so cool. Now I understood how the animals were still alive.

'These are mine,' the little Khat said again, thumbing his chest. 'Because I'm the Khat. But you're my friends, so they're yours too, because I say so.'

I smiled, putting my hand on the little Khat's shoulder.

The boy finally met my eyes. They were a startling blue.

'Family,' he whispered.

I went to the nearest secret hole, getting on my knees and touching the topmost Khol.

'Is real?' Sett asked.

My hand shook. I brought my fingers to my lips and tasted salvation.

I turned to the warriors.

'Grab as many as you can.'

PART FOUR

Chapter Twenty-two

I didn't want to come to this place.

But I needed to come to this place.

I used my fingers instead of my eyes to see. To touch. I thought it would be less painful that way. I thought I might keep a safe distance, but there was no avoiding the sorrow in my chest. The memories flooding in from my fingers were far worse this way. My hands were too sensitive to the truth.

I wanted to be deceived.

I wanted to believe Abb was still alive.

I pressed my palm against the loose panel in my old barracks. The metal slat had more give than I remembered, but the day's heat lingered the same.

What struck me was how much taller I was now. The top edge of the panel used to be level with my forehead, but now it was well under my chin. I kept telling myself that I was a different person, but no matter how big I'd grown, no matter how many trials I'd faced, no matter how many steps I'd taken away from these walls, some version of Spout still lived inside. He hid in the dark, wondering over his scraps of metal and broken glass. He looked at me and saw the reflection of a boy who wasn't ready to let go.

I'd already lost count of how many times I tried to go inside the barracks. Whenever I tried to slide the panel, my arms tensed up and my heart screamed. I didn't have time to delay. It almost made me smile, knowing I had the strength to push through all I'd done, but not strength enough for this.

The panel was the same weight it had always been, but now it was just too heavy to move.

I gave up and turned around, placing my back against wall. The Matty loomed in the shallow sands, standing on top of the same place where I'd once destroyed all of my previous inventions. I'd smashed Crank Fans, Dream Webs and my deadly Stinger, all in a fit of rage and fear.

Back then I hadn't known what I knew now.

Behind the Matty was the path I had once taken into the Southern dunes. My father had led me there, ending at the banks of the River Kiln. I'd wept at the shores, battered and blind, near death from thirst.

It was there my father revealed the truth of the world.

About the Khatdom.

About the Nobles.

About how the Jadans might rise as a people and take back what had been stolen.

And now here I was, back at the barracks where it all started.

I had invented the life my father always dreamt about. I looked up into the stars, a small hope that my eyes might be met with his pride.

The other Mattys were sailing in the air, off to bring Khol – and in turn salvation – to the dead lands of the Khatdom.

Rivvy was off to the Hotland Delta. Tully was headed to Belisk. Sett and Sinniah were off to Langria.

Before flying away, they had all wept with me, calling me Meshua and embracing me in victory.

Ellora had decided to stay behind in the Paphos with Leroi, looking after Bear. Bear was thankfully going to make it through, but she was in no condition to travel. No one would harm them now that they had the Little Khat on their side, and they had promised that while we were off putting Khol in the ground, they were going to do the same in Paphos. Leroi had held me so tight I thought he might never let go.

The pieces were in motion.

Everyone else was on their way to fix the World Cried. They would put the Khol in the ground. Jadans everywhere would weep with joy when they saw new Cry Patches coming to life.

We had won.

But I still couldn't step into my old barracks.

I put my forehead against the hot bricks. The Sun would be rising soon. It was the last time it would hold power. Its backlash would likely be violent and terrible, but there would be no more denying the truth.

Jadans were worthy.

The World Cried would finally have peace.

I knocked my head against the stone. I wanted to march in with a wide smile and open arms, but I was stuck.

The corners of my eyes grew hot.

Then the panel began to slide.

But not by my hand.

I stepped back, nearly toppling over, looking for places to hide. My only option was to jump inside the Matty, which wouldn't really help. I tried to calm my heart as the panel moved and my past opened up.

Moussa.

Of all my old family who could have been sneaking out tonight, it was Moussa.

He crawled out of the opening on his hands and knees. His body was covered in welts and wounds, and he looked frail enough that his bones might collapse under their own weight. There was a burn scar on his arm, one in the shape of the Closed Eye.

I lost all ability to breathe.

Moussa didn't see me at first, but then he turned to put the panel back in place.

We locked eyes.

I was taller than him now. And twice as heavy. To my eyes Moussa looked so thin and frail, even though he would be a Patch Jadan by now. I couldn't believe that this was the same Jadan. But there was no mistake. He had the same frizzy hair, the same beakish nose. His skin was still as dark as shadow.

He blinked over and over, his expression blank.

I tried to say something. Nothing came to my lips.

His thin legs nearly buckled as he stepped over to me. His gait was careful and slow. I'd have thought he was approaching a sandviper. He raised a shaking hand and placed it against my cheek, checking to see if I were real.

I put a hand over his. I nodded.

He eyed my bronze fingers, touching them to see if they too were real.

I nodded.

He swallowed hard. The motion looked like it might break his thin throat. There was no fat anywhere on him. His chest was sunken. He looked over my shoulder at the Matty, eyes brimming with uncertainty.

I still couldn't find words.

He opened his mouth. He couldn't find any either.

The pause was excruciating. The last time I'd seen him was right before he was taken by the Vicaress. She'd tortured him for information. I didn't know if Moussa hated me for dragging him into my mess, but he certainly would have been justified. I'd abandoned him. I'd left him in Paphos and gone off on an adventure. I'd deserted him to a life of suffering, suffering that I could visibly see all across his body. His invisible bruises would be even worse.

He slowly wrapped his arms around my back. His hands were careful and precise. It was almost as if he still couldn't believe I was real. Then he drew me in. He pulled tight, slowly and even, like his shoulders were running on gears. Eventually he gripped me firmly.

'The Jadans—' he coughed into my shoulder. 'The Jadans work upon the sands.'

The crack in my heart went as deep as possible.

After all this time, he remembered. It was the song we'd written together. Me, him and Matty.

The Jadan's Anthem.

'The Jadans work upon the sands,' he said again, his voice choked and distant and full of sorrow.

I swallowed hard. 'Those who need the Cold.'

'Family forever,' he said.

He didn't put the words to melody, as we used to do, but they felt like thunder.

'Older than the old,' I said.

I missed him so dearly. I hadn't realized the extent until he was back in my arms. In that moment words alone weren't enough.

'Older than the old,' I began to sing. 'Strength to the forgotten, who still bleed for the lands . . .'

I paused.

Moussa joined in on the last two lines.

We sang together for the first time in a lifetime.

He collapsed into me, still holding as tight as he could. I could barely feel him; his arms were so weak. The image of Matty with Khatmelon juice dripping down his chin flashed into my mind. I began to smile.

'It's been really hard without you,' he said.

'I know.'

'Things have gotten really bad.'

'I know.'

There was another heavy pause.

'Abb—'

I cut him off.

'I know,' I said.

He pulled back, checking my bronze fingers.

'The Vicaress?' he asked.

I shook my head. 'Me.'

'You?'

'Well, I guess officially it was a Hookman.'

Moussa's eyes went wide with disbelief. 'You met a Hookman?'

'Well, he *was* a Hookman,' I said, my words spilling out. 'But he only did it because I burned myself with Ice in a caravan cart.'

Moussa rubbed the sides of his head, trying to take everything in.

'Spout, where have you been?' he asked. 'Everyone thought you were dead. Abb – I mean, here's the thing. You left and—'

I cut him off, gripping his shoulder. 'I don't have time to explain. My other friends are in trouble, and I have to get back to them. But I came to give you all something.'

His lips went thin. 'Friends, you mean like that Shilah?'

I nodded, unashamed. 'And Camlish Tavor. And a Pedlar named Split. And five ex-Hookmen. And a whole city of Jadans that believe I'm this saviour from the Book of the March—'

Moussa held up a hand to slow me down. He looked ready to gag. 'I don't – what's the Book of the March?'

I opened my mouth but came up empty.

Then he began to laugh.

So did I.

'Do me a favour,' I said. 'Get everyone. Wake them up. Bring them out here.'

Moussa looked up at the night sky. 'The Sun will be up soon.'

'I promise it will be worth it.'

He looked to the side of me, out into the sand. 'What is that thing, Spout?'

I flicked him in the shoulder, the same way he used to flick Matty.

'Just get them out here,' I said. 'I only have a few minutes.'

'Only a few minutes?'

'For now. Don't worry, I'll see you again very soon.'

He nodded, turning to go back inside. Then he stopped, giving me a pained look. 'Don't . . . don't leave while I'm in there.'

I shook my head.

He crawled back through the opening. I let out a long breath, trying to keep my hands from shaking. He left the panel open. I almost closed it, but instead I stared into the dark hole. Temptation overcame my resolve.

I stepped backward. I couldn't face it.

Then a gust of wind kissed my back. It nudged me closer to the barracks. I grumbled up to Gale, dropping to my knees and poking my head through the open space.

I was back in my old room.

Nothing had changed. I would have thought that as soon as the private room opened up, someone would have raced to claim it, but everything was the same.

But it was also much smaller than I remembered.

How Abb and I fit comfortably in here didn't make much sense. I reached inside and touched my old sleeping blanket in the corner. It was ratty, torn and stained. I looked at my tinker-wall, still intact with all of my old projects. They seemed both brilliant and childish. My supply buckets still had all of my raw chains, glass and tools that I'd scavenged from the Paphos alleyways.

I breathed in. The smell was too much.

Old sweat, groan salve and rust on the healing box.

It was still my father's home.

I had to leave.

I backed away and headed straight for the Matty, trying not to collapse. I took one of the Khol from the bag, feeling the Meesh-Dahm pulsing into my fingers.

Without thinking I grabbed one of the Swing Swords. The disc was locked at the end, and so I began stabbing the sand at my feet.

It didn't take much effort to dig out a sizeable hole. I threw the weapon aside and started digging with my hands. Then I pounded my fist against the ground.

Not because it was more efficient, but rather to distract myself. I smeared some of the sand across my lips. It tasted of death. It was easier to concentrate on this.

I widened the hole more. I bashed at it with my fists, my bronze fingers creaking. I clawed at the edges and the sand went under my fingernails.

I began to memorize every lump and dent.

Finally the rest of my family began spilling out of the passageway, gasping in disbelief.

Joon. Jardin. Avram. Levi. Slab Hagan. Phears. Stephin. All the Builders, Street Jadans and Domestics who, along with Abb, taught me not only what Jadans need, but why I should care.

And they all looked so frail. Great Gale could have blown them back inside with a simple gust. Perhaps they had always looked so hungry, so close to death, which made the pangs all the worse.

Some of my family were missing. Some of them I didn't recognize.

Most of the newcomers were around Matty's age when he died, looking to me with the utmost confusion. I must have been quite the sight, looming in the starlight behind their barracks, dirty and bloody, holding a piece of Cold they wouldn't recognize. These children might see me as a sort of demon.

But the others:

'Spout!'

'Micah!'

'Alive. He's still here.'

'Tears above, if Abb—'

'Praise the Crier.'

'It's just a vision. It's not possible.'

Mother Bev walked up to me the same way as Moussa, with a combination of exaltation and disbelief. The deep crook in her back meant she had to take her time.

'Spout,' she whispered, stopping on the other side of the hole I'd dug.

'It's me, mother Bev,' I said.

'Crier bless you, child,' she said. 'You came back.'

'I did.' I held up the Khol so they could all see. 'And I brought you something.'

The rest of my family started walking towards me, closing the gap. They were all overflowing with emotion. Jardin no longer looked at me like I was a child. Kilin appraised my new muscles. Levi wore something other than a scowl for once in his life. Most looked like they wanted to fall to their knees and weep.

Which was fine by me. I needed that to happen anyway.

'I've missed you all so much,' I said, clutching the Khol to my chest.

I could tell that all of my old family wanted to rush me with hugs and questions, but I couldn't let myself fall prey to comfort. I couldn't stay. The Flock was still in danger.

So I held the holy Cold between us like a shield.

'Do you know what this is?' I asked them.

The Patch Jadans all gave fearful nods. They gasped, seeing my hands directly touching the Khol. For a Jadan to touch a Khol in the Patch without gloves was punishable by death.

'How did you get a Frost, Micah?' Joon asked.

'I have so much to tell you all, and I will.' I took a deep breath. 'But for now, we end the Great Drought. Together.'

'End the Drought?' Mother Bev asked. 'Child, what are you speaking of?'

I began to cry. It wasn't difficult. I didn't have to gather anything up.

All I had to do was let go.

I held the Khol out further so the droplets wouldn't strike it directly, but the light at the centre began to intensify with proximity to my tears.

'I don't – I've been through so much just to get this,' I said, sobs flowing freely. 'I don't know if the Crier is real, and if He chose us to do it, but He's ready. He's ready for all this suffering to end. He's ready for us to live. All we have to do is plant this. This Frost is a seed for a new Cry Patch, and it just needs to be in the ground.'

My crying had opened the gates. The rest of my family were breaking into tears. The Khol pulsed with Meesh-Dahm beneath my fingers, reacting to all the Jadan crying in its vicinity.

'What are you talking about?' Levi said, looking at me like I was crazy as Old Man Gum. 'Frosts are in the ground all the time. They fall in the Patch, kiddo. I dug out three myself back when I was a Patchy.'

Slab Hagan gave a sad nod, dropping his head. He didn't seem as gargantuan as I remembered. He wasn't even as large as Kasroot, the smallest of the Five.

'Come closer,' I said.

Cries wracked my chest. I wished I could wipe away the tears so I might look at my family without a blurred vision, but the warm stings in the corner of my eyes had a purpose. 'I know the secret now,' I said. 'It's something that's been right here. The missing piece. Please, everyone, come closer.'

Some, especially the new Street Jadans, watched the Khol as if it were about to explode. The rest threw away caution and tightened the circle. Joon and Sarrah were holding hands. Moussa was holding himself, arms wrapped around his chest.

So much pain. So much loss. So many lies. But now, after eight hundred years, the world would be reborn.

I got to my knees, holding my breath.

Then I put the Cold in the ground.

It was simple. It was quick. It was time.

We were so close to being free. I just had to do one more thing.

Adaam had uncovered this next secret out of desperation. It was Inventing in its purest form. And it had been right in front of us. We'd been saying it since the beginning.

This was the World *Cried*.

The secret was already in the name. I had to cry for the world. I had to weep for my people in happiness; in despair; in love; in need.

In wonder.

So I let my tears fall on the Khol.

And the land shone gold.

The sands tinged, spreading out from the spot where I knelt. The light pulsed in all directions under our feet, reaching the barracks, the dunes and even the guardhouse. Gramble, my old Barracksmaster, was standing outside of his shack with his whip by his feet. His jaw had dropped, paralysed with awe.

'Come closer,' I sobbed to my people, my Jadans. My smile broke wider than it had in my entire life as I covered the

Khol in a light layer of sand. I could feel the gold light glowing in my cheeks. 'Cry with me.'

Moussa was first.

He knelt by my side and wept, touching his fingers to his face and then pressing them down to the sand. I put a hand on his back and pressed tight. I wasn't ready to let go.

The golden hue deepened. A wave of Cold washed across our knees.

Then came the Domestics.

They cried and the world took another breath.

Then the Street Jadans.

They cried and the world breathed again.

Then the Patch Jadans. And the Builders.

Everything was Cold. Everything was light. Everyone knelt around the hole and added tears to the Khol, forcing life back into the sands. They hugged me, and hugged each other, crying out the Ancestors. They sang the old songs, ones I didn't know they had remembered, and the tears kept falling.

I didn't give any speeches.

There were no words as powerful as watching my family gathered around the Khol, weeping and singing, and rolling on their backs so they could look up to the sky and pray.

This was Langria.

This was my first time seeing true freedom.

I kissed Moussa on the top of his head. Then I beckoned for him to sneak away with me. We crept over to the Matty while everyone was distracted. The sand where it was waiting was no longer tinged with hate and heat, but rather it was cool and lovely.

I reached into the Matty and pulled out three more Khol in a canvas bag.

'Here's the thing, Moussa,' I said with a wink, resting the bag at his feet. 'I'm putting you in charge. I have to get back to stop the Noble armies. Take these Frosts and plant them behind other barracks. Tell our people what you've seen. Show every Jadan in Paphos the truth, and have them end the Drought with us.'

Moussa nodded, too overcome to speak.

I gave him a tight hug.

'One more thing,' I said.

Moussa sniffed, rubbing the back of his hand under his nose.

I leaned over the railing and reached into the Matty, waiting for my new friend to climb out. It had taken a few tries at first to build her trust, but now she ambled onto my wrist with little hesitation. Her talons were a bit sharp, but it was a nice pressure more than anything; it meant she was real. Somehow I knew she was a girl.

She stepped one thin leg at a time and then balanced. I cupped my other hand around her weak side and brought her out of the nest I'd made from boilweed shreds. I didn't have a name for her yet – still she cooed and rubbed her bill against my forearm.

Moussa swallowed hard. 'Is that – sand in my figs, Spout. Is that—'

'A bird,' I said.

Moussa slowly reached into his pants pocket, pulling out the metal feather I once tinkered for Matty. It had been Matty's favourite possession. We were going to use it in the board game that never was quite finished, and I wondered if perhaps we'd get all the pieces right in the next life.

'You still have it?' I asked, sniffing.

The ibis nuzzled my arm. It cooed softly again, the warmth in its chest stark against the Cold rising off the ground.

Moussa smiled. 'I never let it go.'

'She can't fly,' I said, gesturing down to the bird. 'What would Matty say about that?'

Moussa stared at the metal feather, comparing it to those

of the bird. His eyes were rimmed in tears. 'He would say he missed you. And that just because a bird can't fly now, doesn't mean it won't ever. He always thought there was a way back.'

I nodded, holding the ibis back over the boilweed nest. She stepped in, gathered her wings around her, and then took a sip from the Khol bucket. The water I'd filled it with was cool and wonderful.

'I have to go,' I said, stepping into the craft. I didn't have it in me to say goodbye to everyone. I wanted to leave with this exact picture in mind, of my family enjoying their first moments of freedom. The first of many.

'Micah,' Moussa said gently. 'I'll see you again?'

'Of course.'

'So what happens now?' Moussa said, gesturing back to the spot over which everyone was weeping.

The land was blinding gold beneath them. Gramble had dropped to his knees by his guardhouse. He was sobbing as well. He poked at the golden sands with his finger, pressing his ruddy cheek against the land.

'Come nightfall,' I said, 'the Crier will know where his people are. Cold will find you. It's over, Moussa. The Drought is done.'

Moussa nodded, taking hold of the bag. 'I won't let you down.'

I put on my boilweed mask and then let the first Asham tear fall on the Desert. It spat up orange heat, and the Matty quickly began to rise.

My family was too distracted by the golden light pulsing in the sands to notice my departure. No one other than Moussa looked in my direction until I was already into the sky.

Once I was high enough, I dipped the copper wire into the Cold Charge, and the glider blades began pushing me North. I checked the ibis, making sure the Desert fumes weren't poisoning her, but she seemed okay.

When I was moving at a good speed, I went to the back railing and looked down.

The golden light had begun to make a pattern. It pulsed at the edges like a ripple in water, but the parts that shone brightest had taken a definitive shape. It was so clear that I laughed. I kissed my fingers and drew them down my cheek.

An Eye.

The golden light had taken the shape of an Eye.

It wasn't perfect, but the shape was clear enough. And it had long single streaks pulsing out in all directions

And funnily enough, my family, kneeling in a circle, made a perfect pupil.

I laughed, deep and loud.

Maybe this was where the whole idea of the Crier came from in the first place. Maybe this was the next big secret; that my Ancestors knew the shape of a Cry Patch being born. That they knew what the love looked like, and matched it with a story.

I would probably never know.

I knew that I was tired.

So very tired.

Tired. Weary. Hungry. Raw. And impossibly happy.

I set a course North and closed my eyes.

Just for a moment.

Chapter Twenty-three

'A father would be proud. Actually, a father is proud, Spout.'

'I always hated that name.'

'I imagine it's funny though, now that you know what it means. I'm glad I made it up.'

'You did? I thought it was the other kids who started it. Because I sweat too much.'

'Nope. It was your old man.' There was a tap on my forehead. 'Planting a seed.'

I opened my eyes.

Abb looked different.

He was younger than the last time I saw him. His face had fewer scars and shallower wrinkles. His hair was thicker and more full than I'd ever seen. And long. It was so long that he had it braided off to one side. There was something else different about him, too, but I couldn't place it.

We were back in our old room. I was sitting on my ratty blanket, while he sat on his, the healing box open at his side like always. He had a piece of boilweed and needle in his hand, practising his stitching.

But this time, the holes he poked in the plant closed up immediately after the needle passed through.

'So you knew all along?' I asked, starting to smile. 'That "Spout" was the translation?'

Abb shrugged, poking another hole with the needle. 'I told you before. I don't speak Ancient Jadan.' He paused. 'But I could guess.'

I tried to get up off my blanket, but there was a weight pressing me down, like giant hands on my shoulders. It wasn't unpleasant, but it was firm, and I couldn't move. There was nothing visibly holding me there, and as much as I wanted to go over to Abb and touch his arm, to see if he was real, I couldn't.

'Good guess,' I said.

'So what happens now?' Abb asked, putting the boilweed and needle back into the healing box.

'I don't know.'

'You don't think you're done, do you?'

'An Inventor's work is never done,' I said.

Abb got up off his blanket and stretched out his back. His tired spine didn't make the same cracks I remembered, which was always three big cracks and then a series of smaller cracks once he really twisted.

This time his back didn't make a sound.

'Look at that,' he said, sauntering over to the tinker-wall. 'This side has its advantages.'

'What side?' I asked, still feeling the weight.

He turned and gave me a gentle look.

Then he picked off one of the crank-fans that I'd once made. He gave the lever a turn and the tiny blades began to whirr. The fan hovered in front of him, and then started to fly around the room. Abb took another fan and it did the same, even though I hadn't designed them to do such a thing. He cranked another and another, until the air above us was swarming. They flew in a single file and followed an oval path.

'I was always a fan of these,' Abb said, pointing.

I smacked my forehead. The contact made no sound.

He picked up my old Stinger next. He shook his head, putting it back and instead taking my Claw Staff. He pulled the camel-leather strap and the claw fingers closed the end. He pointed the staff at my chest.

'Want to see a trick?' he asked.

I nodded.

He thrust the claw into my body.

It tickled as he dug around. He whistled, and I tried to whistle along, but my tongue was too dry. After a moment, he tugged the camel-leather incredibly hard, and I could feel the ends of the staff gripping something inside of me.

He yanked. He pulled.

The thing didn't want to give.

'Hmm,' he said.

'Hmm what?'

I felt pain. But it wasn't sharp, or throbbing. It was a pain that I'd been holding on to for a long time. A special pain. A pain that I felt safe having inside of me, that I'd given passage to, so it might keep me disconnected. It was a lie, but it was my lie all the same.

'Hmm nothing,' Abb said.

His legs took a stronger stance and then he yanked again.

I cried out and gnashed my teeth at him.

'No!' I shouted.

Abb's face went serious. He put both hands on the Claw Staff and drew back with all of his might. I tried to hold on. I tried to keep my secret in, but it was slipping.

After a moment there was a pop.

Abb stumbled back.

The end of the Claw Staff was dripping with a black sludge. It reminded me of slag from a Droughtweed bit. Like a poisonous shadow.

Trapped in the claw was something terrible.

It didn't have a shape, but it was deep. It might have gone on forever.

Abb whistled as he put the end of the staff inside a boilweed bag, and released the tension. Instead of filling up, the bag did the opposite. It began to collapse inwards on itself, folding so tight that it was barely visible. Abb carefully replaced the staff on the shelf and slung the soiled bag over his shoulder.

The pain was gone.

I looked down at my chest.

My skin was radiating gold. It tingled with memories I didn't think I still had. It was a colour I hadn't felt in such a long time.

I pointed to the bag. 'What was that?'

'I think you know,' he said softly. 'And that's the thing about truth, isn't it? Life is complex. Maybe you needed this to get here, to come so far, but you don't need it anymore, son. You can let go now.'

He was right. I was ready.

I didn't want to be, but I was ready.

'So what happens next?'

'Now, I leave,' he said, hoisting the bag. Even though the bag was as flat as could be, it weighed on him, like the entire Pyramid was suddenly placed on his back. 'And I'm taking this with me.'

'Thank you,' I said. 'Thank you for everything.'

Abb winked. And then he went to leave.

'Dad,' I called out. 'Will I see you again?'

He laughed, taking hold of the boilweed flap and lifting a corner.

Behind it was a magnificent sight.

A long, grassy plain. Nighttime. But the darkness was cool, and the whole place looked like home. It was sprinkled with more stars than I ever thought possible. There were people on the plains, Jadans with distant faces. They looked like me, like my father, like Shilah, even like Leroi, and they jumped into pools of water and danced in vests of alder light. I heard the most wonderful music. I smelled the most delicious food. The laughter here was pure. And endless. A calm peace drifted towards me. I shied away. It wasn't my peace to feel yet.

Abb let the door fall. He came over and kissed me on the top of my head.

'Don't worry,' he said. 'I have plenty more jokes for you. Soon. But not for a while. And they're going to be hilarious.'

'I bet,' I said.

As he pulled away, there was a tear on my cheek that wasn't my own.

'I'll tell him you say hello,' Abb said.

'Tell who?'

Abb pointed behind me.

I woke up, staring into the dome of the Matty.

My limbs were frozen, and for a moment I couldn't move. The jolt back to the waking world was so disorienting that panic seized me from head to foot, and I had to concentrate on breathing through my nose before I could gain control over the rest of my body. Bright light nipped at the edges of my vision. I ached to get back to the dream, if that's what it was. Everything in it felt so real; I didn't want to know the difference.

The dome-sail above me was fully distended, the rising heat distorting my vision. I touched a hand to my face. I was covered in sweat. More likely they were tears.

I wiped my cheeks dry and unwrapped the nearest Khol from its boilweed covering, my finger hovering just above the surface. The centre of the Cold began to glow, making the three-lined symbol more prominent. I was overcome with a profound thirst. I dropped my ladle into the Khol bucket, which I'd filled with water before leaving the Pyramid. It was phenomenally Cold, and tasted of the things of which I couldn't speak. I peeled away the silk covering over the boil-weed nest and offered the ladle to my ibis friend. She dipped her bill in and drank deeply. I could feel her coo through the nest. I'd brought some of the feed that the little Khat used, and sprinkled some at her feet.

I stood up and looked out over the railing.

It was daytime. The Sun was blazing directly overhead. I had slept through a large chunk of the morning.

Rushing to check my compass, I saw that miraculously I was still bearing North, the fan blades pushing the Matty onwards, swift and steady.

I grabbed the Farsight and scanned the horizon.

Mostly it was just empty sands around me, but I could see a few caravan passages cutting through the dunes and rocks far below, reminding me of sandviper tracks. There were also a few high beige hills off to the left, leading to a city that I guessed was Marlea. Black statues lined the streets at every corner and were interspersed between the red brick of the actual buildings.

Marlea was known for using black summerstone, which was native to the surrounding dunes. Many Asham sculptors liked to live in Marlea so they could have constant access to the material. There was also a rumour that every Jadan there had permanent scars on their palms from having to dig up the rocks so frequently.

On the outskirts of Marlea were digging camps. Factions of my people toiled in the distance, being whipped and taunted by death. They lined up to go into the summerstone mines, a return line hauling out the terrible bounty. Many of the Jadans were being made to carry the stones back to the city on their bare backs, without any carts.

I let out a long breath and then pivoted the fan blades towards them.

There wasn't time to waste, but I had to do something.

I couldn't land the Matty and chance getting caught by any Asham, and so I closed my eyes and came up with a simple idea.

Quickly I grabbed a few tiny rips of boilweed and started cleaning the spots underneath my cheeks, getting as much of the moisture as I could, hoping that indeed the droplets were tears. I stuffed the saturated strips into vials and stored two away for later in case this worked.

Then I tied a vial around one of my Khol with a strip of boilweed, layering it a few times to make sure the glass stayed in place. I was careful not to touch the surface of the Khol directly, in case I still had tears on my hand. A reaction might stop the Desert heat and send me plummeting to my death. So I moved with great care.

When I finished prepping, I'd neared one of the mining outposts.

I lifted the Khol package and kissed the outside of the boilweed, hoping that falling from such a height would bury it deep enough in the sands to work. Enough for the seed to take root.

I paused, holding it up towards the sky.

And I let the package fall.

Leaning over the railing, I watched the Khol soar towards the ground. The boilweed wrap held tight, keeping the glass against the Khol.

I squinted, and after a tense wait there was a disturbance in the land below. A cloud of sand puffed upward. The obstruction took a few moments to disperse, all the while my throat too tight to even breathe.

Then I let out a howl of victory.

I was too high up to be heard, so I let out another.

Golden lines pulsed outward from the hole in the sands, forming the rough shape of an eye. There was no family of

Jadans crying around the centre this time to make the pupil, but the cratered sand helped with the illusion. My heart beat wildly, different than before, faster and more free. I put my hand over it and savoured the thumping.

More tears spilled down my cheeks as I thought of my father disappearing behind the curtain. I grabbed another strip of boilweed, quick to wipe the drops under my eyes. I saved the tears in another vial, as my idea had worked.

Abb was right.

My work wasn't done yet.

I took one more glance beneath me and then turned the craft back North.

It wasn't hard to spot the City of the Jadans' Rise.

The plateaus were vast, and the walls stout. The place loomed over the surrounding sands, tall and proud, like a single ship navigating a boiling river. I didn't realize how big the city was until seeing it in the daylight. There were so many planes and crags and alleyways, all places the Khat could have buried the Desert, and I was shocked he still hadn't succeeded.

Thousands of Asham surrounding the place were a dead giveaway that the Fall still hadn't happened. Shilah had kept the Khat from victory, and the sieging armies appeared to have at least doubled. A few separate outposts had broken off of the surrounding ranks, having set up their own markets, makeshift temples and stages.

Through the Farsight I spotted that the Asham seemed happy, locked in massive bouts of celebration. They were drinking ale, huffing slag and performing acts that I'd never be able to get out of my head. Their jubilation was verging on madness, and fear rattled my core. Maybe I was wrong.

I turned the Farsight onto the Southern cliffs. I had to work up the courage three times before I tilted the lens enough to see the rocks at the base, holding my breath as I scanned.

To my complete and utter relief, the base was clean.

There were no sign of bones or char.

'No fall yet,' I said to the ibis.

It didn't mean my friends were safe, or even still alive, but for now I was able to hold myself together. I scanned the plateaus for signs of life. There was no movement, even from inside the gates, where the Beggars had lived. Everyone must have been in hiding. I couldn't imagine what sort of mayhem Ka'in and his armies had been unleashing during my absence.

I expected a fresh wave of hate to boil my veins. These Asham were surrounding a city of innocent people, my people, celebrating our fear and pain. I wanted to hate them with everything inside of me. I wanted to yearn for their violent deaths; to thirst for their blood to stain the very sands upon with they rejoiced.

All Asham are supposed to be poison, after all.

But the hate couldn't latch on. It came and went. I felt it, burning as it passed, but that's all it was. Fleeting. Something was missing in me, something viscous and inviting and terrible, that had been inside for far longer than I realized.

The anger came and left, and all that remained behind was a new truth.

These Asham were victims too.

Their lives were also lessened by the First Khat, and in that respect we were all one family. The Asham had been Jadan at one point, before the Drought. Before the Khat had stripped away equality, pushing us down so he and his chosen few could step on our backs. Now Jadans had different skin, and Cold reacted differently to our bodies, but the Asham were suffering as well; in a different way. They were suffering because they had to live with their casual cruelty, with their careless oppression.

Such plagues made for very thin hearts.

The Asham were suffering because they couldn't enjoy the beauty of green hills and cool rivers and freedom songs that once covered the world, nor to know lands that were alive with animals. They weren't experiencing the kind of culture that could be bred outside of their oppression. The Asham suffered because they were told they were better than the world, and because of that they were no longer a part of it. They'd been torn from the rest of the Jadan people. They'd been stripped of their potential for good. They had the gift of community taken from their hands and replaced with a whip and a blade.

And for the first time in my life, I finally understood what was happening.

I wasn't just bringing freedom to the Jadans.

I was bringing freedom to everyone.

And it would require no bloodshed. For tonight, all people would look to the sky and see that the Drought was over.

Tonight, everyone would cry as one.

I dropped the copper wire deeper into the Cold Charge, as deep as it would go, and the glider blades began to buck in their cage. The Matty sped towards the city faster than I'd ever gone. There was no more conflict in me, no more doubt, no more confusion.

Just an overwhelming desire to see my destiny through.

It was time for this world to come to a new beginning. Any Asham that accepted it would be welcomed as brothers and sisters. Those that stood in our way would have to be removed.

Simple. Resolute.

I tightened the cap over the Desert, beginning my descent. I didn't care if the Asham armies saw me approaching. In fact, I wanted them to look up and see not their reckoning, but their Shepherd.

Meshua.

I angled away from teeming crowds. I didn't want to drop a Khol in the midst of their ranks, in case it landed on a tent, or a cart, and then ended up not making it far under the ground, so I angled over the dunes and soared over open sand. I was flying even higher than I had been in Marlea, so the Khol would have had plenty of space to gain enough speed.

No one saw me hovering overhead.

I wasn't surprised.

The Asham were too busy celebrating amongst themselves to look up.

I took the next Khol and made sure the tear vial was tight and secure. Then I kissed the boilweed layering and sent the package plummeting over the side. I waited for the blossoming gold with a smile in my heart.

No Asham noticed the falling Khol. They continued to drink their Cold ale, and eat their ripe Khatmelons. They continued to dance and sing, and to whip the Jadans unfortunate enough to be on the wrong side of the wall.

The sand settled beneath me and another Eye appeared, gold and wide.

I gave it a wink.

And then I flew to the East.

I dropped another Khol package, this time near one of the caravan roads. Still no Asham noticed. The were too busy strutting through the market stalls, trading their Shivers and Chills for exotic goods such as chocolate and honey.

This Khol cut through the sands without making much of a visible impact, and I surmised it had landed in a patch of cloud sand. The Eye that erupted was even larger than the others, the gold more vibrant and visceral, which raised all sorts of new questions in my mind about how the Khol affected the natural world.

I kneeled down and let the ibis climb on my wrist, so she

too could see the rebirth of paradise. I held her chest tight so she wouldn't fall.

'What do you think?' I asked.

Her wings began to struggle.

I kept her balanced best I could as she unfolded herself as far as she could go. Her feathers were a gorgeous red, almost as dark as the alder, and they fluttered as we sailed through the sky. Her left wing couldn't extend all the way, as there was a nasty crook somewhere in the bone, but still the wind found her.

She didn't try to fly away, keeping her pose. The wind kissed her feathers. She was at peace.

'Gale,' I said. 'Your name is Gale, isn't it?'

The ibis cooed.

I set Gale up a little perch so she could stretch her wings as I worked.

I circled North, rounding the Asham armies at a distance. I made the unfortunate decision to look through the Farsight so as to see clearly what was happening on the main stage, and quickly returned the invention to the floor of the Matty. It was difficult to resist the urge to pick up my large variety of weapons and hurl them down on the Ashams' skulls. They had a whole slew of my kin chained up, celebrating in another of their special ways.

I had to focus.

I could do more good with the Khol than with weapons.

I sailed around to the North side of the city. Drawing two fingers down my cheek, I held them out to the distant free lands. I didn't feel the least bit alone.

'Ready?' I asked Gale.

She took her long bill and nuzzled the next boilweed package.

When I was far enough away from the armies, I let the Khol fall.

This one had a delayed reaction after it landed, but sure enough the golden light took shape in the deadland, pulsing just like the others. I gave the reaction a respectful nod, and then finished the circle, dropping another teary Khol into the Western sands.

And it was done.

I aimed for the centre of the city and surveyed the results. The armies of Asham may have been sieging the city, but four bright eyes were sieging the armies. The land pulsed with colour.

If the Asham didn't notice now, they would notice tonight.

Inside the city walls, the streets were not only deserted, but also in ruins. Some of the buildings had crumbled, and there were fires blazing in a few places. The Asham had clearly been having quite the time ransacking the place while they waited for the Fall. There was likely good reason my people had made themselves scarce.

I aimed the Matty towards the high plateau. Gale the ibis tilted with the craft, balancing on one leg.

I couldn't believe the Drought was over. I couldn't believe that such a journey would have a happy ending. I always knew success was possible, but I never thought it likely.

'Thank you,' I whispered.

The lands surrounding the city answered with golden light.

I judged the angle and turned the Matty towards the Sanctuary. I hoped that my friends would see me coming, wherever they were hiding, and come out to greet me. I couldn't wait much longer to see them.

There was no one in the camps surrounding the Sanctuary. The tents and stalls and sands were empty.

I landed the Matty near the gates. It was so good to see this place, even though it had once represented all that I feared and hated about the Asham world. I heard an odd sound in the distance, almost like a sizzle. I couldn't place where it was coming from.

'Shilah!' I shouted, my heart thundering. 'Cam! I'm back! It's over! The Drought is over!'

I gave Gale a gentle pat and then leapt out of the Matty.

The air was swimming with heat. It felt sickly and steaming, like being back inside the Adaamclock.

My forehead answered with sweat, and I had to wipe it dry with my sleeve. My tongue felt heavy and my stomach churned. I wanted to jump back into the Matty and escape the terrible heat, but I held my ground.

I waved two knuckles at Sun, wondering if this was its final attack.

The horrible sky glared down, angry and spiteful. It didn't appear any stronger than normal. Yet the heat from the ground was nearly unbearable. I picked at the front of my shirt, my chest and stomach already sticky with sweat.

The strange sizzle had become louder. I turned from side to side to try and figure out what was making the sound.

I looked down.

It was coming from my sandals.

I lifted my foot up and the noise cut in half. I lifted the other and the same thing happened. I turned to the Matty and realized the sizzle was also coming from the wood being pressed down onto the land.

'No,' I said, throat constricting with worry. 'No.'

The truth of the matter struck.

I'd succeeded.

But so had Ka'in.

He must have gotten a piece of Desert in the ground, one that the Five missed. Or maybe he was able to plant a few Deserts while I was gone. The Khat may have been dead, but still the land was burning.

I chanced touching my bare finger against the ground and

nearly yelped. The pebbles and dirt felt like hot coals, and looking closer, I realized everything had begun to take on that same sickening orange glow as Desert.

This is what my Ancestor's must have felt at the first Fall. Right before the heat forced them to jump.

This was what the Asham must have been celebrating.

Dread and panic knocked into me, threatening to send me over the edge.

But those feelings came and passed. There was nothing for them to hold on to.

I wasn't done yet.

I hopped back into the Matty, taking Gale the ibis and dunking her straight into the Khol water bucket to keep her cool. She struggled at first, but then accepted. I grabbed a different Khol from the stash, hoping it wasn't too late. I didn't know if it was going to be strong enough to combat active Desert. I prayed that I might at least halt the damage where it was. I tried not to think back to my experiments with tubs of land, and reminded myself I didn't have Khol back then.

The land spat heat into my face, cackling at me.

I grabbed my sword and began stabbing at the ground. My arms were slick with sweat and I could feel the bottoms of my sandals beginning to melt. I kept thrusting the sword into the packed earth with all my might. The metal grew hot, and soon I had to wrap my hands in boilweed just so I could hold the weapon. I worked with precision instead of fury. With tact rather than anger.

I scooped out the rubble and eventually had a hole big enough for the Khol.

I hopped back and forth from foot to foot. The heat was so intense that my vision had gone woozy. I didn't know how much more I could take. I prayed for the Crier to steady my hands. I prayed for the Crier to be real.

The heat coming off the ground was making me choke. I had to keep my breathing to a minimum.

I had to keep hoping.

I planted the Khol in the ground and leaned over.

I thought of Shilah and Cam having to endure this deadly heat without me. Their fear over having lost, with no way of saving the flock. They would be so helpless, so afraid.

My tears were quick to fall.

The Khol sprang to life as soon as the first drop struck. I scooped the loose land over the hole to keep all the Meesh-Dahm from escaping. I needed it to flood downwards, to find the Desert and stop this madness.

At first nothing happened.

I was too late.

Then the land began to shake.

I'd never experienced anything like it in my entire life. The plateau rattled, the battle happening right beneath me. The gold was trying to pulse, but the land resisted its momentum.

I stumbled backwards. The colour at the hole was blinding. The air was changing temperatures, but I couldn't tell in what direction, and for a moment the whole plateau threatened to collapse. The land was quaking so much that I could barely stand up straight. The heat was overwhelming. It was like being back under the wool hat, only this time with wool constricting my entire body. I grabbed for the Matty to try and stay upright. Looking in, I found Gale had ducked her neck underwater, trembling in fear.

I could feel the Meesh-Dahm beneath me trapped in a terrible struggle.

The golden light kept getting brighter, but the sickening orange was walling it in, concussing together and trapping it on all sides. The Meesh-Dahm was shaking and tense. It had no place to go. My lungs were ablaze with hot fumes. I tried to breathe, but it was like the world in front of me had emptied of air. Nothing filled me up. I gasped with desperation.

The gold grew even tighter within its bindings. The pressure kept building. There was no sign of release. The struggle ran up my legs and into my arms, and for a moment I was dragged into the fight. Both sides were so much more powerful than me, so much grander and older and more enduring. I was caught between two surging rivers, or two bucking mountains, or even between the stars and darkness. I felt so feeble in their presence. So useless. So aware of my own, fleeting existence. Like a pebble tossed in the Great Divide, as the cliffs chewed.

I stepped towards the buried Khol.

And I was going to finish what I started.

I knelt down, the stones and sand burning my legs, and I howled with pain. The land seared into me, both Cold and heat, and my mind threatened to flee, leaving my husk of a body behind. Scarabs were crawling beneath my skin. Sobek lizards were gnawing on every piece of my flesh. I couldn't see much except for the blinding light; couldn't feel much except for the blinding pain. My soul was on the verge of being banished, flushed out of my body, and parts of me already ached with emptiness. Suddenly I couldn't remember my father's face. I couldn't feel where my arms ended and where the pain began. I couldn't remember what or who I was called.

The only thing that existed was eternal battle.

I was going to finish what I started.

I wept onto the ground.

Golden light burst outwards, an explosion of Cold and life and beauty like I'd never seen. It shot downwards into the land, gaining speed as it moved. The orange was carried away at the tips of the wave, pushing to the fringes of the plateau and eventually disappearing over the cliffs. I gasped with the relief, the most sensational feeling. I fell against the ground.

It was bliss.

I pressed my cheek into the glowing land, finding myself touching Cold. My memories came rushing back. My purpose returned, along with all the moments, dark and light, that made my life meaningful.

The things that made a difference.

I got to my feet and looked over my body, lit underneath by gold. I was unharmed. I raced back into the Matty and checked on Gale, who was cooing. Her whole body was submerged, but her long red bill rested on the bucket rim. I got the Desert roaring, but only opened the cap slightly, not risking much more than a hover. I primed the blades and sailed across the Cold land, away from the Sanctuary.

I knew exactly where I'd find my friends.

Chapter Twenty-four

I landed the Matty two streets away from the secret entrance, just in case the Asham were watching. I couldn't give away the location to the Coldmarch cavern just yet. The Asham needed to see the falling Cold to know the absolute, irrefutable truth of the new world.

I capped the Desert and the Matty landed gently enough. I threw off my mask, and did something that I'd been waiting a long time to do.

I had made a promise, and it was time to honour it.

I opened the lips of the Coldmaker bag, undid the bronze Belisk puzzle box lid, and stared into the empty chamber of salted water. I thought back to the Little Khat's animals and once again I was filled with new questions.

I wasn't afraid of them, however. Questions were the beating heart of inventing.

Maybe the beating heart of everything.

I took one of the new Khol from my stash and put it in Coldmaker. It fit perfectly. I closed the lid with a deep sigh of relief. Then I turned the machine on.

I put my ear up to the machine to listen to the effect. I'd missed that hum.

Inside of the bronze was something I might never understand, but it was something I could use; something that I would always hold sacred and dear.

I was going to make as many Coldmakers as I could.

I would teach the new world about the discovery, and what it had meant for the end of the Drought. Hopefully one day, many years from now, a free Jadan would tinker with my design and figure out more answers, the deep and profound mysteries of Cold that I would never be able to uncover. The future was full of so many wondrous things, so many adventures and discoveries.

I could barely wait.

A golden bead formed at the catch point of the machine. After it grew to a respectable size, I turned the Coldmaker off and pulled the abb loose, putting it in my pocket.

Gale watched me from her perch. I smiled, blowing a steady breath over her red wings. She roused, opening her feathers, and I think she smiled too. I lifted her up and settled her in the boilweed nest. I wanted to take her with me, but if I ran into any enemies or surprises, I might not have been able to protect her.

'Keep quiet,' I said, giving her feathers a pat.

She cooed and nuzzled my hand with her bill.

I covered the nest lightly with silk, and then stepped out of the cart. I slung the Coldmaker bag over one shoulder, and a canvas bag holding a single Khol over the other.

I removed my sandals and took great pleasure in finding that the sand and rocks were quite cool now. The golden hue had travelled throughout Jadans' Rise, lightly tinging even the bottom plateau. Though the colour was barely visible, it proved the Khol had more power than the Desert.

I ran down the streets towards the secret entrance to the Coldmarch tunnels, wanting to shout out and announce my arrival. But I had to keep composed.

Until the Crying tonight, I was just a regular Jadan in the eyes of the Asham. There could have been Khatfists and taskmasters waiting and watching through any one of the shop windows. I doubted they would have remained in a burning city, but I couldn't take any chances. Not this close to the end.

I slipped through the secret door and into the Coldmarch tunnels. There was no sign of life, but the tunnel was long and the flock was most likely scared. They wouldn't know that the Second Fall was over before it started, and they'd be doing everything they could not to make a sound.

I shot down the dark passageway without worry. My feet knew the way.

I took the second bend and found the staircase, carefully stepping down. When I got to the bottom, a flickering light called to me in the distance. It was coming from the main Coldmarch chamber.

The flock was still alive.

They must have been terrified.

I hurled myself at a reckless speed, the edges of the Coldmaker digging into my hip as I ran. My feet slapped against the cool stone. I finally crossed the threshold.

And was welcomed by a face full of blades.

Dozens of swords and spears were raised, ready to skewer me. My enemies were backlit by Sinai, and I could only see the sharp metal raised in my way. I stumbled back into the tunnel, panic in my heart.

And then I realized the shape of the weapons.

Hooked blades.

'MESHUA!' a most welcome voice called. 'IT WAS HIM! I TOLD YOU! I TOLD YOU HE WAS BACK!'

Dunes dropped his blade and barrelled into the tunnel, wrapping me in his large arms. He was so strong that I couldn't breathe, but I pressed my head into his chest and sighed with relief even without air.

I was home.

Whispers of Meshua rose from back in the chamber, spreading out and hesitantly growing. A happy bray that could only have been from Picka cut through the hush, her feet clomping against the ground.

Dunes finally let me go, checking me all over for wounds. He prodded my muscles and checked in my hair until he was satisfied that I was whole.

'We all thought you were dead,' he said, words spilling out. 'And the land was burning, but then when the cave began to cool down, I knew, I just knew it was somehow because of you, and – are you hurt? What can I bring you for your return? I will get you anything in the World Cried!'

I laughed, feeling overwhelmed by seeing him again. 'I know you would, Dunes. I'm glad to be back. But right now all I want is—'

Shilah and Cam burst around Dunes, nearly running straight into me. Cam's jaw was so slack I imagined it might hang loose forever. Shilah didn't look surprised, but rather radiated happiness.

An exhausted air hung about their bodies, dark circles lining their eyes. Shilah's braid was loose and uneven. Cam's hair was barely yellow anymore, matted with sweat. They stood so close that their arms were touching, and they were covered in dirt. They also had similar cuts and bruises along their arms and legs.

Cam launched forward and grabbed me in a hug. He started laughing, too close to a mad giggle. His whole body was shaking; whether from relief or fatigue I couldn't tell. I gladly held my friend as he trembled and sobbed. The hilt of his sword scraped against the Coldmaker in my bag, but I imagined it wasn't doing much harm.

'Shivers. And. Frosts,' Cam said when he finally calmed down. 'You're alive.'

'I'm alive.'

Cam stood in front of me, frozen. He didn't speak for a long moment, appraising me as if there was a chance I was a spirit.

Shilah kissed Cam on the cheek and then pushed him off to the side.

She took me in her arms and rested her hand against the back of my neck. Her hug wasn't frantic, like Dunes and Cam, but rather she drew me in slowly and with purpose. Her body radiated heat. I had so many questions for her, so many things to share; for now I let myself relax in her embrace.

She rubbed the back of my neck. Not sensuous, but in a familial way. I'd never felt more comfort; not even when Abb used to hold me when I was a boy and sick.

'I missed you too,' I whispered into her neck.

'It's been really hard without you,' she said. 'I've been praying for this every second since you disappeared.'

'So you pray now?' I asked, smiling.

'In you, World Partner,' Shilah said, pressing her hand against my cheek. 'I have faith.'

She stepped aside. In turn the Flock hugged me, kissed me, and chewed me out – although the rebuking was mostly by Split, who kept growling: 'Don't you ever leave like that again! Picka was so upset!'

Jia had candied figs ready.

Kasroot shook my hand, leaving a residue of groan soap. It was the first time we'd ever actually touched.

Cleave knelt before me, silent.

Het's hands wouldn't stop making words for a full minute straight.

Leah wrapped me up tighter than anyone, her curvy body clinging to me like she'd been dipped in glue. I had to work very hard to extricate myself from her, and she hung at my back during the rest of the greetings.

Ellia and Ellcia hugged me together after that, hissing 'love you, priss', into my ear.

Picka stood up on her hind legs, braying wildly. She tried to lick my face and succeeded.

Samsah pounded a fist against his chest, emotion in his eyes.

Everyone was here.

The rest of the Flock watched and whispered as I was showered with love. Everyone looked rather battered. There were too many scrapes, bloody lips and burn scars. There were weapons strewn about everyone.

'So what's happening here?' I asked Shilah as Jia shoved another round of figs into my palm. 'Were you planning on fighting your way out?'

'Fight not Fall,' Shilah said, turning to look back at the Flock. She drew her fingers down her right cheek. 'FIGHT NOT FALL!'

The words passed through the rest of the Flock, chanted back and forth. Weapons raised and hands curled into firsts. Their sentiment echoed deeply off the stone walls and deep pool.

'FIGHT NOT FALL.'

I gave Shilah an impressed look. 'You've been busy.'

Shilah shook her head. 'You first, Meshua. How'd you stop the burning? We looked everywhere for the Desert. But Sun-damned Ka'in and his masked bastards got one past us, and then it was too late.'

Dunes lowered his head in shame. 'I'm sorry, Meshua. We looked everywhere, but the enemy did something different this time and—'

I smirked. 'I *didn't* find the Desert.'

Shilah put a hand on my shoulder. 'Seriously. Where'd you find it? *How'd* you find it?'

I shook my head. 'I didn't find the Desert.'

Cam and Shilah exchanged a look, as if trying to decide who was going to ask where I'd left my sanity.

'Meshua,' Leah said from behind me in sultry tones, 'if you show me the place you found the Desert, I will gladly write you a song and commemorate it.'

'I'm telling you the truth. I didn't find the Desert.' I laughed. 'That's not how the burning stopped. I found something else.'

'What?' Cam asked, feeding off my grin, sprouting his own and nudging Shilah with an elbow. 'Langria?'

'Yes,' I said.

Cam laughed, and then did a double-take. 'Wait, for real?'

I nodded, opening the canvas bag I brought and taking out the Khol.

Cam and Shilah both gasped, and Cam thrust his hand into the air and shouted a victorious: 'Yes! Tears above, YES! Does that mean you got the Coldmaker working again?'

I nodded, slapping a hand against the other bag.

Cam looked like he was about to freeze over with excitement. 'We'll have crossbows again. Abb crossbows.'

Shilah stepped forward and reached for the Khol.

'Where'd you find it?' she whispered, aghast.

'The First Khat's Pyramid,' I said matter-of-factly. 'Along with all sorts of animals that were supposed to be extinct.'

'Spout,' Shilah said slowly.

I bit my bottom lip, holding back a smirk. 'I have a lot to tell you.'

'Abb crossbows,' Cam said, putting a hand on Shilah's lower back. 'I'm good with those suckers. And we can get the Wraiths working again. We might actually stand a chance in battle.'

'There doesn't have to *be* a battle,' I said, tears stinging the corners of my eyes. 'It's over.'

Split grabbed my cheeks and bore deep into my eyes,

checking for signs of slag or Dream. Picka's eyes narrowed as well, and she gave a little huff.

'What's over, son?' Split asked.

'The Drought,' I said, holding the Khol out for Dunes. 'Take it. It's real.'

Dunes shook his head, looking nervous.

'Please,' I said. 'Take it through the cave. Let everyone touch it. Let everyone see it. They deserve to know just what the Khat's been hiding all this time.'

Dunes bowed. 'By your command.'

I passed the Khol over. 'Also, the Khat's dead.'

Dunes nodded without hesitation. 'Yes, absolutely, Meshua. If you want the Khat dead, I will storm into his ceremonial tent like a Firegog and—'

'No,' I said, shaking my head. 'The Khat is *already* dead.'

'Micah,' Cam said, swallowing hard, 'what invention did I buy from the Ancient shop that one time? When we first met.'

'A music box,' I said, raising an eyebrow.

Cam nodded. 'Mhhm. And how many humps were in the valley on the original Coldmarch.'

'Three.'

Cam nodded again. 'Mhmm. And have you gone insane?'

'No,' I said, grabbing his arm. 'It's over. The Drought is over. We were so close all this time. I finally stumbled on the answer in Langria.'

Shilah walked forward with her arms open, ready for another hug.

And then she bopped me on the head.

'You went to Langria *without* me?' She pointed to Cam, indignant. 'Without *us*?'

I gave her a sheepish smile. 'It was an accident.'

'An accident?' Her face was nearly shaking with anger, but there was humour cracking the tension. She was trying hard to hold back a laugh.

'Sorry,' I said with a shrug. 'Trust me when I say Langria is not what you think. It's far from paradise.'

'That's what I told you,' Split said.

'And you never told me Lizah was from Langria,' I said to Split, raising my eyebrow.

Split choked, his eyes bulging out of his sockets.

'Micah,' Shilah said, holding my cheeks to get me to look her in the eyes, 'how is the Drought over?'

'They're seeds. The Khol – Frosts, I mean, but the Langrians call them Khol. They're seeds to grow Cry Patches, if they're planted and a Jadan cries on them. And right now I have five planted inside and around the city. Come night-time, Cold is going to fall here. For us. And the Nobles – the Langrians call them Asham – will have to admit that we are worthy and that the world has changed.'

Shilah stared at me for a long moment. Her back went straighter than ever.

And then she bopped me on the head again.

'You planted Cry Patches *without* me! I've been here with Cam trying to keep hundreds of Jadans off the edge of the cliff, fighting Ka'in and the Nobles from sneaking in and stealing our people, scrambling to find all the Desert they put in the ground, and you went off and saved the world *without* me!'

I paused, unsure what to say.

And she laughed, winking and launching into another hug. This time she kissed me on the cheek as she held me close, her braid laying across my shoulder. 'You really are Meshua.'

'We both are,' I said. 'You kept the flock safe. You kept Cam safe.'

'And, I mean,' Cam said, 'Shilah and I *did* get a few good moments while you were gone. Don't let her tell you we had no fun at all.'

Shilah's cheeks flushed with colour and she bopped him on the head next. 'He doesn't need to hear that!'

Cam laughed, teasingly rubbing the spot on his head. 'Ow. I thought Spout said there wasn't going to be a battle.'

Shilah turned to me, grabbing my hands in hers. 'Tell me everything, right now. What was that about animals?'

'Actually, everyone should hear this,' I said.

Shilah took my arm and threaded it through hers, marching through our people, leading me to the dancing platform beside the pool. The huge Flock looked on with wonder and awe. I didn't know all of their names, and there were new faces that I didn't recognize – probably from the Beggars – but I knew that after this night they would each carry with them a powerful story the rest of their lives.

They would tell their children, and their children's children, about the night the Great Drought ended. Of the two Meshuas. These words I was about to impart would be spoken of, and transcribed into scrolls, and passed down through generations. I almost asked Shilah to give the speech for me, as I was a tinkerer, not a speaker, and didn't know how to make words sound important.

But I realized I didn't need to make any grand speech.

I just had to tell them the truth.

And so I stepped up on the platform and told them everything. About Langria. About Khol. About Adaam and the first Cry Patch. About the Khat being dead, and the Little Khat being kept as a secret. About the animals. About Sett and the warriors flying off to the other cities with the Khol.

About how come night, Cold would once again be Cried for Jadankind.

I kept it simple and straightforward.

They hugged each other and dropped to their knees in sheer relief, tears flowing freely. I had Dunes pass around the Khol for every Jadan to cry on. They held it against their chests so they could feel the Meesh-Dahm pulsing for themselves, and although it was over far too fast, I'd never forget their expressions.

Freedom had always been a stranger, a face shrouded in distance. A song covered up by the sound of hungry stomachs.

We were all meeting freedom for the first time, as one.

Shilah broke from my arm, giving Cam a passionate kiss. She ran her hands wildly through his golden hair.

I was happy for them.

I was happy for everyone.

After things settled a bit, I took Shilah, Cam and Dunes with me back to the Matty to gather supplies. We agreed not to talk in case there were Asham still waiting in the city. We got to the craft, and Shilah took one look at Gale the ibis and actually shrieked in delight. I had to wrap my hand around her mouth to keep her quiet.

'You found a bird without me too?' she whispered when I freed her.

'She's an ibis,' I said. 'And her name is Gale.'

Shilah lifted her hand to bop me again, but then stopped at my cheek. She gently rubbed circles into my skin and then gave me a gentle pinch.

'If only I didn't love you so much, partner,' she said.

I winked at Cam.

Cam smiled, reaching out for Gale. The ibis gently nipped at his knuckles but then climbed onto his wrist, tucking her neck into her feathers.

'She likes me!' Cam shouted, pointing frantically. 'She doesn't see me as a Noble! She—'

Shilah and I both shushed him at the same time.

We returned to the Coldmarch chambers with Gale and the Khol, and then broke out the last of the food. Dunes found a few barrels of ale, and we feasted for the rest of the night. The figs were so bountiful they seemed to regrow on their stems. The ale flowed so freely that the barrel seemed bottomless. We piled the Khol on the stage next to the Sacred Pool, holding hands and spinning around them. Shilah refrained from dancing, as she was too busy fawning over Gale the ibis. The bird took a liking to her, as well as to Picka, nestling up on the camel's hump. Cam and I sang beautiful songs with older members of our Flock. Split finally showed us the traditional Crying Dance. Leah pulled out her harp and graced us with entrancing melodies for hours, plucking until her fingers nearly bled. Storytellers got up on stage after the music, regaling tales of small rebellions past, ones that I hadn't even known about. Samsah told a particularly good story about a Builder named Hassin, who'd baked Ancient Jadan curses into the middle of Pyramid slabs.

All the while the Coldmaker hummed on the stage, making abb after abb. I'd put Split in charge of distributing the abbs, and he merrily dished out the golden beads to all the children in the Flock. So many children. They were the best dancers in the room.

But even with all the celebrations, all the family by my side, all the hope, I still felt an odd pang. I was here in the room, but I was also elsewhere. Maybe back at my barracks. Maybe Langria. I couldn't tell for sure.

The world was saved, but my work wasn't done.

When Dunes came back to the cave and announced that night had arrived, I felt a bit of relief.

'Come on,' I told everyone, grabbing the Coldmaker and putting it back in its bag. 'It's time to watch.'

We all held hands as we left the cave. Long links of Jadans traversed the tunnel, holding on to each other, moving as one.

Outside, the Sun was gone.

The stars were beginning to arrive, pricking away the darkness. We spilled out of the alleyways and into the streets, showing our numbers in all their glory. We marched up the plateaus, the long line keeping as tight as possible.

Gale nestled on my shoulder, every once in a while giving my hair an affectionate nip. Shilah kept trying to get the bird to climb over to her shoulder, but Gale stayed with me. It would be a lie to say I wasn't flattered.

I touched the painted feather on the side as we passed the Matty. So did everyone behind me, silently and reverently. It was beautiful.

When we got high enough on the plateaus where the Asham could see us, they began to jeer so loudly that I could feel their hate all the way from the other side of the walls. There were horn blasts and explosive cheers and the armies began to sweep their way to the Southern side of the city, moving in dark clouds. They must have thought the Second Fall was about to happen. They were about to be sorely disappointed.

Shilah, Cam and I continued to hold hands up front, leading the charge.

Leah hovered right behind us, looking like she wanted to grab my hand too, to join in, but she kept her distance. I was grateful for her understanding.

I couldn't help but notice from this height that the eyes made of golden light were no longer stark upon the sands. They'd faded, leaving behind only the faintest tinge of colour. I wasn't worried. In fact, I was happy that the evidence was gone; it would only make the Crying that much more of a shock to the Asham.

We continued to climb the plateaus.

'The City of the Jadans' Rise,' I said to Shilah. 'Perfect.'

She squeezed my hand in agreement.

'I still like Camland,' Cam said with a shrug. 'But I guess it's not as punchy.'

Shilah pulled Cam close and poked him in the ribs. She left her hand on his chest, letting it linger.

The stone beneath us was cool and lovely, and before I knew it we'd climbed all the way to the top plateau. The Nobles far beneath us yelled and and shouted and cursed, continuing their celebration.

We just smiled.

They'd see the truth soon enough.

Eventually the entire Flock gathered where I'd planted the Cold, and everyone took turns pressing their hands against the holy spot, feeling the residual Meesh-Dahm.

The cheering of 'Jump!' and 'Fall!' and 'Unworthy!' could be heard in the distance, but the wind picked up, and the Asham were quickly drowned out. I looked up and gave the stars a sly wink.

And then we waited.

No speeches.

No battle.

No Cold.

The night was young.

The Nobles far below must have been confused, wondering how we could be enduring such heat. They snarled and lit fires, but we were untouchable so far above them.

We waited on. The night grew darker.

'Listen,' Split said, sidling up next to me, looking up at the stars. 'It's been eight hundred years, Micah. If for some reason this doesn't work—'

'It will,' Shilah said by my side.

Split gave an agreeable cough. 'I'm hoping as much as you, but just in case—'

'It will,' Cam said on my other side. 'Work, I mean. It will work.'

Split bowed and then backed away, giving Picka a pat on her snout.

We waited.

Gale's eyes grew tired, and she nestled close against my

neck, cooing softly. I wished for her to be able to open her wings. I wished for her to fly up into the sky and caw out to the Crier. To tell Him that we were waiting.

The Five came up to me next.

Dunes knelt down at my feet. 'We are prepared to do anything you need. Just tell us anything you need to help the Crier see us, and we will get it for you.'

I scoped the stars through the Farsight, trying to spot any new Cold. There was no movement. Only flickering light so far away.

I didn't say anything.

'It's okay, Dunes,' Shilah said, sensing my hesitation. 'Everything is already in place. Just keep a watch over the perimeter. Ka'in and the Nobles' – she looked at me – 'the Asham, will probably be coming soon.'

Dunes bowed and the Five backed away.

Shilah turned to Cam. 'I won't call you Asham, though. Ever. I'll call you something new.'

Cam lit up. 'Handsome? Brave? Necessary for your continued happiness?'

Shilah smirked, taking his hand. 'Keep dreaming.'

'I will,' Cam said with a smirk, gesturing down to their entwined fingers. 'I must be.'

We waited.

The Flock grew visibly nervous. Sounds filtered from the walls below; of gates being opened; of steel boots crunching against stone.

The Asham armies were coming.

I went over to the spot where I'd planted the Khol. It was true that I didn't know for sure if the Idea was going to work, my only proof being from an old Langrian story that might have been lost in translation; but still I didn't feel any doubt. I'd been with the Khol during its win against the

Desert. That experience spoke of something too big to simply stop there. My heart knew the Cold would come.

But my heart, just like all hearts, had been known to lie.

My heart had promised me that Abb would be by my side should a night like this ever come. My heart had told me that Shilah and I were going to be together; not Shilah and Cam. My heart had told me that a young, bright-eyed Jadan whose only crime was being on the small side, would get to live and grow into his smile. My heart had told me that the Crier was real, that He was watching, that He—

I sat down next to the spot where I'd buried the Khol. The Asham were coming. Without a miracle, we were to be slaughtered. This would be our end.

And worse, the Langrian warriors were flying around the Khatdom, burying Khol and proclaiming the world fixed, while nothing had actually changed. My people would start to believe, and then they would come crashing down once again. The mighty blow worse than if I'd done nothing at all.

The Khat, even in death, had won.

The Second Fall was to belong to the whole of Jadankind.

Running my hands over the land, I asked my fingers to stop trembling. They refused to listen. I found a small hole to still them in.

'Please,' I whispered. 'Please.'

I looked up at the sky.

Nothing.

I closed my eyes and let out a defeated sigh.

There was nothing divine about the reaction. The Khol and Desert were simply at odds as materials, and they had nothing to do with Cold from the sky. The effect stopped at city.

I swallowed hard, dread stiffening my throat.

I'd never felt so small.

I went to pull my hand back from the hole.

But there was something small and solid there. Curious, I pinched my fingers together and pulled out a Wisp.

It was dull, brown and ordinary; just like any other Wisp in the World Cried.

Only I hadn't put it there.

I stood up, the excitement rushing back.

I held the Wisp up towards my father.

'This from you?' I asked, madness making me shake. 'IS THIS FROM YOU?'

Nothing.

Gale cooed softly.

A pause.

The air went still; like the plateau itself was holding its breath.

And the sky began to weep.

It was only a few falling Wisps at first. They streaked the air, catching glimpses of the starlight, and landed with little puffs in the sands near the hole.

The Flock erupted with cheers, everyone pointing at the falling Cold.

Some dropped to their knees. Some began to dance.

I made the Crying gesture down my cheek. So did Shilah. So did Cam.

'Thank you,' I whispered, touching the spot where the Wisp had come. 'Thank you for everything.'

Shilah and Cam embraced, holding each other tightly.

More Wisps began to fall around us. Muted thumps came from around the Sanctuary moat as Wisps plummeted into tents. I scanned the surrounding plains. Soon enough there were little streaks in every direction. All around the City of Jadans' Rise, Cold had once begun to fall.

'Everyone!' I shouted, taking Gale off my shoulder and

holding her against my stomach, hunching over so she wouldn't get struck. 'Inside the Sanctuary!'

Confusion rang through the crowds, but Dunes and Jia were already rushing towards the Sanctuary doors to get them open. We filed in quickly, racing through the halls and gathering near the top balcony.

Shilah, Cam and I stepped out to the balcony, to the site of such terrible things in the past. The Flock came out behind us, packing tight under the overhang which covered our viewing platform. They kept switching out the rows so everyone could witness the Crying, and I heard many feet scamper off down the halls to find their own windows.

The awe was indescribable.

Wisps touched down everywhere: in the sands, on the roof above us, and even a few at the stone lip of the balcony, bursting into wonderful little puffs of Cold.

Each Wisp was a dagger in the Sun.

Each was a breath of freedom wind.

The Great Drought was over.

The Asham army didn't take long to arrive.

Their force was smaller than I expected, perhaps only five hundred strong. They came with shields and swords and helmets, flanking the Sanctuary. Ka'in and the Vicaress led the charge.

A large portion of the ranks appeared frightened and confused, which would work in our favour. They kept glancing towards the Crying sky in awe: a feeling I was hoping would turn to peace. The world deserved peace. It was time for us all, Jadan and Asham alike, to rest and heal. Unlike with Inventing, a warrior's work can sometimes be finished.

I hoped that the Asham would see the first new Cry Patches in eight centuries and naturally put down their weapons.

Ka'in had war in his eyes.

Shilah and I expected this possibility, that Ka'in wouldn't be swayed. In the face of uncomfortable truth, some still chose the familiar lie.

Ka'in was a victim in all of this, and I would try to save him if I could.

The celebrating in the Sanctuary behind me had become solemn and silent at the sight of the army marching towards us. Everyone looked to Shilah and I with worry. The Asham just barely outnumbered us, but they were trained, and had superior weapons and armour. If they wanted to, they could storm the building and end us with minimal effort. Even with the Five on our side, we'd never win a true battle.

The Vicaress limped at Ka'in's side as they closed in. The climb up to the plateau must have been difficult for her, as she looked pained in all sorts of ways. The fire still blazed heavy around her dagger, alighting her eyes, but instead of the drab brown they normally were, tonight they burned with an intensity. She couldn't stop staring at Ka'in.

I couldn't tell if it was love or hate. Funny how much they can look alike.

Wisps kept falling on the Asham. The night was now thick with falling Cold, and tomorrow morning there would be thousands upon thousands of Wisps out in the plateau sands to collect. The Wisps kept arriving in large numbers, puffing up where the land was soft and breaking where the land was rocks. Many of the Wisps landed on Asham helmets and shields, bursting into tiny puffs of Cold on the spot. The effect caused a few smiles and many confused frowns.

Shilah took my hand in hers. She and I stood at the front of the balcony, waiting for the Asham approach.

We'd abandoned our plans for battle. At this point, the most powerful force we possessed was from above.

'Ka'in,' I shouted as he stepped away from the ranks and

approached the balcony. 'Welcome to the City of Jadans' Rise. Put down your weapons and let us celebrate this miracle together. We have a lot to discuss.'

Shilah gave my hand a proud squeeze.

Ka'in's smile was wicked and full of self-righteousness. He wore no mask this time, his features a mess of purple burns scars. The cuts and marred skin were glossier than normal; almost as if he'd applied a balm to make the features look even more grotesque.

Ka'in spat at our direction and then ground the spit into the dirt with his foot. He picked up a freshly fallen Wisp and then turned around to his armies, ignoring my remarks.

'My loves!' Ka'in shouted. 'My fair family! My fellow chosen *more* than a few! Tears, tears, tears everywhere! Tonight is the night we are proud to call ourselves Nobles. Because the Crier is here with us, and he is speaking to our blessed people through miracles! He is proving that once again, we are the chosen!'

Ka'in put the Wisp in his mouth, which I knew would burn rather painfully. He swished the brown bead around, holding it in his cheeks for a spell before spitting the remainder back out into his palm. He opened his mouth and wiggled his tongue, which was visibly swollen.

The Vicaress looked at Ka'in as if he'd gone mad. Still, she didn't speak up.

Ka'in spat a few times, licking his lips.

'The Crier has watched his chosen Nobles gather here, so far from our homes, so far from our normal lives!' he continued shouting, although the words were a bit loose. 'And he has begun to Cry for us. He sees us gather at the Second Fall, without our comforts, our delicious gardens, our slaves, and sees us suffering. Well, we have suffered long enough! We are beautiful and this night is beautiful, and now we are one!'

Shilah and I exchanged a hopeless glance.

Split came up beside us and growled out, 'Liar! This Cold is not for you!'

Ka'in waved a delicate hand. 'Thus spoke the traitor.' He turned to the Vicaress. 'Darling, is there really anything worse in the whole World Cried than a traitor? At least the Jadan scum are just nasty scum.' His face grew angry. 'SCUM!'

A few of the Noble soldiers snarled and waved their swords, but many of them still looked up at the sky with unease. They were close to believing; so close. If only I said the right thing. A real leader would know what to say.

The Vicaress said nothing. She looked into the flames of her dagger, as if searching for answers.

Ka'in put a hand over his heart. Then he ripped his shirt and rubbed the purple and red scarring on his chest. 'But to betray one's own kin! The Crier holds special duties for traitor Nobles in the black. Especially for you, Camlish Tavor.'

Cam stepped up to the balcony, opening his arms wide. 'Don't listen to word he says, people. My name is indeed Camlish Tavor, and as a High Noble I can tell you with absolute honesty that the Drought is over. That the Jadans are more than worthy. That there is no reason to fight. The Crier has been on the Jadans' side all this time. Micah and Shilah here have discovered the real miracle. That if Jadans cry on a Frost and it is put in the ground, then a new Cry Patch will—'

Cam abruptly stopped talking. Something flashed through the air. His head gave a violent jerk backwards.

'No!' Shilah rushed towards him. 'Cam!'

Cam took his hand away from his face. There was blood on his palm. He looked down at his feet, clenching his fist.

'That asshat threw a rock at me,' Cam said, spitting blood from his lip.

Ka'in curtsied.

Shilah stood up straight as I'd ever seen. She reached into her braid to go for her dagger.

I stopped her, shaking my head.

'We can do this without violence,' I said, gesturing to the Crying sky.

Ka'in pursed his lips and blew a kiss at Cam. Then he turned back to the armies, Wisps striking their helmets and swords.

'My beautiful beauties!' Ka'in said. 'What a delicious sin. Sounds good, but don't eat it! Anyway, here we Nobles stand in celebration. The Crier has watched us struggle for so long now. Struggle to be away from our families and lives. These slaves had obviously made a deal with the Sun to keep the city from burning. The Sun has been helping them all this time, but now the Crier is helping *us*! He cries this Cold for Noblekind, to help us in our fight! To show us that he cares for us! Now in return, the Khat asks that we exterminate—'

'The Khat is dead!' I shouted.

A rush of whispers travelled through the ranks.

'It's true!' Shilah said. 'The Khat was never here at the city. He died nearly a year ago, and his only son has been locked in the basement of the Pyramid. Ask Ka'in!'

Ka'in's eyes narrowed.

The Vicaress swallowed hard, her blade lowering just a tad.

The whispers picked up behind them.

The Khat's dead?

Could it be true?

I haven't seen his holiness in a while.

It has to be a lie.

Cam stepped up again, but I gave him a gentle gesture to hold back. Instead, I motioned to Split, for him to bring me Gale. The ibis was nuzzled on Picka's hump, sleeping soundly. Split picked her up, and the bird struggled, but she calmed when she was in my hands.

More whispers from the crowd:

What is that?

What is that the slave is holding?

The Wisps began to pick up. They fell everywhere, continuing to crash on helmets, swords and pikes, almost as if the night sky itself was trying to tell the Asham to put down their weapons and come inside the Sanctuary. To join us.

'Noblekind!' I shouted out. My voice strained to the point of breaking. I held Gale above my head for all to see. 'Please, I beg you to listen to reason. You came here for the Second Fall, which will not happen. Ka'in promised you a burning city, but here is a city coming back to life. Here is a city of healing. Here is a city for the animals to return to. My name is Micah Ben-Abb, and I am a Jadan from Paphos. Together with my friends, we have discovered what caused the Drought in the first place, and how it was ended. And we can prove both. Right now there are new Cold Patches Crying for Jadans all across the World Cried. In Paphos, Marlea and even Langria. Put down your weapons and let us talk. You see, there is something called Desert, that can blind the Crier and make it so he doesn't know where to cry. The First Khat travelled the world—'

Ka'in took out a dagger and hurled it at my chest.

It headed straight up with incredible speed.

Cam jumped in front of me.

I gasped and cried out.

The dagger hit the stone at Cam's feet.

Cam watched the weapon skitter harmlessly through his legs, everyone jumping out of the way behind him. Shilah looked like she was about to faint.

I placed a hand on Cam's shoulder, my heart thundering.

The Five burst out of the crowd behind us and stood right at our sides, huddling tight and looking ready to jump in front of anything else for us.

Cam turned to me, his hand over his heart. 'I really thought that was it.'

'That's the second time you've jumped in the way of danger for me,' I said.

'For you, World Partner,' Cam said, slapping my cheek playfully, 'anything.'

'Hey, that's our thing!' Shilah said, crossing her arms. 'Get your own thing.'

Cam shrugged giving me a questioning look. 'My . . . Cold Buddy?'

I chuckled. 'Absolutely.'

'Bah!' Ka'in said, turning back to the Nobles. 'Do not listen to their scum lies, Noblekind!' He picked up another Wisp that fell by his feet. 'Lies and tears. Lies for fears. This Cold cannot be explained. This is not some natural thing! Desert, or whatever the ugly boy called it, is not real, but this Wisp is a sign from the Crier, for us. This was never supposed to be a Second Fall, it was supposed to be a slaughter! We are worthy, they are not. It has always been that way. And it always will! Maybe the Khat has always been dead, because I am the Khat now! And I tell you that I can hear the Crier speaking to me! He has chosen me and is speaking right now! His voice is so deep and powerful, and he is telling us to get our weapons ready and sharpened, for we shall storm the Sanctuary and kill any Jadan—'

A collective gasp rose from the army.

'K-Ka'in!' the Vicaress shouted beside him, pointing up. 'Lo-lo—'

'Quiet!' Ka'in snarled. 'You bumbling—'

And then his head caved in.

A burst of wind and Cold shot out from Ka'in's body, knocking the Vicaress back a step and extinguishing her blade.

Ka'in crumbled to the ground, lifeless.

The cloud of Cold raced across the front lines of the soldiers, biting their hands and faces, making them drop their weapons.

It had happened so fast. But we'd all seen what killed him.

A Shiver.

A beautiful Shiver.

The first piece of Cold bigger than a Wisp to fall in this new Patch, and it had streaked the air with speed and starlight. It landed right on Ka'in's head with enough force to break both itself and his skull.

Shilah and I looked at each other aghast.

Ka'in's head had a large gash at the impact point, viscous red seeping into the sands beside him. Panic flooded the ranks of Asham at his back, wincing away from the sky with fear. They raised their shields and huddled close together, looking to the Vicaress for answers, calling out with alarm.

The Vicaress looked up at the balcony.

Come on, I prayed. Come on.

She looked at her blade.

She looked back at the armies.

She looked at the ibis.

And then she kneeled.

She thrust the dagger into the sand beside her, and lowered her head.

The rest of the Asham hesitated, but then eventually followed her lead. They all dropped to their knees and laid down their arms. Wisps continued to fall in greater quantities, landing on exposed backs, causing small grunts of panic and pain.

The Jadans behind me cheered like never before, but I waved them quiet.

'Noble Family!' I shouted out into the sands. 'Rise. You don't need to kneel!'

The Vicaress reached out and touched Ka'in's leg. She was weeping.

'Rise!' I said. 'We are all one people! We are all ONE PEOPLE! Come inside with us! Take shelter with us!'

They looked worried, as if I were inviting them into a trap.

I bowed.

Shilah bowed next.

Then Cam.

And the Five.

And then everyone behind me.

The Vicaress hesitated.

Finally, she rose and began to limp forward.

The Asham armies quickly followed her, hurrying out of the falling Cold. They threw down their weapons into a large pile on the rocks.

I took Shilah's hand and Cam's hand and together we turned towards hallway.

The Flock parted ways so we might pass, continuing to bow, but this time it was to us. Dunes had his forehead pressed against the stone. Split and Picka were hugging each other tight in celebration, the little camel licking the bald spot on the top of the Pedlar's head. Leah and the sisters were crying with joy.

Cleave touched my shoulder.

I turned towards the giant man.

A single tear crossed his stony face. He got down on one knee.

'Meshua,' he said.

It was the first time I'd heard him speak.

His voice was weak, gritty and full of tenderness.

I drew two fingers down my cheek and he mimicked the gesture.

And then Shilah, Cam and I made our way through the hallway. We walked down the stairs, our hands together.

To greet the new members of our family.

Epilogue

We rebuilt everything.

It wasn't easy, but sometimes easy isn't what Jadans need.

Tensions ran high at first, with Asham and Jadankind staying mostly to themselves, having set up quarters on different plateaus. But when the Sun disappeared in the evenings, and wondrous Cold fell for us every night all around the city in our new Cry Patches, eventually the two factions began to blend.

Shilah and Cam did an excellent job helping to bridge the gaps.

They truly cared for one another. It was love at the very least. Seeing them come together, a Jadan and an Asham, helped inspire by example. Shilah had a knack for leading, and I let her direct the new society. She was fair and kind when it came to the Asham, promising to forgive but never forget. Cam never left her side. Eventually his posture became the same as hers.

Together they were invincible.

The feasts and celebrations were nightly and lavish. Soon some of the once-shame-faced Asham were asking Jadans to dance around the Cold pools. The reverse was also true, with

Jadans inviting Asham to dine at their tables and listen to their stories. All the resentment and hate bubbling under the surface calmed down as the Cold continued to fall in abundance.

The Builders showed the strongest and ablest Asham how to mix clay and shape stone. Quickly enough, the buildings that had been destroyed by fire or heat were being erected once again, even stronger than before. The Cry Temples were restored, although the decorations and statues inside were changed quite a bit. The Builders also went on to strengthen the roofs of every building to resist the Crying, so the big Cold that fell on the plateaus wouldn't knock shingles and stone out of place. Mostly what fell were Wisps and Drafts, but there was the rogue Shiver every once in a while. There were still no Frosts here in Jadans' Rise yet, but for the first time, we were okay without them.

The Domestics showed the Asham, both men and women, the secrets to planting gardens. The Asham had to wear hats and clothes so their fair skin didn't burn under the hot Sun, but they worked without complaint. Even the Vicaress of David's Fall – her real name being Victovius – gave up her mantle and tended to the gardens. No one worked within twenty paces of Victovius at first, but after Shilah helped her plant her first alder, she was welcomed into the fold.

With all the new Cold, extra hands and the soil returning, green plants shot from the ground faster than arrows off crossbows. In the first few weeks, we had a whole field of plump knuckleberries, the seeds brought here by Shaman Eli and Lop, who hitched a ride back with Sett and Sinniah. The other crops fields, which grew figs and dates and pomegranates and orangefruit, spread wide and far into what had only recently been deadland around the city.

Shilah and I deemed these fields the Camlands.

Collecting from the Cry Patches became an honourable

task, one of love and pride. Since it was clear that the Gospels or Decrees held no credence any longer, perspectives on work shifted. Gathering Cold from the Patches was no longer some burden with impossible quotas, but rather it was labour that cleansed the soul. Many of us would dance our way into the Patches in the morning and dance our way home with our buckets spilling over in the afternoon.

Within weeks, Jadans and Asham from all across civilization had begun to flock to our walls. The Langrian warriors had done their jobs well, bringing new Cry Patches and the truth to the fringes of what was once the Khatdom.

Jadans came from Marlea. The Shocklands. Belisk. Mirrluh. The Hotland Delta. The City of the Shade, and the City of the Stars.

And of course from Langria.

The free Jadans showed up in abundance. They arrived with exotic seeds to cultivate, a slew of materials for inventing, and books and scrolls and whole caravan carts of history. Once they settled in, they began to show us how best to carve tunnels beneath the land, so we could expand our rooms and halls and Coldmarch caves. We unearthed an underground river flowing into the sacred pool, gifting us more than enough water for everyone.

We built homes down under the land where it was cool, where the Sun couldn't pox our new society. There were no Firegogs, or Wraiths, or Dybbuks, or any terrible creatures down in the tunnels.

And certainly no Hookmen.

The Hookmen were gone.

The Five, on the other hand, became excellent leaders, helping the new arrivals to adjust to life in the new city. They showed them how we lived and what we stood for. They taught them how to live free lives. Split happily joined them in their tasks. Picka and Gale the ibis were beloved by all.

Leroi, Ellora and the Little Khat brought the animals with them from Paphos. Leroi had built mobile enclosures so they could be transported safely in the shade. Hundreds of Jadans from Paphos, and even some Asham, wheeled them to the gates.

We built large, fenced-in pastures to hold the more dangerous ones, at least until the world was ready to give them their freedom as well. For now, the lands were still dead, but soon enough the fields and forests would return. The animals appeared to be much healthier out of their stone cages, their patchy fur becoming thick and their broken bodies beginning to heal.

The people, especially the free Jadans from Langria, marvelled at the different species. The Langrians loved those animals with ferocity, giving them names and treating them as part of the Flock. The animals obviously couldn't understand them, but it was truly a sight to behold. The Khat's Pyramid had been cleaned out, and everything had a new home here.

And it turned out the line of Khats had been hiding animals in secret chambers around the Khatdom as well. The Jadans and Asham coming to Jadans' Rise brought a number of types. There were stables of withered horses in Marlea. And three skinny rhinoceroses in the Shocklands. And more birds in the Hotland Detla.

There was even another Loonchin from the Southern Cry Temple.

We gave Zeekah the honour of uniting the two.

The lonely grass song wasn't heard again within our lands.

The Little Khat also brought thousands of Jadans and Asham from Paphos, all carrying carts full of supplies and food and clothing; and of course, hundreds of Khol. New markets were set up with wonderful goods, and since there was enough Cold for everyone to buy everything, we just laughed, shared and dreamed.

Mama Jana ran the best shop in the city. Her nails were pristine, each one a different colour.

Moussa wrote us a hundred new songs.

And all of my barracks family were there before I knew it. Jadankind was now free to live where they chose, and everyone was welcome here.

Very soon the encampments stretched as far as the eye could see, and we had to find another source of water. The free Jadans had another river tracked down and an abundance of wells dug up in less than three days.

Leroi had begun to study the Frosts and Meesh-Dahm. Ellora helped him, and the two of them became rather close. Sett lent a hand in their experiments as well.

One of the first discoveries their tinkershop made was that the diseases that only Asham could get, like Firepox, could be cured by drinking water that had been cooled by Khol. They studied their findings vigorously and tinkered non-stop. I had no doubt they'd find every answer they sought.

I had my own answers to find.

Within the City of the Jadans' Rise, art blossomed. Food was abundant, spiced and exciting. Leah taught music and harp to anyone who desired. She also was always around me, always bringing me gifts and smiles, always trying to win my affections with a careful stroke of her hair, or a smouldering look, but I could never fully respond to her efforts.

My work wasn't done. I didn't know what I had to do, and even though I couldn't walk ten paces in any direction without hearing laughter, I still wasn't quite ready to laugh along.

Within months, the city was thriving.

The land flushed green and alive, and when I walked through the covered gardens, which were swollen and lush, I could go a hundred feet in any direction and pick a fruit as big as my fist. At night, Cold broke on the rocks and plains around the city, cooling the air and the newly-found underground river.

Which we named the River Split.

Split cried for an hour straight after hearing that.

There were still some Asham around the World Cried who didn't believe our story. Cam's father wasn't seen or heard from, along with other Asham who were once heirs to the throne. The detractors were only a small portion of the population, and rumour had it they took refuge at the Western Cry Temple. Sett and the warriors were adamant about tracking them down, but I told them no, deciding to let the Asham disappear.

They would have been welcome here, but I wasn't going to stop them if they wanted to suffer alone.

The City of the Jadans' Rise became a place of peace and wonder. We had our difficulties, but Shilah was a strong leader, dealing with problems swiftly and with a generous strength. Her braid grew so long it hung down to her waist. There was never again a blade kept inside.

Our land was truly a paradise, and I knew the Jadan Ancestors were smiling down from the stars. The people of Jadans' Rise started to look at me as if I were a living myth. They praised me, thanked me and bowed at my feet.

And I grew restless.

I tinkered as much as I could, making dozens of Coldmakers, but still there was a hollowness growing inside of me. At first I thought it was just a longing for my father, a sadness because he didn't get to see the place he always knew could exist, but it was more than that.

Abb was off someplace better, behind the boilweed, and

in my heart I knew he was as much at peace as everyone here.

Everyone except for me.

I began to take long walks at night alone.

I would watch the Cold falling, sitting on a stone wall in the Camlands. Sometimes I was caught by Jadans or Asham, who would wrap me in hugs, or fall to their knees weeping at my presence. Some members of the city began painting their fingers bronze to honour my sacrifice.

The hollowness inside of me grew deeper.

One night, when I was walking on top of the city wall alone, in the dark hours before Crying was about to start, I was stopped by Cam and Shilah.

They weren't holding hands.

They were holding Khol.

They told me they supported me. And that they loved me. And would miss me.

They had already loaded up my Matty with supplies.

We hugged and kissed and said long goodbyes, although it was clear I would be back soon enough.

But we all knew my work wasn't done.

Because the World Cried was a big place.

Far bigger than only what was once the Khatdom.

And someone needed to see what was out there. To bring life back to the far reaches. The places that had lost hope long ago.

And so that night I set out with Gale the ibis. We took flight, and as soon as we were high enough, she stepped onto her perch and stretched out her wings. Because one of them was broken, she'd probably never fly on her own, but that was okay. We were rising towards the stars, where we both needed to be.

I looked back on the city just as the Crying began.

It was the most beautiful thing I'd ever seen.

I still wasn't sure if the World Crier was real. Or if everything was just some happy accident.

But one thing was certain.

My eyes had finally Opened.

THE END

Author's Note

Three books. Ten years. The Coldmaker Saga has been an adventure for me in every sense of the word. How does one end such a journey, such a transformation, with grace and poise?

I dreaded writing this section. Perhaps more so than any other section in any of the books. I'd known it was coming for a while, with months to get it done and still I had trouble finding not only the right words, but any words at all. I'd never been affected by writer's block in the traditional sense before, but for once I found myself truly afraid of my keyboard, paralyzed at the thought of bringing this part of my life to a close.

Right now I'm sitting in my favourite place in Austin, Texas, a place called 'Mayfield Park'. It means more to me than anywhere else in the city. Here are sprawling gardens with coy ponds, peacocks, and a woody trail I've wandered countless times while waiting for inspiration to strike, or for chapters to come. I even have a special bench, and special rock, where I come when I'm feeling particularly sentimental – as I am right now.

When I was in my early twenties, I suffered a mental breakdown and ended up in a psych ward on suicide watch. Three years prior I had been put on a very powerful prescription drug for insomnia issues, and after being hollowed out by meds I was too young to understand, I had decided to go cold turkey, unsupervised. I refused any and all drugs that the ward psychiatrist tried to put me on, and so I was released fairly quickly.

It took me about nine months to return to any semblance of sanity. I had been diagnosed with depersonalization disorder— I won't go into the details of my condition here, but will describe it as hellish. As a last-ditch attempt at healing before doing something permanently destructive, I went to, and was saved by, an Israeli acupuncturist who looked into my eyes and understood both my pain and what had happened to my central nervous system. He stuck me full of needles and left me alone in a dark room, and after fifteen minutes I felt myself return, just for moment, just slightly, to my body. It was the upswing that all lasting hope demands.

I did not believe in acupuncture then. I do now.

After that, I moved from New York to Austin to get away from my demons. I went cold turkey from the entirety of my past self. My life was split down the middle, shattered by mental illness, and for the longest time I didn't even have access to memories on the other side of the Great Divide. It is still the deepest wound I harbor, and had not yet scarred over when, out of the blue, a young boy wandered across my imagination fully formed.

He trekked across sand dunes, strapped into shoes that looked like tennis rackets, holding a mysterious golden machine. Somehow I knew that this machine could make life (Cold) in a world that had been diagnosed as terminal.

This boy and his machine became my entire life. For ten years, I did everything humanly possible to put his story together. The work was tiresome, maddening, and endless, a Sisyphean effort, but it gave me direction. It gave me *meaning*. It was my fourth novel, but it felt so much bigger and more visceral than anything I'd ever attempted. It made me feel like I'd never done any real writing before, which I guess is what you want from each progressive book as a writer.

In the four years of grueling effort it took to create the original iteration of the story—a book called 'The Inventor in the Sands'—something unexpected happened.

Dan the person, not just Dan the writer, began to take shape once again.

I started a band and recorded two albums. I made some of the best friends I could ever hope for. I fell madly, deeply, perilously in romantic love (I was pulled kicking and screaming out of that very same love soon after). I experienced other, calmer types of love. I travelled. I hid when I needed to. I met people who cared about me when I could not. I learned to care about myself when others could not. I discovered books that spoke to my tender soul, telling me it was okay to come out of my cave and smile from time to time.

In essence, I started to heal.

Very recently, after handing in Coldmyth to my wonderful editor Vicky, I took a trip back home to New York. To the house I had grown up in. I'd returned a handful of times in the ten years after leaving, but I was only ever there physically, and did not bring anything deeper along. I was driving in to the city with my father (who in many ways is Abb-like) and when we got to the border of my hometown, something unexpected happened. I began weeping uncontrollably, sobs wracked from a well long forgotten.

But the crying was not of pain or sorrow.

I was crying because I once again could *remember* my past life.

I recognized all the landmarks that I had known as a child (the baseball field where I hit my first and only home run, the hobby shop where I had my first job cutting boxes and cleaning Super Nintendos, my old high school where I relatively kept to myself and played lots of saxophone, etc.) and I could feel the kid inside me speaking up, wanting to play. Wanting to get to know me. Wanting to remind me how to love again, in all the forms that love can take back when we're younger and unbroken.

When we got to the house I collapsed on the floor and started looking at everything through the eyes of my childhood self, staring wide eyed and blubbering. My father, bless him, sat close by and held my hand quietly, letting me take it all in.

After a while he looked me in the eyes and said:

'Me and your mother knew you had to go away for a while. Sometimes you have to go away, and that's okay, but I'm glad you're here now. Welcome back.'

He wasn't speaking of my physical self. He had looked into my eyes and saw my pain, and knew what had happened to my spirit, or soul, or Meesh-dahm.

In many ways Micah's story parallels my own, albeit my story is a lot less grand. But still: a young boy is cast out of the life he knows, forced to struggled with faith and identity, and a bit of madness. That boy tries to make something he believes in, to heal, and in doing so has to go away for a while. After many adventures, after loses and loves and trial and error, he finally finds his way home thanks to the help of so many people. Thanks to his family.

And so, as a conclusion to this part of my own story, hopefully leaving this section of my life with a sense of grace and poise, I want to give a special thanks to my friends and family (you'll probably recognize many as character names from the story, go figure) who were most closely associated with the books, and who stayed with me in some way or the other until the very last page.

My father. My mother. Jardin Telling. Sara Hahn. Stephanie Radzik. Danielle Zigner. Matt (Matty) MacDonald. Moses (Moussa) Elias. Ben Barr. Jake McNally. Josh Klaus. Rachel Cohen/Klaus. Daniel Fears. Natasha Bardon. Vicky Leech. Lily Cooper. Thomas Judd. Jack Renninson. My Waking Fable people. My Bad Bonsai people. My House Wine people. My Firehouse people. My extended biological family. The authors who showed me the way: Brandon Sanderson, Patrick Rothfuss, Ted Chiang, Theodore Sturgeon, William Goldman, David Eagleman, Pierce Brown, Sherman Alexie, Neil Gaiman, and so many others.

And of course, you, the reader.

Thank you coming with me on this most unexpected, yet wondrous adventure back home.

Daniel Cohen
December 10, 2019